PREHISTORIC BEASTS AND WHERE TO FIGHT THEM

HUGO NAVIKOV

SEVERED PRESS
HOBART

PREHISTORIC BEASTS AND WHERE TO FIGHT THEM

ISBN: 978-1-925493-93-1

PREHISTORIC BEASTS AND WHERE TO FIGHT THEM

One of Katherine Muir's favorite things about taking a panoramic submersible down was watching the bubbling waterline crawl up the viewing windows, letting her see the old, familiar world get replaced by the new, exciting one under the surface. But that was about the only thing she regretted about the design of her new vehicle, this sleek and solid lozenge built with viewports that were *much* stronger than those of any panoramic-view vessel, but much smaller, too.

Those bubble subs were wonderful for examining coral reefs, fish, and other sea life. Watching the amazing octopus as it changed its color, pattern, *everything* to make itself completely invisible to predators. The times she had watched them deploy such camouflage, the only way she even knew they were *there* was because she followed silently behind them and waited until they felt a threat. Then they slapped themselves against whatever surface was nearby … and *disappeared*. Truly, studying ocean life in the panoramic submersibles was a joy.

But this new vessel, *Deep Thoughts*, was made not to explore ocean creatures, but the ocean itself. Katherine and her husband, Sean, had designed the submersible, working hand in glove with some of the most innovative subaquatic transport engineers in the world. It had been a difficult decision whether to create a one-person vessel or one more like the bubble subs, with room for two. She and her husband wrestled with how cool it would be to explore together, but a submersible meant to reach the floor of the benthic depths 20,000 feet below the surface couldn't be very big. So it came down to either giving up the amount of scientific and observational equipment that would allow a second passenger to ride or giving up the fun of doing it as a couple.

They decided in favor of more science. It *was* to be a research vessel, after all, funded by a variety of philanthropic and academic sources to expand the frontiers of human knowledge about the still little understood landscape and biome at the bottom of some of the deepest water on the planet. Benthic was as far down as one could go and still investigate "normal" undersea terrain. There were deeper fissures and channels, but the deepest average real estate on Earth was benthic, and scientists still knew near to nothing of what went on in the complete darkness at the bottom of this zone.

This wasn't an expedition, despite the fact that they had a small documentary and communications ship, *The Moaning Mermaid*, along with their main launch and support vessel, *Sea Legs*. This was the second of four tests to make sure the submersible—christened *D-Plus* by the whole smart-aleck crew (because it was "below C level," *har dee har*)— could handle the greater pressure and harsher environment it would encounter the farther it descended.

Katherine took the first test run, this to "just" 5,000 feet. Not terribly deep, but deep enough that a major malfunction would force the crew on *Sea Legs* to get the winch going and haul her back up by *D-Plus*'s tether, which also included data lines and fiber optics for communications. At a crisis point, however, the high-tech tether would just be a rope everybody needed to yank on immediately if they wanted to rescue the researcher tasked with making sure everybody got their paychecks.

As expected, however, the first test went off without a hitch, and she and Sean were pleased. Any major hiccups would have been obvious— or at least detectable—at 5,000 feet, so each of the next two tests would be to make sure the things they designed on land worked under the stresses of the deep ocean. Also, going to 10,000 feet exposed the submersible to double the pressure of 5,000 feet, and 20,000 feet would double the pressure again. The second test, with Sean at the controls, would venture almost two miles into the black depths; and the third, this time piloted by Katherine, would dive to 15,000. If *D-Plus* didn't exhibit any major issues during the third dive, then the final test would touch down on the seafloor at roughly 20,000 feet and come back up almost immediately. If everything worked the way it had been designed to work—or most everything; no exploration went off perfectly—then the first real mission would spend a few hours at the bottom and see what there was to be seen. Take sediment samples, look at creatures that somehow made a life at *four tons* of pressure on every square inch, and perform a preplanned battery of observations and measurements. This particular area of the ocean bottom had never been explored, and many in the oceanographic community were watching the Muir mission with great interest.

Katherine took the first dive, and they were supposed to take turns, but somehow her klutz of a husband—they named their boat *Sea Legs* in honor of his many times he almost fell over on any size of watercraft— had managed to run afoul of a line on board the launch ship and dislocated three fingers on his right hand just that morning as they were setting up the winch for the next test. It was 2016, for the love of God! They weren't sailing with Blackbeard here—who got caught up in *rigging* anymore?

2

Nevertheless, there it was: if a second test was to be performed, it would be Katherine Muir, not Sean, who would take *D-Plus* down. Piloting the submersible, even a deep-sea vessel going on what was essentially a controlled drop, required both hands and all ten of the pilot's digits. But they told only their crew chief, Mickey Luch, about the change, since professional mariners, like those who worked the boats while scientists did their science-ing, were still a superstitious lot. Changes in plans made them antsy, to say the least. So she and Mickey just secured her in the sub without any announcement. Once she was in place, he told the crew they were making a switch—*never you bunch mind why*—and Katherine would be executing Test No. 2.

There was a small murmur of protest—the winch greaser (a job title that always elicited snickers but was quite important) and the camera specialist on deck were especially superstitious and vociferous—but Mickey just helped Katherine into *D-Plus*, and the assistants got it locked up tight and ready to go. This crew had overseen 10,000-foot dives many times, and that's why they were hired as a team by the Muirs.

"Let's move 'er out and get 'er down!" their chief shouted, and the A-frame winch structure slowly stretched its long crane out over the water. With a thumbs-up between Katherine and Mickey, the winch whined and the submersible was lowered into the choppy sea.

This would be a very awkward and dangerous point to stop the operation, so it wasn't until that moment that Sean Muir stepped out onto the deck, his first three fingers wrapped in a splint. The next test dive wouldn't be for two days, and he'd work through the pain if necessary—he was no stranger to the sea, and he had "played hurt" through worse than this. The crew was preoccupied with the task at hand, but when they saw the researcher on the deck, they took a moment to bust his balls and laugh at his "horrible" accident.

Some of them weren't laughing, though. Sean knew that this switch—obviously due to the injury they could see with one glance at his right hand—would initiate rituals of touching wood (where they could find it) and prayers to Saint Michael, not to mention whispered oaths and grumblings about the expedition leader at the mariners' table come chow time. Slipjack and Toro and Vanessa—the winch team—looked especially upset, although obviously trying to hide it so as not to visibly challenge Sean.

He nodded at all of them and released them to work on the dive. He and Katherine exchanged "See you soon! Love you!" through the interior camera feed and monitor as she was lowered into the water.

Once in the water, she started testing instrumentation and such while Sean supervised the support crew on the surface.

The winch would be turning for an hour or so, meaning relatively little to do for the boat crew but help the scientists, if needed. Sean took the opportunity to motion for the three shaken-looking members of the winch crew to join him on the lee side of the huge spool, where it made enough noise to render eavesdropping impossible. When they had assembled, Sean said, "So what's the rumpus here, guys? I know it's considered bad luck to change things at the last minute, but —"

"It isn't superstition, Doctor Muir," Vanessa said, and just from that Sean knew she was trying not to be a nuisance but truly was upset. After their first meeting, he had asked the solid, sun-leathered woman to call him "Sean," and she always had. But calling him by his title and surname was like her filing an official complaint. "Last-minute changes mean other last-minute changes, and those make for mistakes. We should've put off this dive until you were recovered from ... did you break your fingers?"

"No, just dislocated them. Should be fine in a day or two."

"Well, then, what I'm saying is even more true—we've had to wait *days* before because of rough seas, Sean ... *Doctor Muir*. Why risk everything now? That's your *wife* down there! How can you tempt fate with her under the water?"

Sean listened intently and respectfully, and she was right about last-minute changes often leading to mistakes, but the words "tempt fate" told him everything he needed to know about her objection. "*Fate* is what it is, Van, and by definition, we can't change it. But you know that Kat and I are equally trained to pilot the sub, and we had equal hands in designing it. Really, it barely counts as a change at all. The weather gives us the chance to do things on schedule—we have to take advantage of that."

Vanessa didn't look thrilled with what he said, but she nodded and even gave him an "Aye, sir." Formal, indeed, but he hoped that its vestigial tone of worry would vanish once plans returned to normal and his wife and he got back into the correct rotation. He didn't like to "pull rank" or tell hard-working people such as these to fall in line or start swimming home. They were professionals upon whom he relied, and he treated them that way. But they had to respect his decisions, too, and he had decided operating *D-Plus* without the use of three of his favorite fingers was not going to get this expedition where it needed to go, not on schedule.

"Thank you, Vanessa, that's all." He said to Slipjack and Toro, "You guys stay here for a second, okay? I need to check on Kat. On the descent, I mean."

He rushed over to the video feed and radio comm, swept up the transceiver and pushed the black button with his left hand's thumb. "How are you doing down there, my dear?"

Katherine's grin on the video was infectious. "I believe you mean 'How are you doing down there, *Professor Muir?*'"

"Of course."

She laughed. "All is well. We're at almost 2,500 feet. Everything is humming along just right. The next 7,500 should be a breeze. How're your poor fingers?"

Sean couldn't help hoping the others on deck didn't hear. "Um, they're great. So, seen any new friends down there?" That was a weird and stupid question, he realized, but he was anxious.

"Well, we're deep in the dysphotic zone, almost to aphotic, so if anything wants to be seen, it has to make the first move and get in front of my lights. All I have is darkness ... as you'd well know if you'd been paying attention. What have you been doing up there while I'm down here? Looking for clues?"

Clues? *What the shit?* He let out a strained exhalation that sounded more like he was choking on something than laughing. "What are you ... clues to *what?*" he said, looking around like a paranoid wino at the crew on deck, a crew of which every single member spontaneously and assiduously looked anywhere else than at him. At charts, maybe, or out to sea, or just moving their eyes off of him and onto something, anything, else. His heart pounded in his ears.

"No, silly, I mean clues about what be around the thermal vents. About your *theory.* You know, the whole reason we're doing this thing?"

The crew members laughed, but not very loudly. More of a smiling and shaking-their-heads kind of reaction. Katherine Muir was a firecracker, as the old sea dogs would say. There were other labels that might fit her, too, but Sean wasn't about to get into it when they were supposed to be running diagnostics and such on the submersible. Besides, she was right. They were here to gather evidence that would either keep his theories afloat or sink them for good. It was a big leap to make on not much evidence, but if they could confirm it or even just find an indication he was on the right track, it would shake up all of oceanography, marine biology, land-based biology, maybe xenobiology, possibly even evolutionary-development biology. There was a lot at stake, and he couldn't let worries about rumors and loose talk aboard ship distract him from a career-making discovery.

He took in and let out a long breath, getting his mind back in the game. He depressed the button and said to his wife, "Right, the theory, *duh*. Sorry. So what do you say to giving us some readings and telling us how our little sinker is doing?"

"Ha! Nice. All right, *Sea Legs*, as we continue the descent, we are now one hundred percent in the aphotic zone. It's completely pitch-black outside. Running lighting-system test in three ... two ..."

Sean remained at the monitor until his wife had thoroughly gone down the checklist, told her "Good job, Kat," and returned to where the two crewmen were to still be waiting for him.

Except they weren't.

"Goddamnit— Toro! *Slipjack!* Get back here *now*, if you please."

Slipjack was just around the corner, looking at the video feed where Sean himself had been standing just a moment earlier. Sean caught him in the first glance he took to look for his fugitives, then barked at him to find Toro and for both of them to get back to their earlier place of "conversation." Less than a minute later, the two crewmen stood before him again, Toro looking a bit sulky and Slipjack just nervous.

"Gentlemen, the decision to have my wife take the second test instead of myself was *ours*, mine *and* hers, once we knew what had happened to my hand. I couldn't do it for now, and she knew it needed to be done, knew the job well enough to take the reins and do it herself. Okay? I understand mariners' beliefs and superstitions; I've spent half my life on boats. So, as far as Kat going in place of me, you know I would never let ..." He trailed off as everybody's attention was drawn to the sound at the winch spool. "What the hell is *that?*"

A tremendous slow ripping sound erupted from the winch, and all hands close enough could see that it was caused by a stripped length of iron-shrouded tether cable on the giant spool, a length that had apparently taken more abuse than it could bear. Their armored support unwoven, the fiber-optic cables were the only part of the tether holding one end to the next, and when that section moved to the top of the wheel in about fifteen seconds, those thin plastic lines would snap at the first pull of the submersible's weight.

Sean rushed to the controls and tried to figure out which levers and buttons would stop the spool from letting out the damaged length of cable. But it was hopeless. The half of his life he had spent on boats was as an oceanographer, not the operation of this equipment. "Where the hell are my winch men?" he shouted, hoping one of the other crew members would locate—

"Aw, *goddamnit*," Sean moaned when he remembered that his winch crew consisted of Vanessa, Toro, and Slipjack, the last two of whom he had just told not to move from their useless positions behind the winch assembly. Vanessa busted her ass to get at the cable and the winch that was slowly feeding it out, although she plainly had no idea what to do except shut it down. Which she did.

The stripped length stopped two feet from where it would have had to bear the full weight of *D-Plus*. Vanessa let out a huge breath of relief, and so did Sean.

"Toro, Slipjack," he was able to say in a normal tone now that the loud winch was stopped, "let's get to work. And if any of the three of you says 'I told you so' to me ... well, I know where we keep the harpoons."

The two men hurried to the spool and immediately saw the issue. As long as they didn't let any more cable out, it was possible that the line wouldn't break. It still could, and easily, but it was also possible that it would not, and they had to be grateful for that.

That was the good news.

The bad news was that they couldn't reverse the winch to haul Kat back up, because in its present position, *that* would put too much strain on the weak area and snap it like a piece of uncooked spaghetti. They were lucky that Vanessa got the winch stopped in time at all, but the next thing to do—if there was anything to be done—was going to prove much more daunting a task.

There was emergency scuba gear on board *D-Plus*, but Kat was more than 2,800 feet down. That meant over *one thousand* pounds of pressure per square inch pressed on the sub. Kat had a wetsuit inside the submersible, but her hatch had all that pressure keeping it closed—and besides, she'd freeze to death even as every atom of air in her body was compressed to the point of complete organ failure. She wasn't getting out, and even if she could, she would die within 30 seconds.

No one could dive down in scuba gear to rescue her, either, and for the same reasons. Another sub could perhaps couple with *D-Plus*, but they didn't have another sub and they were too far out to request one before Kat ran out of oxygen or that cable snapped.

However, there was little risk of crushing: the submersible was rated for the entire 20,000 feet down. And there was a *chance* the whole works could be attached to a new cable and "carried" back to the surface by another submersible device.

Sea Legs carried an old but trustworthy *Johnson Sea Link* knockoff that could, in an emergency, possibly go that deep. The JSL was essentially human-shaped, with a clear-mask helmet for the human occupant's head, and then controlled external arms and hooks that could perhaps slip a sturdier cable (one without any communication lines or fiber optics) onto *D-Plus*, and haul her up.

The problem—and *of course* there was a problem—was that the *JSL* had a crush depth of 3,000 feet. It used to be *the* vehicle for "deep-sea" exploration, but as exploration technology had improved dramatically since the mid-70s, when the university's robotic-looking spare submersible *JSL* was built, the definition of "deep-sea" had also changed, or at least what it meant to science and technology.

Two researchers had touched the bottom of Challenger Deep in 1960, but that was funded by the deep, deep pockets of several sovereign governments and wasn't intended to do any science; it was a Cold War demonstration by the United States and France, just like the race to land on the moon. The Muir expedition could buy only what they could afford with their academic funding—barely enough for the present mission, let alone getting down to the very bottom of the entire ocean. Besides, there were no hydrothermal vents believed to be that deep, so it wouldn't have fallen under the mission parameters anyway.

The Muirs' *D-Plus* could go to 20,000 feet (theoretically, anyway; that was what they were currently trying to test before committing to using the sub for exploration), and they were extremely lucky to have been able to afford *that*. Although not lucky enough, apparently, to have anticipated the need for a backup cable system.

"Guys?" Katherine called from the radio. "What's the holdup? Traffic? Is there too much—?"

Sean swept up the mic. "Kat, we have a situation here."

"Oh. I do *not* like situations."

"We read you at about 2,800 feet, sound about right?"

"You guys are letting out the cable, you tell me," she said with a laugh. "Yeah, looks like 2,840. The descent felt very smooth until we ... well, *you* stopped. I have hours of air left, and I won't try to go outside, I promise. Can we start up again? *What's the rumpus*, like you always say?"

Sean couldn't help but look at the spool with its almost bare-naked two-foot-long stretch of cable. "We're having some trouble with the winch—or the cable—actually, it's both. The winch can't move it forward or back without, um, *complications*."

"Forward or back? Those are pretty much the only options, right?" A note of concern had entered her voice, the playfulness sounding strained now. "Seriously, talk to me, honey. What's happening?"

"The cable," he said. "It's stripped almost bare in one section."

"I see. Boy am I *really* glad that's impossible. But, just for fun, let me ask: one 'problematic' section is all you ... we ... *I* need to be completely screwed, isn't it?" She was without levity in her voice now. "Sean, a thick-ass cable like that doesn't get stripped by … I don't even know *how* you could 'strip' that accidentally. You'd have to know a lot about how we do things and have a lot of time around the cable."

Without conscious intention, Sean looked over at Vanessa, Toro, and Slipjack. They were all looking at him the same way, blankly but with uncertainty in their eyes.

Or maybe with *certainty* in them.

"So, Sean, babe, what's the plan here? The cable's magically stripped, fine. What are we going to do about it? Can the bare area be patched?"

Sean shook his head, even though she couldn't see him, and said flatly, "No."

"Well, shit."

"I mean, it *could*, but that would take equipment, supplies, and room we don't have. Not to mention time—that'd be a two-hour process before we even moved it onto the spool. If you weren't attached to the other end of it, we could use the blow torch to just cut the cable off before the break and then reattach it. No worries. *If* we had all that, and we don't."

"So helpful, thanks."

He loudly mumbled a string of angry-sounding almost-words; then, more clearly not much less loudly, shouted into the comm link with his wife, "These goddamn cables *never* just get stripped like this! They're *indestructible!*"

Kat didn't say anything.

He calmed himself. He took a big breath in and let it out. Then he could say with honesty, "Honey? We've got options. Don't worry."

When she spoke, it was clear from her voice that she had gone into shock. It was almost a whisper, as if she were talking to herself: "Someone's trying to murder me."

"What? No, that's not …" He wanted to say it wasn't possible, but she would give him the same retort as always when he said that: *It doesn't have to be possible anymore. It's actual.* "Listen, let's just focus on getting this FUBAR situation fixed up, okay?"

Kat had head-mounted headphones with a microphone, so her scarcely audible mumbling of "… murder … someone's trying to murder me … someone's trying to murder me …" continued on the radio on deck where everyone could hear it, even though she clearly was no longer conversing with her husband.

He called to Toro: "How long do you need to get the *JSL* ready to launch?"

The big Hispanic mariner looked up at where the knockoff was secured. "If I bust my ass, it could be in the water in forty-five minutes. And you bet *your* ass I'm gonna bust *my* ass, *jefe*."

"But what are we supposed to do when we get down there?" Vanessa asked, not as a challenge but as a consequence of her overflowing anxiety. "Okay, yeah, the *JSL* isn't a tethered submersible, so we don't need to use the cable on *that*. But the whole point would be to pull *D-Plus* and Kat up to the surface, and that would require the bad cable to be cut or separated, and a new one to be slipped into the place of the bad one.

"But even if we had another three thousand feet of cable—which we *don't*, since all our cable for the whole mother-loving mission is on this one useless spool because *this cable is practically indestructible* unless you're *trying* to damage it—how would we attach it? You can't do detail work like that with those *JSL* claws, Sean. And God knows it's too damn deep for an *out-of-vessel* excursion. Three thousand feet in just a wetsuit isn't even close to possible, and that means we can't attach another cable and we can't just spring Kat out of there and into our sub—her lungs and heart would collapse instantly."

Sean's gaze remained on the deck, which is what he did when he was trying to think deeply, or when he was listening intently, or both. He nodded at everything Vanessa was saying, and it wasn't much different from what he was already thinking. For a moment a hope came to him and he said, "What if we went down in the *JSL* and clamped onto the cable holding *D-Plus* and just dragged it back up to where she *could* get out? That would keep there from being any pull on the compromised cable, and the slack as she was brought up could be used to wrap the exposed cable under several more layers on the spool."

"That could work, but what's the operational depth of the *JSL?* Didn't it get discontinued because those poor bastards got caught on some sunken ship, and they were stuck there until they ran out of air? How deep was that?" Slipjack asked in his hint of a western-by-way-of-New Jersey drawl that usually seemed homey and ominous in equal measure but seemed neither at the moment, more like on the edge of panic as he tried to run through all the possibilities in his mind. The winch, after all, was *his* responsibility. Only he and Sean Muir had official access to it around the clock. The others had to be wondering how he'd let this happen right under his nose.

Vanessa said, "That had nothing to do with crush depth, Slip."

"No, but I'm wondering how deep that was, 'cause obviously that dive must've been inside their depth comfort zone, y'know? I think its deepest rating is in the neighborhood of three thousand feet. And she's at, what'd you say earlier, 2,800 feet? So you'd have some wiggle room to save her, boss!"

Sean nodded. That accident killed two submariners and got the original *JSL* discontinued, but they lived long enough as the carbon dioxide scrubbers became inoperable that they knew they would die down there. All they could do was wait for the oxygen to run out. Vanessa was right: it was an oxygen thing, not a crush depth thing.

But those memories came and went like vapor. Slipjack's words barely stuck, although he understood his winch man perfectly. All he could focus on right then was his wife still repeating that she was being murdered, someone was trying to murder her. Only now she was leaving the "trying" part out: "... someone's murdering me ... why are they murdering me? ... someone is murdering me ..."

"I think you got to go for it, boss," Slipjack said, looking ill. "You got to save her somehow. She's in danger because of you—"

"All right. *Enough!*" Sean snapped at him. "You think I don't know that, goddamnit? You and Toro break out the *JSL*—use the launch crane—and make it ready."

Slipjack and Toro moved as fast as Sean had ever seen them move. Vanessa stayed with Sean, since two deckhands with a hook and *Sea Legs'* smaller winch would be enough to get the *JSL* down where they could prep it for a dive and get the pilot situated. An additional person would only get in the way.

"This could work, boss," she said as the two men wrestled the hook onto the goddamn museum piece that was their counterfeit *JSL*. Young oceanographers from the Institute liked to use the thing to spend some time near coral reefs or where they could set down in a couple dozen feet of water and observe turtles and interesting fish do their thing in the light of the euphotic zone. But the Muirs had it on *Sea Legs* because it was always stowed on *Sea Legs*, the boat being used currently by the Muirs but actually the property of the Institute and thus used also by their colleagues and students. He was very glad right then that no one had ever thought it necessary to go through the pain in the ass of taking it off the boat and storing it somewhere else, just to have to haul it out and load it on the boat again the next time a grad student or postdoc wanted to use it.

Moving to help them, Vanessa stopped next to Sean and asked quietly, "Listen, Cap—even if they can get it down and prepped in forty-five minutes, how long will it take to get it down three thousand feet? Another forty?"

Sean looked pale but didn't let his fear get the best of him. No effective mission leader could let anything, even something like this, get that deep under his skin. "Could be an hour."

Vanessa looked at the green-screen on-deck computer monitor. "She's been down there an hour and a half, Sean. Those scrubbers work how long? I don't know this shit, boss, you got to help me here."

"She's got five hours in the sub. More than that and her brain dies from lack of oxygen." He swallowed, shaken from listening to his wife go dissociative with talk of getting "murdered" while sitting in what could soon be her own coffin.

"Shit. So an hour and a half, plus, let's say, an hour to get the *JSL* down to *D-Plus* and get a good hold on her cable. How long's it gonna take for our little *JSL* to pull our chunky sub to the point where Kat can get out and free swim to the surface?"

"I have no idea, Van. I've never done this before. No one has. These armored cables do *not*—"

"I know, Sean, I know. But there's plenty of time for figuring that out once we have your wife back and safe. Give me a ballpark: How long?"

"The *JSL* isn't really made for towing, but since we're pressing it into service, if I had to venture a guess—"

"Which you do."

"—I'd say at least two hours with that heavy load and the limited thrust of the *JSL*. Maybe more."

"That *maybe* is straddling the line between saving your wife and losing her, Sean. You've done, what, a hundred dives in this thing? You have to be the one to go down and get her—you always find a way to keep us going. We haven't lost a crew member yet, so let's not start today, all right?"

He allowed himself a very small smirk and said, "When did I promote you to first mate?"

"When you lost your shit listening to Katherine. Besides, who do you want right now? Mickey is a boat chief, not a submersible expert. I'm not saying he can't learn, but now seems an inopportune time for rookie training.

"Slipjack doesn't dive, but he could be your right-hand man on the surface once we get the *JSL* ready to go. And that should be soon, once they get the batteries installed and run through the checklist."

"Has Toro ever piloted a submersible?"

"No. He's purely a member of the boat crew, promoted to winch team. And I've dived a few times, just not in the pilot's seat."

"Vanessa, I know all this. What are you getting at, already?"

"I'm telling you that *you* need to get suited up, and *you* need to do this. Not because she's your wife, but because she's part of your research crew. *Your* skills and experience are the only things that can save her."

Sean took all of this in, sucked in a deep breath, then let it go. He shouted to Toro and Slipjack, "Let's go, gentlemen! Time is short!"

"Twenty minutes," Toro said without looking up from his work.

"Screw that. Fifteen at the most and I want this in the water."

Slipjack muttered under his breath, but it was plenty loud enough for Toro to hear, and laugh.

"It's a suicide mission, *ese*. You don't want it. Like Van said, you don't dive."

"No, I don't. But I *could*. I want to be the hero for once, save the woman who ..."

"Who ... who what?"

"Who is really friggin' important to this expedition! I want to be her hero instead of just a guy on the boat."

"What, you got a crush on Mrs. Muir? *Ha ha*, that is *muy adorable!*" Toro said with a sympathetic smile. "She is easy on the eyes, man, but come on. And you want to be a hero ... or a martyr, maybe, you mean? 'Cause that's what *el jefe* is gonna be in a few minutes, man. Ain't no way this thing can drag up a full-size submersible."

"This ain't right. The whole thing stinks like rotten fish covered with dog shit," Slipjack said when they turned back to keep prepping the rickety-ass sub that was less likely to rescue the wonderful Kitty Muir than to send Sean *and* his wife to the bottom forever.

He just hoped his check got signed *before* Sean Muir left on his mission to be the center of attention once again. And the Muirs *would* be at the center, all right. He could see the headlines: OCEAN RESEARCHERS DIE IN 'ACCIDENT.'

Except this bullshit is no accident, Slipjack thought, but kept it to himself. He had a job to do here, and doing it well and swiftly could mean rescuing Katherine instead of letting her die, even if the whole situation was Sean Muir's doing, or if not his fault, then at least definitely his responsibility. But he shook that out of his mind and got the *JSL* ready as quickly as he and Toro could.

"Sean ... ?" It was Katherine's voice, still sounding distant but much more cogent. "Come in, babe ..."

Sean spun around from watching them work with the *JSL* (just far away enough that he couldn't hear what Slipjack was saying to Toro) and practically hurled himself the six feet to the mic and started talking almost before he had depressed the button: "Kat! Thank God! I thought you had gone off the deep end!" He winced at his own choice of words.

"I'm okay. I'm alive. Had me a little freak-out there." She sounded *more* with it, but hardly one hundred percent. "Honey, I'm just hanging in the dark. There's nothing to see, not even dinosaurs ... and directly below, there's the vents. Maybe the dinos are nearby, maybe they can sense me ..."

"Don't worry about that, honey—you're not deep enough to give off a heat signature strong enough to attract them, anyway. So just forget about anything except my words, okay?"

"Okay." With that one-word response, she sounded again like the researcher who had first gone down in the submersible.

"Okay, excellent. The cable is ... not operational. We can't haul you up with the winch, and we can't even get you any deeper—not that we would—but never mind—I'm coming down to get you."

"Sean, it's okay. I know the risks every time I go down."

"Jesus, honey, no—I said, I'm coming down *right now.*"

"I'm at three thousand feet, Sean! What are you going to do, put on some swim fins and a snorkel? I can still get some data, even if we can't find your prehistoric beasts—"

"No! Just hang tight"—again he regretted his turn of phrase—"and I'll be there in plenty of time. I'm using the *JSL.*"

"*That piece of [buzz]?* Don't you dare, Doctor Muir—we don't *both* need to die! Somebody on the ship sabotaged the cable. Don't give them a chance to mess with the *JSL* and murder you, too."

"Don't say *murder*, Kat. Number one, you're not going to die; and number two, *I'm coming to get you and bring you up.* Just keep your mind on that, okay? You've got to have two hours of oxygen left. I'll make it in plenty of time."

"I love you, Sean. I'm so sorry."

"Nothing to be sorry about. We got this. And I love you, too, so much. And if I have to die to save you, that's a fair deal to me."

"Well, it's not to *me!*"

"All right, then, we'll both live. How's that?"

"Roger that. Okay, fine, go suit up and get down here already."

"On it." He motioned for Mickey to come off the bridge. "Mick, you've got the comm, all right? Talk to her, keep her calm, and keep reminding her that I'm on my way."

"You got it, boss. And good luck—we know you can do it."

Sean nodded at that and got his ass over to the winch crew setting up the submersible, which looked like nothing more than a 1950s science-fiction robot. He squeezed into his wetsuit and stowed his air tank and regulator inside the *JSL*. There was no real reason he'd need them—or be able to use them—unless and until he got Kat near the surface and opened *D-Plus* to get her out. The extra equipment was fine, anyway; he'd take a load of anvils on board if it would help him get down there. He froze. *Why in God's name didn't I think of this earlier?*

"Holy shit! Mickey, tell her to jettison her ballast, every bit of it, right away!" He literally couldn't believe he hadn't remembered to tell her to do that in the first place. Everybody on board must have thought he was a complete shithead who didn't care whether his wife lived or died. Not that he cared much about that right now.

Mickey relayed the message, and the last thing Sean heard before Slipjack helped him into the *JSL* was her response of "Roger that." It gave him the tiniest peace of mind, which was better than nothing.

Slipjack got him ready and was about to screw the hatch shut but stopped and looked Sean in the eyes. "Go save your wife. Save our Kat."

Our Kat? But Sean nodded, holding back the desire to say, *Why in the hell do you think I'm sitting in this thing?* but he could hardly blame the crew for loving her. She was so good to everyone, always smiling and working as hard as anyone else. Sean saw her occasional tantrums and tears, but that was the difference between a husband and a coworker on a research vessel.

Slipjack screwed on the hatch and stepped back. He and Toro and Vanessa exchanged thumbs-ups with Sean and then with one another when each of them took their assigned positions to deploy the A-frame and crane to lower the submersible into the sea.

Excruciatingly slowly, they lowered the *JSL*. So slowly he would surely never get down in time to Kat, who was breathing the last of her air, waiting for him, so far away.

***

Inside *D-Plus*, Katherine quickly hit the necessary switches and buttons to release the ballast. She'd done it a hundred times in submersibles; the ballast was just seawater, but water actually made for better ballast than any other material, and it didn't shoot a lot of garbage into the ocean they all loved, like the old-school kind did.

But neither of the hatches on the sides of the submersible opened to release the ballast. *D-Plus* was still as weighted down as she was at launch, when the hatch worked perfectly to let the seawater *in* and allow the dive to happen in the first place.

She didn't panic, though, didn't enter any kind of fugue state like before. She just went through the steps again, more slowly and carefully this time.

It didn't make any difference.

The hatch wouldn't open, and of course there was no way for her to get out at this depth and open them manually with the fail-safe tool. "You're just going to have to lift me with my ballast," she said into her headset.

She kept in contact with Mickey up on the surface, but radio waves traveled more slowly the deeper one went—which was why a deep-sea submersible like *D-Plus* was connected to fiber optics for data and video and lines for voice and other communications. These lines were encased in armored steel and were supposed to be as close to indestructible as possible. That was because fail-proof systems were essential in extreme environments like those Sean and Kat were aiming for with this expedition. *Supposed* to be indestructible. At least, that was if no one with specialized knowledge—and some kind of motivation, obviously— got to them when no one was looking.

But delay or not, saboteur on the loose or not, Mickey on *Piranha II* kept the video and other sensors tightly focused on the line that was all that was keeping Kat on *D-Plus* from sinking, fatally, to the bottom. If she had been able to jettison the ballast—which was done with the push of exactly two buttons and a switch—it would have made Sean's job of grabbing hold of the cable just above *D-Plus* with the *JSL*'s clamp-like "hands" and bringing her up *much* easier.

Easy wasn't happening in this FUBAR situation anyway, but trying to bring up *D-Plus* loaded down with ballast might be impossible for an ancient gadget like the *JSL*. Sean would jettison his own ballast when he got to her, so at least *he* would retain some buoyancy.

As was always the case in their line of work, they'd just have to go with what was even infinitesimally possible and make it a dead-certain reality.

It was obvious that rescue of *D-Plus*—and, more importantly, Katherine—fell into this category. No one could blame him for failing, but everyone still would. *He* still would. He needed to show everyone that he could do this, save the day. Mariners were an odd lot who might call off the next dive "because of weather," since they were empowered to make the final decision. Theoretically, this took into consideration the science team's input, of course; but the professional sailors on board knew that, outside of a storm forcing waves over the deck, the scientists would always choose to dive. Thus, oftentimes the "consideration" of the scientists' opinions meant "seeming to listen and then doing what real men and women of the sea thought right and proper." So it was best to avoid discomfort in the sailing crew.

Also, of course, if they lost this submersible—even if it during an unmanned test—it would render funding for of his any further dives highly unlikely. *His and Kat's* funding, that was. She wasn't dead yet. He had to not think like that, *Jesus.*

Not yet, anyway.

D-Plus and similar research submersibles were designed to be pulled up by the same cable that guided them down. That would make it a hell of a lot easier to drag it back up with the *JSL*, which was built for exploration mostly in the euphotic zone, not for its gripping or lifting power. Of course, there never would have *been* a problem like this if the deep-sea sub dived and rose under its own power. But that's just not how it worked anymore, the cable being needed for heavy data and communications demands if not for lowering and lifting the submersible.

Mickey told him which ways to activate the *JSL*'s small water jets to keep the vessel the right distance from the cable. Not that this was in any way a "normal" operation, but the usual and much less difficult way of approaching would have been for Sean in the *JSL* to loop onto the cable itself and just slide down to the research sub. However, that option wasn't available to them since it was a flaw in the cable itself (*Ha! That's the understatement of the year,* Sean scoffed despite himself) that had put the submersible in peril in the first place. One strong tug on that line and it would snap up on the boat and that would be that for his wife; the ballast-weighted *D-Plus* would be much too heavy for the smaller and lighter *JSL* to hold.

They had gotten extremely lucky—or less *un*lucky, he guessed, because this was not a lucky day—that the surface was almost mirror-calm that day. Choppy or "confused" seas, when you couldn't tell which way the water was going to take you, put a lot more stress on the cable.

And that stress was exactly what the damaged cable couldn't take.

The *JSL*'s descent went smoothly, Mickey letting him know how things looked and also relaying any messages from Kat and doing the same for Sean's messages to his wife.

In fact, it went so smoothly that his mind drifted.

Diving to just three thousand feet wasn't going to be any help with the expedition's goals, but they had been on the path to the benthic zone, where they'd found evidence that a line of hydrothermal vents stretched for several thousand miles from just north of Hawaii right up to the Marianas Trench. Maybe continued *in* the Marianas Trench, so little had those extreme depths been explored in any detail.

Heat was at the center of his theories. When the oceans cooled and put the Permian Extinction into motion, most aquatic dinosaurs died off—actually, 95 percent of everything in the oceans and a huge percentage of things living on land, including dinosaurs. But where the ocean remained warm, even hot, was at the bottom, near the network of hydrothermal sulfur vents.

The idea came to Sean Muir five years earlier, when he was a graduate student in oceanography with a specialty in undersea geology at UCSD. He went on a deep-sea expedition with his advisor and two other grad students the professor was mentoring. It wasn't some kind of historic outing, diving in a well-explored area just off the California coast, but it was deep enough that there was no light except for the glow around their four-person submersible caused by the sub's own floods.

Looking at the constant snowy fall of organic material destined for the ocean floor could hold one's interest for only so long, but they weren't underwater for an hour when his advisor said, "Do you see that? This is a fount of life, lady and gentlemen!"

The submersible had many viewports, and they all got a look at the odd orange-yellow light coming from the ocean floor. It was only about 1,500 feet down, but it presented a completely alien world. The vent had *things* all around it, things that looked like those giant inflatable men at car dealerships and such, beckoning buyers just by random movement catching their eyes: tube worms.

It was the same principle at work here—all four of them were mesmerized by the giant sea worms, securely attached to the seafloor but being blown around by the sulfur-rich, superheated water coming from the tectonic rip.

"I wish we could get closer, but that heat would overpower the sub and boil all of us faster than trout in a steam basket," he said. "But *look*—it's an ecosystem like none other. These worms—and amoebas so large they're visible to the human eye—thrive directly on the chemicals pouring out, and then there are predators even down here ready to eat them, starting a food chain without the slightest thing to do with sunlight."

"Predators?" Sean asked in a dreamy voice.

"Oh, yes, there are albino squid down here, octopoids, *jumbo* shrimp relatives, and there are signs of even more complex life. Even vertebrates."

One of the other grad students spoke up: "Wouldn't their bones get crushed at this depth?"

"No, indeed. That's what one would worry about, isn't it? Your rib cage being flattened and your head caving in? But, in fact, you would die of capillary damage and organ failure at much shallower depths than those required to destroy the calcium in your bones. This is because water is incompressible. Not just the water in the ocean, but the water in the human body! This presses against all of the body's systems, including the skin, and meets the incompressible water contained in your organs. They reach a stasis rather quickly, but stasis is not how organs keep us alive! A stopped heart may be perfectly balanced with the water pressure outside it, but that doesn't do its owner much good if all the oxygen has been rendered immobile."

A chuckle went through the submersible, then the third grad student asked, "Then how can anything with organs live down here? I mean, tube worms are pretty simple, and octopoids are incredibly elastic, I know. But things that would *eat* them? I don't see how that's possible."

"But you're working on your doctorate in marine biology! Surely you know that, as Jeff Goldblum so succinctly put it in that dinosaur movie, 'Life finds a way.'"

"*Jurassic Park*," Sean said almost automatically. It and its sequels were favorites of his since he was a kid. But paleontology was a field with precious few positions available, and professors retired very late, if at all; the joke was "Old paleontologists never die. They just turn into fossils."

"Just so. The way the concept was used in that story was a bit silly, but the statement remains valid in a general sense, and is definitely applicable down here. And Sean, since you're a dinosaur aficionado, you see how, with the oceans growing colder after the Cretaceous event, some marine lizards could evolve to take advantage of heat sources far deeper than those they had earlier thrived in."

Sean said lightly but with respect, "That's pretty speculative."

His advisor laughed. "Indeed, it is. But something balances the ecosystem down here, and aquatic dinosaurs have had a *long* time to adapt. I mean, the water didn't turn cold overnight, and maybe the deeper one went at that point—and remember, there was a lot more going on volcanically and such down here during that period—the warmer it would be. Yes, they'd have had to evolve structures other than bones and organs that would work in ways we probably aren't even able to conceptualize at this point … unless one were researching it full-time, say." He gave Sean a meaningful glance. "Also, the giant lizards ruled the earth for 165 million years—you think they'd all just give up without a fight?"

They laughed, but Sean was struck by the idea. Being a graduate student was a time for learning what could be reasonably speculated upon and what was better not to waste one's time with, because the thesis and dissertation were what mattered most. The fortunate few, however, were able to develop something new, something at least *different*, about which they could publish, and publish papers on every change of nuance as their research developed. Sean and every other student in any graduate program anywhere needed something real, and possibly dramatic, upon which to create a reputation and thus become very attractive to those seeking to fill empty tenure-track lines at Carnegie I research institutions.

However, he also had heard many cautionary tales of grad students who went awry trying to prove some pet theory of their advisors'— drinking the academic Kool-Aid, as it were. Embarrassment and wasted time were the least of it. No, the worst was a career up in smoke, one's world-changing dissertation given up for something mundane, something just to get the degree so he could accept the first community-college job offered to him. *If* any were offered. Life as an adjunct earth sciences "professor" was worse than embarrassing to someone like Sean; it would be humiliating and would remain humiliating until the day he retired. Or killed himself. Which would be preferable was a coin toss.

In other words, Sean Muir needed to find something attractive and unusual, maybe even slightly groundbreaking, but nothing so off the wall that it would come crashing down around him and ruin his life. (Any advisor he had would be tenured already and thus wouldn't be affected professionally in the slightest by such a disaster. If he or she were a *human being*, the professor in question might feel terrible about the whole thing, but pity or even heartfelt regret didn't open doors to academic careers.)

But God, *dinosaurs* still existing near the ocean floor! Evolved and adapted, of course, just like every other living thing, but perhaps in the same way that sharks and alligators had evolved—almost unchanged through the millennia, so what you had now was almost identical to what you would have had 300 million years ago. And even if it weren't dinosaurs, finding whatever was at the top of the sea-vent chemosynthesis food chain would attract a lot of welcome attention.

It was a risk; but no risk, no reward. Sean had a *long* talk with his advisor the day after their undersea excursion, during which each argued for and against the idea of building on this speculation as a real program of research. Finally, they agreed the best course of action would be for Sean to change his concentration from oceanography and tectonic geology to marine biology and—thank God he was at San Diego, where this wouldn't get him laughed out of the room—paleoichthyology. Even if he didn't find the predators that just *had* to be there (*life finds a way*), he would certainly discover enough about deep-sea hydrothermal vents to write a dissertation that still broke new ground, so to speak.

A voice snapped him back to reality, the present, where he was in the rickety *JSL* submersible surrounded by black water.

"Sean? Copy? *Sean.*" It was crew chief Mickey's voice, and he must have been calling for a while. "Sean, tell me you're not dead. Sean, *do you copy?*"

He said into the comm, a bit sheepishly, "Copy here, *Sea Legs.* Sorry, I was having trouble with something."

"Sure, okay," Mickey said in the tone Sean would have used himself if he had been on the other end. "Listen, do you still have the sub's cable in view?"

Fortunately, despite his sudden mental walkabout, he did.

"You've got about twenty feet to go, by your instruments. Can you get a visual on *D-Plus?* She should be just below you, dead cen—right in the middle."

He leaned against the viewport and saw the lights that adorned the submersible. "Affirmative, I see it. If I can get down to Kat—"

"No, Sean, there's no time. You need to extend the *JSL* claw in front of you and open the claw, then ease yourself forward until you can get a tight grasp on the cable. Keep descending, too—get as close as you can to the sub, but *stay above her.* Nobody blames you for wanting to *see* your lovely bride after all this, but first we need to get her out of danger by you clamping on. You copy that?"

"Roger. Moving toward the cable—"

"Did you extend the arm and open the claw?"

Dammit. A few seconds later, he called up, "Affirmative. Centering *JSL* to position the claw around the cable ... *got it.*" He could hear a small background cheer from Mickey's microphone.

***

Katherine Muir was running out of air and running out of hope. She had been stuck in one place for more than an hour; this after an hour for descent, and the CO_2 scrubbers were going to remain operative for perhaps one more hour, but perhaps not.

Mickey kept her advised on every move her husband was making in the *JSL* to come rescue her, and it made her cry to spot the floodlights on that obsolete piece of flotsam that was now going to save her life. It came closer, closer, then used some vertical jets to stabilize its depth. The arm of the *JSL* extended and the claw opened. She couldn't see Sean because of the angle and the bright lights, but she felt it was him.

Let me live, the hardcore atheist prayed to whatever deity would listen. *I'll tell him everything. Just get me out of here so I can make amends. Come on, I'm evidence-based. I'll consider that evidence enough.*

She felt rather than heard the *JSL*'s clamp make contact with the iron-clad cable. It felt like a miracle, and she added to whatever deity was responsible, *Thank you. Just a little more, and you'll have a devotee for life, I promise—*

She was cut off by *D-Plus* lurching to port—the side Sean in the *JSL* was on—and then swinging widely to the right before repeating the pendulum motion. Sean must have pushed on the cable instead of just grabbing it.

But it seemed that everything had held, and that the *JSL* had now clamped onto the cable. In a moment, she would feel a tug from just above her, and a moment after that, she would begin her ascent, pulled by the *JSL* all the way to the top, or at least within scuba distance to the surface.

"We've gotcha," Mickey said with obvious relief, but it was nothing compared to Kat's. She shook with adrenaline and felt tears running down her cheeks. "Please put your tray tables in the upright position and enjoy the ride."

Kat laughed hard, very hard. She could feel that *D-Plus* was being tugged upward. Sean must have been hitting the *JSL*'s vertical thrusters in a staccato fashion, which really was not ideal, even though she could see that it might *seem* ideal. However, instead of making it safer—because he was repeatedly stopping to make sure everything was okay—the jerks and stops were adding a lot more stress to her end of the cable. But she remembered now that the problem part of the cable was on the spool on *Sea Legs*, not on *D-Plus*'s connection, so tugs on her end wouldn't cause any important stress on it there. Quite the opposite, in fact. "Mick, tell my husband that I know he likes to jerk it, but this is taking it too far," she said, crying with laughter.

Mickey gave a "Roger" to that, laughing himself. She could hear him relay the message to Sean. "Oh, he loved that, Kitty. Score!"

She laughed anew, maybe even getting a little hysterical with relief, and smiled with each *tug* ... *tug* ... *tug* on the cable from her overcautious, sweet husb—

Slip. The sub *slipped* a little. Kat wouldn't fall very fast if Sean accidentally released the cable for a few seconds, but she would definitely start falling. "*Mickey!* What's going on up there?"

Mickey said, "Stand by," and used the handset to call to Sean: "*Whiskey Tango Foxtrot!* Status, man!"

"I-I had a solid grip. *Solid*—but then something happened to the arm on this goddamn piece of garbage! I got a hold of it with the other hand, the right clamp. The left one is inoperative. Copy me?"

"Copy." Mickey relayed the information to Kat in *D-Plus*.

"Whew. I almost screamed there," Kat said. "I take it he had enough line pulled up when the clamp opened that he was able to catch it with the other?"

"Just so, Doctor Muir. We didn't feel any tug up here, which is good, because that bit of cable doesn't look like it could take one."

"Mickey," Sean radioed.

"Everything is unchanged up here. You had enough slack so it didn't pull the cable."

"No, Mick, this *JSL* piece of crap, I've taken it too deep—the arms' hydraulic fluid is being squeezed out through some fissure. What can I do? I need to know *right now*."

Unfortunately, Mickey knew the *JSL*, which really was a relic and something they should have realized couldn't take the pressure so near its known crush zone without major malfunctions. He told Sean what he knew, careful to lift his thumb off the button he used to talk to *D-Plus*: "Not a goddamn thing, Sean. I'm sorry. Maybe try to position yourself underneath Kat so your buoyancy can keep her from sinking. Shoot your ballast as soon as you get under. As soon as your fluid runs out, the hydraulic pressure will bottom out and that clamp will pop open like the cable's hot."

"Mick, tell Kat to hang in there," Sean said, his nerves all caught up in his voice. "*No!* Don't say that! Tell her we've got a plan."

Their crew chief picked up the mic to tell her, but before he could say a word, the cable going into the water pulled taut.

And snapped.

Mickey screamed into the mic, "*Katherine! Kat! Copy! Do you copy?*" But there was no response, because she couldn't possibly have heard him. The ultimate mission was to go deeper than radio waves could quickly propagate, and so all the communications to *D-Plus* came through the data lines *inside* that goddamn cable. He could feel all of the blood drain from his face as he lifted the handset and tried to yell, but could only croak, "Sean? You copy? What the hell just happened? Goddamn, man, *talk to me!*"

His boss's voice was like a ghost's. "The clamp opened, just ... *so fast*. I was getting in position under Kat to try to hold her up like you said, but the hydraulic fluid must have all emptied. The right clamp popped open ... and she slipped. Jesus Christ, the cable slid right out of my grasp, and I couldn't catch her."

"Wait, Sean. *Wait*. How were you still holding the cable *and* getting in position under *D-Plus?* You'd have to let go of the cable to move under the sub."

"I thought I had more slack, enough to do both." He sounded shell-shocked, then as panic rose, he said quickly and loudly, "What's happening? I can't see the cable anymore—it's got to be right there *and I could catch it—*"

"Not without working hands on that *JSL*."

"—but I can't see the sub, either. What's her status? *What's Kat's status, Mickey?*"

"We lost contact with her when the cable snapped. We lost her, Sean … Jesus, we lost her."

Sean tried to position the old piece of scrap metal so he could see the sub, see his wife one last time, before the lightless depths took her. But he could see nothing. The way the darkness enveloped everything this deep, there was literally nothing for him to see.

***

Katherine Muir was never afraid of the depths, not even down where it was all blackness and nothing lived. She believed in and had helped develop—maybe *more* than just "helped"—her husband's theories about prehistoric animals evolving in order to take advantage of the food at the fiendishly hot hydrothermal vents. Her own PhD had come from a custom-study program of exobiology and geology. Everyone thought she was shooting for Mars, remotely, if not in person. But it was the sea that called her, life below where the sun could reach. She took the lead on several projects with subsequent publications of findings and was much sought after by several universities with elite departments of ocean sciences as well as those working with the Jet Propulsion Laboratory to explore the surface of the Red Planet.

She chose the sea.

And she chose Doctor Sean Muir, who wasn't one of her teachers or advisors, but one who gave impassioned lectures about unusual life possible thanks to chemosynthesis. Sunlight wasn't needed, just energy, and energy was abundant in lines stretching for thousands of miles in the Pacific, Atlantic, and Indian Oceans. That life existed around these vents was well established—but Sean Muir wasn't talking about tube worms and flatfish; he was talking about marine lizards, about *dinosaurs*. He did elicit chuckles and listeners shaking their heads, but the people who held the purse strings at this university often attended lectures featuring the wild surmises of brilliant men and women, Sean being one of them.

His argument for the existence of conscious, complex life-forms (of which dinosaurs were merely the most dramatic and mathematically likely given the timescales involved) along the lines of vents was convincing while also being thrilling. He attracted people with his mind, but also with his generous heart. Katherine fell in love with him the first time she stopped by one of his lectures.

They were no sooner married than they created an ambitious, not to mention expensive, research program that would involve three departments of the school and sponsorship by private businesses as well as funding from the usual government agencies. The funding path charted out, they began work with a phalanx of theorists, designers, and metal-benders to create *D-Plus*, a serious research vessel with an intentionally goofy name that made everyone smile. They went through so many tests on dry dock and just below the surface that sometimes she felt like she lived inside that thing.

If Sean hadn't hurt his fingers, he would be down here, she thought for the hundredth time as she waited at the end of the cable for her husband to come down and rescue her with that Robby-the-Robot *JSL* sub. It was funny that it would be the *JSL* that saved her life. She *hated* that old junk pile; she thought it made them look like amateurs. But now it would be her salvation, the rusty steed ridden by her knight in aquatic armor. She didn't know how to pilot the *JSL*, and *if Sean hadn't hurt his fingers, he would be down here*. She wouldn't have been able to save him. Surely one of the academic support crew would know their way around the *JSL*. But if they didn't, her husband would be lost.

However, he *had* hurt his fingers and so he *wasn't* down here. It was Katherine, thirty-two and almost tenured, married to a brilliant man who would change the way the world understood life and evolution. Her life was everything she could have wished for, but now it was, literally, hanging by a thread.

Then the organic detritus outside the viewport began to glow, and she knew she was saved, she knew Sean had taken that dangerous antique almost to its crush depth to save her. Mickey sent messages down the comm lines to her and then radioed her replies to Sean. Her oxygen and scrubbers would last until they got to the surface—just barely, but if they didn't waste any time, they'd make it.

She felt the tugs and the upward movement of *D-Plus*. The submersible's ballast wouldn't release, but they would work around that; they always found a way to work around any trouble.

Tug, tug, tug. It was going to be slow going, but things never moved quickly in the deep. She was definitely moving in the right direction—

Then the sub *slipped*. That was exactly what it felt like: an ignition not catching, but almost there; a heavy bucket going off the track of a pulley, but just for a second before it corrects itself; holding hands with a toddler who loses his footing but is pulled back up before striking the floor.

The cable must have slipped through or out of Sean's *JSL* hands, but then he *caught it*. He caught the goddamn cable with the stupid robot hands! She let out a huge breath that had a bit of cry in it. Now all Sean needed to do was lift the sub seventy feet or so, and then the bad part of the cable would be pulled back onto the spool where it wouldn't have to bear all of the load. That's what Mickey said, and Mickey had never been wrong on any expedition she'd ever been on.

(Everybody wanted Mickey for their crew chief or even mission chief. He chose to work with the Muirs because he thought Sean's ideas were spot-on, and he wanted to be a part of history. Thinking of that vote of confidence made Kat happy, even as the slip had frightened her almost to screaming panic.)

It was strange inside *D-Plus*, because at this depth, sound was conducted astoundingly well—but it was tones of voice, not the words themselves, that resounded. She could hear Sean talking to Mickey on the comm, but only the tenor of his voice. But tenor was one of anger or fear, or both, and it scared her.

She could hear the *JSL* whine and let out its flatulent thrusts. But then she could hear yelling coming from the *JSL*—

—and two seconds later, she felt *D-Plus* falling. Not *slipping* for an instant like before. No, she and the sub were falling, *sinking*. She immediately tried to raise Mickey on their direct line, but of course there was no response because the cable had broken. The cable that had lowered her down and was to bring her back up had, impossibly, broken, and Sean, just as impossibly, hadn't saved her.

Very slowly, *very* slowly this far down, the sub was accelerating toward the ocean floor. Because of *D-Plus*'s horizontal lozenge shape, without attitude control it went vertical, and she found herself hanging in her buckled safety belts looking straight down into the darkness. After a few seconds, she could no longer hear the *JSL* or Sean inside it. She couldn't hear anything, in fact, but her own breathing. Her own sobbing.

D-Plus would never reach its crush depth, since it was specifically designed to operate at 20,000 feet, to the seafloor, where the thermal vents were. Would she see one of Sean's dinosaurs before her air ran out? Would she see the vents she and her husband had dreamed about, now, before she died? If she could just see the bottom for a second, an *instant*, see the orange light of the thermal vents, she would die with Sean a part of her, seeing the wondrous sights he always promised her were there. That was all she wished for. Just that much. Just that little.

Slowly, ever so slowly, the submersible sank and sank and finally did strike the bottom near the thermal vents, which were just as Sean had described them.

But Katherine Muir saw none of it. The air scrubbers had long since reached their limit, the oxygen completely depleted soon after, and Katherine Muir had been dead for an hour, staring into the dark with sightless eyes, before the sub reached the bottom. She died totally alone, every one of her wishes unfulfilled.

***

Filmmaker Jake Bentneus directed two of the greatest blockbusters in movie history, one (*Lusitania!*) a dramatization of the final voyage of the passenger vessel; and later, an even bigger hit (*Prosopopoeia!*) about human visitors using fictional super-advanced virtual reality to bilk the beings of another planet. Bentneus became fascinated by underwater exploration during the making of *Lusitania!* and learned how to pilot a research submersible in order to see the wreck for himself before filming commenced.

Also, during research for *Prosopopoeia!* Bentneus became deeply immersed in the real-life tech and experience of virtual reality. The twain were to meet, and Bentneus and his team sent Remotely Operated Vehicles (ROVs) to push as deep into the Pacific as possible while he controlled them via a virtual reality interface that made it seem like *he* was skimming along the ocean floor. He could do this because after he had learned to operate real submersibles, he taught himself how to do it while blindfolded, storing that knowledge in his muscle memory. Thus, he could devote his conscious attention to using the robot's cameras for his own eyes, its microphones for his ears.

Essentially, his experience was going for a dive at the bottom of the ocean without any gear on his virtual body at all.

Many known and even some brand-new species of the deep were spotted through the robot's cameras; however, the ROV could reach only the 20,000-foot depths of the abyssal zone. The silty plains Bentneus "swam" above didn't have as many creatures as shallower parts of the ocean, but what he did see amazed and surprised everyone on the team, and the Internet simulcast garnered almost 100 million viewers who watched the entire descent (with live commentary by Bentneus) on their 3D televisions or 2D sets adapted with a special converter made available for watching the dive.

Some got a little nauseated when the little ROV—nicknamed "Nerd Bait," and living up to that moniker—starting shaking after a few minutes at the abyssal zone's floor. The 6,600 pounds of pressure on every inch of the robot was finally breaking it down, literally. Nerd Bait's cameras and microphones bent and twisted, giving a skewed view and loud buzzing before the entire robot completely folded in on itself, like a book slamming shut. In just a few seconds once its crushing point was inadvertently exceeded, the $7 million ROV turned into a pancake of scrap metal.

Experiencing Nerd Bait dying while he was still connected to it affected Bentneus in a way those watching on television weren't, since they could look away, take off the glasses, shut off the set. But Jake Bentneus was lying on his stomach, so he had could get as close as possible to being in the ROV's place. He wasn't physically crushed, of course, but inside his mind he was squashed as flat as a magazine.

His crew winched up the tether—mile after mile of it—along with the tether-management system that allowed the little robot to go so deep while sending and receiving communications through fiber-optic cables. At the end was Nerd Bait, now unrecognizable in its squashed-flat condition, but given a hero's welcome onboard the largest of the three project research vessels. Bentneus had it framed and hung it on his wall like a painting as soon as he got home.

The team's study of the little-researched (because of the huge price) and largely alien (because of its great depths) abyssal zone was a triumph advancing oceanographic knowledge, submersible robot technology, and the widespread interest in virtual reality for extreme exploration. (The moon was mentioned as a next possible "group experience." A Mars-rover–like vehicle with binocular vision and decked out with microphones as well as tactile feedback over bumpy ground would be so awesome, it would *change lives*.)

For Bentneus, however, 20,000 feet down through the eyes of a robot vehicle wasn't enough. True, the floor of the ocean in this part was as far below sea level as the peak of Mount Denali was above it, and Alaska's highest mountain was no foothill.

But Denali was also no Everest.

Jake Bentneus wanted Everest deep.

He wanted *Challenger Deep*.

Challenger Deep is a rip created in the Marianas Trench by active tectonics, a crevasse within a crevasse that already plunges far below the 20,000 feet that killed Nerd Bait. Named after the first ship ever to attempt an estimate of how deep the crevasse went (the *HMS Challenger*, in its 1872–1876 mission), Challenger Deep is a monumental tectonic artifact plunging from the surface of the Marianas Trench in the Pacific past the benthic, abyssal, and hadal zones, the last getting its name from "Hades," god of the underworld. The god of the depths of Hell. These names—which describe depths far less than Challenger Deep—may give a sense of how much farther down Bentneus aimed to dive.

Only two people had gone that deep before, and that was back in 1960, their now-quaint technology allowing the team to stay at the bottom for only twenty minutes before they heard troubling cracking noises and saw water seeping in along the inside of their bathysphere, which they didn't consider necessarily positive developments. They also never were able to photograph or even *see* the bottom because of all the silt their brute-force submersible stirred up upon plopping down. Anything could have been down there—it's *far* deeper than sonar can even estimate well—and they would never have seen it. Still, the two-man team set a still-standing record by descending to the bottom, 36,070 feet deep.

Everest is just 29,000 feet high.

Ghost-white animals called to Bentneus, creatures that had never seen light—and had ceased to possess eyes, since those would prove an evolutionarily useless drain on resources down where sunlight never reached. An ROV couldn't be sent all the way down to the deepest part of the entire ocean, where the seafloor of the Marianas Trench crevasse fell away thousands of feet into that deeper canyon of Challenger Deep.

Bentneus returned from the hugely popular simulcast mission with one purpose, a singular obsession, a monomania that forced itself in front of the making of any sequels to his billions-grossing films … or doing anything else. Perhaps anyone else would be satisfied with skimming the abyssal zone, but the filmmaker demanded the apotheosis of ocean exploration, and had the resources to attempt it.

He would touch bottom in Challenger Deep, and he would stay there long enough to glean real scientific information. Long enough to let settle and dissipate the silt made up of millions of years of diatomaceous sediment, remains of everything from plankton to blue whales. It would take a lot of money, but Jake Bentneus had a *lot* of money and the will to spend $100 million of it in order to put together a crew to build two submersibles—it was vital to have a backup while exploring such an unpredictable environment—and send one down to the most harrowing section of the crushing deep.

The machine they created was unlike any other research vessel ever devised: It was vertically oriented, so it would conserve resources by traveling much faster to the bottom than did the 1960 traditionally horizontal submersible. Most of the length—or height—of the craft was given over to batteries, lights, cameras and other recording and transmitting equipment, and vertical and horizontal thrusters. It was only at the very bottom of the newly christened *Ocean Victory* that a sphere of the strongest steel on Earth would hold its lone occupant. The bathysphere's perfect shape was its trump card against collapsing against the 16,000 pounds *per square inch* that would be pressing against it from all directions at the Challenger Deep seafloor. (As Bentneus liked to say to interviewers, that was equivalent to having the weight of three Hummer SUVs sitting on your thumbnail.)

Ironically, it was the ultimate desire for *freedom* that made Jake Bentneus want to crawl inside a claustrophobic metal ball and sink in a straight line for three hours and then sit in an unmoving can at the very bottom of the ocean, where, at that depth, any imperfection in his sphere would make it implode so fast he'd be dead before even realizing there was a problem.

Not only this, but every move of his would be watched not only by his three-ship crew, but also by an estimated *500 million* 3D simulcast subscribers around the world. Again, the broadcast would be immersive video and sound, but this time a VR helmet was available for $199.99 at Brookstone. It was designed to shut all else out and see and hear exactly what *Ocean Victory* was seeing and hearing every second. In fact, if the silt were still stirred up by Bentneus's extra-soft landing, those cameras stationed higher up on the submersible would actually be able to see *better* at that moment than the filmmaker-aquanaut himself could.

But this, *this* was truly *freedom*. Doing things on his own terms. *Ocean Victory* was to be his in more ways than one. Nothing could crush him or his spirit. Real freedom would be his, a singularity of self and experience no one else in the history of the world had ever experienced.

*   *   *

Jake Bentneus grinned and gave a thumbs-up to the video feed going out to his support crew—and also to the simulcast audience. The simulcast director on board the communications and tech ship *Sea Legs* would switch between cameras and mics for the audience, and a dedicated video archivist would make sure all eight cameras' videos were recorded and saved in their entireties. There wasn't just the 3D feature film of the entire project from conception to completion to think of; this was first and foremost a scientific mission with depth readings and core samples and temperature measurements and such. Bentneus had focused most all of his training on operating the many controls of *Ocean Victory*, which was a full-time job in itself.

Bentneus thought of himself as an *aquanaut*, the deep-sea equivalent of Neil Armstrong or Buzz Aldrin—or maybe Pete Conrad and Alan Bean of Apollo 12, since the 1960 dive technically preceded him. (He had also been in space—it cost him a mere $20 million to orbit with the Russians—but as a "space tourist," not as a member of the crew, helping to expand the boundaries of knowledge.) In *Ocean Victory*, like the lunar explorers, he would operate the machinery, collect the samples, do a little surveying, but then let the marine biologists and oceanographers pore over the data and make theories or whatever they did. But he was the aquanaut here, not a tourist.

His thumbs-up acknowledged by the crew on the main ship, *Piranha II*, Bentneus settled himself into the narrow seat and checked gauges and monitored the operational status of the main systems. They all changed as soon as the submersible was underwater, as made sense. It amused him to monitor the pressure on his cigar-shaped vessel because of how quickly the pressure increased: for every foot *Ocean Victory* descended, thirty-three more pounds of pressure pushed on every square inch of the entire vessel.

Everything went smoothly, unlike the day before when choppy seas made them abort, and now that he was completely under the surface—according to his instruments, since he couldn't see out the small porthole unless he moved the camera out of the way—he felt alone and free. The swaying while being lowered from the A-frame winch ceased immediately upon his immersion, and he was lowered so slowly into the depths that it didn't feel like he was moving at all.

But the gauges told the story, and he watched them with unabashed glee. "All systems operational," he spoke into his on-head microphone, the sound of his own voice jarring in the silence of his underwater cell.

"Roger. That makes it a 'go.' See you once you've made history, Jake."

He grinned. "Roger that."

The trip to the bottom of Challenger Deep would take a mere two-plus hours, cutting in half the time the 1960 duo had needed. The big advantage *Ocean Victory* had was its vertical orientation; the former mission involved an iron bathysphere inside a traditionally shaped horizontal submersible. That took *five hours* to reach the seafloor, allowing them just twenty minutes at the bottom before oxygen supplies and that troubling cracking (due, they surmised later, to the huge difference in temperature of the ocean and of the air inside their sphere) forced them to ascend, which took another three hours.

Bentneus's craft would zip to the bottom—at three miles per hour, but that was zippy for a deep-sea vessel—spend two hours doing science at the seafloor, providing commentary to the crew and millions of people around the world, then zip back up to the ship that tethered him with steel wire and the highest-performance fiber-optic cable.

Bentneus and the crew of the support ships knew that hundreds of thousands of VR helmets had been "rented" for free to many, many K–12 schools and thousands more at a discount to hundreds of universities, so the filmmaker took it as part of his job as an aquanaut to explain to the viewers what they were seeing, while his TV director on the surface worked to switch to whatever cameras offered the most interesting visuals.

"*Piranha II* is lowering me down, but at this point I would continue to descend, regardless," Bentneus told the camera. "This baby has ballast you wouldn't believe. But without the team, I would very easily drift off course—*fatally* off-course—and my telemetry information helps them let me know if and when I need to engage the thrusters. So contact with 'upstairs' is vital. And I get to talk to you guys, so it's a win-win."

The eight cameras looking out at the ocean conveyed images of a variety of colorful fish and also of those gray denizens of the underwater world, eels and small sharks and other predators. Bentneus uttered a stream of "Wows" and "Would you look at that?" but he really got excited when he saw a larger shark swim past the camera, telling the viewers, "The fish are brightly colored to attract mates and look unappealing to predators since many fancy-looking fish are very unpleasant to eat, even for a shark. So other fish, ones without defense mechanisms such as releasing a bitterant or stinging, evolved to look like the fish no one wanted to eat."

From another camera, Bentneus could see that the shark that had passed by was sucking in a big, colorful angelfish. "Um, yeah ... so, obviously, it doesn't work 100 percent of the time," he said sheepishly but quickly resumed using his "expert" voice. "What's interesting to note is that the predators of the deep are mostly gray and white, maybe mottled, but all of it camouflages them from their prey until it's too late for the poor fish to get away.

"They say sharks have changed very little over the past 300 million years, and I believe it. As the seas cooled and many species went extinct between then and now, the shark adapted to the lower temperatures and has remained the 'alpha predator' down here. They stay nearer to the surface for warmth, even with their adaptation to cooler-water survival. Luckily, *Ocean Victory* is much too wide, even with its vertical orientation, to fit between the jaws of any extra-hungry sharks or other predators. *Maybe* a Megalodon—the biggest sea predator ever—could get its mouth around us, but, as it's 100 million years after they went extinct, we're highly unlikely to encounter any.

"Try to notice that the deeper we go, the fewer colorful fish we will see. This is because sunlight can't penetrate very far into the water. Below about 1000 feet—which we'll be at pretty soon—the darkness is almost absolute and the temperature plummets, neither one agreeing with sea life other than squid, octopus, rays, jellyfish, and other squishy creatures. So we'll see a sudden thinning of complex organisms like fish and sharks, because photosynthesis ultimately powers every living thing on Earth—*except* those that live here in the deep." *BAM! That was a super-dramatic way to say that.*

He took a moment to check his gauges and report what they were registering to the crew on the surface. Then he resumed his science lesson. "But although the temperature of the water is going to be actually a degree or so above freezing, oceanographers have theorized there is a system of very hot thermal vents shooting up from the bottom due to tectonic activity below. That is because shifting of the tectonic plates beneath the ocean floor creates friction, which creates heat. A *lot* of heat. Giant, weird creatures like tube worms thrive down there, and who knows? Maybe we'll find something else that likes warm water and doesn't need the sun's energy to survive?"

Bentneus knew this was highly unlikely, at least if people assumed he was talking about vertebrates. But hey, his monumentally popular films were suspenseful, so why shouldn't the long trip down be as well?

In point of fact, he knew it wasn't necessarily exciting for the viewers to see him reading off gauges and transmitting data to the surface, so there were probably a lot of people waiting for him to near the bottom so they could watch his landing and exploration. But if some weird creatures showed up—and it seemed like deep dives always observed some crazy animal or other—that would keep everyone watching.

***

It had been an hour or so of swimming critters, but for another hour now the cameras had shown nothing but darkness beyond the glow that *Ocean Victory*'s own lights gave off. This deep—more than 20,000 feet from the surface—the total darkness meant very, very few animals were around.

There was lots of floating or sinking animal detritus, which the average viewer might find boring, so the filmmaker and his broadcast team elected to show segments that would be in the feature film later.

These were about the planning for the mission, the construction of the submersible, discussion of scientific goals, and so on.

This was by design. Bentneus and the broadcast crew knew there would be dead spots, dramatically speaking, during his descent and then later during his trip back up to the surface, so these pre-filmed segments took the pressure off Bentneus to keep his patter going. They'd cut off the segments if any creature of note passed by or if something went wrong with the submersible, which would definitely make for suspenseful viewing, but even Jake Bentneus didn't care for it to be quite *that* exciting.

"Jake, we're cut away. How you feeling down there?" his right-hand man and mission chief, Mickey Luch, said into his earpiece. When the feed was on, viewers could hear what Mickey was saying as Bentneus did. "Wanna get out and stretch your legs a little?"

"*Har dee har,*" Bentneus replied, but with a smile. "I am seeing a slight anomaly in the temperature gauge, though."

"Should we cut into the segment?"

"Nah, it's the only thing that seems off. Shows the water being a couple of degrees warmer than expected."

"You'll recall that we are lowering you pretty near the vents down there," Mickey said. "Y'know, the mission plan *you* designed and all."

"I'm gonna *har dee har* you again, and don't think I won't. Nobody wants that."

Mickey laughed.

"Actually … yeah, have Kevin up there take us live again," Bentneus said, and waited through the lag for Mickey to tell him they were back on the air. "Hey, folks, we have something strange happening here, something no ROVs or the 1960 expedition ever reported. The temperature gauges—and we got a lot of them—are saying the water is at 6 degrees Celsius, so almost 43 degrees Fahrenheit! That may not sound very warm, but I'm thinking something is malfunctioning with the external thermometers. Mickey, what do you think?"

"Yeah, Jake, the internal ones are working just fine, got you at a steady 24 Celsius." Bentneus harbored an intense dislike for the Celsius scale, because it made impressive numbers look mundane. So he converted the temperatures in his mind: 24°C was about 76°F. "But you're still 6000 feet from the seabed. The thermocline should have settled down pretty close to *one* degree Celsius, but no more than 4C that deep."

"That's between 34 and 39 degrees Fahrenheit."

"What? Jake? Your air scrubbers not working down there?"

"Talking to the viewers, Mickey."

"Oh, right, shi—um, golly," Mickey said, sounding as natural as a third-grader in a school play. "Anyway, that temp is much higher than anyone's ever recorded. I think, yeah, your thermometers are on the fritz."

The camera inside the bathysphere showed Bentneus flipping some switches and even tapping on some analog dials, whether they were thermometer readings or not. "All of them at once?"

"Kevin, cut back to the documentary stuff." Mickey waited a few seconds, then said to Bentneus, "This couldn't be sabotage, could it?"

"*What?* Did we have some—oh, hell, you mean the Muir murder, don't you?"

"It just makes me itchy. Her husband—"

"—is safely ensconced in prison. You and I both vetted this team, so relax. Put that shit out of your mind and get the live link back up. I just saw something *big* pass by down here."

"At 30,000 feet? Maybe it's a giant squid—"

"And *maybe* you could tell Kevin to go live again, *now*, please. Have them review the video and see if you can get an ID on whatever that was." The support vessel *Sharkasm* (motto: "I just *love* salad") could access a computer database that would almost instantaneously tell them what they were looking at in any video or still image. *Sharkasm* was equipped with the most powerful and robust computers and modulator-demodulator technology Bentneus's vast fortune could buy.

If a statistically almost-impossible (but still extant) coelacanth swam by *Ocean Victory*'s cameras, the system would name it in nanoseconds. If an extinct *ancestor* of the coelacanth appeared, the system had the chops to identify that, too.

The truth is that the bottom of the ocean has been explored much less than the surface of the moon. Anything could be down there, and that's what the stack of servers back in Guam in communication with *Sharkasm* would identify and Holly Patterson on board would confirm.

Dozens of albino shrimp and twenty-foot squids (not to mention weirder creatures with no immediate zoological analog) were routinely identified during seabed missions 13,000 feet shallower than the bottom of Challenger Deep. But if they ran across something the computer *couldn't* identify—an entirely new species!—Jake Bentneus would catch it on camera and advance science for *real*.

That is, if anyone knew he was doing it. "Mickey, I'm not seeing myself on my video feed. I am feeling ... *unhappy*."

"Right. Sorry. Here we go." Mickey conveyed Bentneus's concern over the radio to *Sea Legs* and the millions watching were treated again to 3D views of the filmmaker sitting inside his sphere at the top of their screens and the bottom half showing what the exterior cameras were seeing ... which was still just blackness with a light snowfall of organic detritus that he would be touching down on soon.

"Welcome back, world," Bentneus said with a smile. "You're tuned in at just the right time. The temperature, according to my gauges, is—man, oh, man—*seven* degrees Celsius, which is *forty-one* degrees Fahrenheit." All the vital equipment was digital and could be fine-tuned upstairs, but Jake had insisted that old-school brass instruments be installed in his cockpit (even though they were still operated by computer to expand or contact the mercury in their glass tubes according to exterior digital sensors).

The radio crackled. "Jake, recalibration is done on the thermometers. They're all operating perfectly. It really is 7 degrees down there."

"Wow, *forty-one* degrees. Holy cow, that's a true *scientific discovery*—or data, anyway," Bentneus said, "but we have a lot bigger news. Whatever the real temperature is out there, something large, *much* larger than anything you'd expect this deep, passed me by just a minute ago. Our support team is poring over the video data to identify what this could have been. The safe guess is a giant squid or sizable octopus, both of which can go *deep* indeed. Certain species of octopus have actually been seen at the bottom of abyssal zone seabeds, so who knows what we'll find. Exciting, isn't it? Mickey, let's have a look at that video. *Sharkasm* has to be done with the ID by now."

"Um, yes, it's finished ..." Mickey sounded perplexed and nervous.

Bentneus waited, knowing feed viewers also waited. "*And?*"

"It's probably a computer mismatch, but ..."

"Come *on* already, Mickey. We have enough suspense with me daring to go down this deep."

"It was a perfect match with, um ... Jake, it's a Liopleurodon."

Bentneus laughed incredulously, then repeated, "A *Liopleurodon*, as in 'Liopleurodon, the species of *dinosaur* that went extinct ten million years before the meteor wiped out the rest of the dinosaurs?' That Liopleurodon?" The filmmaker was a bit of a dinosaur nerd.

"That's what—I, um—do you want Kevin to run the video?"

Bentneus looked into the feed camera, which always kept his image inside *Ocean Victory* on-screen, and rolled his eyes for the viewers' amusement. "Yeah, Mickey, I think the world would like to see an impossible dinosaur at 31,000 feet below the surface."

Mickey told Kevin to "roll tape," showing his age a bit, and the view popped up on the bottom half of the screens at home. On the top half was Bentneus staring intently at that same video inside the submersible.

It showed the familiar exterior floodlights showing the snow—and then something swam close enough to the camera to be fully illuminated. It moved at a good pace, but not so fast that anyone watching the feed could mistake it for a dolphin or shark or any other familiar sea creature. It had jaws stretching halfway down the length of its stout, striped body; four large paddle-like flippers; and a long, thick tail. There was no way to look at it and think anything other than "dinosaur." (Maybe "sea monster," but those were pretty much the same thing.)

Bentneus, mouth hanging a bit open, asked Mickey to replay it. Then do it again. And again. There was no mistaking that this roughly 20-foot-long animal—whether it was Liopleurodon or something just of similar appearance that *could not exist this deep*—was no familiar fish. The database had returned an ID of "Liopleurodon" because the goddamned thing looked *exactly* like a goddamned Liopleurodon.

Bentneus typed into a console, its small old-school green screen out of view of the cameras, that was created to be used in the event of radio malfunction but was also quite handy for personal communiques:

MICKEY, IF THIS IS A JOKE EVERYONE IS FIRED.

Mickey wrote back almost immediately:

YOU KNOW ME, BOSS.
THIS IS NOT A JOKE.

The filmmaker *did* know that his capable, often ingenious, mission chief would not pull a "hilarious" stunt even in a training exercise, let alone with Bentneus's life depending on him and his crew. He acknowledged Mickey's reply and looked up at the camera. "Well, ladies and gentlemen, we have apparently encountered our first real surprise of the descent. As you saw for yourself, some kind of vertebrate passed very close to me. Our database of every sea creature that has ever lived, coupled with the most advanced pattern-matching software in existence, tells us this is a ... ha ... a Liopleurodon, a fearsome ocean predator from the ... Triassic period?"

A pause from Mickey, then, "Holly says the Jurassic. I bet she didn't even have to look that up." Both men laughed, but Jake's eyes were wide and his face beamed as he watched the feed repeat.

"Wow. Multiple cameras caught it coming up portside, the front camera got a close-up, and multiple cameras on starboard filmed it swimming away." He shook his head, an incredulous smile huge on his face. "This dive is first and foremost a scientific expedition, and what we just saw should keep the paleontologists—*ha!* not to mention marine biologists—busy for a long time!"

He cackled with glee, showing the whole world that he was a big ol' dork and loved every second of it. "See, ladies and gentlemen, this is what I'm down here for—robot probes are great, but none of them registered warmer water than expected. Certainly none of them caught something like this creature on video. But we are breaking new gr—*holy [buzz]!* It's coming back!"

The Liopleurodon had reappeared, its near-albino body coming just barely within the range of the floodlights. It filled Bentneus with awe: this wasn't necessarily an actual *dinosaur*, but if not, then it must have been very little changed from an ancient ancestor that was one. That wasn't unheard of, especially for water-borne lizards and amphibians: the modern crocodile has remained essentially the same since the species developed 200 million years ago. So it wasn't unprecedented in *that* way, but no vertebrates, no *dinosaurs*, could travel this deep, could they? Did water this deep even exist in the dinos' time, or was there even more of it? The pressure was anathema to creatures with compressible air in their tissues, and the water was far too cold compared to …

Bentneus pulled his eyes from the screen and checked the thermometers.

The water was at 15 degrees Celsius. About 60 degrees Fahrenheit.

He pulled himself away from those and checked his depth gauges. These were only approximations down this deep, but they were in-the-ballpark accurate.

This particular ballpark was about 33,000 feet down. *Ocean Victory* sank much more slowly in these dense waters, but the very bottom of the world was just over half a mile away. It *couldn't* be this warm. Bentneus actually shook his head violently to shake himself awake if he was in a dream. It *felt* like a dream.

But it wasn't a dream. The temperature continued to rise, and the pale-striped Liopleurodon moved languidly toward him, pointed slightly to starb—

"*What the* f—*JESUS H. CHRIST!*"

The front camera's view of the Liopleurodon was blocked by something *much* larger than the flippered dinosaur. Because of the 3D hardware installed within every camera, all could see it wasn't just *closer* than the Liopleurodon, but how much *larger* it was just by calculating its distance. And that calculation revealed it to be huge, indeed—it didn't eat the smaller creature, didn't even seem to notice it, but it did turn after a pass to investigate *Ocean Victory*. It must have been twice as long as the Liopleurodon, something like 45 feet from the tip of its crocodile-looking snout (filled with *hundreds* of razor-sharp, serrated teeth) to the sharp points of its tail. Its pass in front and then turn by the starboard cameras meant there was more than enough captured on video for Holly to do her magic on board *Sharkasm*.

"M ... Mickey? Did you see that?"

"Roger that, Jake. *Sharkasm* is already uploading the video to the database."

"That was another goddamn *dinosaur*. These are *dinosaurs!* Holy [buzz]!"

Mickey was glad they had the live feed on a three-second delay so Bentneus's salty language could be scrubbed before it was broadcast, but he agreed: *Holy shit.*

"Roger that," Mickey said. "Boss, I'm going to patch Holly in. She's the oceanographer and marine biologist, not me."

"Okay."

"Jake, this is Holly."

"Hi, Hol. We must have just seen something *very* unusual, right? I mean, more unusual than even a Liopleurodon at"—he checked the gauges—"33,800 feet and ... *my God*, a temperature of 66 degrees."

"Fahrenheit," Holly gently nudged, since scientists and most of the civilized world used the centigrade scale.

"Yeah, right, sorry. It's, ah, just a hair under 19°C."

"Right, good ... um, Jake, you're not going to believe this, but ... the database reports that we just encountered a Mosasaurus."

"I just encountered *what?*"

"*Mosasaurus*. The alpha predator of the Cretaceous period. It didn't live during the same *epoch* as Liopleurodon, Jake. None of this makes sense. There couldn't possibly be enough food down here for *one* predator, let alone two, let alone ... let alone *anything!*"

"Maybe Steven Spielberg should be down here instead of me," he said with a completely false laugh. Steven was a friend, but he got enough attention as it was. "That's the dinosaur from *Jurassic Whatever*, right?"

"*Jurassic World*, I think. I'm not sure—I only watch *your* movies, Jake."

"Consider my apple polished."

She laughed, then said, "Mosasaurus isn't really a dinosaur *per se*. It actually evolved from being a land-based lizard to the huge aquatic predator we ... um ... see today, I guess."

"Well, I'm gonna keep calling it a 'dinosaur,'" Bentneus said with not a little pride. "Are the *Ocean Victory* lights attracting these creatures?"

"I mean, ten minutes ago we didn't even know there was anything down here, but if I had to speculate, I'd say that every living thing, even at the abyssal level, that we've ever discovered is albino, like these maybe-dinosaurs seem to be. Where there's no light, there's no point—no evolutionary advantage—to color. And for the same reason, creatures at these lightless depths are most always blind ... if they even *have* eyes. There's no evolutionary advantage to sight down there. But these, um—"

"Dinosaurs," Bentneus said, not as a suggestion.

"—right, *dinosaurs*. These dinosaurs are plainly not blind. They obviously were attracted by *Ocean Victory*'s bright lights, but it wasn't because of the heat the floods give off. You can tell because they swam *by* the submersible, were checking it out, but they very assiduously avoided *colliding* with it.

"In other words, they can *see*, Jake. They're albino, or close to it, and that's a benthic adaptation. But they can see even though there's no light down here, no reason for them to be able to see. Add to that the fact that no vertebrate could survive at this kind of pressure, and these are *predators*, where are they getting their *food?* And that's not even taking into consideration—"

"*Holly!*"

She collected herself, cleared her throat a little. "Sorry, Jake. Got carried—"

"No, Holly, *look*—what in the hell is *that?*" There was a presence just outside the sphere of illumination, reflecting back a dim ... gray ... *something*.

"I can't see anything. Can you zoom in?"

Bentneus laughed. "The more I zoom, the more light I need. I make movies, remember?"

She shared the laugh, but her voice was cut off by Mickey's: "Jake, we have something interesting for you."

"As opposed to these boring impossible dinosaurs?"

"*Ha*, maybe not, but are you reading the water temperature as 22 Celsius?"

Bentneus was hesitant to take his eyes off the gray shape that appeared and reappeared at a distance just far enough to keep *Ocean Victory*'s cameras from getting a good look at it. But at Mickey's words he glanced at the brass gauge. "Wow, holy ... holy ... *wow*. That's 72 degrees. The water's supposed to be right at freezing, ladies and gentlemen. As in just above 32 Fahrenheit, which is zero Celsius, or maybe zero-point-one."

He looked hard at the feed screen but couldn't see the gray shadow anymore. They were down here ... prehistoric beasts ... it was like he was in one of his own movies. He was startled out of his reverie by Mickey, who radioed, "Jake, we're nearing the bottom. We need you to do the sonar sweep like twenty minutes ago."

"Oh, hell, I was caught up with the dinosaurs," Jake said, a bit abashed. "Doing the sweep right now. Depth gauge shows 35,000 feet, water temp—Jesus—has jumped to 90 Fahrenheit, 32.2 Celsius."

Mickey withheld his own *wow* and read back the telemetry figures they were getting on board *Piranha II*: "Jake, give me a little thrust to starboard. The hot water bumped you off course a few meters."

"It did? How? That implies an actual heat source below …"

"No *way*," the men, both in their 40s, exclaimed simultaneously.

"Do another scan real quick, please, Jake." Mickey's voice was tight with excitement. "And move to starboard *immediately*."

"Oh my God, right, roger that." Bentneus used the horizontal thrusters to meet his chief's urgent instruction. Then he told him, "Scanning."

The data and thermal imaging popped up on everyone's screen at the same time, and everyone who saw it—Jake and Mickey and Holly and Kevin and others on the ships and probably a few thousand viewers who understood what they were looking at in the corner of their screens—exhaled some kind of obscenity. It showed a rapidly rising temperature in the final 800 feet or so *Ocean Victory* would need to travel through to get to the bottom.

Not only that, but the exterior cameras were showing not just the floodlight-illumined water and now, insanely, the detritus being pushed up instead of falling down. Following his curiosity, Bentneus flipped four switches to turn off the eight exterior lamps, and there it was: the water was being lit from below.

"Is this what I think it is, Mick?"

"All signs point to yes. Ladies and gentlemen—"

"Hey, that's my job!" Bentneus said in a jocular tone but meant it seriously, and flipped the floods back on. "Ladies and gentlemen, I have discovered a brand-new hydrothermal vent at the very bottom of Challenger Deep. The whole team has witnessed a historical—"

"Jake, vertical thrusters *UP*, right now!" Mickey shouted into the radio link. "Don't think, don't talk—thrusters full power—GO, GO, *NOW! GO!*"

Jake hit the thruster controls, slamming the levers to maximum capacity, which first slowed his descent and then, after some seventy-five seconds of excruciating slowness, was ascending according to *Ocean Victory*'s instruments. *Very* gradually increasing in speed, but unmistakably upward.

"Go to footage, Kevin. Mickey, tell him."

Mickey repeated the order, and the live feed showed footage of the filmmaker and his mission chief looking over a map of the Marianas Trench.

"We were 700 feet from the bottom, goddamnit! There's things down there we need to see! There's goddamn *dinosaurs* down there!"

"Calm down. Calm down and look at your thermometers."

He did, and they showed 95 degrees inside the submersible. Bentneus hadn't even noticed it, but he had sweat right through his shirt. And outside ... the water was almost at 200°F, 93°C, almost to the boiling point (although actual boiling wouldn't happen at this pressure). If he had descended much farther, the bathysphere would have turned into a convection oven and roasted him like a Cornish hen. "You want me to go live again? You'll behave?" Mickey said with a laugh, but it was he who was quite serious this time.

"Scout's honor."

"All right, then. Kevin says we're live."

Bentneus continued in his amazed tone, but without as many shouted epithets: "We can't go all the way to the bottom, ladies and gentlemen, because there is a never-before-seen hydrothermal vent below us. These shoot out jets of superheated water—like 750 degrees Fahrenheit, and I have no idea what that is in Celsius—and this explains why the temperature down here has only risen as *Ocean Victory* descended the last couple of thousand feet. It should be as close to freezing as water can get without turning to ice." He shook his head as if in resignation, but the tone of his voice expressed exactly the opposite. "We aren't getting to the bottom of Challenger Deep, folks. It's way too hot down there. I can't lie: I'm extremely disappointed by this, but I'm not as disappointed in that as I am happy about remaining alive, *ha!* And this gives us a chance to look for more dinosaurs, since I have hours of life support left to stay down here. We were going to use these precious hours with *Ocean Victory* parked on the seabed. Instead, Mickey, am I right when I say this gives me a chance to do even more of science than we expected?"

"That's more right than you know, boss. Touching down would have been a world's record"—Bentneus audibly groaned in mock-disappointment that was not "mock" in any way—"but now we—I mean *you*—have found the deepest thermal vent on Planet Earth. *Ocean Victory*'s instrumentation, guided by you, will give us unprecedented data. I'm shaking with excitement up here."

Jake grinned and gave a thumbs-up to his interior camera. "Holly, could this explain the dinosaurs we've been seeing?"

"Possibly, but we need to be cautious. We don't know *what* those animals were. It doesn't seem possible for them to be this deep."

"You guys need to stop saying it's not possible. It's freaking *happening*."

The feed showed Bentneus flipping switches and transmitting data to the surface ships, but he always kept an eye on what the exterior camera feeds were showing. There was something down there, something bigger than even the other dinosaurs. Something—

Holly said, "You are making scientific history even without adding these 'dinosaurs' into the mix, you know."

"Why is everyone denying what we all saw?"

Holly paused. For all his enthusiasm and devoted training to bring an unprecedented mission to fruition, Jake Bentneus wasn't a scientist. He lacked the caution of a scientist, instead following the intuitions of a dedicated—but decidedly amateur—enthusiast. "Further study" was a byword, especially when dealing with truly anomalous data indicating that "dinosaurs"—which were, by definition, extinct—were thriving at depths they couldn't have survived back when there *were* dinosaurs. But hell if she was going to tell Bentneus he wasn't a scientist on this mission; what would be gained by such an unsolicited opinion? Nothing, and much could be lost for a marine biologist who wanted to continue being invited on cutting-edge expeditions.

"Holly, you there?"

"Sorry, Jake, had a ... computer thing. Error." *Smooth.* "Listen, let's put the dinosaurs aside for a minute. Or, actually, no, since this is relevant: the water in the immediate area of a hydrothermal is superheated. Only tube worms and other very specialized animals can live right at the tear in the seafloor, because of its volcanic heat. They're the first life-forms that biologists have ever found that don't depend on photosynthesis as the base of their food chain. They use something called *chemo*synthesis, which means using the heat energy and chemicals like sulfur shooting out of the thermal vents. This chemosynthesis feeds the life at the base of an entirely separate food chain from that closer to the surface. Or, heck, on the surface. It is a unique biome at a hydrothermal vent."

Jake nodded at this, his hands hitting switches and buttons to take measurements as he had been trained to do, but his eyes remained mostly fixed on the external feeds. "Thank you, Holly. So this higher-temperature environment ... is that what explains the dinosaurs living down here? Maybe they travel from thermal vent to thermal vent, where the water is just right for them. Maybe they adapted to eating these chemosynthesis plant- and animal-type things?"

Oh my God, Holly thought, *enough about the "dinosaurs" already!* But what she said was, "That could be, I suppose—a system of thermal vents could keep the water warm in their general area, more like what the ocean was like during those ages before the Permian event cooled the seas and wiped out 95 percent of everything living in them."

"The heat supplying the vents comes from friction from shifting tectonic plates, right?"

Holly was surprised but kept herself from saying anything about it— one did not patronize Jake Bentneus, not if she wanted to stay in his good graces. But the filmmaker was correct, and the "dinosaurs surviving in deep warm water" theory had been proposed before. "That's right. I think it was Doctor Sean Muir who first published speculation on this idea."

"Sean Muir? The murderer?"

"He was also a brilliant paleoichthyologist. What we're seeing seems to support his theories, which he has refined and published in peer-reviewed journals over the last seven years—"

"From prison, you mean."

Again, Holly's brain screamed *Enough!* but Bentneus was simply sharing the opinion of many in the paleontology and marine biology and oceanography communities. "Jake, all due respect, but his actions outside the paleoichthyology community don't hold any bearing on the research he's done. Doesn't matter if it was from a jail cell or from Woods Hole—he explains how creatures like our 'dinosaurs' could exist down here! I'd think you'd want to consider his theories."

"Fine, good point," Bentneus said. "Now, it's shifting tectonic plates that create the heat that makes these vents bust open, right?"

"Right."

"How long would the heat from that last?"

Holly's smile could be heard in her voice over the radio: "As long as Planet Earth is tectonically active—that is, as long as the continents continue to 'float' on the crust—the heat will continue. It started before anything had crawled out of the sea and will continue long after humans go extinct."

Bentneus wanted to say something about the *Spaceship: Earth* film he was developing at Disney (since they held the rights to that title, and he was going to use that title, dammit). It was about a "generation ship" preserving the DNA of every human on the planet and a core crew who would "seed" promising planets throughout the galaxy so the human race would never go extinct. But he held back, cognizant that they were on the live feed and people were expecting exciting science talk, not movie hype.

"What I'm saying is that once a vent opens—and we've found they open up all over the ocean floor, usually in a line running along the tectonic edge—it's not going to close for a long, long time. This is a brand-new vent, it seems, or at least new since 2008, the last time the Japanese sent an ROV this deep, but creatures that can withstand the pressure may thrive along the network of thermal vents. That's just speculation on my p—"

"Do you see this? Mickey, do you see this?" Bentneus interrupted, bouncing in his seat and pointing at the portside camera feed. "The big gray one is coming back! Holly, get ready to analyze the living hell out of this footage!"

Mickey hit the video delay button to skip over the expletive, then looked closely at the monitor showing that camera's view, and there was something huge out there. A smaller dinosaur—smaller than the original apparent Liopleurodon, which was mind-blowing when they first saw it but which now seemed like an also-ran—moved aft past the port camera and into the wide-field view of the rear camera array. Like the others, it was very nearly albino but moved around the submersible like a creature with sight.

"Holly, get—"

"Jake, she's on it," Mickey said as gently as possible. Sometimes, working with Jake Bentneus was like trying to move an ADHD child smoothly through the supermarket checkout. "Trust me, she's on all of it."

A moment passed and Holly proved Mickey right by radioing, "Jake, the database calls it a match for Nothosaurus, a small predator from the Triassic period. I know this probably isn't helpful, but none of these animals lived during the same epochs."

"According to scientists who haven't ventured as deep as I have," Bentneus said.

"That is technically true," Holly said, measuring her words carefully, "but the scientific community has been studying fossils for almost two hundred years. Their study has produced consistent results advancing the science—"

"Yes, Holly," Bentneus said, a little condescendingly, "but those are fossils. These are living dinosaurs."

The oceanographer/marine biologist sighed. The last thing she wanted was to annoy or even anger the mercurial filmmaker, but the second-to-last thing was for the real science of this expedition—and these creatures were going to require long study—to be buried under overexcited pseudo-scientific gibbering.

"Okay, yes, good point, but just for the benefit of the many students and possible future scientists watching, I need to point out that technically speaking, there never were any totally aquatic dinosaurs. If we want to be exact in our language, the species of the creatures we've been seeing, if the database is correct in its identifications, are marine reptiles, not dinosaurs."

"*Comme ci, comme ça*," Bentneus said, and was about to add something about the spirit of adventure being more important than this exact term or that specific distinction, but he cut himself off as he took in what was happening not fifteen feet from where he was sitting.

The port camera, the one the Nothosaur had passed by moments earlier, was suddenly blocked by some moving thing of the nearly white, blanched color of steel, its banding barely detectable, and entered the ken of the rear cameras. Before it was finished getting all the way across, still too close to get a good look at, it turned at a sharp angle away from the camera, giving an idea of its size (colossal) but providing no view of its head.

When it finished its maneuver and could be seen in its entirety, it opened its massive jaws, and swallowed whole the nearby Nothosaurus. They could see all of the beast now, and it looked like nothing less than a mammoth great white shark. Mammoth was almost an understatement—the 3D analysis HUD pegged it at sixty feet long, the size of a school bus.

Mickey said with awe in his voice, "That's got to be the biggest great white in history."

Jake smiled and shook his head. "Naw, Mick, I don't even need Holly's computer to tell me what this fellow is. Ladies and gentlemen, I give you the largest predator ever to hunt the ocean: Megalodon."

Mickey paused, listening, and said to Jake, "Holly's database agrees."

Bentneus nodded absently at his chief's words. For the moment, he had no reply and just watched the massive predator swim around and around *Ocean Victory*. Maybe it was trying to figure out what it was looking at—it definitely had eyes and certainly was not blind—or maybe it was trying to check if its jaws would fit around the submersible. (They wouldn't—a man could stand upright inside of this beast's mouth, but *Ocean Victory* was, thankfully, a good bit bigger in diameter than that. However, it could probably knock the submersible over and sever its tether from *Piranha II*, which would be just as fatal to Bentneus.)

The thing was grandeur itself. "This is some pulp magazine stuff going on right now. This is *The Lost World*." He was able to tear his gaze away for a second to look at the camera and add, "Doyle's, not Spielberg's."

Mickey's chuckle could be heard over the comm.

Bentneus returned to the video. "This is amazing ... we're looking at a creature supposed to have died out 100 million years ago. Megalodon, wow. She's so graceful—"

Bentneus was interrupted by the graceful and grand Megalodon slowing down to convulse and vomit, propelling the still-living Nothosaurus back into the warm water and making no further attempt to eat it. The filmmaker stammered and tried to say something coherent, but he failed. After a few seconds of shocked silence, he said, "Anybody want to take a stab at what just happened?"

The radio was silent. Mickey certainly had no idea—he was a boat and submersible engineer; everyone else on board *Piranha II* was a specialist in this or that aspect of sailing and/or deep-sea exploration. They made sure everything worked and the expedition went as smoothly and safely as possible. And Kevin and the rest of the crew over on *Sea Legs* who weren't sailors by trade were in charge of communications, a job plenty as complex and difficult out in the open sea as any position involved in actually operating the boat. None of them were paleo-whatever-ologists, oceanographers, or even marine biologists.

Those folks were on *Sharkasm*, the science teams making measurements, filling entire servers with data coming from *Ocean Victory*, and, of course, identifying any unknown creatures Bentneus happened to come across. The last was Holly's responsibility, and what a job it had turned out to be: they were expecting to see perhaps an unusual octopoid or flatfish or albino shrimp, or even nothing living at the very bottom at all. Instead, she got dinosaurs—or marine lizards, whatever. (Her boss's sloppy terminology was trying to take over her fastidious   brain.)

But she was just one of a dozen oceanographers, meteorologists, and marine biologists on board the science vessel. She was very pretty, but like most women in the field, she eschewed makeup, and all the boys on *Sharkasm* had taken to affectionately calling her "Velma" because of her (sexy? She didn't see it) horn-rim glasses. She was the one on the comm identifying the crazy creatures through her database link, but she had no more authority than anyone else on *Sharkasm* to speculate on the dining habits of extinct animals.

(To be fair, her "affectionate" moniker was hardly harassment—she also had funny handles for most of her shipmate scientists, including but not limited to the bald meteorologist "Sunny," the timid but brilliant female oceanographer "Hermione," and the cute-chubby, astoundingly genius marine biologist "Popcorn," among others. Ocean science seemed to attract as many women as men, and so they all became members of their own gender-irrelevant "old boys' club." She loved it.)

"That's a lot of dead air, fellas," Bentneus said after almost a full minute of silence. The viewers probably didn't care, and, to be honest, neither did the filmmaker. The visuals were overpowering: a Megalodon, 65 feet long if it was an inch, swimming around and around *Ocean Victory*, every camera catching it in 3D. Bentneus had Kevin route the microphone feed into the broadcast, so now the eerie rush of the hydrothermal vents lay a background against the odd whines of the lucky little Nothosaurus. The giant Megalodon didn't make a sound—its movement through the water, even up close to the submersible, released no sound at all. Like its descendant—hell, Bentneus corrected himself, its exact contemporary—the great white, it was a silent hunter. It was a zeppelin-sized assassin. At these depths, with its blind fellow creatures living in the temperate, even boiling, environment around the vents, a sighted, silent killer would be impossible to avoid.

But why had it spit out the Nothosaur? Predators ate smaller predators all the time back in the Cenozoic period. He needed to know, and he needed the millions watching to know as well, to see the science that he was helping to produce here.

"Holly? Anybody on the *S.S. Geek* have any ideas at all? Anything?"

Popcorn motioned for the handset and Holly very gladly gave it over. "Mister Bentneus, this is Orville Blum on *Sharkasm*."

Jake sighed a tiny bit. He had asked, then told, Blum a hundred times not to call him that, to call him by his first name. But he knew that the brilliant fellow was also half a seeded bun away from full-on Asperger's Syndrome, so he let it slide. "Orville, tell me what I'm seeing here, please. You're my only hope."

Blum let out exactly one chuckle, which for him was nearly hysterical laughter. Then he said, "If this is Megalodon we're seeing circle *Ocean Victory*—and I'd be freaking out if I were personally at the center of that circle—"

Jesus, Holly thought, and stifled a laugh with the back of her hand.

"—but let's take this piece by piece, if you will. First, in order for these creatures—or any vertebrate, okay?—to exist at these depths, they'd have to be porous, like a sponge. Otherwise the water pressure wouldn't balance itself out and you would have a wholly different kind of flatfish." At his own joke, he let out a snort, which none of the rest of the crew on board *Sharkasm* had ever heard from him. With wide grins, they looked at each other like, *He's gone mad! MAD!* "Ahem, anyway, so, despite the fearsome size of, say, our Liopleurodon analogue, and certainly the massive Megalodon analogue, they probably lack any real tensile strength at all. Down at the thermal vents, there would be few other vertebrates, if any—if these 'marine lizards' even are vertebrates— so the albino arthropods and tube worms and other native life we've seen down here would be the food these giants live on. And even then, that's not much food. Perhaps we were seeing old instincts still around when 'Megalodon' swallowed that 'Nothosaurus,' but the predator's system isn't evolved to eat meat anymore. This is a most exciting turn of events, Mister Bentneus, please don't misunderstand—but these must be entirely new species descended from the marine lizards of old."

Bentneus blinked his wide eyes a couple of times, then said, "I wanted a scientific opinion, I got a scientific opinion. Thank you, Orville—but wait, I do have a question: why do they all still have the serrated razor teeth? Wouldn't they have evolved better without them if they didn't use them anymore?"

"Heh, that is a common, but unfortunate, misunderstanding of how natural selection works, sir. If the species is under no evolutionary pressure to lose the teeth—that is, if those animals *without* the teeth don't reproduce any better than those with them, then the teeth remain. Perhaps if the teeth are thin, hollow, and filled with water balancing the pressure down there, then there would be no crushing of teeth or interference with feeding. That's what it comes down to—the teeth, especially since everything else down there is blind and can't see these threatening teeth, serve no actual function for chewing or the intimidation of other predators. You saw how the Megalodon analogue—"

"Stop saying that, please."

Popcorn abruptly stopped speaking at the interruption, and everyone in the cabin with him thought his time of speaking with Jake was through. He would go back to his desk and watch the instrumentation, responding when one of them spoke to him, otherwise lost in the colors at his end of the autism spectrum.

But they were wrong. Popcorn rolled his head around and got some satisfying pops, then replied calmly into the handset, "I apologize, Mister Bentneus. I was trying only to keep our terminology in line with scientific protocol." He cleared his throat and said, "Would you like me to continue or is that enough information for right now?"

"No. Please do continue, Orville." He didn't do it for very long since he could barely take his eyes off the circling Megalodon—or what-the-hell-ever it "really" was—but he placed his hand over his eyes and tried to breathe himself out of having acted like an asshole in front of half a billion people.

"I shall, sir. Now, we all saw how the, that is, *apparent* Megalodon swallowed the smaller marine lizard whole. It didn't bite down; it didn't chew. I would hazard a guess, although treating it as a hypothesis would be almost certainly premature, that those intimidating-looking teeth are, in fact, no stronger than *papier-mâché*. They would almost certainly crumble if these animals tried to bite anything with more tensile resistance than one of those tube worms. Does that answer the question adequ—?"

He was interrupted by a shout, almost a scream, from Bentneus that saw him momentarily curl up onto his bathysphere seat. That wasn't all—every person on all three ships who was watching the circling dinosaur either gasped, cursed, or was shocked into silence. It was like every bit of air was sucked up on the surface; and that was almost literally true down in the submersible.

What made every single person watching anywhere in the world jump, do a double take, or just shout in surprise and horror was that Megalodon, the largest and fiercest predator ever to swim the sea, fell into shadow and immediately tried to swim as fast as it could before a titanic pair of jaws clamped down on it. These jaws, filled—overflowing—with teeth that each must have been as big across as a schooner's mizzen sail and just as tall, tore through the Megalodon like a butcher's cleaver through Orville Blum's almost-hypothesized *papier-mâché*. It was impossible to even estimate how huge the biting creature must have been—the cameras couldn't capture the whole thing, even though the monster stretched across three arrays. Its mouth alone looked as wide as the entire Megalodon was long.

The gargantuan creature ripped what was left of the front of Megalodon into a rain of flesh ... but not a drop of blood was released. The inside of Megalodon looked like a pumpkin's sticky nest of tendrils, mostly empty space, making Popcorn nod with satisfaction that at least he had gotten the porous bit right.

Then it spit out the back end of the carcass.

"Mister Bentneus, it seems that the, um ... the *that* wants to bite and chew, but not necessarily consume, the flesh of the Megalodon analo— of Megalodon."

"What the hell happened to *It's got paper-mache teeth?*" Bentneus did scream this time. "Orville, answer me, goddamnit!"

A croak came from Popcorn's throat and that really was all she wrote for the polymath scientist as far as communication was concerned.

Holly gave Popcorn a supportive squeeze on the shoulder and took up the phone. "Jake, how big is that thing?"

"*Holly?* I asked Orville a goddamn direct question!"

"Jake." She waited. "*Jake!* This is new to all of us. Now please focus and tell me: Can you get any read of how big that ... *thing* is?"

For Bentneus, the bathysphere, the instruments and readouts, even the fact that he was epically deep in the ocean, all of that fell away. His knees were up to his neck, and he stared at the monitors showing the thing—dinosaur? Marine lizard of unusual size? Brobdingnagian leviathan?—blocking out three cameras at a time with its ashen gray hide—not quite albino—as it took up swimming in a circle around *Ocean Victory.*

Around Jake Bentneus.

"Jake, come on, boss, what've you got for us?" Holly wasn't at all sure that he had anything for them, for himself, for his hard-working brain to keep it from shorting out. "Jake."

When the voice came, it was reedy, almost ghostly. "It, it can't be that *near* me, near *Ocean Victory*, you know? For it to circle as close as, like, that itty-bitty Megalodon, there's no way. It would have to have a turning radius the size of my *vertical* sub here. It would have to be just wheeling around and around with no way to stay in place."

"Okay, that's good information, Jake," Holly said. "So we know it isn't right up on you."

"But H-Holly ..."

"Jake?"

"... nothing can be that big. *Blue whales* aren't that big. If it's circling and the cameras still can't get a good look at it ... it's too big. It just *can't be that big.*"

"It's cool, Jake. This is science in action, right? Everybody around the world is seeing you break new ground—"

"Can you get Mickey back on the line, please?" His voice sounded weak; this was something that no one who worked with him had ever heard before. Holly realized as she switched the comm over to Mickey on board *Piranha II* that her boss, the creator and boss of this entire enterprise, was going into shock.

"Jake, this is Mick—"

"I'm *turning*, Mickey. *Ocean Voyager* is turning."

Mickey exchanged glances with the others on the bridge. "Did he just say *Ocean Voyager?*"

They all nodded; that's what he said, all right.

Jesus Christ. "Take it easy, Jake. What do you mean, *Ocean Victory* is 'turning'?"

"The monster ... it's creating a whirlpool around me with its circling. Can't you see that up there? *I'm spinning around and around!"*

Mickey could see it now, having taken his eyes off the instrumentation to try to see if he could tell what in God's name that thing was down there. "Jake, here's what we're going to do. I want you to ping the, um, fish. Give it one sonar ping and let's see if we can get a handle on—"

What viewers on the surface and all around the world heard next was "Get me the [buzz] out of here, goddamnit! Right the [buzz] [buzz] [buzz] now!" Kevin on board *Sea Legs* must have been playing the censor button and time delays like Mozart on the harpsichord. And Mickey knew he wouldn't be able to stop his performance any time soon. "Mickey, you dumb [buzz] [buzz]ing son of a [buzz], you [buzzzzzzzzzzzzzzzz]— holy [buzz], you can see it! *GET ME OUT OF HERE!!!"*

"Drop the ballast, Jake—all of it. *Go!"*

Bentneus had trained long enough that, even through his terror, his body could operate the machinery even if his mind had taken a (hopefully) short vacation. He hit the right buttons and turned the right knobs to shoot the blocks of sand and other ecologically sound ballast from the submersible. If he hadn't been able to do this, no one on the surface would have been able to do anything to haul him up.

Even with the ballast successfully dropped, Bentneus knew— Mickey *knew* he knew, even if the aquanaut wasn't aware of it in his panic—that it would take more than two hours to bring *Ocean Victory* back to the surface safely. That was more than an hour faster than the descent, but at 16,000 pounds per square inch, the hadal, then abyssal, then "merely" benthic depths fought you every inch of the return journey. It could not be rushed.

Also, getting him out of there at too high a speed would probably turn Jake Bentneus inside out from the sudden change in pressure. Mickey barked orders to begin pulling *Ocean Victory* back in. Maybe they would get a better look at whatever that monster was, but Mickey didn't really give a [buzz] about that. All the data brought in on this mission would be totally overshadowed by the world's most famous deep-sea explorer dying on a global-event broadcast. It would be like Neil Armstrong tripping off the ladder and accidentally tearing open his spacesuit live on television. Buzz would still have collected the rocks and whatever, but that wouldn't be the headline. And *DINOSAURS DISCOVERED!* wouldn't be the headline if everyone, millions upon millions of people, together watched Jake Bentneus lose his mind and then lose his life.

Over the year of planning and the months of training for every conceivable difficulty or potential disaster, the scenario of "giant prehistoric beast snaps tether, knocks submersible over, and traps Oscar-winning multibillionaire film director Jake Goddamn Bentneus at the bottom of the ocean, where he dies horribly" hadn't come up *once*.

The winches were turning now at his supervision and command, albeit excruciatingly slowly, and that gave Mickey a moment to breathe. Then he remembered what Jake had shouted: *You can see it!* He dashed back in from the winches and instantly saw what his boss was talking about.

The leviathan, monster, dinosaur, whatever it was, had stopped its circling of *Ocean Victory* and moved away from the submersible. Its entire body couldn't be illuminated all at once by the battery of floodlights, but eventually, as it swam into the darkness, parts of it were visible. As it swam back into the illuminated area—a sphere of gray that was now moving upwards, though almost imperceptibly—the entire head was visible for a moment.

That moment, time slowed by the horror of all who were watching, was quite long enough to see that it had a head the shape of a shark's; a long rough snout, like a crocodile's, jammed beyond capacity with a nightmare of row after row of immense, brutally sharp teeth; and, as it moved through the edge of the lights again, still too near to be taken in all at once, a body that must have been more than 150 feet long. Like a shark's, maybe; or no, its fins were more like a sea turtle's, even though it still had a shark's dorsal fin and tail.

On board *Sharkasm* Holly saw those paddle-like flippers the thing had instead of fins and thought: *This is the most powerful creature that has ever lived*. It wasn't any dinosaur, "dinosaur analogue," or marine lizard she or anyone else had ever seen. It was something completely *other*. Fortunately, the mysterious, goddamned scary giant seemed not to care any more about the weird yellow "creature" that had just visited its habitat. That was good. *Jesus on a pogo stick, that was better than good.* Holly let out a breath she wasn't aware she had been holding.

The world scientific community would be studying this footage, this entire expedition and its geological, oceanographic, and biological landmark discoveries, for years to come. Jake Bentneus had always maintained there was more to the bottom of Challenger Deep than just silt and octopoids, but Holly was sure even he could never have dreamed of the bounty his expedition—and it was his, even if he was a textbook egomaniac—would haul in.

Ocean Victory was moving away from where the leviathan was swimming. Holly was glad to see that Jake had stopped screaming obscenities and had even stopped gibbering now, his feet once again set down securely on the floor of the bathysphere.

He cleared his throat and said, his voice very weak at first but then growing stronger as he spoke, "Ladies and gentlemen, I apologize for my … well, my *freak-out* a few minutes ago. Ah, some people have asked me if I feel claustrophobic inside my metal shell here, and the answer is no. But encountering what we did, and the predatory way that that thing was circling me … well, now the full documentary we make about this mission is going to have to include a psychoanalysis of yours truly. Not real excited about that, but it's part of public record now, so shrink away at my head, I guess. I could have PTSD or something, I guess. Anyway.

"Finding this kind of sea life—finding dinosaurs—is going to rewrite a great deal of what we thought we knew about life in the deepest parts of the ocean. And as I leave this astounding biome and my gargantuan friend down there, the discoveries already boggle the mind. We've found new hydrothermal vents with complex life all around them. It would seem that those who theorized that hot, then warm, water would give rise to an entire chemosynthetic food chain were right."

He very specifically was referencing the field and theoretical work of the disgraced Doctor Sean Muir, but there was no way he would mention such an ignominious name to cause himself or the expedition further embarrassment. But the homicidal son of a bitch had been right.

"I name this heretofore unknown apex predator *Gigadon*. Anyone watching could tell it was considering eating *Ocean Victory*—and me inside of it, hence my reaction. But it didn't. It's like it knew I was on its turf as a peaceful surveyor." He sighed with satisfaction. "I know the scientific authorities or whoever get to name it officially, so I'm sure it will be called something like *Gigadonus bentneusii*, but to me this singular creature is just *Gigadon*. Megalodon is named for being so huge, and this big bastard dwarfs Megalodon."

He looked at the monitors and saw that Gigadon was cruising around at the level where the submersible had been hanging. Still swimming like a sentry, but not rising to follow *Ocean Victory*.

"Now we have the long journey back to the surface to reflect. The heat of the vents is still in the metal and foam and other components of *Ocean Victory*, according to the many thermometers we have aboard. The temperature inside here is still over 100 degrees, and it is stifling as hell. But all this heat *plus* our very hot floodlights mean that we can study the trail, the conical shape of the heat signature we leave behind us as we ascend.

"Every part of this journey has changed the history books, folks. I'm gonna ask my mission chief upstairs to roll some more documentary footage while we make what I sincerely hope will be an informative but uneventful trip back to the surface. When we can see light from above, we'll bring you back to *Ocean Victory* and the rest of my ascent. See you soon."

Kevin gave a thumbs-up that they were now broadcasting the documentary footage of how this historical milestone was planned out and executed. At that, Mickey said, "Holy crap, Jake."

Bentneus laughed. "That pretty much sums it up."

Mickey made a hmm sound and said, "Hey, something interesting is going on down there, according to our sonar. Can you aim the bottom floods straight down?"

"What's up?"

"Maybe nothing. Point the lights, willya?"

Bentneus did and was surprised to see the huge gray shape swimming directly below them on the bottom camera's feed. "Whoa, there's Gigadon! The water's a lot colder up here. I wonder why he's following us up. He doesn't seem to be in any kind of attack position, just swimming his giant ass in a circle below us."

"Well, you did mention the theory about dinosaurs following heat sources."

"Oh, yes, from the unmentionable Doctor Muir. It's kind of tragic that we're the ones to confirm that whack job's signature idea. I'm sure he would have liked to do it himself, if he hadn't, y'know, murdered his wife and everything."

"Okay, yeah," Mickey said, "but you also just mentioned how *Ocean Victory* is radiating heat from the encounter and the lights and even from inside the submersible."

"So you think he's following me?"

"I'll leave that up to the science folk, Jake. But my guess is that he's enjoying that 'cone of heat' you were talking about, just following the warmth. He's rising as slowly as you are, so I imagine he'll stop when the sub cools off enough to lose his attention."

Bentneus liked that idea. "He's kind of doing us a favor. We're getting a real look at how huge this thing is, now that we can sort of see his whole body in the light. Goddamn, he's big. I wish we had something to scale him against."

"Maybe you could ping it again, see how far away it is?"

Bentneus should have thought of that, but instead it was his chief sailor. Great. Mickey was a smart, smart man, but he wasn't Jake Bentneus, even if he did come up with a good idea first now and then. "Good thinking," he said. "And then we can use the 3D video system I designed and had built to figure how big our giant is through calibration with the sonar ping."

"Aye, sir," Mickey said, and called for sonar to ping the beast.

Down in the submersible, Bentneus could feel the ping pass through the water, then felt it again when it bounced off Gigadon. "So whatcha got for me?"

"It's a lot farther away than it looks."

"That's a relief," Bentneus said and laughed. "I don't necessarily want him swimming up my tailpipe. We know where he lives now— we've got time to put together a research plan and maybe build *Ocean Victory II* and *III* and so on. He won't be able to elude us now that we know he's there."

"Jake, I know the 3D stuff that you completely designed and deployed will tell us exactly how big it is and such, but ..."

"But?"

"It's *huge*. Much bigger than we even thought when it was passing by the sub. For it to appear *that* big from this distance, it's got to be as long as a city block."

The filmmaker laughed at that. "You been smoking the local seaweed? There's nothing that could be that big and survive the pressure down there."

"I'm just telling you what it looks like from up here."

"Good, good, that's what you should be doing. But let me tell you, from down here, Mick, nothing could be that big. He would have to be practically hollow. And we saw how he chomped that Megalodon in half, so it's not *papier-mâché* teeth we're talking about here. I'd put him at, say, a little bit bigger than the Meg that he killed. A school bus and a half, maybe."

"But Jake, we can't even get a shot of its whole head! It would have to be a hell of a lot ... no, whoa, that can't be right. We're gonna ping it again, Jake. Hold on."

"What's wrong?"

"Hold on, Jake."

The *ping* rang twice again, once going down and once on the way back up. Only this time there was a lot less time between the two sonar signals. That meant something wasn't as far away as it had been just moments before. "Um, Mickey? My video feed just shows him swimming in a circle still. Why was the ping so quick?"

"Don't freak out—"

"*What?* I have *never* lost my cool on a dive, not *once!*"

Mickey and everyone who had heard Bentneus *monumentally* freak out when he was being circled by the Megalodon could have contradicted him, but there was no advantage in it for anyone, so all remained silent.

Not that the occasional freak-out was anything to be ashamed of. Little things, and sometimes major things, commonly went wrong on a ship and certainly during a dive, but Jake Bentneus had most always kept his nerve and his steely resolve. He had to smile despite himself inside the submersible: *What, do these guys think getting a studio to sink $300 million into one movie is easy?* He had balls of steel! So he *could not* freak out, because by definition steel balls prevent that.

"All right, just trying to get you ready."

"This does not sound like good news."

"The creature—"

"I call it *Gigadon*."

"Yes, right, of course—well, *Gigadon* is rising rapidly, in a spiral. The ping must have hit a lower part of its body when it was at an angle to us, so it indicated that the thing was farther away than it really was. Because it's so goddamn long."

"What do you mean, 'rising rapidly'?"

"It's coming right for you. *Ocean Victory* is positioned directly above the center of its spiral."

"Oh, bullshit, I'm looking at the same video feed you are, and he looks exactly the same size as before."

"I'm switching you over to Holly. Talk to the scientist, Jake."

"This is Holly. You copy?"

"Copy, Jake here. What the hell is Mickey babbling about?"

"Boss, the reason you can't see all of this thing—"

"*Gigadon*."

"—is because half of its length isn't illuminated by the sub's lights. You're seeing only a part of it. But look closely and you'll see it looks a little bigger with each circle it makes. That's because it's closer to your lights. It's getting closer to you, Jake."

The world fell away for a moment as it finally clicked for Bentneus. In a few seconds, he shook himself out of his stupor and did his thing: "Okay, team, what are we gonna do about this?"

"Still just Holly here."

"Then get me on the goddamn bullhorn—*everybody* needs to get their heads together on this one! Is that thing coming to the surface? Can we get the sub and me out of the water before he gets to me? *What does he want, for Chrissakes?!* Science people, *report*, goddamnit!"

The scene was chaotic aboard *Piranha II* with divers readying scuba suits and the winch crew set to bring Jake up this last leg a lot faster than was prudent, but at least inside the bathysphere he wouldn't get "the bends" as they tried to pull him to the surface faster than whatever the hell this thing was.

On *Sharkasm*, quant nerds hustled around, tripping over one another to look at data, to check the sonar pings (Mickey had ordered another ping and the Gigadon was closer still, now only about 250 feet below *Ocean Victory*), to find something to do even though almost every single person on both ships couldn't even think of anything that could possibly help in this situation except hauling Jake's ass out of the water.

Onboard *Sea Legs*, which once had been the main ship of well-funded research expeditions but for a Bentneus operation was relegated to communications duty, they just kept the cameras and microphones recording. Bentneus had told them to keep going no matter what, and this was definitely a *no matter what* situation. In fact, Kevin made an executive decision and broke in on the documentary footage they had been showing. He took the whole show live again. Whatever was about to happen, the world was going to see it.

Kevin knew this could very well be the last time he ever worked for Jake Bentneus. Or anywhere else in the industry. But this is what Jake was talking about—showing the real adventure of a scientific expedition! Kevin would at least go out having done the right thing, even if it meant the video would steal some of Jake's thunder ... and Kevin knew he *hated* anyone stealing one decibel of his thunder. He put the live feed through to the broadcast channel, which then sent it worldwide with no more than a two-second time lag.

What was happening was the most incredible thing Kevin had ever seen or, perhaps, would ever see.

On *Piranha II*, Mickey was getting a very bad feeling indeed. The heat from the lights was attracting the monster? They couldn't be *that* warm. *Ocean Victory* itself must have cooled off traveling through tens of thousands of feet of very cold water. Had the creature found itself in the euphotic zone and genetic memory or something triggered it to go toward the sunshine? What the hell was attracting Jake's "Gigadon" to the submersible?

A crackle in his earpiece. "Mickey, Holly here."

"Go ahead, Holly."

"The, um, Gigadon is less than 100 feet from the sub now, and climbing at a much steeper angle than earlier."

It was on the video feed, its massive, spear-tooth-filled mouth pointing right into the bottom camera now. Its eyes were as dead-looking as a shark's, but they were definitely not dead. The son of a bitch could *see*. He could see *Ocean Victory* and was swimming up at it. "A hundred feet, you said?"

"*Less than* 100 feet," she answered.

"Jake is almost to the surface, so close. Twenty-five feet. He could get out and swim the rest of the way holding his breath." Not that he would want to get out of the submersible while the universe's biggest shark-thing was hanging around. But it was a moot point anyway—the hatches were bolted from the outside. "Guys, can we get him out of there *fast*, like *now?* Toro, get that winch going *now*. Vanessa, full speed on the cable. And where's Slipjack? Goddamn that guy! *Slipjack!*"

"Right here, chief!" And he was right there, on the other side of the A-frame and winch that was pulling Jake out of the water. "You know, bringing Jake in and all!"

"All right. Sorry," Mickey said, then turned again to the feed from the bottom camera on the sub that showed nothing now except gray skin and *so many* teeth. "What are you doing, you ugly bastard?"

Then it hit Mickey, and he knew exactly what the Gigadon was doing. *It was playing with its food.* Once it saw the bright light coming from the surface, something switched on, something ancient, something that wasn't hungry for tube worms. It was hungry for that weird, warm yellow fish slowly rising away from it.

So the thing followed and followed, and when it sensed the prey was about to leap out of the water, it—

"*HOLY JESUS THIS ISN'T HAPPENING! This is NOT happening!*"

What exactly was "not happening" was Jake Bentneus, hands raised in thumbs-up at the crews and the on-ship cameras (and then at the camera inside his bathysphere), was being pulled out of the sea ...

... but the monster came, too, right behind him.

The Gigadon was so large that it barely had to lift its whole mouth out of the water. It just opened those crocodilian jaws, water flooding in, and nipped *Ocean Victory* from its impermeable, unbreakable rare-metal-alloy tether like it was plucking a grape off a vine.

Every single person on every ship, as well as most every single person who had been watching the simulcast or who tuned in now for the triumphant return from the deep, was shocked into complete silence. They did nothing, moved not a hair, because there was nothing to do, there was no reason to move. Also, they were watching something that literally no human had ever seen before. Really that *no* eyes had ever seen, because a hundred million years ago there wouldn't have been a fifty-foot-tall submersible to be dragged underwater in the crushing jaws of an impossible dinosaur.

And this dinosaur, this *Gigadon*—a name that Bentneus was right about, it would stick—was a perverse son of a whore. It stayed at the surface, its gray back longer than the three expedition ships lined up end to end, and watched the watchers as it chewed the metal and unbreakable plastic like an old man at Denny's eating a club sandwich with his mouth open. They could see everything being crushed and chomped on, including the solid iron ball of Bentneus's bathysphere.

"Jake is in there," Holly said to no one, and no one replied. Everyone knew that the celebrity explorer was right then being rolled around in the mouth of the Gigadon he'd discovered. "He could be okay if that thing lets him go in time before Jake's air is used up! The bathysphere resists *16,000 pounds per square inch!* Nothing could bite through that, or even dent it!"

"Actually," Popcorn said, and in his defense, he looked very sorry to be the bearer of bad news, "bite strength is a function of jaw width. A normal crocodile—which, you'll notice, this animal resembles in its mouth area, at least—can exert 3700 psi. The ... let's call it a Gigadon for the time being, even though that's not even close to proper Latinate termi—"

"*Popcorn!*" Holly snapped, and her colleague nodded rapidly. "Sorry, time is of the essence. The Gigadon's jaw, if it is analogous to the crocodilian jaw, is as wide as *Piranha II* is long. Much, *much* more than four or five times bigger. But even if it were 'just' five times bigger than a crocodile's jaw, the arithmetic relationship in bite strength would put it at well over 16,000 pounds per square inch."

"Holy hell," Sunny the meteorologist said, without even feeling his mouth move.

"Exactly," Popcorn said.

As if on cue, the bastard lizard let the bathysphere roll to its side teeth and chomped it like a gumball.

The metal—the strongest possible—crunched and folded inward. It wasn't squashed flat anywhere, but it looked like ... a gumball that's been chomped on with a person's molars a few times: its skin was still identifiable, and it still maintained a vestige of its original round shape, but, as in the case of the gumball, no one would say it hadn't suffered irrevocable damage.

Then, as if this was something the Gigadon did every day, it vomited up the pile of parts that was formerly *Ocean Victory* into the water and spit—hurled with an exhalation—the crumpled iron bathysphere straight onto the deck of *Piranha II.* Then it slipped its head back under the water and disappeared. Holly thought later that it perhaps went right back down to the hadal depths, but there were less deep hydrothermal vents in lines all down this part of the ocean.

But at the moment, all any of them on board *Sharkasm* could do was observe the damage that the hurled several-ton ball made of 2.5-inch solid steel caused the deck of *Piranha II* and wonder if there was any way Jake Bentneus could have survived. His seat had been in the very center of the sphere, so it seemed possible—if not at all likely—that he could have lucked out and avoided the parts of the bathysphere that were coming in at him.

Maybe he didn't even need to be actually crushed inside the ball, though. Holly felt that she personally would have died of a heart attack, maybe an aneurysm, when the Gigadon took its first bite. And she would have been *glad* to go that way, too, instead of being chewed to death and then spit out like a spent was of gum.

"He's alive!" Mickey shouted so loudly that the crews of *Sea Legs* and *Sharkasm* heard him loud and clear.

They had no way to get him out of the crushed metal, but their boss was alive. They called for military assistance from the base in Guam, the land closest to them, and which happened to be under American authority. Bentneus may have been of Canadian origin, but to the hundreds of millions watching the drama unfold, he had entered the pantheon of all-American heroes.

***

EIGHT MONTHS LATER

The entire cost of the disastrous but scientifically epochal *Ocean Victory* expedition was less than $60 million out of the pocket of Jake Bentneus. The other $40 million ended up getting paid for by corporate sponsorship, scientific grants, and the donation of much of the equipment from the Muir deep-sea project. The family of Katherine Muir thought she would have wanted the gear not to be sold for parts but kept intact for further scientific missions.

Sixty million dollars was a lot of money. However, to Bentneus, it had represented less than 3 percent of his net worth. Interest alone on some of his more boring investments paid back more than the cost of the expedition in the past eight months, anyway. Bentneus was in the top 1 percent of the 1 percent thanks to his extraordinarily profitable films and investment in other studio blockbusters. He had an almost-perfect track record when it came to picking what movies to put his money behind. He had a gift for the business side of entertainment, some wags opining that it far exceeded his abilities in the *entertainment* side of entertainment.

But he who laughs last laughs best. The various snarky reviewers who opposed the public's enjoyment of spectacular, thought-provoking science fiction and sinking-boat movies had to be aware that not only did Bentneus laugh last, but he laughed all the way to the bank.

His net worth was more than two *billion* dollars, and while much of that was connected with investments, he maintained a great amount of liquidity in cash, gold, and bearer bonds. He could walk into the bank and withdraw a billion dollars. (Now, of course, it would have to be via a wire or other remote access, but the point was that he could have that much in cash to spend within an hour of his request.)

He who laughs last laughs best.

Except Bentneus couldn't actually laugh at all anymore.

Having a machine doing your breathing for you didn't allow for laughter, no matter how technologically advanced the machine was. Neither did a face that couldn't show emotion because it couldn't move except when computer-controlled rods implanted in his jaw and sticking out through his muscles and skin moved his mandible up and down according to the instructions from the implants in his brain.

The advanced breathing machine was controlled by the same computer, a massive parallel-processor device, and it also followed instructions to help Bentneus "talk" while also keeping his system oxygenated.

He could move his tongue, at least, and after months of practice and therapy, his speech had become downright coherent when all of the mechanized and digital elements worked in concert with his own maximum physical effort.

His arms and hands were gone, as were his legs and his feet; and he wouldn't have been able to feel them even if they had still been there. His body had been pulverized to the point where a team of the most brilliant and expensive doctors on Earth actually told him that he should be *glad* he couldn't feel anything, because his mangled nerves would have been firing strong pain signals constantly, trying to get his brain to notice that a whole lot had gone wrong.

He could also move his eyes around in their sockets, courtesy of another set of rods hooked up to the computer. These rods ended in attachments stronger than steel but lighter than foam. These operated his eyelids, blinking for him so his eyes wouldn't have to be sewn shut or removed entirely because of drying out and subsequent infection.

His brain, however, had escaped direct injury, Bentneus managing to avoid getting his head crushed by Gigadon chewing the bathysphere and reducing much of his body to barely operative pulp. But he was lucky— *ha! what luck!*—that the collapsed metal ball actually held him together. This, and this alone, kept him alive while rescue helicopters used super-magnets to lift the bathysphere off the deck of *Piranha II* and bring it back to Guam, where Bentneus's personal surgeons and a team hastily assembled and flown in from the best research hospitals in the world awaited him. Another team was put together as well, this one sporting beards, tattoos, and muscled arms the size of a smaller man's legs: these were metalworkers armed with blowtorches, liquid nitrogen, and more hammers and massive tools than had Vulcan himself.

They alternately heated and froze the thick iron until it cracked, then got into the crack with automated expansion devices that held the space open while they worked more cracks into the iron, eventually getting the cracks to meet and—with doctors who had already taken control of Bentneus's bodily functions through snaking tubes and wires through the broken viewports prepared to transport him—breaking the bathysphere open like a Gigadon egg.

These hardened metal men, all of whom looked stronger than the iron they forged, to a man either fainted or vomited and then fainted at the sight of what was inside. The doctors and whole medical team also felt their stomachs lurch at the sight of what had happened to Bentneus's body, but in accord with their training, within seconds they stopped seeing the broken and squashed mess in front of them as a human being. They were able to work on extricating him by looking at Bentneus as just a *body*, as a complex-but-broken machine that needed to be repaired enough to keep its miraculously uninjured head and brain alive.

It was two months before the filmmaker regained consciousness, finding himself in a private medical facility with the best of everything he would need and absolutely nothing he wanted. What was there to want, anyway? They had put Humpty Dumpty back together again, but not as a nice smooth egg—no, the shell was too badly damaged; so they did the best they could with his scrambled innards. But, like a scrambled egg, a scrambled human cannot be made whole again—no matter how much he wishes it so. That was a longing that could never be satisfied, a torture that Humpty Dumpty was spared by dying from his fall.

He thought at first that he was blind, but the doctors who spoke into his ears told him that his lids had been sewn shut until—and *if*—they could find a way to keep his eyes from drying out (since he couldn't blink).

There was nothing for the phalanx of experts to do therapy *on*, really (except for the psychologist, who gave him monologued pep talks full of personal growth and self-esteem cultivation, for all the good *that* did for a man who couldn't move or talk or see), so his many friends who were electronics and robotics gurus, biotech visionaries, and cutting-edge nanobot theorists got together and devised a system that would allow

Bentneus to regain control over some tiny fraction of his body. Anything would be better than nothing.

It was another two months before these tinkerers presented to the medical team the unethically human-tested (several of the gurus had areas on their heads where hair was regrowing over thin scars) but fully functional face-manipulation and brain-implant technology. The doctors were appreciative of being given a chance to do something for their patient, and they wanted to be hopeful about the results, but their knowledge and experience made them skeptical, and they had to ask Bentneus for his specific and repeated permission to undertake such a risky endeavor. This they had to do by holding his mouth open and instructing him to use his tongue to signal right for *yes* and left for *no*. The patient gave his immediate assent.

The whole time these masters of their science-fiction-like trade (oh, the irony) worked on the equipment that would allow him some small re-entry into the world, his uninjured brain held onto one thought.

This thought let him feel as if he had the tiniest sliver of *freedom* from within despite being trapped in his dark and almost complete isolation. He concentrated on this thought during sessions with "Doctor Slogan," as he had taken to thinking of the psychologist who babbled feel-good treacle at him for *two hours* six days a week. He rolled it around and focused on this idea when his relatives—his parents, a brother, and an ex-wife, but no children—stopped in and sat with him. Sometimes they had long one-sided conversations with him in tones one would use when trying to make a comatose person "hear" you through their unconsciousness, even though the doctors assured them he was quite conscious, just completely "shut in." Other times, his mother or big brother would just be there in the room sitting near him and reading or possibly doing crossword puzzles. This was actually soothing, and he appreciated it greatly. To be fair, he appreciated everything anyone was doing on his behalf, whether it was paid work for them or not. Spielberg stopped by and told him one of the funniest jokes he had ever heard— Bentneus tried to signal his amusement through wagging his tongue against his cheeks, like how an excited dog wags its tail. The nurse pointed it out, and Steven was like a marksman who was proud and pleased to have gotten a bullseye. Jerry Bruckheimer, his ex-wife, who was herself an Oscar-winning film director, Arnold Schwarzenegger, Bill Paxton, and many others came to his room and spoke encouraging words. Tears leaked out from his stitched eyes. They say Hollywood has no soul, but Jake Bentneus knew different now, the one highly ironic but intensely lovely facet of this entire black and lonely existence. The tech guys who would give him a second birth into the world also stopped by frequently to update him on progress and tell him jokes that one could appreciate only if you knew some concepts of higher mathematics and physics. They all became friends, even though he had never looked upon them, shaken their hands, or said one word.

But all that time, through two months of Stygian existence, the *idea* cooked in his brain. He went to it when he felt depressed, knowing he lacked any facility even to kill himself; when he felt happy after a visit from friends who had made Super 8 movies with him when they were teens; when he felt nothing at all; and, most of all, when he felt horribly betrayed by that monster from the deep ... the *idea* gained detail and traction. He didn't care how much it cost, because he no longer could do anything with money.

He could no longer do *anything* with or without money, actually. Except for this one thing. Except for the execution of his *idea*. That would be everything and then his mangled body could give up the ghost, as it were.

When the unprecedented technology was in place, the room was made totally dark. *Totally* dark: the door not only warned against entry, but was in fact bolted solidly from the inside. The edges of the door were sealed all around with blackout tape, and a metal cover had been installed over the room's large window. All potential light sources such as electronic devices were removed or, in the case of his life support readout equipment, were rigged to display in infrared. The doctors and mechanics who surrounded him wore night-vision goggles to allow them to see what they were doing; it would be malpractice of the highest order to rescue a patient from blindness by immediately blinding him with light of any kind.

Bentneus felt the rods being installed on his face, his jaw, and, once they cut through and removed the stitches over his eyes, the butterfly's wings of his eyelid servos. This last was the most exciting to him—sight to a filmmaker and explorer was everything, and his eyes had been forcibly closed from the time he had been put into a coma four months earlier. (Like the hydraulic fluid that couldn't keep the *JSL*'s clamp closed, his autonomic nervous system couldn't hold his eyes shut when he was comatose, and leaving them open was not an option.)

He had technically been reintroduced to aliveness (if not "life") after two months of coma, but the restoration of his sight would be the real rebirth, the thing that allowed him that one iota of freedom outside his own mind. The thing that would, along with the ability to speak given by the specialized aspiration control system and scaffolding of rods implanted into the connective tissues of his face, allow him to pursue the *idea*.

The medical team was represented several days ago by his personal surgeon; the tech team by the head of the world-renowned Robotics and Intelligent Machines Lab at UC Berkeley; and his friends by the stalwart chief of deep-sea exploration support, Mickey Luch.

Mickey was the first to point out the obvious irony of his last name since he had been on the crew of two very *unlucky* high-profile deep-sea exploration disasters. However, he also stressed three things: one, it wasn't pronounced "luck" but like "luccch," with the "ch" sounding like that in *chutzpah*; second, he had been chief as well as crewman aboard dozens of expeditions that went off without a hitch and provided much for ocean science and marine biology; and third, he was now often hired on as crew or mission chief on research vessels *because* of the experience he had gleaned from the Muir and Bentneus horror shows. He had viscerally vivid knowledge of how to detect sabotage, how to control a crew when a dive went totally pear-shaped. He had to turn down a detailed sonar and temperature mapping of the line of ocean-floor hydrothermal vents, something he would have loved to be a part of, so that he could be there for Jake's milestone.

And the job offers were plentiful since that day's worldwide *live* revelation, the very-near-death of Jake Bentneus convincing all that this was no hoax. The informal theories and formal papers supported and endlessly analyzed the footage and those who were there that day were interviewed again and again. The whole world now knew that there really were dinosaurs (or, as they were called by only the starchiest of scientists, "apparently Cenozoic-age marine lizards") down at the bottom of the ocean, following sea vent to sea vent, and there had been a great deal of interest in not only Gigadon but in all aspects of the *Ocean Victory* (speaking of irony) expedition.

Not too long after the surge of interest, the name "Sean Muir," the moniker of the polymath scientist who first theorized about ocean dinosaurs having survived and adapted at the hot-water vent, was at the top of Google searches for more information about hydrothermal vents being a habitat for dinosaurs. There were several interviews held at the prison by especially hungry journalists, but most of the major outlets didn't want to sully the fun of *DINOSAURS ALIVE!* and so ignored the convicted murderer or talked about him in tones that one would use for discussing the ideas of a visionary who had long been dead.

Thus, Mickey Luch got job offers not only because of his expertise, but also because it gave a certain cachet to any expedition to have on its crew the man who was at the center of the discovery of the dinosaurs. Mickey didn't know how many times he had talked about his experiences on the Muir and Bentneus adventures, but he liked regular jobs with good pay, so he told them afresh on every new boat he worked.

So now, Mickey Luch, in-demand mariner *extraordinaire*, was on dry land because his friend and former boss was about to get a little bit of his life back. Since he had no official role in the removal of the stitches and the week-long gradual introduction of light to Jake's long-unused visual system, Mickey just let the big man know he was there and would be there all week. Unless there was a *lot* of money to be made, in which case he was outta there and would send him a postcard.

Bentneus waggled his tongue back and forth to show he was laughing inside his useless shell. Mickey caught it and told Jake he did, and it made the crew chief laugh harder as he took his appointed out-of-the-way corner of the room.

They had to do the procedure inside Bentneus's (admittedly spacious and easy-to-sterilize) room because his heart had been replaced by a "centrifugal pump," which was easier to replace or repair than other artificial hearts that allowed the recipient to enjoy some mobility, something that was not going to happen with Jake Bentneus.

The pump kept his body technically alive by circulating his blood, but this kind of artificial heart, much like the "axial flow" device the doctors considered at first (but then rejected because it wasn't available as quickly) did not produce a pulse. Not that Bentneus cared, but it sometimes spooked out people who came to visit. They couldn't see his ruined body under the blankets, but they could see that something was "off" aside from the obvious. Once they were told what it was, they were spooked no less but at least knew what was making them uncomfortable.

His crushed kidneys had been removed, and a hemodialysis machine was always right next to his bed, actually staying connected to him most of the time. His genitals weren't even identifiable when (after employing very temporary but effective techniques to keep him alive long enough to airlift him to Guam, the nearest land and home to a world-renowned hospital) they cracked his egg open and gingerly scooped him out. His penis was now replaced by a catheter connected to the plastic bag that had taken the place of his bladder; his prostate gone; his testicles gone; his liver replaced by an experimental "HepaLife Bioreactor"; his stomach replaced by a 3D-printed facsimile made from stem-cell technology in Singapore; his permanently collapsed lungs (actually plastered together like two flat, wet pancakes) replaced by an extracorporeal membrane oxygenation machine, which would also take over the duties of the centrifugal heart pump once the latter failed, which they always did in time; his upper and lower GI tracts just a collection of colostomy bags and tubes; and his legs and arms removed before they could go gangrenous and replaced by nothing—they all knew, including Bentneus, that they would never be used again. Besides, since he could never be moved out of his room because of all the artificial organs and systems keeping his head alive, he would never be in a situation where he ever would need the limbs for cosmetic purposes. He would never sit in a wheelchair, could never be wheeled down the hall into surgery in case of an unexpected failure in any of the devices. No, this hospital room, nice as it was, would be his nice prison cell and then his nice morgue. With his eyes sewn shut, it had been his nice coffin in which he was buried alive.

They got his eyes open on a Thursday, and *slowly* the doctors introduced light while Bentneus wore the same specialized sunglasses designed for the Chilean miners trapped in darkness for more than two months in 2010. By the next Friday, eight days later, his eyes had grown fully accustomed to the light, and he could see that Mickey was *still* goddamn there, the loyal son of a bitch, and when his brain ordered an automatic smile, the servos on his face pulled it into an odd but identifiable smile. He had been working with the roboticists and therapy personnel to train himself on the system since they had attached its manipulation rods to him and stuck a dozen sensors into his brain—which were then connected to the super-parallel computer taking up almost the whole wall next to Bentneus. He couldn't see it because he couldn't turn his head, but he could feel the heat and could hear the cooling fans running through a special hole cut right through the hospital wall. The temperature was kept in the 50s (Fahrenheit) in his room, uncomfortable for anyone without a jacket but just fine for someone whose spinal cord was mashed from the coccyx all the way up to C1. The computer had to stay cool to work, and the computer had to work for what remained of Jake Bentneus to work.

Once the entire system worked in sync and Bentneus could "talk" by mentally moving the servos that the rods used to move his mandible and blow air consistently over his larynx, and when he could see again, Mickey finally took his leave. "I'll be back to visit, man," he said, not knowing what to do with his hands, since Jake couldn't shake, fist-bump, or high-five; since he couldn't really hug him without interfering with all of the tubing and equipment attached to Jake's body; and he couldn't even—he didn't know—pat him on the head or something for fear of throwing off the finely calibrated system of motors and rods keeping Jake able to communicate.

So he said he'd be back. "That brain of yours is intact for a reason, Jake. You can't go on any more expeditions, but you can go VR and see everything better than you even could in the sub. And you can help *plan* research trips. And movies, too! Life isn't over for you, Jake. Too many people love you for that. You stay alive, we stay a big part of that life, that's the deal, okay?"

Bentneus was glad the rods made his fake smile look the same as his real smile, because he didn't want to make his loyal friend feel bad. However, there was one thing that would put a real smile in place of the "being nice" one.

"Mick, before you go … I need a favor."

He turned away from the door he was about to open. "You name it, man."

It took a few minutes for the filmmaker to get it all out relying on the speed (or lack thereof) of the facial servos, but he got it all out and Mickey understood every last word.

"I'm on it, my friend," Mickey said, "but … *wow*."

Bentneus smiled.

And it was a real smile this time, which actually *did* look different from his merely polite smile. It's just that the whole time since he came out of the coma, he hadn't experienced one single thing that had made him happy enough to smile. Now he had unleashed his *idea* on the world, starting with Mickey and the people he would contact, and then going out and out to the entire planet.

The *idea* was finally something worth spending money on. The *idea* would take half of his net worth, and he would still be a billionaire. (Eight months without any leisure spending tends to keep a portfolio fat.)

The *idea* wasn't a substitute for real freedom, but it was finally something worth staying alive for.

***

"Welcome back. We've all been following the Jake Bentneus story from his initial excursion simulcast that supplied evidence that dinosaurs still existed, living at the bottom of the ocean. Of course, on that same historical expedition, tragedy struck when the biggest dinosaur— possibly the largest animal ever to exist on Earth—attacked and crushed Bentneus's submersible … with him inside. In the ten months since then, the famed director of some of the biggest hits in Hollywood history has gone in and out of a coma, been paralyzed from the neck down and cannot breathe or move his facial muscles without the assistance of advanced technology, lost his arms and legs, and had almost every major organ in his body replaced. Every day he is alive is a miracle, but the filmmaker says now he has a purpose bigger than any one person, any one race, any one *nation*.

69

"What is that purpose? Tonight, as media outlets around the world have been teasing since the announcement was made two weeks ago, Jake Bentneus will reveal all in his first live appearance since his catastrophic encounter with "Gigadon," as he has named his nemesis. He has purchased fifteen minutes of airtime on *every* network in the *world*. And not just news networks or official broadcast networks in every country. His 100-person team was dispatched some eight weeks ago to buy time on those traditional broadcast channels, but not only those: every single cable channel, from international giants like CNN to channels like beIN Sports USA, which has fewer viewers than there are people in Daphne, Alabama. No offense meant to any viewers in Daphne, of course.

"The Bentneus media-buying team has also bought fifteen minutes of airtime on every radio station in the United States and every legal station it could find in the rest of the world. There will be a simulcast video on not only Bentneus's website, but on thousands of websites that didn't charge a nickel but came to the Bentneus Foundation to seek permission to carry the simulcast, which of course was given enthusiastically along with a link to the Foundation's site. The total cost of this fifteen-minute media buy has been estimated at between 150 and 200 *million* dollars. Wags have pointed out that this amount could go a long way toward ending malaria, which has been fellow billionaire Bill Gates's philanthropic priority for decades. It could also go to fixing a crumbling American infrastructure, feeding the poor, housing the homeless, and countless other world-changing causes. Of course, this unprecedented broadcast could be Jake Bentneus announcing just such a program of philanthropy.

"Unfortunately, we must take note that many, many viewers will be tuning in not because there are no other entertainment choices, but because no one other than his medical team and circle of long-term trusted confidants has *seen* with their own eyes the extent of the injuries Bentneus suffered at the end of the simulcast almost a year ago. Everyone saw him at his best then, beaming with excitement and pride at having found dinosaurs in the deepest part of the ocean. It would be hard to have missed that coverage, either in its live form or during the many times it has been rebroadcast with subtitles in the one hundred most used languages and dialects to everyone everywhere.

"But human nature is what it is, and we shall see for ourselves in a few moments what the world has been murmuring about since the accident: What does Jake Bentneus look like now? His internal organs have been mostly replaced, and it is only by relying on machines that he can talk at all, move his mouth, even blink his eyes. But putting aside the sensationalism and prurient interest in his condition, we will finally hear what it is that the explorer-filmmaker has spent so much money to tell every human being.

"I see we now have less than one minute until the universal airtime. It's 9 p.m. here in New York, 8 in Chicago, 7 in Denver, and 6 in Los Angeles, the entire spectrum of prime time in the United States for maximum exposure. Experts don't expect ratings to be low anywhere on the globe, however, due to the master director and his team not spilling one spoiler about the content of Bentneus's address to the world.

"All right, my producer is telling me the feed is counting down from Guam, where Bentneus will spend the rest of his life; moving him, even out his hospital room door, would probably kill him. All right, we're cutting away. Keep it tuned here for analysis afterward from our panel of experts, who will tell us what we just watched and what they, having heard it at the same time as you, think it means."

***

The man who had served as Jake Bentneus's assistant director on three films was behind the HD camera, and it was he who told the interns to cut the lights to ten percent and then counted down from three, two, waited a moment, and pointed to Bentneus to begin. The only person in the room who knew the main points of what Jake was going to say was Mickey Luch, and Mick had had to work as a *landlubber* with one hundred shiny-suit (and -skirt) media buyers for eight weeks. He wasn't giving *anything* away after all that. He could hardly wait to get back out onto the water, and he knew Jake was right now going to give him that golden opportunity.

On-screen, Bentneus's face could not be seen. There was just enough light to orient the viewer that this was being broadcast from a hospital room, his hospital room. He started "talking," and as he did, the interns followed their instructions and brought the lights up *very* slowly.

The hissing, sibilant sound of his machine-aided speech could be heard before his face could be seen:

> There is nothing wrong with your television set.
> Do not attempt to adjust the picture. This is what
> my voice sounds like now, so do not attempt to
> 'correct' your sound system. The lights will be
> increased as I speak to you, giving the most
> important address of my life. This method is
> being used to keep from shocking anyone, but

also to keep you watching long enough to hear what I am saying before you get distracted by seeing just what is left of me.

My name is Jacob Bentneus. My friends call me 'Jake.' People who were once my bitter, even despised, rivals call me 'Jake' now as well. I can do them no harm anymore, that harm being making better artistic decisions and gleaning greater financial gain than they could. Steven, you know I don't include you in that list."

His aerated and monotone laugh was the most disturbing sound anyone in the room had ever heard. Of course, the pitch and volume of his voice stayed as flat as old roadkill, but a laugh like that ... hehhhhhhhhh hehhhhhhhhhh hehhhhhhhhh ... Who knows how many people watching felt shivers down their spines?

"I appreciate everyone letting me talk to them this evening. I have more or less 'taken over the airwaves,' but I paid for it, and your favorite television shows will begin again shortly.

As you can see me more and more, I ask that you think about what the monster I named *Gigadon* did to me. I took the submersible *Ocean Victory* down deeper than almost anyone ever dived anywhere—but you know that whole story, I'm sure. You also know that a new hydrothermal vent was discovered by my expedition. And that the ideas of a homicidal madman turned out to be absolutely true. Sean Muir's logic and research were confirmed that day, the last day of my life. The day when I found out dinosaurs still existed on Earth, their descendants having adapted to the crushing pressures of the bottom of the ocean but otherwise unchanged. One of these adaptations was continuing to bite, although their adapted systems rejected whatever they tried to ingest.

Gigadon followed me to the surface, attracted by the warmth of *Ocean Victory*'s lights and residual heat from the submersible being so near the hellish temperatures at the hydrothermal vent. A hundred million people watched my sub as it was pulled from the water and then seized by the leviathan's cyclopean teeth. It chewed my sub, and it chewed me in my supposedly indestructible iron bathysphere. Then it spit me out and went back into the deep.

The world reveled in this discovery, celebrated it, dreamed of what it meant while I was in a medically induced coma for two months. I was blind for two more months, and then I was reanimated with the robotic equipment designed by my friends at Berkeley. Interns, please bring up the lights the rest of the way so the world can see what Gigadon did to me."

They turned the lights up to the set point that Bentneus's former AD had marked for this video.

And there was Jake Bentneus, staring into the camera wearing special opticals that blinked and focused his eyes for him since he had no control over even that small a movement. When he spoke again, the wheezes and hisses were easier to ignore since the motion of his mouth was visible. He was gaunt; his playfully tousled hair was gone to keep his implants unobstructed, and his face, for all the technology developed and applied to allow him to communicate and show expressions, resembled nothing more than a ball of dough being poked at by the fingers of the rods.

I used to make movies about cyborgs. Now I *am* one. Hehhhhhhhhh …

Now that you see me, Planet Earth, you will understand better what I am about to tell you. I am a man with billions of dollars that, other than for the fine care I receive from the best—and best-paid—medical staff in the world, are completely useless to me. That's why I want to give *one billion dollars* to you."

His servos put that horrible smile on his face, thoroughly horrifying viewers even as they remained compelled to watch this poor, poor man who just said he was going to give them a rich, rich mountain of money. The AD and film interns—as well as the doctors and nurses present—looked at one another in perplexed wonder. Mickey looked down at his feet, refusing to give any of the game away at this last minute.

Once again, in case you can't understand me with my machine-driven speech, I want one of *you* watching right now to have one billion of my dollars. We can even leave it in an offshore account in my name if you like, to keep the taxman at bay. I promise I won't go to any ATM and take any of it back. Hehhhhhhhhh …

Why am I making this offer? Why did I buy fifteen minutes of airtime, half of which has ticked by as I told you things you already knew, to make you this offer? And, most of all, you must be wondering: *What the hell is this offer in the first place?*

Reasonable questions all, and I shall give you my reasonable answer right this moment: I want one of you, or a team of you, or a small army of you, to kill that Gigadon. It means a great investment of time and money, certainly, but not the rest of your lives if you go down there with the intention to kill this [BUZZ]ing thing. And not a billion dollars of money, either. How you get out there and how you get to Gigadon is your business, and I and my Foundation do not want to hear your plans.

The only thing I want from you is for you to bring me the carcass of Gigadon. I want the whole thing, the whole goddamn corpse; I want scientists to get as much out of this bastard as humanly possible. But even if they don't and it's left for the gulls, I will pay *only* the party who brings it to my coast of Guam, and I will pay *only* if my team of ichthyopaleontologists and marine biologists agree that what is brought forward is the prehistoric beast captured on that very, very popular video.

And, assholes of the world, don't bother making a hoax version; Gigadon is more horrible than you can imagine when you haven't seen him up close and personal, and you will just make a fool of yourself. And do jail time— yes, you will. I have funded the campaigns of many judges in California as well as here in Guam. Not bribes, because I didn't ask for any particular return on my investment. But I do think a scumbag trying to steal from a pile of flesh would not receive leniency in that judge's courtroom. I do not own them; but I certainly share their concern for fairness about who goes to prison and who does not.

But enough of that. The Marianas Trench and, within it, Challenger Deep, are under the jurisdiction of the United States of America, as is Guam, where I will die within five years, my doctors tell me. So, at my request, the U.S. government will allow any registered party, whether it's one person with a harpoon or fifty people with ten exact copies of *Ocean Victory* on their ship, to hunt Gigadon starting *one week* after Registration Day, which is one week from today.

Why one week? The question really should be: *Why waste a week?* The answer to the last question is that I want to be fair and let all the competitors get down here. And the answer to the first: It's because five years is my *maximum* time to live. With the Rube Goldberg mélange of tubes and computers and machinery keeping me alive, I could get an infection and die an hour later. A power outage in one of Guam's south Pacific megastorms would be the end of me. Anything could happen at any time. And while that's true for everyone, I'm the one who can hear the tapping of the Reaper's scythe as he walks the corridors of this hospital.

What I'm saying is that I want to see Gigadon dead and gone from this world, just like the rest of the dinosaurs. Why not all the others down there, too? I want all to please feel free to kill every unnatural monster down there, but even mighty Megalodon is a timid and tiny flower compared to Gigadon.

Gigadon. I curse you to hell, devil's beast of the deep.

There was still three minutes left according to the red LED clock on the wall opposite Bentneus, put there so he could see how much time he had to go on the broadcast.

I haven't much time left—literally … hehhhhhhhhh … but my system is breaking down … I will decline most shockingly as the remainder of my body refuses, part by part, to obey the orders given to them by these remarkable machines.

So listen carefully, record this, write this down: Registration Day is in one week, on the first of April. Yes, that's right, April Fool's Day. But it's not on that day because I'm making a fool of you. You will absolutely get your billion dollars if you succeed in this task. No, the fool is going to be that monster, that lousy abomination of the deep that killed me.

Registration Day will be held on the grounds of Governor Joseph Flores Beach Park starting at dawn and continuing as long as it takes to register all those who arrive before 11:59 p.m. Chamorro Time Zone. You can boat in and dock near the beach. You can fly in to Won Pat International. You can ride a goddamned magical unicycle. The only rules are time of registration; length of the hunt, starting at 12:01 a.m. CTZ on April 8, one week after Registration Day and two weeks from tonight; and you have to bring me the whole [BUZZ]ing fish. I don't care how you do it, the same way you don't care if your billion dollars is in twenties, hundreds, or old hundred-thousand-dollar bills with that weaksauce Woodrow Wilson on them. That's the kind of stuff you know when you're filthy rich. I guarantee you'll like it … hehhhhhhhhh …

I have thirty seconds of airtime left. Everything you need—registration forms, government crap, maps, *everything* is on the website KillGigadon.com. Go there, then come here, and avenge my pathetic death.

Goodnight, and *death to what needs killing.*

Everyone in Bentneus's hospital room and probably 90 percent of the people who watched the whole address were stunned speechless. The doctors and other medical staff were wide-eyed but with their mouths remaining shut by will alone. But two female interns looked at the bedridden man, and the waterworks started. The AD behind the camera just kept nodding as he stared off into nowhere.

And Mickey clapped. He didn't start with a slow clap, showing how ironic and cool he was; he went full bore and applauded Jake Bentneus, loudly, for turning it up to 11, going to infinity and beyond, and letting out a full-throated, revenge-fueled barbaric *yawp* that would never, ever be forgotten.

***

"Welcome back. Well, *wow.* We've seen it and heard it from the man himself. Jake Bentneus is offering a one-*billion*-dollar bounty to anyone who can find, kill, and bring back the body of the sea-monster dinosaur Gigadon. We've assembled a panel of experts to tell us what we just all watched and provide their fine-tuned analysis of this historic—*pre*-historic? ha ha—telecast and reward offer. Jim Blabenfus of K2TV in Casper, Wyoming, can you help our viewers understand this better?"

The studio cameras were pointed at the leftmost panelist, a bow-tied and suspendered man, who had twice received the *Agriculture Roundup*'s "Ranchy" Award for his reports on misfiled paperwork at one barley farm's box supplier. Two other experts were also sitting at the curved desk to the anchorman's left. Blabenfus cleared his throat and looked down at his notes, which viewers could see consisted of exactly one line of black ink. "I think the most important thing to understand about this event is … um …" he trailed off as he checked his notes. "Is that the 'Steven' he mentioned in the opening where he talks about other Hollywood filmmakers is most likely Steven Spielberg, of *Hook* and *Amistad* fame."

"Excellent point," Judith Bombast said, she being the author of several books on current events, including *How to Spot a Muslim* and *Why You Should Spot a Muslim*. "Following the thread of what Jim was saying, Bentneus was most likely mentioning the Jewish hero Steven Spielberg in a bit of an ironic manner, but also with respect, letting him know that he did *not* consider Spielberg 'beneath' him somehow in talent or success."

"That would be pretty ridiculous. Steven Spielberg is one of the most successful film directors of all time," said the third panelist, a mild-mannered reporter named Clark Kent—not *that* one, as he was always saying. And people believed him easily since *this* Clark Kent was a 350-pound black gentleman who wrote the popular sports column "This Week in Semi-Professional Badminton" for the *Watauga Democrat* of Blowing Rock, North Carolina. "But yes, I think Jake was very clear that this was *not* the case."

The host nodded at Kent's comment and turned to the camera to say, "We'll continue with our usual level of professional analysis when we return in just a moment. Keep it here on FOXNews."

***

After the camera crew had packed up and gone, Bentneus's media advisors called in to give him the good news of his 98 percent share of the viewership measurable worldwide (Bentneus was required by what his staff called "Jake's Law" to respond with, "What was that last 2 percent doing?").

So people had heard the message. Good, good, good. But would they have the guts, the balls, the *money* to have a realistic chance at catching and killing Gigadon? Bentneus knew that, obviously, slum dwellers outside Rio de Janiero wouldn't have the resources to put together a deep-sea mission (but if they somehow did and won the billion dollars, he'd say God bless and here's your check); however, those with realistic chances included the Americans, the French, the Japanese, not to mention the independent ocean research institutes in Sri Lanka, Madagascar, and of course from his own final homeland right here in Guam.

His false stomach couldn't have butterflies, and even if it did, he wouldn't be able to feel them. His artificial heart didn't race, his pseudo-lungs didn't draw shallower breaths than it always did, and he didn't even have a sphincter to tighten up; but Jake Bentneus was excited as hell. The rods and catches on his mouth and cheeks showed his uncanny-valley smile.

"Knocked 'em dead, Jake," Mickey said, coming out of his corner now that everyone else was gone. "That big fat son of a bitch is as good as dead."

"Hehhhhhhhhh hehhhhhhhhh ..." Bentneus wheezed. "Now. I have a question for you, Mick."

"Shoot."

"Would it be a conflict of interest for you to captain a team of vessels very likely to take the prize? You're my right-hand man, but organizing a media buy hasn't given you any particular advantage over anyone else. Your abilities as a mission chief have only been strengthened by the Muir thing and Gigadon murdering me."

Mickey hated it when Jake said that last part, but he accepted the compliment graciously, then said, "You're gonna have a team in the hunt? I don't think my being on a team would be any ethical problem, but *you* having a ticket to the Gigadon lottery would be a big ol' conflict of interest. Like *Gigadon* big, if you'll excuse the comparison."

"Hehhhhhhhhh ... no, it's perfect. And no, I'm not pulling a stunt like entering my own team to win my own money back. All the money can kiss my colostomy hole. What I'm looking to do is provide support to the right people to get that goddamn thing."

"For science," Mickey said, and they both wheezed with hilarity.

The servos on Bentneus's face returned it to a serious expression. (A blank one, actually, but definitely not a smile.) "We've got two weeks."

"That should give anyone with enough scratch a chance to get over here."

"Yes. But that's not what the time's for, Mickey. We've got two weeks to get Sean Muir out of prison."

***

Like a mistreated dog, Sean Muir had gotten used to chains.

Hands in cuffs that were chained not only together but also to a chain going around his belt. Chains from his belt went down to cuffs on his ankles. If he tried to run—there was nowhere to run, but *if* he tried—he would exhibit the speed and agility of a man who had been on the toilet running with his pants down to answer the phone.

Bars, too. He was so used to bars after four years that he didn't even notice them anymore, the way you notice the side of your nose only when you think of it first. His cell didn't have bars—it had a swinging metal door that blocked any view. (Not that there was anything to look at, but *if*.) But everything else had iron bars: doors, walls between anything and anything else, windows, any portal to somewhere; they were all barred.

Sean Muir was at one time baked brown by the sun from sailing across oceans to find the sweet spots the ships' equipment told them might be a thermal vent on the bottom. But now he was a ghastly, ghoulish white from not seeing the sun for so long after the incident a year earlier that had earned him a place in solitary. He got an hour a day for exercise, but although he at least got to see the sky, the walls were too high for him to see or feel anything of the sun at that time of day.

Sean's attorney had managed to get him full access to the prison library interlibrary loan to check out books, photocopies of articles from journals, and even DVDs from libraries anywhere in the country, all of which were mailed to him. (He was escorted—in chains each time—to a tiny viewing room and watched the videos taken by old friends and former colleagues that kept him up on the latest sightings and evidence for or against his and others' more interesting theories and speculations.)

After much legal wrangling, he was also allowed a manual typewriter, a supply of ribbons, and paper, paid for by a bank account belonging to his friend and crew chief, Mickey Luch, into which Sean had transferred money during the short time between his conviction and sentencing. (His ankle had sported a flashy GPS transmitter then.) It was good to have access to that money—not that there was anything that he wanted to buy in the prison commissary, but he was allowed to conduct his business by postal mail only, which he knew must make him look like some kind of Unabomber-esque neo-Luddite, if he wanted to submit essays and articles for peer review by the editorial panels of oceanographic, marine biology, and ocean geology journals. However they disagreed on his pet area of research, no matter that he was in prison for a heinous crime, his peers in the academic world still greatly respected his meticulousness and logical argumentation in interpreting established research and cutting-edge discoveries to support his speculations.

He did wonder, sometimes, who would really consider him a "peer" anymore outside of the research journals' editorial boards and contributors. For the last four years, his true peers had been murderers, rapists, and category-fluid paranoid schizophrenics. (It occurred to him that the final category might apply to some academics, too.) That aside, he had published regularly, more than a lot of tenured faculty, about the same subjects that he had obsessed over since that long-ago submersible dive with his professor in graduate school: thermal vents, dinosaurs adapted to live at the bottom of the deepest oceans, how the animals might be coaxed into swimming at depths where they could be better studied.

***

As Doctor Frankenstein said, "They *laughed* at me in school!" After Katherine had died, his "crackpot" theories—those self-same papers respected by his former colleagues—were held up as evidence that he had lost connection with reality. The prosecutors, who would ultimately triumph, made his publication record into a mark *against* him, showing his obsession, they said, with wild ideas. According to the district attorney's office, the incident that killed Katherine Muir was murder, not an accident. No, he had gone off the deep end and murdered his wife by sabotaging the equipment and then claiming an injury that morning that conveniently kept him from performing his appointed test dive, tricking his wife into taking the submersible down to her death.

Sean was jealous of her, they said, because she also published and was considered his partner in more ways that just being his spouse. He was afraid she would take the limelight off him when the "magic dinosaurs" (as they repeatedly called them) were discovered, they said to explain his motive. When his fingers were examined upon his arrest and extradition a few days after the aborted expedition returned to Guam, the doctors back in the U.S. said there was no sign of injury. "Broken" and "dislocated" were intentionally conflated in the minds of the public, and then in the minds of the jury.

Sean's lawyer argued, correctly, that dislocated fingers set and splinted almost immediately after the injury wouldn't show evidence of trauma. However, when this was brought up at the trial to dispel the notion that Sean had planned to switch places with his wife, the prosecution had already planted in the minds of the jury the idea that this clever, educated man would have had little trouble arranging things to *look* like an accident.

No, he was a madman—although one who should go to a maximum security federal prison, not be treated or even held in custody at a facility for the criminally insane—and when madmen start thinking everyone is against them, they eliminate the closest enemies first, the prosecution claimed. In Sean Muir's case, the jury was told, Katherine Muir was that closest enemy conspiring against him, so he murdered her.

The credulous jury was swayed by this argument and also because "Doctor Muir" was a member of "elite academia," where reality was unwelcome if it conflicted with the "ivory tower" and its elaborate and ridiculous "theories" that did nothing to better the lives of others. Dinosaurs hiding out in the ocean? *Preposterous!* Complex life springing from nothing because it eats from vents farting out sulfurous chemicals? *Fishy, indeed!* In other words, the whole research program stank to high heaven, *just like Doctor Muir's excuses and fabrications regarding his wife's death.*

The defense's problem was that they couldn't get anyone who had been on the expedition to actually testify that they had seen Sean Muir sabotaging the cable. In fact, the defense called on Vanessa Jones and Toro del Toro, members of the "winch crew" on the ill-fated mission, who swore under oath that not only did they not *see* Sean Muir doing anything with the cable, but they didn't even know *how* such a thing could be done. The sabotage—if sabotage it was—affected a section of cable that was almost 3,000 feet up the cable and thus under half a ton of iron-anchored tether wound above it. There was no way to get to it without unspooling such a huge length of cable right there on the deck. The noise of the winch would have alerted whoever was on watch, and that was if the sailor on duty hadn't already seen the lights such a job would require or simply somebody skulking around the deck. Sean's attorney, hired by the university and good at his job, ended his questioning of Vanessa and Toro with a statement put as a question: "So, in your opinion as not only a veteran sailor and member of multiple deep-sea expeditions but also as a member of the 'winch crew' who knew that equipment inside and out, is it *literally impossible* for anyone to have altered that cable during the entire trip?"

And both of them answered with the same words: "Yes, sir, it is impossible."

For anyone familiar with the disaster of that day—and the legal teams on both sides were familiar, indeed—the absence of the third member of the winch crew, Phillip 'Slipjack' McCracken, in the list of witnesses called by the defense was glaring.

Slipjack certainly was on the list of prosecution witnesses, and the State called Phil McCracken right after cross-examining Vanessa and Toro, who couldn't be tripped up or made to contradict themselves in any way. This was either a sign of telling the truth or of expert coaching. It didn't matter to the prosecutors, anyway, because they had Slipjack, who would destroy his mates' hour of testimony in less time than it took to haul in a flatboat-full of bottom-dwelling catfish. "Your Honor, we call veteran sailor and third member of the winch crew working on the Muir boat the day of the alleged murder."

Slipjack was put under oath and sat on the witness stand. His hair, already greasy, was slicked back, and his suit hung on his taut frame like he had borrowed it from an uncle. His teeth looked like they had been brushed under duress. As uncomfortable as his being make to look presentable seemed to render him, however, every word he uttered was smooth and confident. Not once did the prosecution refer to Slipjack by his nickname.

"Mister McCracken, can you tell the court your opinion of Doctor Sean Muir, the respected scientist and groundbreaking marine-biology theorist who was in charge of the *Sea Legs* expedition?"

"Yes, sir," Slipjack said. "He was one of the most capable captains I ever seen—saw. I mean, he wasn't the actual sailing captain, but he had a handle on every, um ... oh, yeah, *aspect* of the entire expedition."

"He and his wife, the late Katherine Muir, were involved at every stage of the planning and execution of the mission, including the construction of all specialized equipment?"

Slipjack cleared his throat and took a sip of the water provided for witnesses, seeming choked up at the mention of Kat's name. "Well, they both are brilliant—I mean, she was as brilliant as her husband before she got murdered—"

The judge admonished him and told him not to use that speculative word, as the court was to decide if her death was due to murder.

"Right, Your Honor. Sorry, Your Honor."

"Please continue your testimony, but I ask that you do take care."

"Thank you, Your Honor, I will. Kat—everybody called her 'Kat'—was brilliant, but her end of the planning and such was mostly on how it could be done, what the testing parameters and suchlike would be, and in designing the submersible. They worked on it together, you know, but she was more on the theoretical and design part. The actual building and such was more Doctor Muir's job. He oversaw every step of the construction of the equipment to be used onboard the ship. A man named Mickey Luch worked with him to get the support boat, she was called *The Moaning Mermaid*, and *Sea Legs* exactly as Doctor Muir—he had everybody call him 'Doctor Muir'—"

The defense attorney stood and said, "Objection, Your Honor! We have heard from several other crew members who referred to him as 'Sean' here and, one would assume, during the expedition."

"I'm going to chalk that up to human memory, counsel. Objection overruled." But he didn't ignore the objection. "Mister McCracken, you will stick to telling us what *you* saw and what *you* know, if you please."

"Oh, right, yes, Your Honor." Slipjack cleared his throat and took another sip of water. "He had *me* call him 'Doctor Muir,' as I recall, you know. But what I'm saying is that Kat was mostly on the design phase, and Doctor Muir worked on that as well as overseeing all the actual physical stuff."

The prosecutor continued, "And this 'physical stuff'—does that include the cable used to lower and raise the submersible that both Doctors Muir designed together? No matter—the cable was what it was—but Kat and Doctor Muir decided what functions that cable had to have, correct? Fiber optics for audio and video and also data lines to transmit the mountain of other information needed on a scientific mission. Is that accurate?"

"Yes, sir. Like most of the other equipment used on the trip, Kat and Doctor Muir designed it together, and then he implemented and oversaw the building of the equipment. Definitely that included that cable, which needed to be about 22,250 feet long—the 20,000 feet the main dive was going to be plus enough extra in case *D-Plus* drifted a bit because of currents and such down there at the bottom. I know the cable was built by Doctor Muir, 'cause by that time Vanessa and Toro and me had been hired on, and we assisted him, since the cable deployment was gonna be our main job."

"That was very clear, Mister McCracken, thank you. How was the cable protected from the stress that would be put upon it?"

"Sir, it was what we called 'armored' with an inner wrap of nylon—"

"Nylon?" the prosecutor asked, trying to sound surprised even though he never asked a question of a witness to which he didn't already know the answer.

"Aye—ha, excuse me—*Yes*, sir. Nylon is stronger than steel in this kind of application, and heck of a lot less heavy. But yeah, that was the interior protective sheath, and on the outside was iron cord wrapped tight by machines Doctor Muir adapted for our cable."

"Could you tell the court the difference between 'cord' and 'cable'?"

"They're pretty much the same thing, except cable's usually stronger and thicker. But it's still cord. You couldn't have anything inside cord, I think. That would make it what seahands call 'cable.'"

"Thank you for that, Mister McCracken. This special cable machine, designed and implemented by Doctor Sean Muir, where was it? Where was this cable made?"

"Oh, in an industrial space rented by Doctor Muir."

"Rented by Doctor Muir, or by the university departments whose resources were involved in the expedition?"

"Oh, yeah, sorry—I believe it was rented by the college. I'm just a seadog," Slipjack said with a smile. "They don't tell me the financial details. But, you know, those research vessels aren't that big, and you hear things."

"Of course. But Doctor Muir had the keys to the car, so to speak. The university had invested all its trust and authority in Doctor Muir."

"Yeah, you could put it like that. Nobody was in there unless Doctor Muir let him in. He was the first one in and the last one out every day."

"Was the facility under guard twenty-four hours a day, seven days a week?"

"Um, as I remember, that didn't start until construction began on the actual *D-Plus* sub, when all its parts from the suppliers and factories and such were delivered to the, what you said, the *facility*. But up 'til then, nobody was really worried anyone was going to break in and steal cable and fiber optics or whatever."

"But Sean Muir stayed there overnight sometimes."

"Yeah, but that's true of most leaders of expeditions. They think of shit—sorry, Your Honor—they think of *stuff* at all hours and don't want to be too far from the hardware, you know?"

"Indeed. Now, the court just heard from your colleagues how it was supposed to be *literally*—and this is 'literally' in the original sense, meaning 'absolutely true'—*impossible* for that cable to be tampered with on a ship during an expedition."

"I agree with that."

"But it's possible that the cable could be sabotaged—"

The defense attorney stood and barely said "Objection!" before the judge shut him down with an upheld palm and said, "Sustained. Counsel, please refrain from speculation. It has not been established that any 'sabotage' was committed in this situation. You may continue."

"I apologize for that, Your Honor." He turned to Slipjack and reframed his question: "Do you agree that *if* any kind of tampering with any equipment occurred, including with the cable and its constituent contents, it would have had to take place before the enormous spool was transported to the ship and installed?"

"Yeah, that's right. I've worked with Vanessa on several expeditions, and she knows the procedures regarding the cables and winches and such as good as I do. I agree with her a hundred percent that, even if it was possible to unravel that much cable, it couldn't be done without the whole crew on the boat hearing it. Not just the guy on watch—*everybody* woulda heard it and lots of us woulda come up to check out what was going on. Messing with it on a fully crewed ship *would* be impossible, and if you don't mind my putting this in, it wouldn't be possible even to get to where that, um, *problem* was at under all the other cable on the spool."

"No, that's fine, Mister McCracken. Thank you for sharing that with the court. If I may, Your Honor, I'd like to summarize the points made by the witness—"

"You know very well that you cannot, counsel. You can do that in your closing argument, which, I will remind the jury, is never to be considered *evidence*. All right?" He waited for each juror to acknowledge this before telling the defense counsel in words, "You may continue," but his expression advised, *You're pushing it, and you'd better stop right now.*

Defense counsel's words were "Thank you, Your Honor," but he realized from the judge's tone and expression that he was overplaying his hand, and since he was already holding two aces, there was no need to trip over his own two feet. "Okay, just a bit more, Mister McCracken. Would you consider yourself an expert on deep-sea tether cables?"

"I've worked with them on ten trips and helped in their … dang … Oh! In their *manufacture* when elements like data lines and such have been run inside the twisting metal exterior. I've helped with that on all of those missions that used them. So I don't know if I'm an expert, but I can lead you through the whole process right now without even closing my eyes to think."

"Thank you, but I don't believe that's necessary."

"Just saying."

"Certainly. As an expert, in your opinion could such a flaw as that which caused the loss of the submersible and Katherine Muir be introduced at some point in its manufacture? And, following up on that, could it be done in such a way that no one would notice until it was unspooled during a dive?"

"Objection! Your Honor, he's calling for speculation."

The judge looked at the prosecutor once again, but his expression was neutral this time. He asked, "Counsel, are you asking a hypothetical question, or are you asking if that happened with the voyage in question?"

The prosecutor hesitated a moment, then said, "A hypothetical question, Your Honor."

"I hope so. Objection overruled."

"Mister McCracken, let me make it clear to you that I'm asking if this is a physical possibility. I mean, it is an iron sheath that can take the abuse, corrosion, and strain placed upon it in highly volatile circumstances. I'm not asking if you conjecture that this is what happened on the expedition led by Kat and Sean Muir. I'm asking you, on a material level, whether you, as someone who has years of experience with these matters, think such a cable can be compromised? Tampered with in a way that no one would notice until it was in use?"

"Yeah. Yes."

"I see. Thank you," the prosecutor said, glancing at the judge, who seemed content enough to let him continue: "Knowing the procedure as you do, is there a time during the manufacturing process of thousands of feet of this cable that a single person could *interfere* with its structural integrity?"

"Yeah, there—*yes*, there are a lot of such times. It just has to be before the iron is wrapped around it and left to set. Once the iron has cooled down, you're not cutting through that or breaking it or such."

"Are you trying to tell us that this is what happened to cause the tragedy on *Sea Legs?*"

"No, I am not. I'm just talking about cable in general of this specific kind."

"Very good." The prosecutor stepped close to the witness stand, but in such a position that the jury's view of Slipjack was unhindered. The sailor looked the part of an expert mariner, someone more comfortable on water than on land; that was why they had dressed him in a too-big suit in the first place. "This will be my final couple of questions, all right, Mister McCracken?"

"Thank God ... ness. Goodness. Thank *goodness*." A couple of chuckles could be heard in the gallery.

The prosecutor also smiled and rattled off the final questions, with Slipjack answering them thoughtfully and carefully so as not to rouse the ire of the judge.

"Mister McCracken, were there any periods of more than, say, an hour when you *know* Doctor Sean Muir was alone in the facility where the cable was made?"

"Yes. He slept there sometimes, like I said."

"To your knowledge, did any of those times when you *know* Doctor Muir was alone in the facility occur during a period of the cable's manufacture? Specifically, were any of those times before the application of the iron armoring you mentioned?"

"Yes. Many periods of those ... periods. And such."

"That iron armoring that, once left to cool and harden, would be well-nigh impossible to cut through or snap?"

"Yes."

"To your knowledge, was Katherine—*Kat*, as she was affectionately known to all—ever alone in the facility during those times when the cable could have been damaged?"

"Alone? Naw, I mean, no. She'd really have no reason—"

"Don't speculate, Mister McCracken. Just answer with what you *know* to be the case."

Slipjack nodded and took another sip of his water. "No, she was not ever alone to my knowledge in the workshop."

"Did Kat have access to the facility that would have allowed her to—"

"Counsel ..." the judge growled.

"Sorry, Your Honor," counsel replied, satisfied that the words of his question had been heard by the jury so they could fill in the rest of what was *really* being asked (which is exactly why the judge cut off such "Trojan horse" speculation put forth as a question). "Mister McCracken, do you *know* if Kat had access that would allow her to be in the workshop alone?"

"She did. She had the same kind of key her husband did."

"How do you know that?"

"I saw her use it. When she was looking for Doctor Muir inside the building. He was there alone a good bit, like I said."

"There was no bell or buzzer or other signal that the door was being opened?"

"What, like at a hardware store to let 'em know a customer is there?"

"Yes, that sort of thing."

"No. That is, I can tell you I *know* there wasn't. During the day and sometimes pretty late, people were going in and out. Some of us smoke—I smoke—and so went out front for a cig. But there was also contractors and parts people working on the materials for the sub itself. It was all in one industrial park kind of place. Bells and buzzers going off would have driven Doctor Muir and Kat and the rest of the people what needed to concentrate right up the wall."

"All right. So, to your knowledge, there were at least two keys to the facility, the workshop where the cable was assembled?"

"That's right."

"Again, to your knowledge, were there any other copies of that key in circulation?"

The prosecutor paused to take a walk back to his team's table and picked up a brass-colored, large key inside a clear plastic evidence bag. "If it may please the court, this is the key that was found to be in Doctor Sean Muir's office when he was arrested." He returned to his place next to the witness stand and asked Slipjack, "Do you *know* why Sean Muir would still have this key once the project was no longer using the manufacturing facility but before the incident that killed his wife?"

"Well, sir, the university kept the lease going on that place because there was still the equipment inside. If this mission was a success, from what I heard, there would be follow-up missions that would need to use that same equipment. So, instead of returning the huge machines—they were rented, too—the college kept the lease going on the warehouse and workshops and such."

"Understood, but why would Doctor Muir still have it in his possession?"

"Counsel," the judge warned.

"Excuse me, Your Honor. Mister McCracken, do you *know* of any purpose for which Sean Muir would have been keeping this key? No such key was found in Kat's office or the Muir home during the investigation."

"I don't know what he'd need it for."

"Did you know that Kat Muir's key was reported missing to the security authority in charge of keeping track of keys to university-owned or -leased facilities?"

Slipjack looked honestly surprised. "No, I definitely did not know that."

"Oh, yes, there is a record stating that the defendant turned his key in at the end of the manufacturing process for the expedition." Then he pulled a face. "But Kat Muir never turned hers in."

"Well, that sure isn't—wasn't—like her. She always liked to have her *i*'s dotted and her *t*'s crossed and such. She was always careful, no matter what she was doing."

"Yes, I would imagine that misplacing a key to a facility full of very specialized, *very* expensive equipment would be reckless, even for a comfortably tenured academic, wouldn't it?"

"It doesn't seem like it would be real responsible, but that's why you report it missing, so they can change the locks."

"Did you know that the defendant reported the key missing only after returning to San Diego following his wife's death?"

"Wha—? I mean to say, no, I was not aware of that factoid."

"Just two more questions. No, *one* more, sorry, Your Honor," the prosecutor said with a nod and returned his attention to the witness. "Do you have any knowledge—*knowledge*, now—of how, if Kat Muir's key was reported missing and Sean Muir's key was turned in according to protocol, there could be a *third* key? One the security folks in charge of every key at the university didn't know about?"

"They could've gotten a copy made at Home Depot or like that, I guess."

"Aren't these kinds of keys marked 'DO NOT DUPLICATE'? Surely, you've seen those many times."

"Yeah. Yes, I mean, many times."

"So one couldn't legally get a locksmith to do it, and certainly not Home Depot, where they probably don't even *carry* this kind of key, and for that exact reason. "

"Oh, yeah, I guess not."

"So there could have been a third key or not?"

"What? I—I'm really confused right now. I guess there *could've* been a third one."

The prosecutor held off the defense lawyer and judge by immediately smiling and indicating the man on the bench, "Don't speculate, Mister McCracken. You don't want to get on the wrong side of *this* esteemed gentleman."

Again, a small laugh rose from a few in the gallery.

"Okay, then, I just mean there could've been a third key."

"Even though, to your knowledge, it would be illegal to have such a key made?"

Slipjack laughed, a bit uncomfortably. "I'm … I think I lost track of what you was asking me."

The prosecutor smiled sympathetically. "I was asking if there was, to your knowledge, any way a third key that could have been used by either the defendant or the victim. Was there? Did you have that knowledge?"

"No, sir, I got no knowledge of how there could be a third key."

"So Kat Muir had just one key, the one to her office; and the defendant had just one key, the one to *his* office."

"Yeah, that's what I seem to be saying."

"Thank you, Mister McCracken. No more questions, Your Honor." Then, with a nod acknowledging the ladies and gentlemen of the jury, the prosecutor returned to his table and, giving off an air of dispassion, examined some documents shown to him as if on cue by the other prosecutor seated at their table.

"Counsel, come visit the bench," the judge said to the prosecutor, and when the lawyer got to the bench, he whispered in consternation: "What in the good graces of God was *that?*"

"I don't know what you could mean, Your Honor." He kept his face as still as possible. No smirk would do anything good right now.

"You know *damn* well what I mean—that whole business with the keys! You got the witness so turned around he didn't know what you were even *asking* him."

"I was just trying to cover all the possible contingencies, Your Honor."

"You were trying to make it seem like Sean Muir did some subterfuge with his and his wife's office keys to make it look like he was in the building alone with the cable."

"If this witness is confused, then the jury is *certainly* confused."

The prosecutor looked, like, *totally* shocked, and said, "I didn't think of that, Your Honor. I hope they didn't get the wrong idea."

The judge closed his eyes and breathed through his nose for a moment, then said calmly, "What is the *right* idea, counselor? Who had what keys? And when?"

"Exactly the question I was trying to answer, Your Honor."

"Go, sit down. Get out of my face." The judge shook his head with his eyes closed for a moment, then said, "Defense counsel, the witness is yours."

The defense attorney, dressed in a gray suit as fine as the prosecutor's was off-the-rack and navy blue, thanked the judge and approached Slipjack at the witness stand with a facsimile of a friendly smile on his face. "Mister McCracken, may I call you Phillip or Phil? Or by your sailor's name—'Slipjack,' isn't it?"

"Yeah," Slipjack said, his tone and mien already suspicious. "I mean, that's my name and such, but I don't know why you want to call me that. We aren't friends, and you ain't—aren't—a seagoing man, I can see that. Unless it's on a yacht."

The judge had to suppress a small smile as he said, "Just answer the questions asked of you, Mister McCracken."

"Yeah, that's not important, Mister McCracken, although I do wonder what 'Slipjack' even means. I've heard 'Skipjack,' but never '*Slipjack*.'"

"Counsel, don't get cute. You don't seem to be asking a question, which, I may remind you, is your job here."

"My apologies, Your Honor. Mister McCracken, did you know that 'Slipjack' means 'A person so unattractive that he looks like he was working underneath a car when the jack slipped'?"

Slipjack, who was no model but wasn't *that* bad to look at—especially after being bought a couple of beers and shots at the Bayside Bar & Grill, which had for as long as anyone could remember sported a hand-lettered sign in its front window that said "GRILL BROKEN"—shook his head, looking surprised and embarrassed. "I did not know that. I didn't think it meant … anything, really."

"Now, *skipjack*—that's a kind of tuna, isn't it?"

It was the prosecution's turn to make an objection: "I don't see how this could possibly be relevant."

"Overruled, for the moment," the judge answered, and fixed the defense attorney with a sour look. "Counsel, will there be a point here other than trying to insult the witness? That's kind of, I don't know, 'contemptuous' in a courtroom like this, don't you think?"

The defense attorney made reassuring motions and said, "There is, indeed, a point, Your Honor. Now, Slipjack—"

"*Counsel.*"

"Wha—Oh, excuse me, Your Honor. Now, *Mister McCracken*, that nickname isn't exactly a compliment, is it?"

"Don't sound like it, no."

"A *skipjack*, on the other hand, is a kind of tuna, the kind that merchant fishermen *love* to haul into their boats. In fact, 'skipjack' also refers to a kind of fishing boat, did you know that?"

"Yeah. Yes. I know boats and merchant fish and such."

"Is it possible that whoever gave you that nickname meant to say 'Skipjack'? As a good seaman's moniker, you know?"

"It's possible," Slipjack said.

"But it must've gotten around on the boats you've worked—nobody was saying, 'Are you talking about Phil McCracken? Surely, you mean "Skipjack." After all, "Slipjack" basically means "really ugly."' Right, 'Slipjack' must have been repeated about you and it stuck? Mister McCracken?"

"Objection!"

"Sustained. Counsel, did I just hear what I think I heard? Are you calling the witness ugly?"

"No, Your Honor. I'm asking if those around him called him ugly."

"You're right on the edge, counsel, and you know I will not hesitate to put you up at the Hotel County Jail for contempt of court."

"Your Honor, there is a point I'm trying to get at, and I believe this line of questioning is the only way to find out if my surmises are accurate or not."

"Get at it *very* soon."

"Certainly, Your Honor. So, Mister McCracken, I will reformulate my question: Was it the case that the nickname 'Slipjack,' which we've established means 'ugly,' was given to you by your shipmates or others with whom you associated?"

"I don't think I'm ugly," Slipjack said in a tone somewhere between sulky and pissed off. "There been a lot of women who don't think that, either."

"I don't doubt that for a moment, but please answer the question, Mister McCracken."

"Yeah, it's possible. I mean, that's the only people what would give me a nickname at all. But they were just kidding around."

"I believe that. I really do. It was kind of a way to bust your ... well, y'know. Some harmless ribbing that almost every ship's crew—or any group of men and women crammed together for a good period of time—

takes part in. Takes everybody down a notch and makes them all the same kind of unlucky son of a gun who's found himself in lousy surroundings. Just teasing. Could it have been that, maybe, Mister McCracken?"

"Objection, Your Honor! He's asking the witness to speculate—"

"Naw, it's okay," Slipjack said. "That's all it was. Everybody got nicknames that meant 'stupid' or 'slow' or 'lazy' and such. Nobody would stay on their high horse very long. It was good for working a boat like equals, yeah."

"Thank you for answering that, Mister McCracken. It shows you're probably a good sport. Are you?"

Slipjack shrugged and said with a smile, "Yeah, I guess."

"I thought so. I mean, going by a name for 'ugly person,' you have to be a fun guy, a sport." The defense attorney's smile and nod at Slipjack looked like he wanted to slap him on the back or bump fists like a fellow cool dude. "I do want to ask, though: When a shipmate gets nicknamed something like 'Slowpoke,' is that based on anything, any, I don't know ... maybe *sluggishness* on the part of the person receiving that handle?"

"I'm sorry, sir. I don't get what you're saying."

"You know, 'Slowpoke,' wouldn't that be funny and also make sense as a nickname for the slowest deckhand on the boat?"

"Oh, right. Yeah, that makes sense."

"Sure, it does. Somebody who, I don't know, was the poor guy who started off on the ship cutting bait all day, he could be called 'Stinky,' right?"

Slipjack laughed and said, "Oh, yeah, there was almost always a Stinky on every fisher boat, let me tell ya."

The defense attorney laughed with him a little bit, then said, still smiling, "So even though these aren't *compliments*, certainly, they show a brotherly kind of joking around that actually means the other sailors accept you as one of them, would you agree?"

"Definitely."

"And like all good jokes, these nicknames have at least a little bit of truth to them, right? I mean, you wouldn't call a shipmate who would slip on his own mopped deck 'Slowpoke,' right? It wouldn't make sense. 'Slowpoke' has got to be the name for a slow guy if it's going to be funny or catch on with the crew—do you see what I mean?"

"Yeah."

"So when they nicknamed you 'Slipjack,' did you know what it meant? It's sort of urban in origin, so a sailor could be excused for not being familiar with that as being something people were called."

Slipjack sensed something coming, he didn't know what, and so he had stopped smiling. "Actually, I, uh, actually thought it was 'Skipjack' for a while."

"But you found out what it really was soon enough, is that right?"

The seaman pulled an abashed face and looked at his hands in his lap. "I did, sir," he said. "Soon enough. We got a computer hotspot on the fancier boats, so I looked it up."

"You did. Of course, you did—who wouldn't, if they somehow had earned this name from people he thought were friends?" The defense attorney shared a sympathetic look with Slipjack, making sure the jury could see it. "What did it say, when you looked it up?"

"It said just what you said. It's for people so ugly that they look like a car mashed their face. But it was just a joke, like the ones we had for the other guys. I kept it even when I got out of fishing, so guys wouldn't think I was all full of myself. I like it now."

"You don't think it's an accurate nickname, anyway, isn't that right? So no hard feelings."

"Yeah, that's just how it was."

"But you do admit that everybody else's nickname was based at least a little on reality. 'Stinky,' 'Porky,' things like that."

"Um, yeah. That's right."

"So they actually thought you really were kind of ugly, if they called you 'Slipjack.' That's how I see it. Is that how you see it?"

"I never really thought about it."

The judge grumbled, "All right, that's enough. Do you have any other lines of questioning, counselor, or is this just going to be you berating the witness about how unattractive you think he is?"

"My next question, literally my next question, will bring it all together, Your Honor. If you don't find it relevant, then I'll stop the cross-examination there, no more questions at all."

The judge looked dubious, but he said, "Counsel for both parties, approach the bench, please."

The prosecutor, who looked more perplexed than upset at the lack of apparent point to the defense attorney's questioning—the witness was *not* an attractive man, he agreed—tried not to show his confusion to the judge.

The defense attorney did what *he* could not to show smugness or how in love with himself he was at that moment.

First, the judge addressed the prosecutor: "Do you want me to let him ask this supposedly final question, or should I cut him off here?"

He answered, "I'm curious myself to see where the heck he's going with this. Your Honor. I think one more question would be all right, but I believe that should be his last question, *period*. I don't presume to tell the court what to do, but in my opinion that would be a fair deal."

"I'll take that under consideration." He then turned to the defense attorney and said, "Can you live with that? Is your next question important enough to be your last? If I cut you off after the witness's answer and don't let you make one more peep to this witness than "Thank you" or to me than "No more questions, Your Honor" before he leaves the stand, are you going to try any shenanigans? I have exactly one last good nerve before I send you to county for the next thirty days, so you'd better be meaning whatever you say to me."

He nodded soberly. "I accept the terms, Your Honor."

"All right, then. Thank you, gentlemen," the weary judge said. "Let's get back to work."

The defense lawyer stepped back into position. "Thank you for your patience, Mister McCracken, ladies and gentlemen of the jury. I have one last question and that's it. The nickname 'Slipjack,' whether meant in a friendly way or as an outright insult, is based on what many *may* see as a certain, let's say, appearance that improves in opposite proportion with the brightness of a room's lighting—"

"Your Honor!" the prosecution yelped.

"—so real quick, here's my final question: How did an ugly mug like you get Doctor Katherine Muir—the beautiful, well-paid, respected, and, by all accounts, *loving* wife of Doctor Sean Muir—to carry on a sexual relationship, a full-blown *extramarital affair*, with you for the last three months of her life?"

Phillip 'Slipjack' McCracken practically jumped to his feet and tried to lunge at Sean Muir's defense attorney but was held back by a quick-moving bailiff. The prosecutors almost knocked their chairs over as they shouted *"Objection! Your Honor! OBJECTION!"* again and again. However, that was largely drowned out by the eruption of shouts and shrieked obscenities from both sides of the courtroom gallery: Sean's family screaming bloody murder at the accusation, no matter that it completely destroyed the credibility of the prosecution's star witness; and Katherine's family roaring in fury at the blackening of their dearly departed's good name.

"ORDER IN THE COURT!" The judge banged his gavel again and again and again, yelling, "CLEAR THIS COURTROOM! *CLEAR THIS COURTROOM NOW!*" also again and again and again, and to just as little effect. However, he did get the two uniformed officers who came running at the riot of noise to get both sides of counsel into his office NOW and to get more courthouse police to clear the room NOW. He also yelled to his bailiff to escort the witness out the back to a secure space and keep him from getting killed for as long as possible.

Sean Muir, for his part, had been coached to be inexpressive during the trial, even to seem to zone out. *Except* when witnesses testified how wonderful Kat had been, sharing stories of this kindness or that generosity—*that* was the time, they said, to cry or let his anger out (silently). The jury would be watching, and taking notes subconsciously, notes that would come to the forefront of their minds during deliberation over his guilt and then, possibly, in the worst-case scenario, his sentence.

Sean wasn't an actor, however, although he did get teary during the opening statements, when *both* parties extolled some of his late wife's many virtues. The State lamented that such a wonderful woman could be betrayed and murdered by her husband; and the defense insisted that no one who knew her, *least of all* her devoted husband, could harm a hair on her head, and this was a tragic accident that an overzealous district attorney had blown up into a headline-grabbing travesty of justice.

Otherwise, he just listened quietly, zoning out being something he did not want to do and probably, given his restless mind, couldn't do. It wasn't difficult to keep calm after the opening statements, since everything thus far had been technical details, expert opinions on the materials used in the winch, cables, and submersible. Sean could see that the prosecutors were trying to find if there were any flaws in the design, perhaps intentional flaws introduced by the defendant to make his wife's death look like an accident; and his defense was looking to show that not only was all equipment ideally designed and built, but also that Kat had taken part in every step, making it unlikely any flaw could have been intentionally incorporated into the works that she wouldn't have noticed and pointed out. Slipjack was the final witness in the part of the trial dealing with what was damaged, possibly even sabotaged, and who would have had the opportunity, motive, and ability to perform the sabotage, if sabotage it was.

Slipjack was called—strangely, by the prosecution, with the defense to perform cross-examination—and answered everything in a way that matched Sean's statements well. It was only the final run of questions, this seemingly irrelevant and insulting line of inquiry, that was all set up for this bombshell to be dropped. Kat was having an affair with *Slipjack?* Sean's attorney had been correct to imply that the winch chief had a face only a mother could love, and only if paid to do so. But it was more than that: Slipjack had an oily quality about him, something Kat had once commented to Sean about over wine among other inappropriate observations about their crew, and even if she just wanted something physical ... she turned to *Slipjack?*

It was true that Sean pulled long, *long* hours working on all aspects of the expedition, but the same was true (although less frequently) of his wife. They were academics with the funding to make the research voyage of a lifetime. They would be able to gather evidence to support the logically connected, but thus far physically unsupported, conjectures that some other scientists called a "theory," using that word in the sense of a "systematic explanation ready to be tested." He appreciated their enthusiasm, but he knew they knew that he needed hard data, and a lot of it, to move the "prehistoric beasts surviving near hydrothermal vents" idea from an interesting thought experiment to a theory that could be supported or not supported by reality.

Ichthyopaleontology, and evolutionary biology in general, were different from mathematics or physics, in that nothing could really be disproven—the Higgs boson was theorized to exist only within certain energy parameters. If it wasn't to be found there, then either that part of the theory was incorrect and the Higgs boson might exist somewhere else; or that part of the theory was correct but the Higgs boson didn't exist.

But paleontology of every stripe was a matter of finding evidence, usually in the form of fossils but also with chemical and statistical analysis, that could be pieced together to form a larger picture of what had happened, what life-forms were involved, how they lived and when they died. Alternate explanations could also be reasonably introduced—unlike with math or the hard sciences—and duked it out with the prevailing theories used to suss out the secrets of things that lived one hundred million years ago or more.

Sean was glad to have a marine biologist and oceanographer as his wife (apart from being glad to have the excellent person Katherine was as his wife in the first place). This combination of specializations and meeting of the minds allowed Sean to add credence to his ideas and was used by Katherine in paper after paper as her star rose in academic circles. It wasn't a one-way street: each Muir did anything possible to lift the other up, and it had worked beautifully until the day that Sean wished Kat had never shown any interest in his crackpot ideas.

He remained seated at the defense table as the gallery was cleared out and his main lawyers were called away to meet with the judge. He found himself staring at the empty witness stand. His Katherine had been having an *affair?* Why would she do such a thing? She was no wilting flower—she could have shared her issues and desires with him. They were academics; they could have worked something out from the catalogue of sex-partner scenarios. And she had shared a bed with his trusted crew member, the winch man *Slipjack?* He just couldn't get his mind around it. Until the bailiff and officers returned to the courtroom to safely escort Sean and the assistant defense lawyer out of the building, he just stayed where he was, stunned into silence, asking himself the same questions over and over again, and coming up with nothing.

***

The judge's robes and demeanor made him resemble nothing so much as a pitch-black tornado, and anyone in the halls who happened to be in his way got the hell *out* of his way with the same speed and urgency that they would have shown had an actual tornado been coming at them.

The two lead attorneys followed him, trying not to look like they were being called to the principal's office, but the speed at which they had to follow His Honor left little doubt in anyone's mind that they were being taken to the woodshed.

The judge swept behind his desk but didn't sit down. When the prosecutor and defense counsel arrived, he barked, "Shut the goddamn door, and sit your asses in those chairs."

They did as they were told, trying to maintain their dignity but failing.

The judge didn't even notice their expressions through the flames of his anger. He stabbed a finger at the defense attorney and said, *"Mister Kreide,* what in the name of God was that just now? I had half a mind to let the witness put his hands around your grandstanding neck!"

"Your ... Your Honor, I know it was dramatic, but—"

"Dramatic? For Chrissake, you accused the witness of screwing around behind the back of *your own client!* The defendant may be guilty of murder—*may* be, and it's the jury's job to decide—but you just pulled this thing out of your rectum and *humiliated* the poor son of a bitch!"

"Your H—"

"Don't you talk, counsel. Don't you say a goddamn word until I *tell* you to talk. I should've held you in contempt six times in the past half hour, and if you don't make the next thing you say containing a Mother Teresalevel of convincing credibility, it's unlucky seven for you, and you *are* going straight from this room to jail. You understand me, Mister Kreide?"

The defense attorney nodded.

"All right. Now, you didn't imply an affair, you didn't goddamn *allude* to it, you said, *How can an ugly-ass bastard like you get my client's classy wife to spread her legs on a regular schedule?* I want to stick you in a hole for a year and let you count up all the ways you just violated not only the decorum of my courtroom but also your own Bar Association's guidelines and rules! I guarantee a year won't be enough, but I'm going to give you *one* chance to defend what you just did during a *trial*. Not a magistrate's hearing, not in opening or closing arguments—where it would have been entirely inappropriate, anyway—but in a trial that you might have just forced into a goddamn *mis*trial, wasting the taxpayers' hard-earned money, wasting weeks of time that fifty public servants could have used to improve the county, not to mention your own client's goddamn money!"

"Mister Käse," the judge said to the lead prosecutor, "I need to ask you a couple of things before I let your opposite number make one more peep." He came around the desk and half-sat on it in front of him in a way to express casual interest, nothing big.

"Yes, Your Honor," the prosecutor said as seriously as the defense attorney had nodded a moment earlier. (Contrary to what fans of courtroom-based dramas may have been led to believe, lawyers on both sides of the aisle were colleagues and often friends. Trial attorneys Käse and Kreide—"one *K* short of an ACLU lawsuit," this judge had said to them in a much lighter moment during a much less complex trial—were friends, and neither took pleasure at the other being chewed out or embarrassed. At least outside of court.)

The judge took a deep breath and began: "Did this alleged 'affair' ever come up in discovery? Did it arise in *any* depositions from *anyone* involved, from *any* witnesses, including this 'Slipjack' fellow? Do you feel that any evidence of this out-of-the-blue accusation was withheld from the prosecution? Or did you know that this subject was in the air surrounding the case but thought it wasn't relevant to pursue? Go ahead, just tell me. You're not the one I'm *extra* pissed at." He took a moment to glare at the defense attorney, who just didn't feel like meeting His Honor's eyes at that exact moment.

"Your Honor," the prosecutor said carefully, not wanting to attract any of the wrath he had so far avoided, "this was the very first anyone at my table has heard anything at all about any affair. And we spent a lot of time looking for motive. We also couldn't find anything out of the ordinary regarding the office and shop keys."

"All right. Why, then, do you think Mister Kreide—a very well-compensated, high-profile attorney who, to my knowledge, has never been accused of flagrant contempt of court—would pull this kind of a stunt? There was no reason for the defense to discredit an expert witness called to describe the manufacturing process of this cable. I can see the need of a prosecutor to have the court hear how and when the cable could have been tampered with or otherwise compromised, the whole thing with the keys, and so on, of such an expert witness. You follow me?"

"So far, Your Honor."

"All right. Why, then, do you think, the lead defense attorney could possibly have done this—based either on evidence that he illegally withheld from the prosecution, or possibly based on no evidence at all?"

"I don't know, Your Honor. If I put myself in his shoes, I believe that I'd see that my client was guilty as ... *heck* ... and would start grasping at straws, do anything to tear down a prosecution witness."

"Hmm. Was it, maybe, a trick question? Like a 'When did you stop touching strangers on the bus' kind of thing?"

"It could be, Your Honor. I don't want to speculate too much in front of defense counsel, sir."

"No, of course," the judge said. "You'd never ask any trick questions of anyone, not of a fellow attorney, certainly not of an unsophisticated witness doing his duty to the court by testifying, would you?"

The prosecutor let out a breath of laughter, which dissipated when he saw that although the judge was giving him a smile, he was asking him a question that he expected to be answered, and answered right now. "I—I wouldn't—well, Your Honor, I don't believe I would, not on purpose. It wouldn't be ethical."

"No. No, it wouldn't," the judge said. "Very *un*ethical, in point of fact."

The judge kept his gaze on Mister Käse, and he couldn't lower his eyes the way his defense compatriot had without being rude. But something was coming, he could feel it. So he nodded. "Very unethical, Your Honor."

"Glad you agree. You know another dirty trick? One played against the witness, the jury, the judge—hell, anyone within listening distance? There are so many a clever lawyer can pull, aren't there?"

He gulped like a cartoon turtle. "Yes?"

"Oh, indeed there are. Here's one: You implied, strongly—almost *stated*, actually—that the reproduction of keys marked 'DO NOT DUPLICATE' was illegal. Then you asked the witness if he had any knowledge of that not being true."

"Your Honor, I believe I asked him if he had any knowl ... edge ..." The judge's expression was not one approving of interruption. "But yes, Your Honor, I did."

"You know damned well it isn't illegal. Not even unlawful. Hell, it isn't even unethical if you don't use the duplicate key for nefarious purposes. But *you* got your witness to agree that it couldn't be done, or wouldn't be done, anyway; and so cut off any answers to your 'key' questions that depended on a spare key having been made." The judge seemed to be done and waiting for him to respond.

He cleared his throat quietly and said, "Yes, I did, Your Honor. I was trying to show that the defendant must have kept the key to the manufacturing building. I'm trying to show he kept it to eliminate—" He stopped dead and looked at the defense counsel. "I would rather not share my prosecution strategy with the defense, Your Honor."

"No, of course not. I'm done with you, anyway, but please do stay with us, Mister Käse. Maybe you'll enjoy learning a new dirty trick."

He couldn't laugh, because it wasn't a joke. And he couldn't show any resistance to the judge's words, because the judge was not inviting him to enter into a conversation about "dirty tricks." So the prosecutor made no expression at all and very subtly nodded to acknowledge the judge's words.

"All right, then we all agree that you two have both acted like jackasses." The judge turned once again to the defense attorney. "Now, Mister Kreide, what evidence do you have, whether you have shared it with the opposition or not, that there was a sexual relationship between Mister McCracken and the late Katherine Muir?"

"Evidence? I have no hard evidence, Your Honor."

"Then what ... the ... *hell* were you doing in there? You accused the witness of sleeping with the defendant's wife. You can't slander the dead, but you sure as hell can slander a living witness."

"It was reckless, Your Honor, but I asked because everything suddenly made sense to me: the whole business with the keys, why Sean Muir *and* his wife both were in possession of keys to the building even though there was no need for either of them to have even *one*. The prosecution has as good as said that the defendant kept his to remove any trace of evidence that *he* had tampered with anything. But what I believe—and now that I've thought of it, if I'm not going up the river for thirty days, I can find evidence for it—is that Slipjack McCracken and Katherine Muir used the building for their trysts. There are long couches in there, and we know they were used by the defendant and others to catch some sleep when pulling an all-nighter working on the expedition. McCracken was in love with Kat, and he saw her husband as an obstacle to their getting together. That's why, I believe, McCracken tampered with the cable. He could do it without anyone knowing if he had Kat's key copied, a key she had pilfered from her husband in the first place."

The judge leaned back and crossed his arms. "*You* don't even know which keys were which, let alone who 'illegally' made copies. There isn't one iota of this horseshit that will stand up in court—you have to know that, Mister Kreide."

"Maybe it won't, Your Honor—"

"*Definitely* it won't, Counselor."

"Yes, okay, I apologize for following an idea that I hadn't even fully worked out, much less had any evidence for. I started doing my closing argument during the questioning of a witness. I am very sorry, Your Honor, and I apologize to Mister Käse as well," he said, looking at the prosecutor, who gave him a noncommittal nod. "But it wasn't out of contempt, sir—I had a sudden revelation about what actually happened, and why."

"A sudden revelation that just happens to exonerate your client."

"Your Honor, if I may just give you the last piece of the puzzle, the thing that made me improvise and go down the road of making McCracken admit he was ugly and others saw him as ugly."

The judge looked at the prosecutor and widened his eyes. He said, "*This* should be good." He motioned for the defense attorney to go right ahead and collect however much rope was necessary for him to hang himself.

"What seemed really hard to reconcile in my mind was not why McCracken was in love with Katherine Muir, who was practically model material. That was self-evident. But why in the heck would *she* be sharing a bed with *him?* I know people can have affairs without necessarily being unhappy in their marriage, and I know sometimes the paramour isn't as attractive, smart, interesting, or well-heeled as his or her other number. Look at Hugh Grant and that nasty hooker—he was in a long-term relationship with Elizabeth Hurley, one of the most attractive women in an industry with a lot of attractive women."

"You're talking in circles now, counselor. Sum it up; let's go."

"Yes, Your Honor. But even if Kat Muir was slumming, which does happen, why did the liaison take place at a building that both of them *knew* Sean Muir had a key for? It seems unnecessarily risky, *especially* for a spouse who is sleeping around for the thrill of being with someone beneath her."

"So to speak."

"Ha! Yes, Your Honor, very good. McCracken insisted on bedding her at the manufacturing building because he was in love with her—as often happens with the 'slumee,' someone who is not even close to being in the slumming party's league. He was delusional, having convinced himself that if he was in love with her, then she must be in love with him, and was only afraid to break from her husband for a deck swab because it might put her reputation and career at risk."

"I see where you're going with this," the judge said. "Get there, already."

"So, since he was largely in charge of overseeing the manufacture of the cable, the *lifeline* that kept *D-Plus* from sinking irretrievably into the depths, he would place the flaw, one that would weaken the cable enough to break entirely, at a spot that wouldn't come into play during Katherine's first test depth but that would be unrolled during Sean's deeper second test. Sean hurt his fingers, though, and Kat took his place in the submersible, and there was nothing Slipjack—Mister McCracken—could do to stop it that wouldn't expose him as a saboteur and a murderer."

"Holy cow," the judge said. "That is one heck of a convincing argument, isn't it, Mister Käse?"

"Sure, and when I was a kid, I could explain exactly how Santa filled billions of stockings and left presents all over the world in one night. It was a *very* convincing argument."

"All right. Now, Mister Kreide, you ... wait a second," he said, and looked at the prosecutor with eyes narrowed in amusement. "What was this super-convincing argument about Santa? I want to believe!"

The prosecutor smiled and spread out his hands like he was stating the most obvious thing in the world. "*Magic*, Your Honor. Magic doesn't worry about physical laws—that's what makes it *magic*. And Santa is well known to be a magical personage."

"Wow, you missed your calling, Mister Käse."

"Did I, Your Honor?"

"Yeah, you should have been sent to the asylum back when you were a kid," he said, and laughed heartily. "All right. Back to you now, Mister Kreide. Your argument is very convincing in an Agatha Christie / Sherlock Holmes kind of way, but surely you know not one iota of that is admissible in court."

"I do, Your Honor."

"All the evidence, including the key business introduced as a trick by the opposition, is firmly against your client."

"I can't say that, Your Honor."

"I know, I know. That really *would* be a breach of ethics, and I don't want it in my quarters or my courtroom. But the fact remains." He turned to the prosecutor and said, "However, if I know your opponent here—and I do—he's going to find a way to work this theory into something admissible."

"Probably, Your Honor," Mister Käse agreed with a rueful smile.

"Do you two want to work out a plea deal, both of you cut your losses and walk away without a whole goddamn egg on your face?"

They did.

***

Four years later (out of the ten he was sentenced to in his plea deal for voluntary manslaughter) and one day after the Bentneus Transmission (as they were calling it), Sean Muir was led in his familiar chains to the designated visitation room to meet a visitor, most likely his lawyer, the man who had shared with his client all of the confidential conversation with the judge and prosecutor in chambers. It didn't really matter who it was; Sean would be still glad to see him or her. Solitary made a body downright thrilled to see anyone at all.

The guard looked through the visiting room door's tiny viewing window, made a guttural noise of acknowledgment to himself, unlocked the door, and yanked it open for Sean, shuffling in his chains, to enter.

He had two visitors, both of whom he knew, or at least recognized, after being cut off so long from familiar faces. The first was his defense attorney, Bill Kreide, who hadn't kept him from prison but did get the charges reduced and his sentence a third of what it might have been. Because it was Kreide, the guard would stand *outside* the room to grudgingly satisfy the rules of attorney-client privilege. Sean didn't mind that at all.

The other man was Mickey Luch. He had a little streak of gray in his well-kept black beard, but his stocky frame and genuine smile were unmistakable. He hadn't seen Mickey since he was put away, and now he cried out, "My god—*Mickey!*" He couldn't hug him with his cuffed wrists on chains attached to more chain wrapped around his waist, but Mickey's smile was just as warm and maybe as teary as Sean's. "I can't believe it's you! Not in a letter, but really *here!* How—what are you doing here?"

Mickey kept smiling as he talked, a hopeful note in his voice. "Mister Kreide and I have something we want to discuss with you."

Sean looked back at his attorney, kept on retainer paid for by the sale of *Sea Legs*—the equipment belonged to the university, but the boat was his—and most everything he owned that wasn't imbued with sentimental value. It had paid big dividends in getting Sean access to the library system and that beautiful typewriter, both of which kept him from cutting his wrists with the wrong end of a plastic spoon. Kreide was setting up a laptop with a screen bigger than Sean had ever seen on a portable machine.

Four years was a long time for technology. Or for a man. The loss of that much time—and the greater amount still to go—hit him with a nauseating pang of regret. But he shook himself out of it and said to

Kreide, "Movie time? Did you find evidence to exonerate me? The security video?"

"No, unfortunately, no matter how many times I check with the building management, they keep telling me the system keeps only the previous 24 hours' worth of recording. It hasn't magically changed, Sean." His ironic tone leavened when the laptop finally cooperated and the two-way video chat finally registered the cameras and microphones at both the prison and on the other end. He said, "Sorry to snap at you, Sean. Technology makes me crazy, but the limit of visitors accompanying your lawyer at one time is *one*, and since I needed Mister Luch, I couldn't bring my usual computer guy."

They all waited while the attorney fiddled with the hardware, then the software.

"There we go," Kreide said at last, and turned the laptop around to face Sean. There was another chair bolted to the floor on the side of the table opposite the prisoner, but Mickey stood with his back to the corner—you could tell he was a sailor who felt more comfortable in tight spaces—and the lawyer just stepped back a few feet. Someone wants to speak with you. Make a proposal to you that you might find compelling."

Sean blinked in surprise. Was this one of the academic presses he had contacted about his book on present-day sea dinosaurs, the ones theorized by him and confirmed by the *Piranha II* expedition? They must have been very enthusiastic about the draft he sent, since it explained the "impossible" things that the huge simulcast audience saw right along with the explorers and also supported certain ideas Sean had been proposing for years before the tragedy of his failed deep-sea project. He sat up straighter in the chair bolted to the floor, although he doubted it was possible to look dignified while wearing an orange prison jumpsuit.

"Doctor Muir, please meet Jake Bentneus."

Sean's eyes goggled. He had actually met Jake Bentneus briefly years before, when the technical advisor on *Lusitania!* had invited him to a meeting to talk about ROVs and what it would look like on-screen with them exploring the wreck. Sean had been pleased to speak to the filmmaker and his crew working on the movie, who wanted this information for extra verisimilitude during a framing scene of the present-day sunken ship that would run on either end of the main story, which took place on soundstages and used CGI to portray the romantic adventure making up most of the film. They had all shaken hands afterward and Sean was brought by limousine to the airport for the short jaunt back to San Diego, and that was that. Memorable for a paleoichthyologist, not so much, probably, for a super-famous movie director.

However, the man on the laptop screen said, "Actually, Doctor Muir and I have met, haven't we?" The pumps and other machinery provided a background of white noise through which his words seemed to rise like an air bubble in the ocean.

"Yes, we have," Sean said, pleasantly surprised. "I didn't think I made much of an impression on you."

"Ha! I became obsessed with the whole thing, as you obviously must know. And obsession leads us down a dark path, doesn't it?" Bentneus indicated his useless body as well as possible through the facial rods and servos, but Sean would have gotten his meaning even if they had been speaking over the radio. He nodded and indicated with *his* expression that his surroundings were a testament to what the filmmaker was saying. "So, Doctor Muir—*Sean*, if you don't mind—you had a chance to see me in my present state last night, I presume?"

Sean had no idea what he was talking about. How could he have *seen* Jake Bentneus?

"Mister Bentneus," Sean's attorney broke in, "Doctor Muir has been under solitary confinement for more than a year. He doesn't have a television or radio available to him."

"Hehhhhhhhhh … please excuse me, Sean. I heard there were some people who hadn't seen my broadcast. Now I know why we fell short: solitary confinement. Hehhhhhhhhh …"

Sean didn't have anything to say to that hilarious and thoughtful comment, so he didn't say anything.

"Mister Kreide and our mutual friend Mickey will fill you in on the details, but the only thing alive on my body is my head. One of your prehistoric beasts chewed my bathysphere like it was one of Mama's meatballs and spit me out. I'm lucky to be alive at all. Lucky, *lucky* me! Hehhhhhhhhh …

"But you could have told me that your surviving dinosaurs wouldn't be able to digest me, couldn't you? It was all right there in your academic publications, warning me, if I'd taken the time to read them. Of course, it doesn't matter if you don't get digested if they crunch you to death."

"Yes," Sean said, not really liking Bentneus calling them *his* dinosaurs. Galileo discovered the four moons of Jupiter, but they aren't known as *his* moons.

Wait, damn, yes they are. That's why they were called the "Galilean moons." Another beautiful conjecture ruined by inconvenient facts, Sean thought, and he could feel the trace of a smile on his face. It had been a long time since he'd smiled.

Coming back to his surroundings, Sean said, "I, um, *proposed* that in order to live under the incredible pressures near ocean-floor hydrothermal vents, their bodily structure would have had to adapt in such a way that ingesting nonorganic matter—like the plastics and metal in your submersible—would be impossible. Even a man in a thick wetsuit wouldn't agree with a present-day dinosaur's stomach. But I also conjectured, and I'm sorry that I was correct, that they would still have the instinct for biting. That's because I believe there would be no evolutionary pressure, no advantage to reproductive efficiency, to lose their teeth over generations. Or to stop biting with them, since any time they did bite down on or swallow organic matter soft enough to be absorbed by their adapted digestion system, they still got fed. It's like kittens playing—they are fed in bowls, but they still have that hunting behavior because they can hunt without eating, but they can't eat without hunting. Of course, it's only been a hundred years or so since the concept of an exclusive 'indoor cat' arose." He finished and looked at the blank expressions of the two men in the room and the one on the laptop screen. "Sorry, excuse me—I haven't talked to anyone in quite a while."

Bentneus "smiled" and said, "Of course, it's no problem. In the time since my disaster, I've realized that I didn't have the single element, the one thing that would have greatly helped myself and my whole team not only to find your dinosaurs, but to gain knowledge about them without being eaten. Or without getting chewed like a stick of Juicy Fruit."

"One thing?" Sean couldn't think of any one thing that would have kept the Gigadon (he liked that name) from attacking Bentneus inside his vertical sub.

"*You*, Doctor Muir. I should have had *you* on my boat when we went out there to Challenger Deep. Once we saw that there really were dinosaurs down there—actually, once we discovered a newly formed hydrothermal vent—we could have consulted with you right there and then, or not gone any farther without at least contacting you on the satphone. If we had known more about what was down there, countermeasures could have been considered and built into *Ocean Victory*."

"Countermeasures?"

"*Weapons*, Doctor Muir. We had a golden opportunity to bag a specimen that would greatly advance science, but it all went to hell, as you well know. I had read some of your work, but read it like Buzz Aldrin might have read Jules Verne's *From the Earth to the Moon* the night before liftoff; it was an amusing sideline among much more mainstream research I did about the Marianas Trench in general and Challenger Deep in particular. If I had been paying real attention, we could have brought weapons and made everything go ... more *swimmingly*. Hehhhhhhhhh hehhhhhhhhh ..."

God, that "laugh analogue," as Popcorn would have called it, was creepy as hell. Sean ejected that extremely awful "ableist" thought from his brain (he had been a prof at a California university, after all, and knew better) and said, "I never imagined my theories would be quite as 'on the nose' as they were. The expedition that landed me here was to test conditions in the environment, see if what assumptions I had made about the vents and life around them were correct—not necessarily assumptions about dinosaurs, but about the ecosystem existing without sunlight. In essence, I was looking to support my less, um, *mainstream* ideas with new information I collected myself. My wife and myself, I mean."

"Of course," Bentneus said. "But, tragically, your mission objectives never came close to being realized because of the loss of your submersible."

"Yes," Sean paused, "but especially because of what happened to the person inside of it. My wife."

"I did say *tragically*, Doctor Muir." If he still had hands, he would have cavalierly waved away Sean's correction. "They don't imprison you for ten years because you just mishandled a piece of machinery."

"Look, I didn't—"

"No, don't worry about defending yourself. You are not being attacked. I, myself, didn't fulfill my original mission of touching down in Challenger Deep. We were less than one hundred feet away, but you don't set your sub down on a 750-degree vent you had no idea was there in the first place. Yes, we discovered and got footage of your dinosaurs, so my name will be in the history books ... just not the way I would have chosen."

Sean nodded. The situation was highly ironic, but what had happened to Bentneus was also so appallingly atrocious that he couldn't really say anything that wouldn't feel like piling on. He didn't know what he was supposed to be saying or thinking or how he was supposed to be reacting, anyway; he literally had no idea why Jake Bentneus was talking to him. It didn't matter—he was enjoying the hell out of a conversation with a person who wasn't a prison guard or a lawyer. Obviously, it was about the dinosaurs, probably about the 'Gigadon' about which Sean had read stacks of journal articles, but beyond that, it was a complete mystery.

"My life is over, Doctor Muir; surely you can see that. Billions of people saw me in this condition for the first time last week, and they understand. I'm assuming you can understand why I haven't long to live. But showing my desperation and burning desire for my goal to be realized, that was the real point of letting the world into my private hell. I will ask Mister Kreide to supply you with a transcript—it explains everything about what I'm seeking and how it can be delivered to me. But if I may give you the abridged version?"

"Y-Yes, of course."

"I spoke a moment ago about the wish that I had outfitted *Ocean Victory* with weaponry," he said, and waited for a nod of acknowledgment from Sean, which he made as soon as he realized there had been a pause in the filmmaker's monologue. "Yes, well, I want a second chance, Doctor Muir. It is impossible for me to be moved from this one spot in one hospital room in one hospital in goddamn *Guam*. But we have full-immersion VR now, and I will still be a part of this dream realized."

Sean searched his short-term memory—had Bentneus said what that dream was? "You mean the wish that you had brought along, um, *countermeasures* down into Challenger Deep?"

"Hehhhhhhhhh … no, that's merely a dead man's regret. But this dead man wants to see a submersible just like mine outfitted with not only weapons but also heat generators on an epic scale. 'Epic' as in unprecedented: why would anyone want to heat localized areas of the frigid, sunless depths of the Pacific Ocean? But also epic in that I have worked with an army of engineers, applied physics professionals, metalworkers, you name it. I've worked with them to create portable, one-use batteries of such power that they allow a one-person submersible to be underwater for 12 hours.

Also, we created the technology to allow the bathysphere will be filled with water, body-temperature water, in which the pilot sits. This keeps his temperature normalized, not going through highs and lows, and the water is constantly recirculated through pipe works that have earned over one hundred new patents for their ingenuity … and their value. I just can't help but make money. Hehhhhhhhhh Hehhhhhhhh …"

"Wow, I'd love to see the specs on that—"

"Mister Kreide, please provide our friend with any documents he needs." Sean's attorney made a note on his iPad. "Have you ever seen my movie *Abyssal Zone?* It's from a few years back, but it's proved prescient—admittedly, it was aliens down there instead of dinosaurs, but you get me. It was way ahead of its time, as my films have always been."

Don't say anything sarcastic, Sean reminded himself. "Huh, yeah, I see what you mean. And yes, I saw that movie in the theater, if I recall correctly."

"Hehhhhhhhh ... good man," Bentneus said.

Sean realized that part of the creepy feeling he couldn't shake stemmed from the fact that, apparently, the advanced breathing technology couldn't be modulated and so there was no inflection to Bentneus's voice. That meant Sean couldn't get a good read on what was said lightly and what was meant to be taken utterly seriously. "Good movie," he said, not having any idea where the filmmaker was going with this.

"Do you remember the part where Harrison Edwards has to breathe the water itself because of the pressures involved?"

"Oh, yeah, that was tough to watch. How Edwards jerked back when he first filled his lungs—he looked like, 'Oh, hell, I have made a *huge* mistake.'"

"Yes, but it worked out, didn't it?"

As Sean remembered, the aliens executed what was essentially a *deus ex machina*, rescuing the humans from the depths and magically keeping them from decompression sickness. But it did work out with the breathing the water thing. "As I remember, he could breathe like he was a fish himself."

"Right," Bentneus said, and Sean bet that he would have shouted that with an upraised finger if he could. "That's what we're going to do with this new submersible, inside the bathysphere. The pilot will be able to breathe the water so his environment can be constantly cooled, even as heat is pouring out of the sub."

Sean smiled. "The idea is to get the dinosaurs—the Gigadon for sure, but every other dinosaur that can be killed, too—to follow the warm water up as close to the surface as possible, where they can be killed from the boats on the surface. Yes?"

"It's taken directly from your research, Doctor Muir."

"Oh, I recognize it. Of course, my speculation that the heat-vent-loving dinosaurs would follow the path of a heat source—like the Gigadon did before its, um, *attack*—didn't include instructions on how to *kill* anything. That wasn't really the focus. I was trying to work out a scenario in which they could be studied nearer the surface."

"No, I understand," Bentneus said. "But you *could* kill it."

"I suppose. I mean, if it's alive, then it can be killed. If one had a way to lift its gills out of the water, that would be more efficient—more possible, actually—than trying to destroy it with guns or bombs or whatever might be carried on a modified commercial fishing boat. A person would—"

"No," Bentneus wheezed, and despite the breathing machine, the sharpness of his contradiction snapped. "Not *a person*. Not just *any* person. *You*, Doctor Muir."

Sean's mouth opened into a smile, and he looked to Mickey and Kreide like, *What the hell?* Mickey smiled widely and Kreide nodded, indicating that Sean should return his attention to the laptop screen. "Um, Mister Bentneus, you do know that I am four years into a ten-year sentence, right?"

"Hehhhhhhhhh ... hehhhhhhhhhh ... *hehhhhhhhhhh* ... Doctor Muir, you are thinking small. You are thinking *poor*. Let me ask you: Did you do what they all say? *Did* you murder your wife?"

Sean wasn't offended. It was a question you asked of someone in prison if you had any doubt or curiosity, or if you maybe just wanted to hear the person admit it out loud. He glanced at his lawyer, who closed his eyes and gave a slight nod.

In other words, *Go ahead. They can't try you twice.*

Sean cleared his throat. "In point of fact, I did not. Maybe it *was* my fault, inadvertently, for not checking every foot of cable for flaws. But it's a new process, armoring fiber optics and other data lines within an iron cable. And unspooling twenty thousand feet in the workshop—"

"The details aren't needed, Doctor Muir. I didn't think you killed anyone. I don't know if *anyone* killed your brilliant wife. I think it was a freak accident, and you damn near saved her even still."

"Thank you, Mister Bentneus."

"You call me 'Jake' now, and I'm gonna call you 'Sean,' all right?" His face was pulled into a smile. "I mean, since we're going to be partners in this undertaking."

Sean didn't laugh, surprising himself. "I don't know much about *killing* prehistoric sea life, but I can definitely help you with information about what I believe their behavior would be at the bottom. What it would *have* to be, in fact, if they are descendants of dinosaurs—I mean, *marine lizards*, but I'm a paleoichthyologist and if I'm not giving a lecture, I exclusively call them 'dinosaurs.'"

"Hehhhhhhhhhh ... that's great, Sean. That information will definitely be needed." He paused for dramatic effect, and achieved it. "We're both imprisoned, aren't we?"

"Ha, yeah, I'd have to agree with that ... Jake."

"But do you know the difference between my prison and yours?"

"Other than the obvious? No."

"One million dollars put into the right hands can release you from yours."

Sean looked at his lawyer and said, "What is—?"

Kreide said, "Hear him out, Sean."

He fixed his eyes back on the laptop.

"Mister Kreide is a good man, Sean. He doesn't believe you committed murder, or even were responsible through neglect. He is, in many ways, your real advocate inside the courtroom and out."

"This I know," Sean said with a smile bigger than the modest one his lawyer allowed himself.

"When I contacted—well, my *people* contacted—your very busy and very expensive lawyer about getting you out of prison, he didn't say 'Impossible!' or 'Don't waste my $400-an-hour time!' He didn't even tell his administrative assistant, his paralegal, or his phalanx of subordinate attorneys to take the call. The son of a ... gun took the call himself. If I had one finger left, I could count it and have a tally of how many bigshot lawyers would have done that." He paused to allow a nurse to suction out anything accumulated in his windpipe, then continued as if nothing had happened. "You lose your humiliation reflex in the condition I'm in. Anyway, let me cut to the chase, as all those Hollywood types say. Hehhhhhhhhh ..."

Sean smiled. It was a good joke.

"I want you to head up an expedition to Challenger Deep. I want you to direct your crew to find Gigadon however you can. I have given Mister Luch a blank check—a black AMEX, actually—for you to outfit *Sea Legs*, which I bought for a song after your ... forced retirement. This will be the information center of your new expedition. Obviously, I know that much new science and technology is needed for any historic dive."

Sean waited until it was clear no more was forthcoming before he spoke. "I'm sorry, Jake. I'm not really following you. Are you suggesting that I work with your people through teleconferencing, give them my ideas for a research ship converted into a vessel meant to kill giant prehistoric beasts? I'm very happy to do so, if the warden allows it—"

"Screw the warden."

"O-*kayyy*, but if we're going to set up a VR headset or the like for me to kind of be a part of the actual mission, that will take data lines that I don't know the prison system will allow."

"Screw the prison system."

"Um, Jake, where is this going? I am completely—"

"In over your head? Hehhhhhhhhh ..."

"So to speak, yeah. I feel a bit at sea, if we're going to pun ourselves to death," he said, acknowledging Bentneus's wit, "but I really need to know what you're talking about. What's the big—I mean, it must be *giant*—picture here?"

"So what is this grand dream of mine, one that I have spent hundreds of millions of dollars on? Why am I visiting you virtually this morning?"

"Those would be a couple of my questions."

"I like to build a little suspense. You can take the filmmaker out of Hollywood, but you can't get Hollywood out of the filmmaker. Hehhhhhhhhh ..." His facial servos and rods moved from "smile" back to affectless, and thus serious, expression. "Although I think it should be obvious by now: I want you to help me kill as many dinosaurs as possible. That said, the only one I really care about is Gigadon. He's not like the others, in addition to his being the size of a goddamn ocean liner."

Sean felt the icy hatred inside Jake Bentneus as he spoke of the leviathan. This was *Moby Dick*—level hatred.

"I want your expertise and my resources to kill that monster. I want you to kill it and bring its head to me where I can see it on the beach outside. We'll have to set up a goddamn hall of mirrors, but I'll see that bastard's dead face." The manipulators on Bentneus's own face must not have had a setting for angry sneer, because that was the only possible expression to go with what he had just said.

"As I said, I'm very glad to help, but I don't know what exactly I—"

"Doctor Muir—Jake—I want you to be on the boat, on the ocean, over the Marianas Trench, and get that goddamn Gigadon's head."

"That would be great, but—"

"No 'but.' All you have to do is say the word that you'll do this for me, and you will be driven out of those prison gates in twenty minutes."

Sean shook his head to release himself from this bizarre dream. Nothing happened. He tried it again while blinking his eyes hard, like he had a piece of grit in them.

Nothing happened.

"How is that even ... Oh, wait, is this the 'million dollars' thing? Are you *serious?* You want me to undertake the expedition of a lifetime, see the dinosaurs I've talked and dreamed about for fifteen years? Like as a favor to you?"

"And kill them, yes."

That was unfortunate, but not *that* unfortunate. "I'm in, Jake. *Wow*, am I in! I don't know how long it will take me to find the other ships and crew needed for the—"

"It's already been seen to. I had a feeling you would be interested in my offer. Have you heard about the reward?"

Once again, Sean looked to Mickey, who was nodding and smiling again—Sean wasn't sure he had stopped smiling the whole time he'd been in the room—and to his lawyer, who said, "*Have* you heard about it, Sean?"

"I haven't heard anything about anything except current research in my field for the last year. I've been in solitary, and let me tell you, that is some *solitary* solitary."

"Well, I'll be the first to tell you then," Bentneus said with what seemed like pleasure. "If you find and kill Gigadon—and bring its head to the beach right outside my window—I will pay you a billion dollars."

"Pay a *what?*"

"One *billion* dollars, Sean. Think 'Doctor Evil'–type money here."

Sean laughed, really laughed hard, and had to take a moment to collect himself. "Okay, that would be … unreal, quite literally … but even a billion dollars won't mean much to me for six more years. Not that I wouldn't take it—I'll take it!—but I'm not sure what I'd do with it during the rest of my time here."

"Wake up, Sean. You will be leaving this prison in fifteen minutes or so. Take my mission, and it's *for good*."

"Wh—how—wha—"

"Don't worry about it, Sean. Mister Kreide will fill you in on all the details, all right? And Mister Luch has volunteered to drive you where you need to go. You have thirteen days to get the expedition ready."

"Wait, I don't even have the design for *D-Plus* anymore, let alone your *Ocean Victory*. It's going to take *months* just to get the design and materials together, even if you have *Sea Legs* and a crew at the ready."

"Hehhhhhhhhh … what, do you think this all came to me last night? You've got your old ship as well as two other badass ships, fully crewed. And a vertical sub based on *Ocean Victory*, but with the water-cooling and breathing systems I mentioned."

"Whoa, the *Abyssal Zone* thing? That's really real?"

"It was real back in the day … just not a whole lot of call for it. But don't worry, you'll get almost two weeks of training."

That didn't sound like enough time to learn to *breathe water*, but he certainly wasn't going to raise any objection. "Isn't a bathysphere of half-inch-thick iron almost too heavy to bring up, let alone one filled with water?"

"Hehhhhhhhhhh … *this* one has a full inch of iron. And your pilot ball will be filled with water, it's true. But don't worry about the weight—this sub has magnesium-hot *rockets* on its bottom. It will shoot you upward, not very fast in that kind of pressure, but definitely upward movement all the way. The best part is this: It will superheat the water behind you all the way up. Where the weapons are. Of course there is, as we said, major weaponry on the sub itself. That might be enough to bag a Megalodon, or at least enough to get him to back off; but the Gigadon weapons are on the ships. Your job, other than running the whole goddamn show, is to lead Gigadon up to where they can end his unnatural existence."

"So I'm bait."

"That's right, *chum*. Hehhhhhhhhhh ..."

Groan. But it did make Sean smile. "What about the crew? Will they get a cut of the billion?"

"Of course. I know you were never a treasure hunter—not that kind, anyway—but that's assumed. Half of the billion will go to the twenty-seven crew members, if you guys end the hell-beast."

"Good, good." He wouldn't have known what to do with a billion dollars, anyway. Now, five hundred million was more reasonable to deal with ... He grinned at Bentneus. "I'm in! Where do I sign?"

"Yes, smart. Mister Kreide has prepared all the paperwork for the bounty. And I've hired Mister Luch to be your chaperone, if you will, on land and also at sea."

"*Mickey?*" His bearded friend smiled and gave him a thumbs-up. "Ha, *fantastic!* But 'chaperone'? What does that mean?"

"You have to understand I have quite a bit invested in this operation, not even taking the bounty into consideration. I need to protect that investment, don't I?"

All at once, it dawned on Sean what the filmmaker was saying. "Ah, got it. The prison's got to have tabs on me so I don't take a ship and run off to the Philippines or Indonesia."

"Not the prison, Sean. Everyone's palm that needed greasing has been greased. It is *I* who needs to keep tabs on you. Mister Luch will take good care of you and not let you do anything stupid, and he's your ... shall we say 'best friend'?"

The two men exchanged another smile. "Nobody except Mister Kreide ever came to visit me in the past year—only lawyers could visit. But I had letters from Mickey *every week*, some of them sent *while he was at sea*. That tells you all you need to know."

"Excellent. Mister Kreide will outfit you with a GPS ankle cuff. Waterproof, obviously. If you do get of a mind to run, it won't take a whole lot of effort to find you and put you back in solitary for the rest of your sentence and then some. And the only way anyone without the code is going to get you out of that thing is by sawing off your foot."

"I'm not running anywhere."

"It's just a precaution. I believe Mister Kreide has the paperwork, which you will sign and Mister Luch will witness. Five minutes and you're out, Sean. All the papers and books from your cell have been transferred in file boxes to the trunk of the Humvee. All you need to do is change into the clothes we brought for you, get in that, and go. That's it. Mister Luch will let you know other details and things you need to know while he's driving you to the airport."

"The airport?"

"Doctor Muir, you will be in Guam before the sun sets here. Time to get to work."

"Well, all right!" Sean said, and gave Bentneus a thumbs-up. "Here's to *Ocean Victory II.*"

"Hehhhhhhhhh ... hehhhhhhhhhh ... hehhhhhhhhhh ..."

Sean felt like he had missed something important. "Jake?"

"*Ocean Victory* died with me that day, my friend. No, you'll be piloting something much better. I call it *Ocean Vengeance.*"

***

The ride in the Humvee was more comfortable than anything Sean had felt in years, of course. But the best part was spending time with Mickey Luch. They told stories—all of Sean's were about prison life, but Mickey found it damned interesting, indeed—and the six hours to LAX went by faster to Sean than a jaunt across town. And McDonald's, *McDonald's* from the drive-thru. Kobe beef at the White House couldn't have tasted better.

On the way, Mickey showed Sean the videos (on a passenger-side 15-inch screen, *wow*, this thing was "off the chain," as Sean's students used to say) of Bentneus's broadcast and all the footage they had of Gigadon plus some featuring the guppy-size-in-comparison Megalodon. He couldn't believe his eyes, but perhaps more visceral was that he couldn't believe his back and his ass, the way they melted into the soft leather seats.

The Humvee belonged to Mickey, making Sean whistle because this was no secondhand automobile. "It's part of Mister Bentneus's compensation package. Like you, I get to do things I'd pay to do *and* cash the hell in!"

"It all seems too good to be true," Sean said, enjoying the speed of the car and the smell of the air through his open window, like a dog sticking its head out the window of the family car. "All this *and* I get to see the dinosaurs."

"Well, bud, it falls to me to give you the caveats and whatnot," Mickey said, not without a certain note of regret in his voice. "Part of my job in exchange for such nice payment. Not the especially fun part."

"Oh, hell," Sean said with a laugh, but it fell away when he saw the real discomfort on Mickey's face. "Is it that bad?"

Mickey just said, "Remember all those papers you signed?"

"Of course."

"You notice how none of them was for your release from custody?"

He hadn't. "I assumed that was in some of the documents somewhere. It was all about the billion dollars and payment, that was what I noticed most of all, right?" He tried a laugh again, but Mickey stayed as serious as a Baptist teacher at a high school dance. "Oh, God, tell me already."

"You know all them palms Mister Bentneus greased to get you out of there?"

"Yeah ... a million dollars' worth."

"Actually more, but forget about that. They got greased a couple of ways, man. First, they let you walk right out like you just did."

"Right ... what else could there be?"

"Well, Jake Bentneus is kind of an 'all or nothing' kind of guy. People do what he wants on his movie sets—back when he could direct them, you know what I mean—because if they screw up, if they bring him a coffee with two Equal instead of one, their ass is out the door along with a big black mark against their getting hired onto any other movies from that studio."

"*Shit.*"

"Yeah, no kidding. That's harsh. But I was instructed that *I* be the one to talk about the consequences of failure."

Sean's hands went ice-cold.

"Mister Bentneus didn't say anything about this, but when we get to Guam, we got to get you registered in the competition."

"Competition? For what?"

"That billion dollars? Well, last night on TV he offered that up to anyone who can find the Gigadon, kill it, and bring back its head. Registration is tomorrow, and God knows what is going to show up."

Sean said, "But ... including me with access to Jake's bottomless pockets, there must be no more than five parties in the world who could do a dive like that with only *two weeks* to prepare. People are going to *die* trying to get down to the bottom of Challenger Deep."

"Well, you *did* say the dinosaurs probably follow the heat vents at twenty thousand feet. We could just do 20,000 feet—that's way deep, yeah, but not *Challenger Deep* deep."

"Yeah, but I doubt there's anything at 20,000 feet anywhere near the size of this 'Gigadon' thing. Maybe size increases proportionally with depth? I never imagined anything like that could survive ... hell, *anywhere*, but down there where there's so little to eat, how could something get that *big?* I don't even have a wild guess about how this thing even exists." He considered for a moment and added, "Besides that, people are going to die trying to get just to *twenty thousand* feet if they don't know what they're doing."

"That's their problem," Mickey said, which had to be verbatim what Bentneus had said to him. "What we need to do is make sure *you* get the job done. If a bunch of amateurs get themselves killed, all that does is thin out the field for you."

"Wow, Mick, I've never heard you like this. What the hell are 'the consequences of failure'?"

"I hope you won't feel misled, Sean."

"Why would I feel misled?"

"Because we *misled* you. I was given strict instructions—"

"Yeah, yeah, fine—out with it, already."

Mickey shifted in his comfortable seat, then said as matter-of-factly as he could manage to speak: "One of the papers you signed was a confession."

"It was? There were a hell of a lot of papers."

"That was by design, Sean. Bentneus *wanted* you to skip ahead and just start signing randomly because of how excited you were to get out of that damn place."

"He called that one right," Sean said, feeling a little embarrassed to have been so easily manipulated. "But a confession to what?"

Mickey's mouth moved, but he was obviously hesitant to make any sounds that would answer Sean's question.

"*Jesus*, Mick, come on."

"If you fail to be the one who kills the Gigadon—even if no one kills it or even finds it, you go back to prison."

"Aw, hell," Sean said, now watching the freedom of the outdoors with longing instead of simple appreciation, "that's dirty pool, man."

"Yeah ..." Mickey said.

Sean picked up on the trailing-off of Mickey's response. "Oh my God, there's more?"

"The confession that you signed ... it, um, God ... it was you confessing to escaping the prison and while you were on the lam ... *gah* ... molesting a five-year-old girl."

Sean goggled and silently screamed until his voice could catch up: "*What the hell? Why? Why would you let me sign that? Why?!*"

"I'm sorry, pal."

"You're *sorry?* Why did he want a confession like that in the first ... oh, *goddamnit.*"

"Yeah."

"He's going to punish me for failure by getting me put away for the rest of my life. *If* I survive to the end of my life, a child molester in prison. You know what I mean—it'll end a lot earlier. Not that I would want to live very long ... *Goddamnit,* Mick! What the hell am I supposed to do?"

"Sean, chill for a second," Mickey said, and, despite himself, Sean did. "Listen, nobody has a better chance of getting this thing than you do. There's two weeks of shopping and outfitting that you get to do to deck the ships out however you want. You can get *missiles.* You know what it takes to dive to the bottom, and Mister Bentneus is *backing* you!"

"Okay, true. Yes. I can do this." He didn't have a choice, anyway, did he? "I can do this. *We* can do this. We've got the best of everything, right? Best boats for the mission, the submersible made especially to attract—and then escape—dinosaurs, a crew that must be fantastic if they know they're going to share in the $500 million prize ... this is good!"

At the "crew" comment, Sean saw Mickey get that indigestion-type look again. "What? We don't have a crew? *Oh, for the love of God,* what are we—?"

"No, we got a crew. Handpicked by Bentneus ... so to speak."

"So what's the problem? You're going to be my mission chief, right? I can't do it without you. I'll be—"

"No, no, I'm your guy. And we've got Holly Patterson as our science chief. Did you ever know Holly?"

"What? I've never worked in the field with her, but we've exchanged letters and papers. It'll be amazing to meet her!"

Mickey smiled—he liked Holly a great deal—but here came the thing he didn't want to say. "There's a really excellent winch-and-cable crew, too, the best in the business."

"Is that bad? You look like that's bad."

"Slipjack McCracken is the winch boss."

Nothing. Blankness.

Blackness.

"Jake Bentneus insisted on him. Paid him a pretty penny upfront to get on a boat with you, too."

"Slipjack? That *son of a bitch?* Why? *Why the hell* would Jake want the man who *screwed my wife* to be on a boat I'm even going to be *near?"*

"I told you," Mickey said. "He's the best in the business."

Sean put his face in his hands. "This can't be happening."

"Besides, he sued your lawyer, Mister Kreide, for slander for insinuating that he was ... y'know, *doing* anything with Kat."

"That dirty bastard made *money* off banging my wife?"

"No, Sean, listen: He says he *didn't* have an affair with her. He won the lawsuit—against a friggin' *lawyer*."

"Why has no one ever told me this? God, it's tortured me in there, tortured me ..." Fresh out of prison, about to fly overseas to see the dinosaurs that would have made his career and still could if he stayed free, Sean Muir cried anyway. His Kat hadn't cheated. It was like he had gotten her back.

Of course, Kreide put forth the affair idea because he was trying to establish that Slipjack had motive and opportunity to sabotage the cable, and thus it was completely in Slipjack's interests to vociferously deny the affair ...

But that didn't matter. He had Kat back. And for his freedom as well as $500 million, he could work with the slimy asshole. He could work, and he could win. The only person better suited for the job than he was the one who had hired him (and that was Bentneus as he was before the, um, incident). He dried his tears, and he and Mickey were laughing together again by the time they got to the airport.

***

Across the Atlantic Ocean, on the same day that Sean Muir was driven out of the gates of prison—that is, the night after the Jake Bentneus broadcast, celebrity angler Jeffrey Plaid walked right by the secretary's desk and into the office of ROAR! Network's director of programming and sat himself in one of the plush seats across from her desk.

Sasha Climber was on the phone when her No. 1 star busted in and plopped himself down in front of her, but she smiled when she saw his actually *happy* grin, so rare in the cutthroat basic cable entertainment environment. "Sorry, Consuela, I have to go—sí, take the baby to *el medico* if it's so *importante*. Yeah, good, right, bye." She hung up the phone and said with delight, "Jeffrey! How's the killer-fish business?"

"Getting better every day, love," he said, and as casually as possible added, "You happen to catch the broadcast last night? Jake Bentneus, or what's left of him."

120

"Oh, Jeff, that's terrible. But yes, of course, he bought fifteen minutes from us. Great viewership in the framing commercials, too— you bet we'll be basing some ad rates on those."

"Good, good. So this challenge ... I think I should go for it."

Sasha thought at first he was joking, but Jeffrey Plaid never joked when it came to exactly the crazy-ass ideas that begged to be joked about. "Are you talking about the 'challenge' of diving to the bottom of the ocean and killing dinosaurs?"

"Indeed, I am. Think of how good it'll be for ROAR! We'll film the whole thing—if I get this Gigadon bastard, obviously the network gets a nice slice. And even if I just get a Megalodon or Plesiosaurus or whatever the hell is down there, it'll make for one hell of an episode. Maybe a two-hour special. Maybe an *all-day* succession of commentary and episodes, like the Super Bowl for the Yanks, eh?"

"That's stellar and everything, Jeff, but we can't afford the outlay for a fully equipped research vessel and experimental submersible or the like," she said. "You must know that. How could we pull this off?"

"Ha! Listen, my dear, I'm Jeffrey Plaid! All I need is something that floats and some big, big hooks. Okay, that's an exaggeration—I will also need depth charges to heat up the water and such. But I have some friends at the Flash Fishing Research Institute who already have in their possession one of those robots that goes down with cameras and so on. We borrow that, get some swots and boffins to hook up the wires to with computers and the like, use that footage for some underwater prelude before I get my diving piece on, and hook one of those big bastards with our film crew right there, recording everything! *Come on*, Cheryl—"

"Sasha."

"Exactly! So is that a 'yes'?"

Sasha didn't say what was in her mind to say. She did say, "How much will this whole thing cost, Jeff? It's got to be a truly grand amount of money just to fly you and the crew to Guam to register."

"*Indeed!* We're ready to start today! I already got the robot last night, anyway. You'll get the invoice today or tomorrow, I believe."

Sasha put her head in her hands.

"But listen—this Bentneus bloke is *passionate*, Sherry. He doesn't need someone like me to 'register' and all that. No, I recognize that passion—because of my own. I'm sure you've picked up on it."

Sasha groaned.

"So we can hire a big boat and get that fishy codger caught, and *POW!* the ROAR! Network's got $20 million to, hell, I don't know, put on whatever you put on when my program isn't showing."

"That's our cut, out of a billion dollars? Twenty million?"

"Before taxes, natch."

"He's not going to pay out to anyone who didn't follow the rules, Jeff."

"No, no, no—all that matters to him is that the bugger what chewed him up and spit him out. Kill that bastard and drag it onto the beach, I guarantee you that's all he cares about. He's got this whole ... I dunno, *apparatus* in place with the competition and all to get as many people as possible going after his Gigadon. Registration and the week delay in starting is just his nod to fairness and equality or some such bollocks."

"So how much?"

"The best part is that we won't leak a frame of footage. People will just know that it happened, that Jeffrey Plaid, the man who eats river beasts for dinner, killed Gigadon." He watched for a reaction, then added, "I do actually do that, by the way, eat those for dinner. On occasion."

"Good to know, Jeffrey. Now please tell me what you want from the network to make this happen."

"That's the great part, Susan," he said, and made a "presto" gesture with his fingers. "It won't cost ROAR! one dollar."

That perked Sasha up a bit. She didn't really mind being nice to Jeffrey Plaid—he wasn't a bad sort, but she wouldn't make the mistake again of thinking he took into consideration anyone else's concerns. She sat up straighter and blinked with wide eyes. "No? No money from us at all?"

"No!" he said with a big TV grin, then made an equivocating expression. "I mean, yes, a lot of money, but it would only be a loan. Two million dollars, to be paid back with interest, and that's on top of the $15-million cut the network gets of the billion."

"I thought it was $20 million."

"All right, deal," Jeffrey said, and before she knew it she was shaking his proffered hand. "This is going to make ratings history, Sasha!"

She smiled falsely at him as he left, then dropped it. He was *such* an asshole. "Hope you get eaten by a goddamn brontosaurus," she said quietly and just to herself, but hearing the sentiment out loud still made her very happy.

***

The two million was in Plaid's expense account by the end of the day. Okay, yes, he had to sign papers saying it was to be considered an advance against future royalties and all that, but it paid for Guam—the closest land to the Marianas Trench—and got him, the team, the robot thing, and a bunch of science types onto a nice boat that they immediately took to what Jeffrey insisted was the best dive location for dinosaurs. They got another boat for an army of video guys, not just cameramen but editors and special graphics people and all that. They'd have so much footage of this adventure, this triumph, that they could run it all day on ROAR! and he could still save the best stuff for a feature film he'd produce with some of that billion dollars he was set to win.

"Okay, Jeff, we're rolling," Nigel Tremens, producer of *Scary Fish Alive!* (ROAR!), said, then played the part of off-screen interviewer. "Jeffrey, this is going to be a groundbreaking expedition, right?"

"Well, I don't know if I'd say that—maybe a *water*-breaking one," he said from a seat positioned to show the sheep on the beach, waiting in line to "register." "But yeah, it really is. That San Diego scientist, the one in gaol for knocking off his wife ..."

"Sean Muir?"

"Yeah, that's the one. He came up with the idea of deep-sea dinosaurs, man-eating dinosaurs, just monsters so voravenous—"

"Voracious? Or ravenous?"

"Exactly. So much of *that* that they laid in wait for millions of years for mankind to get down there, so the beasts could gobble 'em like a tin of sardines. Then that poor movie fellow, Jack whatever ..."

"Jake Bentneus?"

"The very one. He showed the world that these things *exist*, things bigger than we could've ever expected, right down there by the hydrothermal vents. Of course, the biggest of them all, the Gigadon—the same big fish we're looking to bag on this very mission—made a meal out of him and spat him out. That was his bad luck, but we now have a foolproof plan. I was able to formulate it by taking to heart the lessons learned by the earlier expeditions."

Jeffrey waited a few seconds, then prompted his producer, "Next question, mate."

"Oh! Sorry. What, um, is your plan for finding Gigadon? You say it uses some of the research done by Sean Muir and the techniques used by filmmaker Jake Bentneus."

"Good point. We know now that the dinosaurs are attracted to heat. That's why they hang out at the bottom of the deepest ocean. Those vents get plenty hot, as I'm sure everyone knows by now. So all we have to do is create a heat source and lead the things up to the surface. I'll be waiting in the water with my gun filled with explosives-tipped harpoons, and when he comes near enough, I blast him, and the deal is done. We'll bring it onto shore and present it to Jake Bentneus, collect our reward, and end the day knowing we've eliminated the most fearsome predator in the sea."

"What's the most dangerous part of this 'fishing trip,' as you call it?"

Jeffrey laughed photogenically. "The whole thing's dangerous. Just taking a boat out onto the ocean like this, even that's dangerous."

"Why is that dangerous?"

Jeffrey wrinkled his brow. "Goddamnit, Nigel, stick to the questions on the cards. Who are you all of a sudden, David Frost?"

"Sorry, Jeff."

Jeffrey smoothed his receding gray hair and took a deep breath. "Okay, let's go."

"You were talking about how dangerous this all is."

"Right, right, yes." He let Nigel count down and picked up where he left off. "Just taking a boat into the Pacific like this, even that's dangerous. Sharks and the like, but now we know killer dinosaurs hunt these depths, too. It's my personal opinion that Malaysia Flight 370, the one that disappeared? It crashed into the water, all right, but no one ever found any wreckage because Gigadon swallowed the whole blasted thing."

"It seems the obvious answer now, doesn't it?"

"Well, I wouldn't say *obvious*, since I discovered it first. But sure, it makes all kinds of sense in retrospect. You can't *not* see it."

"Indeed. Jeff, what other dangers will you and your crew face out here?"

"Do it again. Leave out the 'crew' bit. It's just confusing to the viewer."

"Of course, yes." Nigel cleared his throat. "Indeed … um, Jeff, what other dangers will *you* be facing out here? Is it fair to say that you will be risking death every second you're in the water?"

"More than fair, actually. Once Gigadon senses we're up there—that *I'm* right there in the water, just filling out a pair of Speedos and holding the instrument of his demise—"

"Hold on one moment, Jeff, excuse me. Won't the viewer become confused when you're not wearing a scuba suit in the water in the footage?"

"Oh, no, that won't happen. I want some drama. I'm gonna refuse the wetsuit because I want to face the dinosaur one-on-one, *mano a mano, tête-à-tête*, man against beast—you're still rolling, right? We can edit around this good part, make it look super-spontaneous but also from my heart?"

"Certainly."

"Ah, good … man against beast, face-to-face, Coke versus Pepsi, whatever—pick your favorite expression and it will mean 'strong man versus giant dinosaur.' Because that's what we've got here happening in just a few minutes. We're set to drop the robot, the remotely operated video—"

"Vehicle."

"Nigel, I swear to God, if you interrupt me again, I'm going to throw you overboard and interview myself." He took his producer's smile as he nodded to mean all was well between them. "All right, then. We're set to drop the robot, the remotely operating video vehicle, and we've got some juice on it that'll get it down to the bottom in forty-five minutes. That may sound slow, but the water gets thicker the farther down you go until it's like molasses. It takes a while even for a specialized remote robot-operated video vehicle to get to the bottom once the water gets extra-sticky like that.

"Nigel, it's like sending a rocket into space. It has to be covered with shields and the like, then cast them off as space gets safer to fly through. Our robot has the same thing, and it shall throw off its shields very near the bottom. The secret to its speed is the *shape* of those shields. And the rockets, obviously. But the brilliant part is that the robot will take all this deep-sea footage of dinosaurs and the like and then hit a totally separate set of rockets once it catches sight of Gigadon. This shall make a *very* hot path for the giant monster to follow, leading right where I want him—in front of my harpoon rifle."

"That is very exciting. I—" Nigel said, getting cut off by the text notification on his cell phone.

"Oh, for Christ's sake. How the hell are you getting service out here, anyway?"

"Um, Jeff, we're less than a kilometer from the shore."

"Oh, right. Behind you is just open water, so I keep thinking we're far out to sea. More used to rivers, eh?"

Nigel nodded absently as he read the message, which left him smiling. "Oh, boy."

"What? What is worth an 'Oh, boy' during a hot interview?" He took a drink from his bottle of mineral water.

"Guess who's just registered over there on the beach?"

"No idea. And I don't really care, Nigel. Let's—"

"Gary Lucas."

"*Gah!*" Jeffrey choked out as his water went down the wrong tube. "He's—he called himself a *better angler* than me! He must really believe it, too, the son of a … *We're going live, right now!*" He ripped off his mic and stomped off to "get that goddamned robot in the water! *Now!*"

More to himself than to Jeffrey, Nigel mumbled, "Going live where, on the ROAR! Network? We aren't set up for that kind of broadcast—"

Jeffrey rushed back in and got right in Nigel's face. "You want to keep working for me?"

"Technically, I work for the network. But yes—"

"Jesus, shut up! Get on the line with your superphone and get us a news team from the island. Look! I can see them on the beach, covering this Chinese fire drill of a 'registration'—get them and their cameras over *here!* By the time Lucas even gets his boat wet, we'll already have taken the prize—*live on the air!*"

"Why don't we use *our* video crew? We can upload the video to the ROAR! website."

Jeffrey let out a roar of his own, a roar of frustration. "The *Web?!?* Can this piss-pot network's three bloody servers handle *millions* logging on to see the greatest feat of angling ever performed?"

Nigel sighed, he hoped not too loudly. "I'll get in touch with the newspeople."

"Yeah, you will," Jeffrey said in an unmistakable bellow of anger. He left the cabin and went to yell at the ROV crew, demanding to know why the ROV wasn't at the bottom sending back footage yet, apparently forgetting how "sticky" the maple syrup of the ocean depths could be.

He stood on the deck with arms akimbo, watching the swots fumble around with the ROV controls. Nigel would need a few minutes to get a live feed going, so Jeffrey called his own video crew over to film him looking with concern at the ROV feed, explaining what was happening as soon as the scientists—who had no mics on—explained it to him.

When the filming finished, he shook his head in distaste. "*Pfft.* Gary Lucas, indeed."

***

In line at Governor Joseph Flores Beach Park, Mickey Luch and Sean Muir were glad they had gotten there a little later than they could have. "I haven't seen this many people all together who wouldn't shank me in the liver for a bag of potato chips in years," Sean said, making Mickey laugh hard. "I mean, any of these guys would shank me for a hundred dollars, forget about a billion, but that's only if I don't shank them first."

"I'm just gonna say it."

"Say what?"

"Lima Oscar Lima," Mickey said.

126

"What in the name of my sweet Aunt Sally are you talking about? 'L.O.L.'? Is that a code?"

"Oh, hell, sorry. You haven't been on the Internet lately."

"Yeah, from February of 2009 to yesterday, more than four years. So no, I haven't been on the Whiskey-Whiskey-Whiskey of late."

"Well, they got this thing called 'the Internet' on computers now."

"Har, har. Oh, my sides are aching."

"It just means 'Laugh Out Loud.' It means I found your 'shanking' joke pretty damned funny."

"So ... instead of actually laughing, y'know, out loud, you say 'LOL'?"

"Yeah, TLAs are really popular since texting took off."

"TLAs?"

"Three-letter acronyms."

"I can't believe I've been missing all of this uproarious humor since I went away. I might ask the warden to take me back."

Mickey did laugh out loud this time and said, "Anyway, there's every kind of person here, isn't there? I mean, jeez, there's black people, a gal in a wheelchair, and those have to be Australian or New Zealand, what do you call them ... Aboriginals. What, are they gonna catch a giant dinosaur fishing from a canoe?"

"*Wow*, that was really, *really* racist."

"Juliett Kilo, man, just having fun."

"Nope, not even going to ask what 'J.K.' means. But good—if you turned into some kind of psycho while I was gone, I'd have to, y'know ..."

"Shank me, got it." He laughed again and looked at the thirty or so people in front of them and the, at least, hundred behind them, with more hopeful registrants arriving steadily by boat or automobile (which couldn't park anywhere near the park today).

Despite Mickey's "J.K." comment, Sean did notice that people from every category he could imagine were in line: lots of rich white men with amazing pecs and biceps; lots of poor brown men, maybe South Pacific islander fishing crews; lots of working-class commercial fishermen *and* women—they were good people with infinitely tough jobs, and Sean had always worked well with them; some well-heeled brown people, again men and women, who might have been doing the whole thing as a lark. Or they may have been serious, who knew?

And then there was every kind of Asian one could imagine. That was a racist thing to say, perhaps—more a *racial* observation than anything malign and racist—but he meant it with respect. The East depended heavily on fishing for sustenance as well as, if they were lucky, some profit. And from his time doing research at sea all over the world, he'd worked hand in glove with researchers (as well as veteran expert fishermen and mariners) from:

- Taiwan;
- Mainland China, to whom one mentioned Taiwan under threat of all research assistance being cut off immediately;
- Japan, who had access to amazing ROV deep-diving robots as well as whale hunters, from whom he'd needed information on hunting *big* prey, despite wanting to gag from shame every minute he talked to them;
- South Korea, who always impressed Sean that so much scientific genius and insight could fit inside a normal-size human skull;
- The Philippines, who had everything from junks to advanced research vessels;
- and Indonesia (not really East Asian, but whose fishermen knew the waters above the Marianas Trench better than anyone)

By the time Sean and Mickey got to the tables in front, the turnout behind them had swelled to hundreds. How many boats were going to be out there, trying to see—to *catch*—a sea creature that had been seen *once*, and that one time was at depths unreachable by almost any sub or ROV in the world? Not to mention that the expedition ended in horror. There were a lot of man-eating fish species and countless other dangerous genera in the waters of the Pacific before any deep-dwelling dinosaurs were even taken into account.

Sean just hoped that not too many entrants into this insane hunt would get themselves killed. He noticed that very specific waivers regarding personal injury, loss of property, and loss of life were part of the paperwork. Sean flipped through it but didn't have a chance to read much of it before he signed. It didn't matter, anyway—being killed by any of the creatively dangerous creatures in the sea would be preferable to going back to prison, especially for the rest of his life, *especially* framed as a child molester.

And he couldn't just enter, couldn't just place—he had to *win*. He had to kill this underwater mountain of death. There was no second place, let alone a ribbon for "Honorable Mention" or "Participant." He needed to win at any cost ... but he had no idea how dear that cost might be.

No sooner had he and Mickey officially signed up for The Bentneus Prize, as it was being called now, than they were to get to the shipyard and get the apparently already tricked-out boats and submersible ready for the most important mission of his life. Of the lives of any people in those lines at the park and the beach. Of Jake Bentneus's life, from the prison of his hospital room.

He and Mickey were headed for the shuttle stop, where *many* registrants had parked their vehicles. For one day's notice, it was quite well organized. And, of course, it was one week's notice to everyone else; who knew how long the filmmaker had been plotting all the details of his revenge?

Before they had taken ten steps away from the registration table, however, a murmur among the registrants in line grew into exclamations in twenty different languages and dialects, then "oohs" and "ahhs" from just about everyone. Even the four Bentneus Prize registrars stood up at their table to see what everyone was making such a fuss about.

The registration table was several hundred feet from the water line, and the prospective registrants stretched all the way to the water line before taking the line 90 degrees to the left and to the right, getting lengthier in each direction. Thus, the registrars were able to see past the mass of humanity only by standing on their chairs as they looked out to sea. First they murmured, then they exclaimed, and then they whispered "ooh" and "aah" themselves.

Sean thought he had seen every flavor of race and economic level already that day, but this sight put that idea to a quick and permanent rest.

It was a submarine. Not a research submersible. Not even a bubble sub. From the dark waters of the South Pacific, a full-size gray lady rose, water streaming down as she broke through the surface. Mickey was equally transfixed, and Sean was glad they were already registered so they could walk down the beach from the park and get an unobstructed view.

From the top hatch of the massive submarine—Mickey said in admiration, "That's a goddamn Chinese Type 033 Romeo-class submarine, displaces 1,800 tons"—two sailors leaned out and inflated a red rubber lifeboat. Then two men wearing drab gray double-pocketed uniforms and caps, so probably officers, climbed out of the sub and down a ladder connected to the raft.

"You really know your Chinese subs," Sean said with a laugh.

"I know them well enough to know the 033s have been obsolete for decades and are *way* beyond their range down here. Hell, I think they're breaking five different treaties just by popping up off an American-run territory like Guam."

"I thought submarines could last for months and go anywhere. Not *anywhere*, but for sure places they aren't supposed to be. But yeah, stay under a year if they had to."

"That's true of modern subs, man, but these dinosaurs—*ha*—are diesel, not nuclear. No, this ain't out of China. There's only one country using those things. I'll bet you dollars to donuts this is frickin' North Korea."

As the raft approached the beach, Sean could see that the two men in gray were accompanied by a sailor in his white work uniform and cap. The sailor operated a small outboard engine that had been handed down to him.

"Holy crap, it *is* North Korea. What in the holy hell are *they* doing here? We're not in their territory, not even close. The whole area, the Marianas Trench, all that is held by the United States. What are they doing here?" Mickey repeated, talking half to Sean and half to himself.

It didn't take long to figure out that they were there for the same reason everyone else was. The boat came up onto the beach, and the officers—wearing rubber boots so as not to dirty their uniforms—stepped out, somehow with their backs ramrod straight the whole time, and marched all the way up to the people waiting in line to get to the registry tables.

"They're entering the competition," Mickey said, his awe renewed. "Now I have literally seen everything. Underwater dinosaurs, a man with no organs, and now North Koreans in a giant submarine signing up for a fishing contest."

Sean was no less amazed, but said with dawning realization, "I remember reading that North Korea has an annual GDP of *twelve* billion dollars. That's less than *Vermont*. That's less than Botswana or Mozambique."

"Okay, hold the phone, Rain Man. How the hell do you know what different countries' GDPs are? You didn't even have your smartphone out to cheat."

"I don't *have* a smartphone, genius. And the GDPs of all these countries are from 2011, I think, so two years ago, pretty current."

"That don't explain how you know them off the top of your head."

"It was included in some papers sent to me while I was in solitary. They listed each and every country's GDP, because they used that information to calculate what percentage each country spent on oceanographic research."

Mickey scoffed a little, but with a smile said, "I don't think a country can get more landlocked that Botswana, boss. If North Korea spend twenty-five cents on oceanic research, I'll eat one of those DPRK assholes' stupid hats."

"No, you're right, but every country was listed anyway. Some were just zero percent."

"That still doesn't tell me how the heck you remember all that."

"You've never spent a year in solitary confinement, Mick. There's time, so much empty time, you could memorize a thousand digits of pi. I lay in my bunk at night and saw if I could get the right amount for the right countries. A hundred nights of that, trying to sleep when you've barely moved all day, you remember that information like you remember your first day on the inside. It's burned into you, and you'll never fail to recall every detail."

Mickey was completely silent. What was there he could say?

"Anyway," Sean said to get them going again, "a country with a GDP half that of our least populated state, they'll feel a billion dollars coming into their economy. That's, what? Like adding eight percent to their economy."

"Which the government would snatch up and spend oppressing its people."

"Have I ever told you about what I do when I work with Japanese whalers?"

"What?"

"Hold my goddamn nose and get on with it."

"Yeah," Mickey said with a nod. "Besides, we're assuming the government wants to compete. Maybe this is like *Red October*, with a rogue crew or whatever stealing the submarine to defect?"

"Look at those two jerks—they march to the head of the line and loudly claim that a sovereign nation must come before any individuals. And look, they're getting what they want, too. Of course, they might have sidearms to, um, assist with compliance."

"Sounds like a North Korean operation to me."

"Sound like the Wild West to me." Sean looked back out to sea, at the menacing steel vessel. "You have a smartphone, right?"

"Don't leave home without it!"

"Would you check out the operating depth of whatever sub you said this was?"

Mickey pulled out his phone and dutifully started tapping. "Yeah, prepare to be unimpressed: the whole Romeo class—of which the 033 was sold to North Korea for *scrap*, but they got running again somehow—is rated as having a normal operational depth of about a thousand feet. Its maximum tops out—or bottoms out, I guess—at about 1,600 feet."

"That's less than Kat's first test dive back in the day, and that's their *maximum?* Are the North Koreans *suicidal?*"

"I would think so."

"Nice," Sean said with a smirk. "I mean, they obviously know the operating limitations of their own submarine."

"Again, I would think so."

"Then what could they be doing? You can't launch submersibles from a sealed submarine, unless you're going to shoot them out of the torpedo tubes. That wouldn't make any sense, anyway. It would destroy whatever electronics you had in the projectile submersible."

The two humorless North Korean officers took the copy of their completed paperwork and marched back down to the beach where their rubber boat and equally humorless sailor awaited them. They launched and were back inside the submarine within minutes. Then the enormous iron hulk pulled out to sea and disappeared under the glassy water.

Mickey and Sean exchanged flabbergasted looks with everyone around them. They headed back to the shuttle stop, but not before taking in the crowd waiting in line, perhaps five hundred entrants still waiting to sign up. Some looked like they didn't have a plugged nickel but were entering the chase anyway. The sea around Marianas Trench was going to be filled with God knew what kind of boats, ships, and at least one Communist country's jalopy submarine.

A billion dollars was worth it. Even if some didn't have the chance of a slug making it through the salt flats of Utah, there was still some chance, some ray of good luck that could shine down on those who had lived all their lives in shadow.

A billion dollars was worth doing it. It was worth doing *anything*.

***

Jeffrey Plaid had been training his whole life for this moment. Well, not "training" so much as "being on telly holding a scary fish," but that counted. Both required being on a boat. Both were dangerous—he had never had any mishaps himself, except for that time he got a nasty bruise from being hit right smack dab in the middle of his left pectoral by a fish jumping out of the river.

Man, that *hurt*. Let that handsome swine Gary Lucas laugh all he wanted—it was an *injury*, taken in the line of duty. Since then, Jeffrey *knew* pain. He was like one of the historical fisherman, perhaps of cod, suffering through all kinds of weather (for him shooting his show in the

States, usually sunny or a bit overcast, but the point remained). Like the mariners who were responsible for half the wonder of fish 'n' chips, depending on that next catch for their livelihood or to avoid having to run a repeat, Jeffrey Plaid had suffered just as they did, that is, if any of them had been struck in the middle of the left pectoral, just above the nipple, by a fish assassin *leaving its entire world behind* to take out the best angler in the world.

Only, that best angler was even more great now. Now he had robots.

"Did it dive?" Jeffrey shouted from where he was reading his magazine. "We have video or what all?"

"Affirmative. We have an uplink!" Nigel shouted back.

"Wha?"

Sigh. "Yes. The video is coming in." The team on the deck watched the monitors with excitement. "It's tossed off the shields, and we can see the light from the hydrothermal vents. You should come see this."

Jeffrey, clad in only his red custom Speedo, walked out to where the monitors and swots were. He squinted and said, "Not much to look at, eh?"

One of the video people (scientists? Dear God, this was wearisome) said a bit defensively, "The video quality isn't going to be as good when the ROV isn't tethered. We have to wait for the signal to reach us from twenty thousand feet down. The density of the water at that depth—"

"I know, very sticky indeed. Then what kind of delay are we looking at, since the radio signal is bogged down?"

"It's not actu—"

"Or *whatever*. Info, now, let's go."

"There's about a four-minute delay at this depth. So we're seeing what the ROV saw four minutes ago."

Jeffrey's eyes widened. "So Gigadon could be eating the robot right now and we wouldn't know it? Then we'll never lure it up here! We've got to hit the rockets, start the heat trail for it to follow!"

"Sir, it's unlikely that we'll even encounter anyth—"

"All hands! *All of the hands!* Get me and the camera crew in the water *now!* And where's my bloody explosive harpoon-rifle thing?"

Nigel came trotting out from the cabin. "Got it, Jeff. I'll hand it to you once your tether is securely fastened to the boat."

"The robot doesn't have to use a tether, but I do?"

"Unless you want the Gigadon to drag you to the bottom and eat you at his leisure."

Jeffrey considered this a moment and said, "But you'll remove the tether line in post?"

"Of course."

"All right, then." He turned to the crowd at the monitor. "Oi, you, video people, how much time have we got?"

The tech actually seated in front of the monitor said, "Sorry, sir, until what?"

"Until bloody Gigadon is up here, you dolt."

The tech opened her mouth to answer, but from out of nowhere Nigel the Producer was there and whispering into her ear. She nodded at Nigel and called back to Jeffrey, "We've got at least four minutes, sir! But yes, you should *definitely* get ready *down there* in the water. It could come, you know, at any time."

She whispered to Nigel, "We *are* actually seeing some anomalies. We did a sonar scan, and even though the resolution isn't spectacular from this depth, there *is* something moving around near the vents. You can't see much except light splotches using an ROV with no data tether, but that light has been blocked a few times, and for a good amount of time."

Nigel almost laughed. This would be like choosing a needle from a haystack on the first try. "All right, then! Camera folks are giving me the thumbs-up, looks like Jeffrey's ankle is on the tether with the other end tight on the boat ..."

One of the robot techs heard Nigel and said, "Light her up, boss?"

Nigel paused. "Light her up?"

"You know, set off the rockets to bring the dinosaur up here so Jeffrey can kill it. Make the heat trail and everything."

"Ohhh! Now's as good a time as any, I suppose. Yes, *light her up."*

"Aye, Cap'n," the tech said, weirdly, but another joined him at the ordnance station, and they counted from three, two, one—and mashed the big red button.

Nothing happened.

Nothing happened on the monitors. Nothing moved or changed, although something big was definitely occluding the light between the thermal vents and the robot's camera.

"Oh, right," Jeffrey mumbled to himself. There was a *delay.* As in, *You won't see everything in real time.* Nigel used the extra time to check in with Jeffrey, got a thumbs-up, everything good there; the camera crew and their feeds, also good; and then back to the robot camera's monitor.

"Ooh, see that?" the video tech said breathlessly.

"I see ... *something,* I think. What is that? Is that anything?"

"I think it's our friend, the Gigadon," she said through a smile. "See, it just turned, and you can see the thermal vent's light shining on the dinosaur's hide. Actually, if you look carefully, you can see that it's swimming right toward the camera. I can't believe that crocodile snout thing on a giant shark's body!"

The onboard marine paleontologist (which is slightly different from an ichthyopaleontologist, the hairline distinction in their precisely defined fields of study making any sense to—and holding any interest for—only marine paleontologists and ichthyopaleontologists themselves) said to the video tech, "'Snout thing on a giant shark'? Jenny, that's *not even wrong.*"

"We'll talk when you can tell me the difference between a coax cable and an Ethernet cord," she said, and everyone around laughed, except for Nigel. *Did they hit the rockets, 'light her up,' whatever the blazes they were supposed to do?* He could see that nightmare mouth coming very close indeed to the robotic diver.

"Em, is that thing going to eat our little robot?" Nigel asked, actually expressing less trepidation than he felt.

One of the rocket boys came to look at the screen as well, then glanced at the impressive glass casing and metal indicators of his diver's watch. "It just might, if our signal to launch doesn't—"

On the screen, the nightmare visage of the Gigadon was flooded with light and the view from the ROV was, in seconds, above and looking down at the dinosaur.

"We have a launch!" Rocket Boy shouted, and a general cry went up around the boat. "Are the heat generators employed?"

"Yep," the assistant robot tech said. "The water between that bad boy and our sack of rivets is getting superheated."

"Roger that! And the monster is following. Gigadon is on its way up!"

Nigel stood, transfixed by the Gigadon—and this was definitely the same creature that was in the Bentneus footage—and even more stunned by Jeffrey Plaid getting this one so right, when usually a fish practically had to come up and hit him in the chest for him to catch it on his own.

Okay, that's a bit unfair, Nigel scolded himself. *He's a smart guy, but his marketing abilities put his fishing to shame.* That was better; Nigel was nominally C of E, but he believed in karma. No sense tempting fate.

Like swimming without, at the very least, a *thick* wetsuit when waiting for a vicious dinosaur to show up (the camera crew had ensconced themselves in two of the world's strongest shark cages, but nothing like that would be allowed to impede viewers' sight of their favorite angler). The Speedo showing off Jeffrey's Hemingway-level hairy chest and his lumberjack muscled arms looked great on camera, but would he be too tasty to spit out?

Of course, the Gigadon *had* spit out Jake Bentneus inside his inedible shell, and Nigel bet the poor bastard wished it hadn't. So what the hell. If there was one thing he had learned in his five years as the field producer of Jeffrey Plaid's various hit shows, it was that the man was going to do whatever the blazes he wanted to do.

So Nigel relaxed. He watched both the host with his scuba tank and the film crews in their two separate ultra-strong shark cages get into the water, tethered by unbreakable carbon nanotube cables into the very structure of the ship. *Nothing* was going to swallow them and get away. That didn't mean they wouldn't get killed, but that billion dollars would go to the ROAR! Network—minus a *very* generous share to Nigel, thank you very much—and they could set up The Jeffrey Plaid Foundation for Kids Who Can't Fish Good (Nigel thought the film *Zoolander* must have been based in part on his employer) for all he cared.

That Gary Lucas comment about being a better angler was legendary around the ROAR! offices. But getting the Gigadon—there would never be a bigger or more lucrative catch—would prove him wrong, wouldn't it? Even if Jeffrey's role was, essentially, being bait.

But that was thinking negatively. Jeffrey hadn't failed to catch whatever scary and/or disgusting creatures lurked in rivers—or if he did fail, they could get him catching something else and redoing some of the lead-up—so maybe he could do this.

Yes, that was positive. Good.

"Nigel?" the video tech called. "Nigel!"

The producer zipped over to the monitors, but it took him a moment to comprehend what he was seeing. More than that, actually. What it took him a moment to do was to realize he wasn't going to comprehend what he was seeing. So he asked the video tech: "What on God's green Earth am I looking at? What's with the overexposure? This is going out live, you know."

She smiled in acknowledgment. "The flare is from the rockets on the bottom of the ROV. They get it to the top faster—maybe five minutes until it hits the surface and shuts down automatically. And they make a *lot* of heat."

"So where's the monster?"

"Our sonar says it's moving toward the surface, but I can't tell how close behind the ROV it may be swimming."

"Hell's bells. What should I tell Jeffrey?"

"Um … nothing? Ask the comm tech. I'm just the video gal."

"Right, thanks." He crossed the ten feet to the communications setup, where the techs were just shoving a live feed without commentary or editing onto the Internet—and a *lot* of people were logging in to every mirror server the ROAR! Network, its parent network, and *their* corporate masters had running, and there was probably some slow viewing going on. "What've we got, Web gurus?"

"We've got two static shots from different angles of a hairy man in a speedo, holding a thing, the harpoon or rifle or whatever. Split screen, so we'll catch all the action. If there *is* any action."

"Oh." Nigel didn't know what, if anything, he should say. The whole "live" thing to win Jeffrey's stupid pissing contest had left him right off the pitch. He had no control over anything, even if he had authority as producer. The various techs were just waiting, as they all were, to see if Gigadon was going to show up so Jeffrey could blast it.

"Whoa!" the Web tech blurted, and similar outbursts came from just about everyone on the boat. Nigel whirled around, catching exclamations of varying crudeness but all of them expressing surprise and shocked delight. He started toward the video tech's station, but then he saw what everyone had seen on their screens just a moment before, as it made its way to the surface.

The little but super-powered ROV launched out of the water only about a hundred feet away from the boat, its magnesium rockets still blasting. The heat coming off the robot was almost painful to the crew on the boat, like they were sitting too close to a raging campfire, but in a few seconds, the rockets sputtered and died; and the ROV spun down into the water on the other side of the boat.

Nigel laughed with all of the others at the spectacular feat the ROV (and its designers and engineers) had performed. If there was anything that was going to coax the leviathan to the surface—

"Nigel!" the video tech cried, and Nigel ran from the spot he had been frozen to when the robot exploded from the water. When he got to the tech's side, he could see that she had switched from the sonar and other instrumentation displays to the live split-screen feed. There was Jeffrey, who had his explosives-tipped harpoon pointed down and was blowing huge rivers of air bubbles from his mask—he may very well have been hyperventilating.

"Can you patch me into his earpiece? He needs to—"

"He didn't wear one, sir," she said. "We told him it would take five minutes to get it checked and ready—"

"Oh, in Christ's holy name! Then there's no way we can know what he's looking down at. Do the camera guys have their earpieces?"

"I don't think it matters now."

"What? How can you—oh, *hell,*" Nigel said, the sentence kind of trailing off as one camera on the split screen changed its angle from Jeffrey to whatever the TV host was pointing his weapon at. And there it

was: the crocodile-faced, nuclear-aberration-size shark body, all of it the size of a building higher than any in the town Nigel was from. Its jaws opened—so wide, wider than wide, wide enough to take in a PT boat, if not a battleship. Camera 2 did a good job of keeping on the important area of the Gigadon—its teeth visible in that gaping maw—while Camera 1 stayed on Jeffrey as he let loose with the harpoon.

The projectile looked top-heavy, but it was weighted properly and shot true through the water, finding its target dead-on. Jeffrey had been smart—it happened sometimes—and aimed at the end of the crocodile snout, which was the most sensitive area for crocs *and* for sharks and thus the most likely spot for the giant to receive an injury, maybe even a fatal one.

The harpoon hit the Gigadon square on the "nose" and blew up in spectacular fashion. The explosives first created an expanding sphere of violence through the outward force of the explosion; and then, as the vacuum created by the rush of water away from the blast collapsed, the shell contracted at the point of impact. This let Jeffrey and everyone else see what damage had been done to the monster.

Which was just enough to make the dinosaur react by closing its massive jaws about ten degrees. Then it shook it off—literally; Gigadon gave a small shake of its massive head—and swallowed Jeffrey Plaid whole.

***

Oh, you son of a whore was the exact thought that Jeffrey Plaid's panicked brain chose for this moment. The words rushed through his mind as he screamed through his regulator; then the whole thing popped from his mouth like a baby's Binky. His Speedo was filled. He had time for one attempt to use his arms to somehow get away, but there was no speed a human could move in the water that would have saved him.

All of this happened before he was even sucked into the prehistoric beast. The thought, the screaming, the soiling, the single futile swing of his arms. Then he was drawn in, between the rapidly closing mega— *giga*—jaws, and the lights were out.

He floated inside the creature, not knocking into anything even as he felt himself being swished around. *Ha!* his mind shouted. *He can't eat me! I'll be spit out!* All he had to do was put his regulator back in, which he did, and breathe normally. He had plenty of air left.

He felt a tug on his ankle. *The tether!* His leg would be ripped off before the monster got away—which he hoped meant that it would be unable to get away and be killed by some of his crew … somehow …

Oh, wait, no—it's gonna spit me out. Right! And like magic, there were its jaws opening again. He readied himself to try to avoid any of the teeth in row after row at Gigadon's jawline. He was pushed forward as the old water went out and the new water came in. *Ha! Here we go!* He hadn't gotten so much as a scraped knee.

The jaws opened farther, he was pushed forward faster—

—and then one of the motorcar-sized shark cages (with the screaming Camera 2 crew inside) rushed in on a wave of fresh water.

A few seconds later—the son of a whore hadn't even bothered to close its jaws—the second manned cage came in. And *then* the bastard shut its mouth and plunged them all into darkness. The first cage ran into Jeffrey at full speed, breaking the leg that wasn't tethered—it hurt like the devil's hangnail, but at least it wasn't the tethered leg, which would have come off the bone like a boiled chicken's drumstick. Jeffrey screamed expletives of agony but had enough presence of mind to keep his regulator in his mouth and to keep breathing.

The goddamn thing would *have* to spit the cages out. That's what had happened with Bentneus—chewed almost to death first, but still—and the cages were too much nonorganic matter, he was sure. It couldn't keep them in its belly, or its mouth, or wherever they were inside the cavernous beast. It couldn't be *totally* hollow.

And it wasn't.

One of the Camera 1 crew had calmed down enough to switch on the light on their cage, giving them all a look at the thing's stomach. It had to be a stomach, but it was formed like a hammock instead of a wineskin.

Barely registering that he was moving at a rather high speed toward the hammock—it even was crisscrossed with "netting," maybe so the water could flow through it and aid digestion? He had moved beyond the cage's light—the cages weren't being sucked back the way Jeffrey was—but he could feel himself still moving, and when he reached the stomach-thing, his front side got splayed against it like he was a spider caught in a web.

Wait ... can spiders get caught in webs? his adrenaline-soaked, rapidly deteriorating cognitive apparatus wondered. *Don't they ... know ...what's sticky ...?* Then his mouth shot out the regulator again—and for the final time—as he screamed in pain that was beyond pain. This made the pain of his horribly agonizing broken leg feel like being tickled by a feather.

That stupid jumping ass-fish slapping into his pec was the worst injury he had sustained in his five years doing the show. But now ... *aighhhh!* ... he felt burning, *sizzling*, that started on his skin and went deeper in a very short time. *You're digesting me? You bastard!* was what his brain tried to cough out.

He was right, too. And in the moment before he was dissolved too much to live, his mind sent Jeffrey one final thought:

Gary Lucas will never *let me forget this.*

***

The now-late Jeffrey Plaid was right about the cages: the Gigadon couldn't digest them and *would* spit them out. However, this would not be before its jaws clamped shut, teeth interlocking, and it dove back into the blackness with the practically indestructible nanotube cables anchored to the shark cages trailing from its mouth. On the other end of the cables, which were laced through the structure of the boat for extra security, was the ROAR! Network's floating command center full of screaming video techs, babbling communications techs, and one shaking-with-fear TV producer, Nigel Tremens.

They were screaming even before the Gigadon took the shark-cage cable shut tight in its teeth and made back for the bottom. But they *really* screamed—not to mention clutched onto anything they could for dear life—when the cables pulled on the rod 'n' reel that was the ROAR! boat. First they heard a low grinding from everywhere at once, and even the video techs turned away from the screens, which were showing nothing but black with an occasional spotlight of a moist surface. (That was the camera crews dropping their cameras and the shark-cage floodlights swinging around and sometimes illuminating random nothings that were in the line of the camera.)

The grinding of the cables running securely through the ship was followed by a sequence of events that lasted two seconds, if that: the metal hull indented slightly, then buckled altogether, the boat capsizing not in the direction of the dinosaur but toward the side that buckled first. This meant the boat whirled and capsized, throwing some off the craft entirely, then finished the circuit with the boat right-side up again. Those who weren't thrown off—mariners and crew in cabins or who somehow were able to hang onto something—didn't stay safe for long, however; as soon as the nauseating spin was done, the hull crumpled and the entire vessel was pulled under the water as if by the Kraken.

Those who held on or who had been protected in their cabins on the ROAR! boat died in one of the following ways, depending on how long breath could be held, or scuba gear grabbed, or air bubbles existing nearby:

1. Drowning.
2. Survivors of #1: Hypothermia.
3. Survivors of #2: Pressure sickness.
4. Survivors of #3: Crushing. (Well, not "crushing" per se: At depths below about 300 meters, incompressible seawater meets the incompressible water of a human body and its organs. Something's gotta give, as Ella Fitzgerald said, and it did—the air in the unfortunate longest-lasting survivors got compressed and thus lungs collapsed, sinuses collapsed, and everything else relying on uncompressed oxygen failed.)
5. No one survived #4.

***

The ROAR! Network didn't do the live broadcast; as Nigel had tried to get through to Jeffrey, there was no time to set up the infrastructure. But, as usual with the angling celeb, Jeffrey got at least some version of what he wanted: connections were made—both literally and figuratively—and the Internet got every horror as it happened.

The night after registration for The Bentneus Prize, Mickey got the very posh hotel's Wi-Fi going, and both Sean Muir and he watched the footage again and again in the two-bed suite. After a while absorbing the information and pondering how his theories about the deep-sea dinosaurs might help provide them with a plan of action, Sean said, "Our job just got a lot easier *and* a heck of a lot harder."

"Oh, good Christ, I don't know if I want to hear the second part."

Sean smile-laughed, something between *Tell me about it* and *You definitely don't, ha ha, El Oh El.* "Mick, how many times has there ever been a report about a creature bigger than a whale coming up to the surface and eating boats?"

"Moby Dick?"

"That was a whale. Also, that was fiction."

"Heh, right. All I can think of is old-school sailors—like *thousands-of-years-ago* sailors—sharing stories about the Kraken and Greek water things that would lead a boat to dash against the rocks, or grab it and pull it right under."

"So, nothing. No sketching on a bit of scrimshaw. No inscribed urns. Nothing other than traditional representations of dragons or serpents. Nothing like what we—what *millions of people*—have seen twice now, a leviathan's leviathan rushing from the depths to destroy and then diving back to the bottom."

"I been on the water a long time, Sean, heard lots of stories, old and new. Nothing like that. And nobody would bother *telling* a story like that—it's not believable enough to scare anybody. A giant shark, sure, but the size of this thing? It wouldn't even make a good joke."

Sean nodded. "Exactly. No one has ever seen this, not even once. It's not even been talked about in a cautionary tale or as a legend. There were marine lizards millions of years ago, basically water-dwelling dinosaurs, yes. But they went extinct 64 million years before upright apes climbed down from the trees."

"All right. This is unprecedented is what you're saying."

"Essentially, yes. But now we see evidence that leads us to conclude that some sea dinosaurs—predators, in fact—adapted to the cooling oceans by going incrementally deeper each year, maybe each century, eating what there was to eat at that depth. I bet that in the middle-lower depths, past the euphotic zone, where photosynthesis stops, they ate each other, too. But then things were getting too cold even in the middle depths, where it was warmer than it is now but not what the dinosaurs would have felt comfortable in.

"But these predators, I mean the creatures' adapting descendants, sharpened by millions of years of evolution to detect slight differences in water temperature that indicate prey in the area, may have sensed something warm below. *Far* below. This is the basest speculation made from precious little data, but I believe that's when they found the hydrothermal events."

Mickey smirked and said, "I don't think you're gonna get much disagreement with your theories these days, boss."

"Ha, yeah, well, there's a billion reasons for all of us to hope they're on the right track," he said. "Here's what I'm saying, though: It might have taken a million years, it might have taken *tens* of millions of years, but eventually the dinosaurs we've seen—Liopleurodon, Mosasaurus, Megalodon—adapted to the extreme depths. Even so, their genetic memory of thermophilia—"

"They like heat," Mickey interrupted before Sean spent time explaining the word.

"Exactly. So, they were drawn down here by their predisposition to warmth, and this was made possible by the glacial adaptations ending in completely altered physiognomies. And even that's weird, because, other than albinism, their exterior appearance has changed little from what we would expect to see on an actual marine lizard of that time."

"This is cool—amazing, mind-blowing—and I'm no evolutionary theorist or whatever, but *why* did they go down to the bottom? There must have been food enough at that middle depth for them to be there for a long-ass time."

"Yes, that's the billion-dollar question, isn't it? Even twenty years ago, I don't think we would have had an answer to that. But since the discovery of hydrothermal vents and the mass of chemosynthetic life that surrounds them for miles, we can answer it. The predators, which I'd be willing to bet are as rare as tigers and other exclusively carnivorous animals in the territory they roam, eat every kind of sea life that populates these vents. Because the prey runs along seams of tectonic plates, it forms a line that these new species of dinosaurs can move along as they need to."

"The things at the vents would have to grow pretty damn fast to keep a bunch of, basically, ginormous sharks fed," Mickey said, impressed with himself for seeing that.

"Yes! That would have to be true for any of this theory to hold together, and in fact, thanks to ROVs and some history-making dives of humans in submersibles, we *know* it to be true. The incredibly active and nutrient-rich environment that these tube worms and their brethren grow in is a riot of organic chemicals. In the heat of the vents, it's almost like a bag of popcorn; an immense amount of life bursts forth just from the organic material being exposed to high temperatures."

"'The Popcorn Cooker of Life.' That would make a good title for your next paper."

"*Our* next one, Mick. That is, if I'm not rotting in some hole for the rest of my life for child molestation. I doubt they give molesters the freedom to do research and publish."

"I want to say that Bentneus must have been kidding, but I've been working with Jake for a number of years now. He wasn't kidding."

"Yup." There was a long silence in the room, the only exception the hum of the air conditioning protecting them from the humidity of Guam. "But that's our, *my*, life situation now. No way out but through."

"That's like ... Zen, man. Deep."

"You'd be surprised the things you learn in prison."

"I hope I never hear them."

"I hope that, too. Because, especially in solitary, you hear all of it again and again and again. In your head, I mean."

"No offense, boss, but you're creeping me out," Mickey said, feeling like an invisible hand was squeezing his stomach to make the contents blow from his mouth.

"Yeah, sorry, jeez. This has been a really big adjustment over the past what, thirty-six hours?" He looked for a clock and spotted the red numerals on the alarm clock radio. "It's past midnight?"

Mickey laughed and said, "Yeah, it's been a slog, hasn't it?"

"I need to get a watch."

"Don't you worry. The North Koreans, Jeffrey Plaid, all that's put off outfitting the boats ... and you. Tomorrow is *shopping day*."

They shared a laugh, but then Mickey said, "Wait, was that the easy part or the hard part? And ... what was *it*, exactly? That they exist, and we can make scientific sense? So we're not fighting totally unknown monsters—we know we're going up against prehistoric beasts?"

"Well, that is a good thing. I mean, we're essentially dealing with cryptids here. They look like dinosaurs, and there is zero doubt in my mind that they are the adapted descendants of the marine lizards, the predatory dinosaurs, whose names we're using for convenience."

"I get that, but hell, if it looks like a predatory dinosaur, got jaws full of teeth like a predatory dinosaur, eats everything like a predatory dinosaur—"

"My point is that it's *good* we have some idea of what these things are, at least. But Mick, listen—they're hollow inside, or just about, from what we've seen. It makes sense, since the pressure would be equalized if the animal was filled with water, but this is a physiology we know *nothing* about."

Mickey rubbed his eyes. "I'm hittin' the wall here, boss. So there's no good news *or* bad news?"

"No, I'm sorry, Mick, I'm still processing what we saw happen to Jeffrey Plaid, what his cameras picked up while they were inside the creature. Here's what I'm trying to say: Now that what we're calling Gigadon has come to the surface, feeling the warmth of the water up here ... it's *remembering*, Mickey. With Bentneus, it was a one-time thing, never to be repeated. This rare monster crept out of its lair and followed the heat of Jake's sub.

"But it happened again when Plaid sent down an ROV specifically designed to give off enormous amounts of heat. When they hit the rockets to make a trail of warm water to the surface, Gigadon *remembered* and followed right behind, not doing the tentative circling like it had beneath *Ocean Victory*. No, it remembered what this meant and again came to the surface, and fed on the organic life there, spitting out the metal or plastic or whatever since its system apparently can't digest that. But it pulled that network boat right under and, I'm sure, snatched up every organic item—the crew on the boat—that it could right after it released those shark cages."

"Goddamn, Sean, I'm begging you: get to the point. The monster remembered coming up. Okay, agreed. So good or bad?"

"That's the thing—it's *both*."

Mick momentarily forgot his weariness. "If you stop there, I'm sorry, but I swear to God I'm gonna smother you with a pillow as soon as you fall asleep."

Sean laughed and said, "It's *good* because it'll be a *heck* of a lot easier to kill this thing if it comes to us on the surface than if we had to go down to the bottom of Challenger Deep to do it. We're a canned snack down there—*if* we could even get down there for the third time in history."

"And it's bad because ..."

"It's bad because Gigadon knows and remembers that there's an 'up here,' full of heartier fare than tube worms. It might need to be led up by a heat source, but it might not. If it doesn't need 'hot bait,' if you get me, it could attack at any time. We've seen it consume only smaller nonorganic items—submersibles, shark cages—but with a mouth like that it could suck down a Navy destroyer."

Mickey blinked, comprehension dawning at last. "So, even on the surface, we don't kill it first, we're a goddamn canned snack up here, too."

"Sweet dreams," Sean said with an ironic smirk and lay down.

Mickey shook his head, wryly smiling as well as he turned off the lamp. "Muir, if I was you tonight, I'd sleep with one eye open, ya rat bastard."

***

At 10 in the morning—sharp, like according to the atomic clocks buried beneath mountains in Colorado—an extremely shiny limousine pulled up to the hotel, as Bentneus had told Mickey Luch to be ready for.

"Whoa," Sean said. "At this rate, I'll be sitting in a Bentley before the day is out." He nodded thanks to the doorman who opened the door for them and slipped inside. The interior made the shiny and sleek exterior look like the front of a crack house. He settled in and felt like he was being gently massaged by a giant with Palmolive-soft hands.

Mickey slid in as well, and the door shut. The limo started moving immediately without a word to or from the driver, whom they couldn't actually see behind the black partition. At Sean's quizzical expression, Mickey chuckled and said, "Don't worry—the driver's got instructions as specific as ours. No need to distract him with how nice the limo is or anything. Believe me, he knows. Besides, if you really need him, just open or close the partition with that window toggle."

Sean considered doing it just to do it, but restrained himself. This wasn't a vacation, as much as it may have felt like one. "So where is Mister Bentneus's silent driver taking us?"

"Oh, this limo doesn't belong to Jake, and the driver doesn't work for our mutual friend, either. This is from the ... store, I guess you could call it? ... that we're going shopping at. *Ocean Vengeance* is already there, outfitted with the basics. The sales liaison, a Mister Abu al Khayr, will let us know what else we can put on her."

"That doesn't sound like a native Guamanian name. Kind of has an, I dunno ... Middle Eastern ring to it."

"You think?" Mickey said with lips pursing into a smile.

"Okay, so I'm getting a watch. I know that. What other equipment are we getting? Weapons for the boats?"

"That's the biggie. You'll have *Sea Legs* and *Sharkasm*, but also there's an armed boat called *Iceberg*, which, again, has the basics but which we're gonna load up with anything and everything we want."

"*Iceberg?*"

Mickey smiled, knowing what he was about to tell Sean was extremely stupid, but it was what it was, and he said, "Anything that runs into it is gonna get sunk."

"Oh, *gawd*. So, we've got our command and launch ship, our science ship, although we're doing 'accidental science' at best ... do we have a communications ship? Tell me it's *The Moaning Mermaid*, that would be nice closure."

"Yeah, no, it's a sleek new thing Bentneus outfitted for this mission. Or, I mean, he designed it and got it outfitted with 3D cameras and satellite whatsits and the like. He christened it, um, the *I Spit on Your Grave*. I think his mind is slipping from all that fake blood and air, honestly."

"No, I get it. He'll *take* Gigadon being killed 30,000 feet below the surface, but what he really wants is for it to come up into the light, where it can be killed in high-definition and glorious 3D. He wants to 'spit on its grave' by capturing its death on film forever."

"Yeah."

"I think let's just call it *Spit*."

"Yeah."

The limo stopped, and, a moment later, Mickey's door and Sean's door were opened practically simultaneously. A man in a limo driver's outfit—leather gloves, service cap, dark sunglasses, black suit, white shirt, black tie—was at Mickey's door; and a sharply dressed man— well-cut gray suit, open-collared shirt that probably cost more than the average American family earned in a week, gold aviator sunglasses, and those shoes that have tassels on them—of indeterminate race was at Sean's door.

"Welcome to War-Mart," the (Israeli? Arab? Tanned Russian?) gray-suited man said to both of them once Mickey came around to Sean's side. His smile was as warm as any greeter's at Saks or Neiman Marcus, and why not? He had a warehouse full of deadly tech goodies, and probably a rhino-stopping semiautomatic pistol tucked into a holster right under that slick jacket.

"Glad to be here," Sean said, and shook the man's hand, as did Mickey, who had a grin of excitement on his face that proved infectious to their host.

"Very good," he said through a little laugh. "My name is Abu al Khayr."

"Your English is very good."

"It should be. I'm from Bay Ridge, in Brooklyn!" Abu al Khayr shouted with a laugh; Sean and Mickey joined in. They couldn't believe they hadn't picked up the New York in the Arab's voice. "Anyway, I feel the excitement coming off you guys, right? Now come on inside and let's pick out your dinosaur killers."

***

"I feel like James Bond being led around by Q," Sean said.

Mickey couldn't even speak, he was so overwhelmed.

The equipment wasn't how they expected, piled on industrial-strength shelving to be found by inventory number, taken down, and examined. No, the War-Mart "warehouse" was more like a showroom, or maybe like the highest-end wristwatch boutique in a mall on the Las Vegas Strip. There was stacked shelving all along the outskirts of the room, but in the minimalist main space, weapons and gadgets abounded—with, unbelievably, a full replica of *Ocean Vengeance* in the very middle. Its ports and connections were all clearly labeled with Arial Black numerals on white cardstock, so Sean and Mickey could see where and in what quantity the toys could be added to the sub.

This had all the sleekness of an Arab presentation floor. Their new friend, Abu al Khayr, may have been born on the Fourth of July twenty feet from Abe's statue in the Lincoln Memorial; but Sean and Mickey both knew this was an operation by Arab-as-Arab-can-be Middle East gunrunners, who were probably watching their every move on security camera at that moment.

But Muslim, Christian, Hindu, B'nai B'rith, Rastafarian—it didn't matter. Religion was left at the door at War-Mart. It didn't matter to the arms dealers whom one was pointing the missiles at, as long as buyers paid top dollar for what they used. Guam was an American territory, to be sure, so gunrunning must have been frowned upon, at least technically. But what could be more American than arming all sides of a conflict, no matter how many sides there were?

God bless the Black AMEX card, Sean thought, mesmerized.

"Gentlemen, as you can see, we have customized the showroom with weapons and other offensive and defensive equipment that will fit onto the submersible."

Sean and Mickey made mumbles of assent and appreciation.

Abu al Khayr said, and pointed out the first item, on a two-foot pedestal and lit from above by spotlight. The pedestal was slowly turning. *The pedestal was turning*, showing every angle of the martial doohickey in front of them. "This is the MAL 9000—"

Very politely, Mickey said, "My good friend"—he'd sailed with many a Muslim and knew some respectful salutations—"we don't need the part or model numbers. Just the functions, if that would be agreeable to yourself."

"Of course," Abu al Khayr responded with a smile at Mickey's care with language. He gestured to the sleek and silvery three-foot-long MAL 9000, which resembled nothing so much as a 1950s-movie rocketship. "This, gentlemen, is a missile that can be fitted to the outside of your submersible. Shoot it into the mouth or the snout of any sea predator, and that will be the last you see of him, except for bloody chunks."

"How many could our sub carry?" Sean asked.

"To balance the weight—they're rather heavy, although this custom design is much lighter than other underwater projectile weapons—I would recommend one on each side of the craft. Pointed in opposite directions so you can hit any unwanted visitor with no more than a 90-degree turn."

Sean and Mickey both nodded and made notes on their paper pads, any portable device with a camera being strictly forbidden, for obvious reasons. They withheld their amusement, but making any turn to aim would end in them becoming a dinosaur Happy Meal. They would have to wait until it swam into their sights.

"And please allow me to let you in on a secret, my good friends. My team has done extensive research on how to kill mammoth sea creatures—or ones on land like Godzilla, *ha ha*." He gestured with his hands as he described the strategy for which the custom weapons were designed and built:

"I understand that the physiognomy—is that the word?"

"Actually, it is," Sean said with a smile.

"*Alhamdulillah!*" their host said with a proud smile. "Anyway, the physiognomy of your dinosaurs differs on the inside of their bodies. However, it is wise to treat them as one would a modern shark the size of a blue whale. This kind of musculature would be singed, even painfully burned, by a bomb or underwater mine—but not killed.

"No, what *Ocean* ... em ..." he closed his eyes to bring it up. "... *Vengeance!* Yes, what *Ocean Vengeance* needs are not bombs but *missiles.* A missile goes deep because of its high velocity and *then* explodes, doing real structural damage in the musculature as well as in their cartilage or bone structures. This is why we have no bombs for you on the show floor."

"Sounds reasonable," Sean said, and Mickey concurred.

"Please excuse this indelicate question, my good friends, but do we need to talk about the prices of these items with installation on the submersible?"

It tickled Mickey to flash the AMEX and say, "We do not."

Everybody grinned at that. "Excellent!" Abu al Khayr said with joy. "So let us move to the second item, no less important that the first, but something had to be first, right?"

"Ell Oh Ell," Sean said as awkwardly as a man with crutches getting on an escalator.

Abu al Khayr looked at him quizzically for a moment but, noticing Mickey's valiant attempt not to laugh, said, "Thank you for your appreciation at my timeworn humor," then gestured proudly to the new item on the second rotating pedestal. "This is an incredible weapon that is actually of *my* design, *alhamdulillah.*"

Abu al Khayr's creation was a sphere roughly two feet in diameter, like a big cannonball or a very small bathysphere that could comfortably take a housecat to the bottom of the ocean. "For my amusement, if you will pardon it, might you like to speculate on what this weapon is? I will give you a hint: It will be covered with a 'skin' of organic matter before being offered to the Gigadon."

"So the creature will eat it and not spit it out?" Sean asked, himself amused by the mystery.

"Indeed, my good friend! Once the organic skin has been eaten away through digestion and the metal comes into contact with the digestive acids, the weapon deploys. And, then, all hell breaks loose, *u'dhurni.*"

"You already said bombs would be ineffective," Mickey said, musing.

"Yes, and this has proved a very effective high-tech weapon."

"Mmm, high-tech?" Sean said. "Does it give off radiation?"

"Indeed, it does not."

"Gah!" Sean cried in mock frustration. "I give up."

"Me, too," Mickey said with a smile.

"It was an unfair question," their host admitted. "There has never been a weapon like this before. And I know you will laugh at this, but the reason it has never existed before is that it is exceptionally useless in almost any situation except for the one you—and the other Bentneus Prize competitors, of course—find yourselves in. It has taken almost 90 million dollars to bring into being."

Silence. In other words, the sound two excited but befuddled men make when they have no idea what to say to something singularly odd. Finally, Sean said, "How did you know to create it just in time for this expedition of ours?"

Abu al Khayr smiled. "Calling us at War-Mart was the second thing that Jacob Bentneus did, instructing that this and other weapons rush through R & D and production, following his awakening from coma."

Mickey chewed on this and said, "Wow. What was the first?"

"If it were me, screaming at how the Will of God had burdened his humble servant." He let out a self-deprecating laugh. "Then the second thing I would do would be to beg God to forgive me."

"So ... what is this thing?" Mickey said.

"We call this 'The Honeycomb.' I have already explained what happens when the organic skin—which, by the way, is actual animal fat and flesh with glue made from animal sources alone—is eaten away and the creature's digestive chemicals touch the metal surface." Abu al Khayr clapped his hands in delight and satisfaction. "As soon as the metal is breached, a kind of foam under incredible pressure inside the metal shell expands, blasting the covering away and—um, do either of you have small children?"

"What?" they said at the sudden turn, almost in unison.

"Sorry, my good friends. I have two small children, so I am familiar with these. My children are fascinated by those toys, those things that are the size of a Tylenol capsule but, when submerged in water, grow to thirty times their size, into an elephant or a monster—or a dinosaur, in fact."

"That's what this 'foam' is?"

"Well, those silly things were the inspiration for this solution to what Mister Bentneus tasked us with, but the material and expansion mechanism are entirely different. What happens with the Honeycomb is that once the organic skin holding the material compact is breached, a chemical reaction with salt water activates the foam.

"It's a recursive process once the foam is activated: there is a very small, solid three-dimensional pentagon made of incompressible plastics in the center of the sphere of foam. The foam closest to each pentahedron touches everywhere on that shape. Once the activation starts, it's much the same process as when ice forms, its crystalline structure coming from imperfections in its container and undergoing a phase shift.

"In this case, our one 'imperfection'—that is, the frame of one honeycomb cell—creates a 'phase change' that races through the material, arranging every group of atoms from a quasi-liquid state into solid rigidity arranged into the pentagonal shape. You recall how I said that the material is packed densely inside the sphere, yes? In fact, it is so tightly packed that a sphere the size of the one you see here has enough foam in it to impenetrably fill the Lincoln Tunnel to a depth of almost half a mile."

The two visitors were impressed, even awed, but didn't see the connection.

Their host picked up on it immediately and smiled. "You're wondering how this helps you in the hunt."

They nodded.

"If you can get this into the mouth of your giant dinosaur, it should not spit it out because the organic shell is flesh. It should move into the beast's digestive system—whatever its structure, every animal on Earth digests its food through some sort of corrosive effect—where it will be activated as soon as there's a breach in the skin.

"In seconds, the phase-breaking foam will, essentially, explode into a three-dimensional honeycomb shape in which the cells multiply out from the central imperfection like ice, again, spreading over a lake. These cells will expand to fill not only the monster's mouth and digestive system, but *everywhere*. Every nook and cranny inside its entire body will within seconds be filled with this. It doesn't matter if it has lungs or gills or a direct-oxygen circulatory system like an insect.

"Needless to say, the creature will be unable to breathe, eat, even swim, since nothing within its body will be able to move as it's held fast by this invasion of our material. It will be dead within one minute, I would estimate, *inshallah*."

"Nanotechnology?" Sean asked, despite the fact that he was as stunned as if he had been whacked on the back of the head with a baseball bat.

"Indeed, Doctor Muir! Phase changes make up one of the most active research areas in applied physics, and this 'foam' is activated at the molecular, even atomic, scale. We are quite proud of it."

Mickey raised his hand a bit and said, "But isn't it dangerous? Like *highly* dangerous? What about when the foam fills up the Gigadon and starts expanding into the ocean, then keeps expanding and expanding until everything is smothered by honeycombs?"

Abu al Khayr gave Mickey an appreciative grin and shot him with a thumb-and-forefinger "Bingo!" pistol. "Good question, Mister Luch. In nanotechnology, they talk about 'the gray goo problem.' It would be a world-ending effect of nanobots that use material around them to form more nanobots, which then use the material to form even *more* nanobots until the entire planet has been converted into nanobots."

"Right! That's what I'm talking about. It would be suicidal to set this off, wouldn't it?"

"Fortunately, no," the War-Mart rep said. "Unlike the idea of self-replicating nanobots, our Honeycomb foam causes a phase change only in the compressed material available within the sphere. Then it stops and remains rigid for, perhaps, one week? Surely no more than that. At that point, its structure cannot hold, and it undergoes another phase change. Whereas the first was from liquid into solid, this last is from solid into gas. The dinosaur killer will effervesce and bubble up to the surface and disperse."

Sean nodded at the sheer genius of it, but ... "So this foam, this Honeycomb material, is it toxic?"

"Oh, yes," Abu al Khayr said, widening his eyes for emphasis. "Our foam makes liquid mercury seem like Coca-Cola. Interestingly, just the toxins might be enough to kill even an enormous animal such as your dinosaur, but you wouldn't want to just dump it into the water. It would kill everything within a square mile almost immediately. However, when it undergoes the phase change as we've designed it, it becomes entirely chemically inert. All the atoms are spoken for, if you will." He beamed at the excellence of his own answer.

Sean kept nodding, as he did when chewing something over, then said, "What about when it phase changes from solid into gas there at the end?"

"May Allah forgive me for sounding rude, but what about it?"

"Well, I mean ... is it still chemically inert at that point?"

"Oh, no, not at all. Once it has atoms to exchange with its immediate environment, it is utterly deadly. However, at the depth this weapon is meant to be used—when your beast is no deeper than 100 meters—the bubbles will rise so quickly that most of its chemical volatility will be lost, and a harmless combination of nitrogen and our proprietary mix of carbon and oxygen will disperse once it hits the surface. Shooting it in the open air would result in the same harmless dispersion. So nothing to worry about there, I assure you. War-Mart has deep pockets, and we do not intend to give any away by being the target of any lawsuits."

He finished with a laugh that was politely shared by Mickey but not at all by Sean. "So when the gaseous remains of the foam are rising to the surface, highly deadly toxins are being released into the water of one of the richest aquatic ecosystems on Earth."

For the first time, Abu al Khayr's genial manner slipped. "A thousand pardons, Doctor Muir, but do you want to kill this Gigadon, or don't you? Mister Bentneus assured me you were both quite seriously committed to this task."

"We are," Mickey said, and when he looked at Sean, the former professor realized concurring would be in everyone's best interests.

"I mean no disrespect, gentlemen, when I say that the lives of one hundred, one thousand, *one million* fish mean as little to your sponsor, and to myself, as would the extinction of an entire species of rainforest beetle never known to man. They should mean as little to you."

"I understand," Sean said. "But, if I may, hasn't Mister Bentneus's entire mission in sea exploration been to preserve the precious life found there?"

"My good friend, that mission ended when that *thing* fatally insulted him on behalf of the entire ocean. You and I are participants in his new and fervent mission, all right? Yes?"

"I see," Sean said.

Abu al Khayr's pleasant expression returned. "Very good. Please allow me to show you the variety of heat bombs, sonic cannons, and—"

Mickey said in his best Doctor Evil voice, "How about some sharks with frickin' lasers attached to their heads?"

"Ah, yes, I have never heard a customer say that before," their host told him with great restraint. "In all seriousness, the issue with lasers underwater is that water refracts light so completely that even a good-powered weapon wouldn't do any damage beyond thirty meters or so. However, that's why I'd like to show you our sonic cannon, which uses pressure waves that propagate especially well in water. Water itself becomes the weapon, which is ironic for this mission. In any case, let me tell you the specs—"

"That's not necessary ... um, my good friend," Sean said. "We'll take all of it."

"All of it?"

"Will it all fit on the submersible?"

"No, no—some of it is meant to be mounted on the bottoms and sides of your expedition's boats. So you want all of these goodies, even the ones I haven't showed to you yet?"

"Yep. Be sure to include the manuals," Sean said with a smile of his own as Mickey moved to hand over Bentneus's black AMEX.

Abu al Khayr motioned that the card was not necessary. "We have your employer's payment information on file, Doctor Muir, Mister Luch. We shall have everything installed at your vessels' berth in plenty of time for you to learn how to use them, perhaps as early as forty-eight hours or, at the latest, four days."

"Earlier would beat the hell out of later," Sean replied.

The Arab's smile flickered again. "Of course," he said.

Mickey laughed at his friend's brazen show of impatience, no doubt triggered by the cavalier way their host waved away the death of an entire ecosystem to fulfill the vengeful plans of a man driven mad by bitterness. But Sean was working to fulfill, even direct, those plans. As was Mickey himself. All soapbox talk aside, every last living thing that died in the service of their mission was a being they had all agreed to kill.

***

The week passed with not only intense slowness (typical before a major dive) but also great rapidity as they prepared *Sea Legs*, *Sharkasm*, and the boat they elected to call *Spit* for their martial campaign. The science folk on *Sharkasm* were torn, of course, between approving of the technology they were going to get to play with, mouths agog, and the fact that they would be using it to end a magnificent creature they would rather study than kill.

The communications techs and general support crew on *Sea Legs* just wanted their cut of the cash and a little fun shooting at things and dropping bombs on them. The oceanophile nerds were on the science boat, not theirs.

And then there was *Spit*. She had been built specifically for this hunt—that latest factoid that Sean had learned supporting his hunch that Bentneus had this whole adventure in sight from the day he awoke. Did that include springing Sean from prison?

You bet your ass it did. Personally, Sean wouldn't have complained if the filmmaker had wanted help planning and gotten him out, like, two years earlier. Then "the incident" never would have happened, and he wouldn't have spent a year talking to the walls in solitary. Yes, he got good research and reading done in there, but he found himself longing to hear the white noise of his cellmate holding forth on "the Jews" until Sean fell asleep.

However, *Spit* almost made up for it. Gleaming, resplendent in the sun, and outfitted with every gewgaw Sean ever could have thought of, let alone been given to use. *Sharkasm* had the scientists and the equipment, but every one of their readouts was reproduced in the large and luxurious cabin from which Sean would oversee the operations.

And there, secured fast to the A-frame that would lower it into the water, was Bentneus's masterpiece of hatred and anger, *Ocean Vengeance*. The yellow submersible was indeed covered in the ordnance Sean had seen at War-Mart and much more besides that could kill Guam's entire population of 181,800, forget about a single gargantuan dinosaur.

As was expected, as was unavoidable, as was dreaded, Sean eventually had to interact with Slipjack McCracken. They shook hands and spoke civilly, even if it was extremely awkward. The appearance of each man might make one think that Slipjack had been the one in prison. He had a haunted and gaunt look and an unhealthy-looking paunch. His hair had grown down to his shoulders and all but abandoned the top of his head. Sean, on the other hand, had obviously made the most of his daily hour of solitary exercise and looked more fit than when he was put into human storage.

Slipjack's skin was sun-beaten, almost leathery; but Sean's was as pale as milk, not having the sun on it for so long. He had to apply sunblock on any and all exposed skin now that he was out in the open, or he would pay painfully for his carelessness.

They spoke about some technical details regarding the launch mechanism and how the weight of the various weapons was balanced in such a way that *Ocean Vengeance* would descend straight down, and fast. Once the baiting job got done in the depths, then the submersible would jettison God knew how many dollars' worth of lethal hardware as ballast and rise to the surface to share in the Bentneus Prize.

If they could somehow bring Gigadon's head up to show to their benefactor. How were they going to do that, even if they could find and then kill the beast?

"It's a special ... *cable* ..." Slipjack answered with discomfort about discussing custom diving cables with the man who had been convicted of sabotaging an earlier custom cable to kill his darling Kat. He shook himself out of it and continued, "It threads *through* the sub, so the sub doesn't bear any of the weight of the fish head. It's all on the A-frame and threaded through the boat."

"Jeffrey Plaid did the same thing with his cables on the shark cages," Sean said, wanting to be contrary but forced to do it passive-aggressively when he would have loved to just do it aggressively.

"Jeffrey Plaid shoulda stuck to rivers."

Sean let out a huff of amusement, then stood in silence, his eyes pointed at the A-frame but not really looking at it.

It was the same with Slipjack. Silence. Not sure how to continue the conversation or to wrap it up.

"Look," Sean said, "before we're in any life-or-death situation, I'm just going to say to you what I think. Then you tell me whatever might be rattling around in your head, keeping you from focusing 100 percent on the mission. All right?"

Slipjack paused to look like he was considering the idea, but in fact he thought it an excellent suggestion. "All right, then. Shoot."

Sean said, "I think you were having an affair with my wife—*how* that could have come about, I have no idea, but it came about. I think you used some kind of sleight-of-hand with that key trick the lawyer talked about, did it somehow to enter the expedition building and sabotage the cable to be used for the second dive. I don't know you would've done it, but I believe in my heart that you did it. You knew I was supposed to do the second dive, and you wanted me dead and out of the way so you could have Kat all to yourself. As weird as that concept even is to me."

Slipjack nodded while chewing on his lip the whole time Sean was speaking to him. "That it?"

"You don't think it's enough?"

"I don't think nothing when it comes to what you say or don't say. I just let you say your piece and try not to punch you in the throat."

"Yeah, all right, same here. Go, talk, this is your one chance … no bull."

"Okay, fine. I didn't know nothing about some 'key trick,' and I think that lawyer pulled the whole thing out of his ass to confuse the situation, okay? Second, I think you messed with the cable so it would come apart on the second dive, the dive you were supposed to be on. You faked getting your fingers hurt—funny you didn't say nothing about that until you needed to get into the sub—so that Kat would take your place and die."

"Why? *Why* would I do that?"

"I don't need to defend what I said. I just said what I think, same as you."

"Fair enough. But will you tell me why you think I'd kill my own wife, who everyone knows I loved more than anything in the world?"

Slipjack balked dismissively. "She told me things. We talked a lot."

"Between banging sessions."

"Damn straight." Slipjack spit over the side. "You wanted to know why I know you killed her—that's how."

"That wasn't anything to do with *why*, Slipjack. *What* did she tell you that makes you so sure I sabotaged my own chance to make scientific history and prove all my naysayers wrong? What could she possibly have said—if she said anything in the first place, which I highly doubt she even did."

"Doubt it, believe it, I don't give a rat's ass one way or the other."

"*What did she say, goddamnit?*"

Slipjack smiled and spit into the water again. "All right, you wanna know, here you go: She said the hydrothermal-dinosaur idea was hers, and you used it so you could get tenure at San Diego. She was already tenured there, and she wanted you with her. So she gave you the go-ahead to take her plumb-crazy idea to impress the committee over there."

"That's insane—"

"That ain't all, boss. When you finally got the funding to go looking for the prehistoric beasts, she was gonna take half the credit since it was her theory in the first place. There was no way you were gonna let that happen—you wanted the spotlight all for yourself—and so you set up the 'freak accident' that killed her."

"None of that is even remotely true. If you are telling the truth, then Kat was lying to you. Maybe she was mad, maybe she wanted you to feel like you should hurt me, but I was the one who got it all started—I was the *hero*. I was the one who would secure complete academic freedom for both of us!"

"You wonder why she started taking me into her bed? There's your answer. She loved you, but you were shutting her out from the glory and fame and such. Maybe you loved her, maybe you just used her, but you frickin' *murdered* her to get all the attention for yourself."

"I guess it worked, then."

"Just not like you thought, huh?" Slipjack said with a sneer. "Anyway, there, you got it; we told each other what we think. Now can we work together to get rich enough to never have to see each other again?"

"I said what I wanted to say. So, yes."

"Well, I could say a hell of a lot more, but why waste my breath when we both know what really happened? One of us is lying, and one is telling the truth, and we both know who's who and what's what. I can work near you, I guess, for the money up for grabs."

"I'm not going to say what I really want to say right now," Sean said.

"Yeah, me neither. But we both know what we'd say, anyway. Now go to hell and let me do my job."

Sean continued to not say what he really wished he could say, because Slipjack was right: they had a job to do, and the sooner they did it, the sooner they would each be done with the man he'd most love to see die in pain.

***

It took most of a day to get out to the coordinates of Challenger Deep, the three boats of the expedition—if it could be called that instead of a hunt for monsters—traveling in a line, like the fleet of a military blockade.

The travel time wasn't wasted time for the crews and the scientists aboard *Sea Legs*, *Sharkasm*, and *I Spit on Your Grave*, however. Aside from the equipment check after redundant check for the techs and the actual sailing activities of the boats' professional sailors, Sean Muir spent hours with the scientific crew on *Sharkasm*, making estimates of how much heat needed to be distributed where, how big Gigadon actually was, and how to best kill it *and* drag it back to Guam for their payday.

Initial answers to these questions were "A lot," "twice the size of a blue whale," and "no friggin' idea." Unhelpful as these were, they were at least a start, because they now knew what they didn't know and could therefore take action to learn it.

Holly Patterson—now *Doctor* Holly Patterson, having been just a last-year graduate student when sailing on the Bentneus expedition—ticked off a few reasons why they were as clueless as they were: "It seems that Gigadon spends most of its time near the bottom, where the hydrothermal vents are. This makes sense, since Jake Bentneus encountered the dinosaurs, including Megalodon and Gigadon, just fifty yards or so above the newly discovered vent.

"The problem we face is that the creature is too deep for our sonar and other equipment to see fine enough detail to know where Gigadon might be."

Sean said, "So we'll know when it's coming only when it's well on its way."

Holly nodded. "We should have our plan ready to go as soon as Gigadon registers on our equipment, which will be sounding the area all the way down."

"So, how long do we have from first seeing that it's headed our way to when it comes to kill us?"

"That's the thing," Holly said with a twist of her lips showing annoyance with how little they knew. "The creature has surfaced only twice that we know of. The first time, perhaps without any idea of what it was doing, Gigadon spiraled up in the warm wake of *Ocean Voyager* for the whole time it took to winch Jake back up to the surface, a couple of hours. It was very slow, even careful. It didn't know what to expect, or maybe it didn't even expect anything in the first place. But when it reached the surface, ancient genetic memories—that is to say, *instincts*—got triggered and sent it into attack mode. Poor Jake was the worm on a hook hanging from *Piranha II*, and the fish took the bait."

"The second time didn't take as long, and Gigadon took down an entire boat that time," Mickey said with arms crossed, glad to be included in the scientists' meeting, but in no way making any claim to being one of their number. It took a mariner's *cojones* to speak up among the geniuses with even this bit of observation.

Holly was quite fond of Mickey and was glad he gave a bit of input—eyewitness evidence from one of the Gigadon's appearances at the surface. Not only that: it was Mickey who busted his ass to get real-time intelligence on what happened to end the hotshot mission of Jeffrey Plaid and his entire ROAR! contingent *and* sailing crew. "Exactly, Mickey—I mean, Chief Luch—"

"You mean 'Mick,'" Mickey said.

Holly laughed. "Just testing the waters, so to speak. But Mickey is right—that first attack took hours to occur, Gigadon finally going for the submersible only once it was in the bright sunlight. But Jeffrey Plaid's fate was sealed in, what, minutes? Half an hour?"

"It *learned.* Two interventions into its territory and it learned, it *remembered*, that following a heat source would bring it to a place to exercise its destructive skills," Sean said, almost not believing his own words. "Anything we send down there that heats the water—once Gigadon feels it, he is going to follow it."

"Question is," Slipjack said from the doorway, making the five people in the room jump, "what do we do with the goddamn thing once it gets here?"

"This is a science meeting," Sean said firmly. "What are you even doing on this boat? Crew meeting is at 1300 hours on *Spit*."

"Yeah, well, I ain't just crew, am I, Doctor Muir? That winch don't run right, trip's over. You seen what happens when the winch and cable don't work just right, haven't you?" He actually feigned disinterest, cleaning under his fingernail. "I mean, I don't care, but, if you think about it, you need to know what I can lift and what I can't, am I right?"

Sean checked the gaze of the three scientists and his mission chief. Each of them gave a reluctant nod, even if these were accompanied by a rolling of the eyes toward heaven. "All right, Slipjack, come on in."

"Don't mind if I do," the winch boss said, and stood at the large table covered with various indecipherable (to him) charts and readouts and such. "Besides, I got something juicy to share with the big brains anyway."

That aroused their interest, each man and woman eagerly giving Slipjack the floor.

"The winch and cable setup on *Spit* is the best money can buy. Hell, everything we have is the best, except maybe our commander—"

"Say something we need to hear or shut your mouth and get the hell out of here," Sean said to him.

"Fair enough," Slipjack said, holding out his palms in mock surrender. "So, we got the best winch ever on *Spit*, one able to lift and lower the most weight of any boat on the ocean 'cept oil tankers and aircraft carriers. But what are we gonna be trying to lift with this son of a whore? How freakin' heavy has that thing gotta be? How are we supposed to drag it back to Guam?"

"All we need to bring is the head," Mickey said.

"Yeah, but how heavy is that? Even the *Spit* winch has a limit. And, who knows, maybe something could go wrong with the cable?"

"Get your ass out of here, right now."

"Sean, wait," Holly said. "He's the chief of the winch team. He's raising important questions, ones we don't have the slightest idea how to answer. There's just so little data about Gigadon—we know approximately what its size is, but is it *really* mostly hollow inside?"

"It has to be, in order to survive at those depths," Sean said. "And we saw evidence from Plaid's video that this is mostly right. It seems to have some kind of organs—which it would have to possess, obviously, to live—but they are gossamer things, able to withstand the pressure, so we can't really establish a useful estimate of Gigadon's weight not knowing what its internal structure is like."

"Agreed," Holly said, her voice betraying that her mind was off chewing on the problem and wasn't 100 percent present. "We'll need to drain the water out of it somehow. Actually, we'll have to *force* it out of Gigadon to have any chance of pulling it out of the water. And how will we cut off his head? Do we have anything capable of doing that on board? A giant saw or something?"

"We've got everything in our little convoy here," Mickey said with a big smile. "Jake really left no stone unturned. Guess what we have from War-Mart, Holly."

"I don't know, what?"

"Nice guess. We have a *maser*. Do you know what that is?"

Everybody was listening intently, even Sean Muir, who of course had been with Mickey when Abu al Khayr had shown it off amid all the other super-advanced weaponry. It wouldn't be "sharks with frickin' lasers," but something even better: a 360-degree-swiveling *maser* cannon that used the newest applied science to operate in temperate conditions instead of supercooled laboratory environments.

"It's like a laser, I believe. I didn't get my doctorate in physics, Mick," she said with a smirk. "Or from a subscription to *Discover* magazine."

Even the responsible adults in the room made sounds to indicate that perhaps Mickey would be in need of aloe to soothe the pain of the sick burn Holly had just laid down on him. He laughed and said, "It *is* like a laser, but instead of being amplified light, it's amplified *microwaves*."

"Is that good?"

"I forgot—biologist, not physicist. Well, the intensity of an electromagnetic wave is in direct proportion to its frequency. Like their name says, microwaves have very small wavelengths, and thus high frequency, much higher than that of visible light in lasers, and so they are a lot more powerful and destructive."

Holly blinked at Sean. "Did he do a home-study course or something?"

Sean said, "I think I've heard these *exact* words before, but it's hard to tell for sure without hearing it with an Arabic accent."

Mickey roared with laugher and said, "You get the point, though."

"Not really," Holly said.

"A *laser* might be useful for putting a cigarette burn on Gigadon's tough exterior. But specially if the dinosaur is mostly hollow, a maser will slash right through its hide and innards and burn its way out the other side." He waited for Sean to jump in or for Holly to ask more questions. When they didn't, he finished: "We can cut the monster's head off and bring it to shore. For our billion dollars."

"So much for science."

"That's not totally correct, Hol," Sean said. "The knowledge of every scientific savant on *Sharkasm* is going to be needed to kill this son of a bitch. It's not being done for new science, that's true. But we'll learn enough to rewrite the marine biology books, just by figuring out how to destroy Gigadon."

Three bells rang, an old-fashioned touch on this most advanced vessel. "That's the first crew mess," Slipjack said. "You gonna talk, Boss Man?"

"If you're asking me if I'm going to address the crew as the director of this expedition, and chiefs *always* address the sailors and scientists and everybody else working with them, then yes, Slipjack, I am. You're asking this *why*, exactly?"

"'Cause I wanna *address* everybody, too."

"The hell you will."

"See?" Slipjack snapped at Mickey, who had no idea why the question was targeted at him. Slipjack then turned back to Sean. "'The hell I will?' I'm the goddamn *winch chief* on this mission. Holly's gonna speak, 'cause she's the science chief, right? And Mickey—I don't know what the hell he's chief of—"

"He's mission chief."

"—'cept stroking your ego. I'm the winch chief. I'm gonna talk. Or I'll go put my feet up for the rest of this thing, and you can operate the winch yourself. It's really advanced, and I've learned it inside and out while you were still cooling it in solitary. But you go ahead, asshole, don't let me talk, and you have fun with the winch."

Sean literally bit his tongue to keep from saying anything that would destroy this mission and send him back to prison as a "cho-mo" for the rest of his life. *No. Don't take the bait from this piece of garbage*, he told himself. *Breathe.* Calmed as much as he was going to be right then, he said evenly, "You're right, Slipjack. I apologize for letting my personal feelings cloud my judgment."

Slipjack seemed a little taken aback, even though he knew Sean Muir would never call his bluff, and so the result wasn't a total surprise. "All right, boss. Apology accepted."

They didn't shake hands or any of that crap. But Sean did shake hands with Mickey, Holly, and his communications chief, Kevin. "Mess time. Let's get to it."

***

Night was falling by the time just about everyone pushed into *Spit*'s mess area, which was big enough to accommodate all of them, since it was also set up as a last-resort staging area for equipment if the weather turned too disagreeable for that work out on the deck.

Like sat with like, the professional sailors in one corner of the room, the scientists and techies in another, the communications crew in another (Kevin sat with them, not with the other boat chiefs, because he didn't have anything particularly interesting to say other than maybe *Keep your comms on the right frequency*) and then the chiefs of the mission in the final corner, standing in front of their table. The actual captain of their little seafaring fleet was the chief of the maritime captains, of course, and he stood with the other three. Sean Muir was there too, of course.

Mickey rapped an empty coffee mug against the table to get everyone's attention.

"This is it," Mickey said, speaking first since his words were the most general. "Tomorrow we start hunting Gigadon. If we succeed, we will all be richer than our wildest dreams. If we fail, we get nothing. This is fair, because we have been outfitted by Jake Bentneus himself with tens of millions of dollars of equipment. We have the best of the best in every department. If we blow it with that kind of advantage, we deserve to float home with our heads down.

"But that ain't gonna happen. We're gonna beat this damned dinosaur and bring its head back to rot on the beach." Mickey laughed at himself. "That came out kind of more dramatic than I intended. Anyway, the mission director of our expedition wants to say a few words. Sean?"

Sean Muir stood from leaning against the table and cleared his throat. The only sound heard was the water slapping against the sides of the boat. Every set of eyes was on him, every ear cocked to hear what this near-mythic figure was going to say. He had predicted the deep-sea dinosaurs; he had gone to prison because of the cable sabotage murder; he was a cipher.

"I'm very happy to be leading this expedition. We will learn a great deal as we hunt Gigadon, findings that will astonish the world. But first and foremost, we're going to bring Jake Bentneus what he has paid us to bring him. Our science chief and her team will direct us, our sailing captain and his sailors will place us right where we need to be, our communications chief and his team will record it all for posterity, and our winch team will make it possible to actually catch, kill, and bring this thing to shore. The winch and other equipment operators will also be in charge of ordnance." He could feel a tenseness in the room at these words and smiled. "Don't worry. We have former military weapons experts working under the winch 'chief,' but they're autonomous. We won't have Slipjack blasting us with the giant laser."

Slipjack spit right on the deck and then spit out words that sounded a lot like "duck shoe."

Mickey jumped in. "Actually, boss, it's a *maser*. Wait 'til you guys see it in action. Holy smokes."

Sean nodded in thanks for the distraction from Slipjack and continued, "If any of you have a concern about how I'm doing things, get with your chief and have them talk to me about it. If the problem *is* your chief, then just come to me directly. Or email me from your ship's connected computer. And that's it, I guess. Oh, one last thing. I know it's the elephant—or maybe the whale—in the room, and let's just get it out of our minds right now."

The room couldn't have been more silent if they were in dry dock.

"I did *not* murder my wife."

If the sound of eyes going wide open could have been heard, it would have been the only sound in the grave-still room.

Sean looked at every crew member as his gaze swept the room, ready for any rebuttal or question. None came, and Sean nodded. "Thank you. Holly, you're up."

The science chief stood from her leaning position and said, "Hey, I'm Holly Patterson, the chief of science and tech on the mission. What I want to say is that all of us should be open to teaching and learning at every point of this unprecedented mission. If there's something technical that you need to know, radio us at *Sharkasm* or, if we're here on *Spit*, just come up and ask us. We may very well do the same to you if there's something we need to know that falls within your wheelhouse. The more we share information and knowledge, the more able to autonomously do our part we will be. That's all I wanted to say." She stepped back and leaned against the table once again.

Stepping up next was the captain of the sailing crew speaking to the need to work together—and keep the ships as a whole together as much as possible—during even calm seas. "Because the huge flotilla of lubbers is already arriving. They're going to be packing a lot of stupid into each of those tubs, and we need to stay out of their way. Most of them should give up soon enough, since maybe they know fishing, maybe even shark hunting, but none of them have any idea what taking down this big bastard is going to require of them. And of us. So give them the right of way so they can screw up faster and get the hell out of here." Quiet laughs spread through the room, and the captain smiled before turning solemn as he said, "I believe in every member of this crew: science, communications, operations, sailing, all of you. God bless this mission and everyone on it."

Mickey applauded with everyone else as he stood from against the table. "All right, that's what we—"

"Luch, you pile of shit," Slipjack snarled as he took a long step forward to the place where the others had spoken, "it's *my* turn."

Mickey's eye twitched, but he put on the appearance of good humor and said, "The floor is yours, Mister McCracken."

Slipjack scoffed and mumbled, "Damn right, it is." He shook off the attempted insult to his person and hooked his thumbs around his suspenders. "You all know me. I'm Slipjack, chief of the winch crew and over the weapons guys and all that. I want to *address* an area of possible concern around here. By that, I mean the cable."

A murmur spread through the mess.

"I'm taking special precautions to make sure that we don't have no problems like what happened on the previous Muir mission where the boss's wife was ..."

Silence. They could practically hear Slipjack weighing his words.

"... killed. Where she lost her life due to an issue with the cable. I'm assuring everyone here that a close eye will be kept on every inch of that line as it unspools. And it's gonna unspool only if we got to send somebody down, probably *el capitan*. But all of us, we're hoping that the Gigalodon—"

"Gigadon," Holly couldn't help but whisper at him.

"—is gonna come to *us*. It's got a taste for the surface now, that's what the eggheads say, so we on the *operations crew* or whatever it's called are gonna be ready."

Nods and a smattering of applause followed. Mickey stepped back up and—

"One more thing," Slipjack said, and eyed them all. "Just to clear the air, like Muir did."

He had the floor. Mickey stepped back, silently hoping Slipjack was going to say something about the weather conditions or something, but knowing damned well he wasn't.

"Katherine Muir and I were in love."

Mickey actually had to hold Sean back in his sudden fury.

"Kat and I were in love, and she wanted to leave her husband, our Captain Supreme. For *me*. But she couldn't find the will to hurt her husband's precious feelings. I don't know what woulda happened if things didn't go FUBAR back then, but the only thing that kept us from being together was her telling her husband about us. That was before we headed out for the expedition. She told him and then she was, like I said, *killed*. Sean Muir was convicted and sentenced, if that means anything to anybody. If it wasn't for Jake Bentneus and his revenge mission, our Dear Leader would still be rotting in solitary."

He turned and looked at Sean, who was still behind Mickey's strong arm but wasn't trying to get at Slipjack anymore. He just looked weary and resigned to this asshole saying whatever the hell he was going to say so they could all get out of there.

"Speaking of which, Cap—why *were* you shut down in that hole for an entire *year*? They mighta kept you in solitary for the rest of your time there. You musta done something seriously bad."

Sean's heavy-lidded eyes now reflected his weariness, even surrender. "There was a fight in the yard. A guy got shanked—stabbed— to death. We were in lockdown for a week, and then they took me to solitary."

"Why you?"

"Jesus Christ, Slipjack," Mickey said.

"Come on, boss, why *you?*"

"Because I'm the one who shanked him."

The room exploded into shouts and frenzied activity. Some of the men rushed at Slipjack and others pushed them back. Or maybe they were trying to get at Sean Muir.

Mickey yelled over the chaos, "That's it, get back to your boats! Let's run a smoother mission than this briefing, for Chrissake, or we're all gonna die out here! *Dismissed!*"

The crew filed out, some throwing glances at Slipjack, others at Sean. But they left in a relatively orderly manner, leaving just the chiefs in the mess. When Sean looked at each of them, he saw the disappointment and suspicion in their eyes.

Mickey stepped up to Slipjack, his bulk making the skinny winch chief look even smaller. "Get out of here, asshole, or God help me, I will pitch you over the side of the goddamn boat."

Slipjack hurried out, but at the door he called back, "You all heard that—Mickey Luch just threatened to kill me." Then he slid out of the room.

Mickey turned and said, tears just about forming in his eyes, "Shit, Sean, why didn't you tell me about this?"

Sean smiled and said, "Because it's a lie. I never stabbed anybody, even though there was a fight where a guy got killed. I wasn't even in the yard at the time."

The sailing captain furrowed his brow, plainly unable to get his mind around whatever the hell was going on. "Doctor Muir—Sean—why … *why* would you say such a thing, tell a lie like this in front of your entire crew?"

"I want Slipjack to stay far away from me. He tried to take my wife away, and when she wouldn't go, he set up the cable to kill me on that test dive so he could have her to himself. But he didn't figure on Kat replacing me in the sub, and he killed her instead."

"S-So the affair?" Holly said in distress. "That was *true*, what Slipjack said?"

Sean nodded, but then shrugged. "I don't know, maybe. I still think he was blackmailing her into sex with him. He was delusional, thinking she loved him, and so he tried to murder me, ended up murdering her. That's all I got."

"*Blackmailing* her? With what?"

"I don't know. He might have gotten ahold of some of her early, unpublished speculation ... about marine lizards living near sea-floor hydrothermal vents."

The disappointed and even frightened looks in his chiefs' eyes were replaced with looks of sympathy and camaraderie. Holly gave him a hug, the crew captain shook his hand, and Mickey patted him on the shoulder as they left Sean alone in the mess.

But a few seconds later, Mickey came back. "Boss, I need to ask you something. We've been friends a long time, so I just want a simple answer, not a lie."

"All right."

"Why *were* you in solitary for a frickin' year?"

"I tried to escape. Almost made it, too."

"*Jesus*, man, you didn't have *that* long to go! What the hell did you do that for?"

A tenuous and twitchy smile danced on Sean's face. "You don't want to know, Mick."

The mission chief put a heavy paw onto his boss's shoulder. "I really do, Sean."

Sean sighed, then took a good, deep breath in and out. Then he smiled again at Mickey and said, "I know where Slipjack lives. It's not too far from the prison. I could've made it on foot."

Mickey didn't have to ask the question. Sean answered anyway.

"I was going to torture the son of a bitch until he signed a confession saying he tampered with the cable. And then I was going to hang him from a belt in the bedroom closet of his shithole flophouse apartment."

Mickey's eyes were wide, but narrowed as he tried to make sense of what Sean was saying. "But ... they'd know it was you, unless you slipped back into the prison unnoticed. That's got to be impossible."

"I'm sure it is. I didn't really have that part of the plan worked out."

Now the mission chief looked askance at his boss. "That doesn't sound like you."

Sean kept his face totally still, his eyes boring into Mickey's, unblinking.

"Boss ...?"

"It wouldn't matter if I went back or not. Slipjack would be dead, Kat is dead, and prison—especially solitary—*drives you insane. Literally, insane.* There really isn't any place for you in the world after that."

"Boss ...did this actually happen? I'm not calling you a liar."

"It would be okay if you did. I *am* lying."

"What?"

"I'm lying to you. I never escaped or even tried to escape."

"Then wha—you—*bwahahahahaha!* You got me! Oh, my God, I'm crying here ..."

Sean's smile was as weak as watery tea. "Okay, enough whimsy, eh? Cappy was right—it's gonna be amateur hour out here tomorrow. I already see lights from at least fifty buckets out there. Let's get some rest and start winning this damn thing." He clapped Mickey on the back as he headed out of the mess.

"But, Sean ..."

"Yes, my son?" he said, and snorted a laugh—at what, Mickey had no idea. "Sorry, that was funny. Yeah, what's up?"

"Well ... why *were* you in solitary for the past year?"

Sean turned and leaned against the bulkhead, his tone still light. "Oh, yeah, that." He scratched his head and said, "Well, it was because I took the fall for stabbing a guy to death during a big fight in the yard."

"Wh-what?" Mickey said, then gave a wary smile. "You're messing with me again."

"No, no," Sean said, smiling. "The guards couldn't see who exactly had done the shanking, but they heard from enough cons it was me. Assholes. But nobody really had anything on me, there was no *proof*, so they couldn't extend my sentence or anything like that. What they *could* do is toss me in solitary for the next six years or so."

Mickey stood stock-still. His emotions had gone up and down, back and forth so much in the preceding hour that he was unable to register any particular emotion. It felt like a dream, a nightmare where nothing gets completed, where you just keep trying to do one simple thing and fail until you wake up. But this wasn't a dream. A nightmare, maybe, but the waking kind.

"Okay, you murdered another prisoner."

"That's what they say." Sean held out his hands. "I'm sorry if I've disappointed you. Shit happens in prison. You do things you *never* would have thought yourself capable of. It's a horrible place, especially for an innocent man."

That's right, Mickey thought, *you were innocent when they locked you up.* He remembered he had heard many times of prison being called "the animal factory," where someone who had committed a crime (or, in Sean's case, didn't) learned to become a *criminal,* to lose his humanity. "I'm no one to judge you, man. Thank you for telling me."

"I'm glad to tell you," he said, pausing as he saw the look on Mickey's face. "Are you wondering if this story is true?"

"No," Mickey said, "it's not that. I was just wondering why you, um, you know ... killed that other guy. To *death.*"

"That's usually how killings end."

"*Ha*, right. But did he ... I don't know ... try to make you his 'bitch' or whatever?"

Now Sean let out a good laugh again, and Mickey smiled and nodded, waiting for an answer. Sean recovered and said, "I didn't even know the guy. Or maybe I did, just seeing him around. But I could see the guards' sight line was blocked and so they wouldn't be able to see what was going on. The weapon was spare shop glue and newspaper rolled to a point to make a nice shiv, and it got used on the poor bastard. Just rotten luck on his part, not that anybody's luck in that place could be called *good*."

"Okay, sure, but *why?*"

Sean shrugged like it was obvious. "I wanted them to put me in solitary."

"Wait, what?"

"It's the only way I could get some serious work done. It was far too distracting in with the general population to really read and write in the concentrated way scientists need, though God knows I tried. But I couldn't, so I found a way to secure my own quiet space to continue my research."

"I ... that's some dedication, I guess? I don't know what to say."

"It's harsh, I know, but we always have to *keep our eyes on the prize*. That's what I did getting sent to solitary, because think about it: without the serious additional publication I did on my theories, would Jake Bentneus have sought me out and sprung me free? Can't let your personal feelings or prejudices throw you off that focus. My focus is getting *free* for good. Do you have *your* eyes on the prize?"

"I think I do ... I mean, yeah, I'm not gonna *murder* anybody, but yeah, winning it all, getting the Gigadon, definitely."

"Good man," Sean said, and clapped him on the shoulder a third time. "Now let's hit our bunks. Big day tomorrow. Idiots on parade—and maybe even someone else to compete with! *Eyes on the prize!*" With that, he left the room at last.

This left a blank-eyed Mickey standing alone in the mess, watching the lights from the cavalcade of inadequate fishing vessels in the half-mile around them and listening to the cursing of their crews as the boats bumped into one another again and again.

He thought that maybe he was losing his mind, just like it seemed Sean Muir definitely had. But no—if he was losing his mind, he wouldn't feel so anxious for this mission to be over, whether or not they collected one dime from Jake Bentneus.

***

When the blackness of the sky over the ocean first yielded to a thin gray in the east, a member of the dogwatch mariner crew on *Sharkasm* stepped out onto the deck to make a visual scan of their surroundings, like a real sailor did, instead of staring at computer screens and tallying numbers that meant nothing to anyone aboard except for the scientists.

Not that those things weren't important to a crewman who wanted to keep getting hired on to cushy academic projects, but to scan the ocean with his own eyes felt more authentic, even if there was nothing to see …

… except something *was* out there, impossible to see in the still-dark water, but its sharp tip—the way it swayed it had to be attached to something below—stood out against the gradually lightening sky. It looked strange, but as his eyes continued to acclimate and the rosy-fingered dawn approached, he could see it wasn't alone. He could see now that they were everywhere, these tips of whatever, surrounding the Bentneus expedition's ships. Everywhere he turned, he saw them, and—

Jesus, they were boats. The tips he saw were antennas, radar dishes, and even some sails. There were dozens of small vessels dotting the water in the half-mile or so that the *Sharkasm* sailor could see from his position.

Did these jackasses know what they were supposed to catch out here? There were some larger boats grouped together, definitely well-financed teams like their own. But they sat mostly silent. As the stars above were overwhelmed by the imminent sunrise, he could hear the crews of the smaller boats, shouting out to one another across the distance that separated them.

He could pick out two words in particular: *Shark* and *circle*.

The smaller boats chugged vaguely toward one another, and it took just a few minutes until the crewman could see that they were, in fact, trying to form a circle. Not an easy maneuver, but the boats pulled it off well. There must have been some actual experienced mariners out there, maybe professional fishermen leading "expeditions" of their own for wanna-be Gigadon-hunters who paid for the chance to land a billion-dollar prize bounty.

Morons, in other words, he thought, but these morons were doing something very particular that he couldn't quite figure out. What was with the circle of boats? Why did he hear, very clearly and more than once now, the word *shark?*

That's when the stench hit him, of course right when he was taking the final gulp of his coffee, making him gag and cough out the precious caffeine. The sharp, pungent, godawful smell was like he was standing knee-deep in a red-tide flood of a million different species of rotting fish.

Then he heard a splash. Then another … and another, getting faster, sounding like someone scraping scalloped potatoes into a garbage disposal.

He knew that sound, and as soon as his brain identified it, he recognized the stanky smell. It was chum, buckets and barrels of leftover fish parts and blood.

Chum was used at the very break of dawn by hunters to attract sharks to the surface. Sharks hunt mostly at night, so at dawn they are still near enough to the surface to sense the bloody entrails as wounded prey, easy pickings they can't resist.

These assholes were trying to hunt the Gigadon like it was a giant shark.

Now he heard splashes from numerous boats—maybe every boat— in the flotilla forming a 200-meter-or-so circle half a mile off *Sharkasm*'s port side. They must have all had harpoons to use together, or maybe had a net strung between their fishing vessels to catch the monstrous creature, because they were definitely working in concert to bring up the biggest shark ever known …

… except the Gigadon wasn't a shark. It wasn't a fish. It was a goddamn dinosaur. From listening to the scientists strategize on board the boat, he knew dropping chum and churning water wouldn't even be noticed by the monster, because the Gigadon responded to heat, especially when the source was near enough to tempt it to the surface. These shark-hunting techniques wouldn't work on the dinosaur.

But, out there in the South Pacific, this massive dumping of bait would work on sharks. On a lot of sharks, all at once.

His cup dropped from his hand and tipped over into the water as the crewman was already running to wake the captain and tell him they were about to encounter a feeding frenzy so massive that it could capsize boats and add everyone on those boats to the blood-drenched water.

He didn't know what the hell to do except rap his knuckles on Cap's door—loud enough to wake him but not such a banging that it would show disrespect—and hand the problem over to someone who would know what to do. The crewman had never been so glad not to be a captain in all his sailing days.

***

The maritime captain of each of the three Bentneus team vessels was a different person from the chiefs of the main launch, science, and communication ships (Mickey, Holly, and Kevin, respectively). *Sharkasm*'s sailing captain was Captain Brady, who, upon assessing the situation presented to him by his able watchman, immediately contacted Captain Looper of the main vessel, *I Spit on Your Grave*.

Brady hated that name for a boat—any mariner knew to avoid violent or vengeful names for ships, as that was tempting the spirit of the sea—and so called it *Spit* like everyone else ... except when a real situation was afoot. "*I Spit on Your Grave*, this is Brady aboard *Sharkasm*. Over."

"We copy, *Spit*." It was Looper himself at the radio, which meant he had been awakened and called to the bridge by his own alert dogwatch crewman. "Affirmative on Sharknado. We see it coming our way. Over."

Brady bet the other captains could hear the smile he tried to suppress as he said, "Any suggestions? Over."

There was silence on the radio for almost ten seconds before Looper offered, "Stay the hell away from them? Over?"

The two other captains gave bemused chuckles before agreeing that this was the most prudent—if not, perhaps, the most humanitarian—course of action for the Bentneus vessels regarding the Feeble Flotilla. "Coming out here with nets and harpoons to catch a dinosaur the size of a small island? No amount of warning about itty-bitty great whites is going to help," Looper muttered. "God, have mercy on Your morons' souls."

***

On the ocean, dawn comes slowly, widening in an arc as the atmosphere refracts the sun's light, and then *bam*—it's sunrise, and the morning sun is yellow-white, raging already in its brand-new day.

The stink, however, wasn't of anything brand-new. It didn't matter how many times Sean Muir had been assaulted by that stench in his time around serious mariners; he was glad to smell it now. It was horrid and made him just about gag, but goddamn if he wasn't out on the ocean again, far away from that concrete hole. He felt *alive* there on the deck of *Spit*, watching the circle of optimistic, hard-working fishermen (and not a few weekend warriors in small but fancy sport-fishing yachts) who were busy dumping the last of their chum into the already foamy and red water inside the circle. He felt *alive*, goddamnit.

But he would die again, wouldn't he, if he failed to land this Gigadon? He had long prophesized their existence, based his ruined-then-resurrected career on them, but knowing how and why these adapted marine lizards existed didn't do him much good in actually bagging the very largest of them. Bentneus's Moby Dick was bigger—and a hell of a lot more willing to follow heat signatures all the way to the surface—than anything Sean had ever considered. He still didn't see how greater size would lend an evolutionary advantage to creatures that ate the gossamer chemosynthetic life growing around the hydrothermal vents.

There *was* a reason, of course, but even an ichthyopaleontologist needed data to work out what that reason was, and Bentneus's ill-fated mission was the first to find any evidence at all. And since Sean's earlier attempt failed catastrophically and he had been kept away from the water for four years, this was his opportunity to get some of that hard data.

Thus, the dying filmmaker's goal lined up neatly with his own: get the Gigadon, bring it (or at least its head) back to shore. For Bentneus, to fulfill his revenge. For Sean, to test his theories and create new ones, get back into the life that had been stolen from him and get working again. Not just logical conclusions based on data collected by others, but real hypotheses and conclusions made on his own discoveries *in the field.*

All of that was if they could beat the other well-funded missions from research institutions like Woods Hole and The Field Institute, from wealthy academic programs like his alma mater in San Diego—he could see their familiar boats a good distance away from Chum Central. He actually wished his boats were farther from the shark-fishing schemers, even with *Spit*'s new hull of armor.

Many of the crew not on duty or asleep on each ship had come to the starboard railing of his boat, the port side of *Sharkasm*, the aft of *Sea Legs*. None of the assemblies were heavy enough to make the boats seriously list, but he hoped each mariner captain was keeping an eye on his boat's center of gravity. Everyone watching must have known something horrible was going to happen, or they wouldn't have been out of their bunks, away from their computers, not getting ready for the dive that would send Sean down to the exact spot where Jake Bentneus sealed his doom.

That's a hell of a lot of bait. If Gigadon responded to blood in the water, then even it would rise with the intention—the goddamn determination—to feed on anything it could. But everything Sean had learned or extrapolated from his own theoretical work said that a creature 36,000 feet below sea level would be extraordinarily unlikely to even *sense* barrels of fish and blood dumped by boats.

Sharks, however, were quite a different matter. They can sense a *drop* of blood from three miles away, that three miles representing the bottom half of a sphere with its equator at the surface. In other words, a shark can sense the tiniest amount of blood in seawater over nineteen square miles at the surface and into the depths well past the euphotic zone, where all sharks (and most every kind of fish) spend their time.

And these guys were dumping a *lot* more than one drop of blood into the water.

"Should we radio them, sir? Tell them to leave off?" a female member of the *Spit* crew asked him tentatively.

"Nah," Sean said as he watched the last barrel, now emptied, tossed into the water. So they were fine environmentalists as well as savvy dinosaur hunters. "I assume they're not in this just for the fun of it, so they signed up like everybody else ... Who are we to say their technique is wrong and they have to stop immediately?"

"Aye, sir," she said, "but we're just north of Papua New Guinea. That's, like, in the top ten of shark populations in the world."

"Indeed, it is, sailor."

"So there could be *so* many sharks around here. *SO* many."

"Should make for a good show, right?"

"Er, I—sir, should I get the rescue rafts ready? Or raise Air/Sea Rescue on the comm?"

"If you want to float out to an unprecedented feeding frenzy in an *inflatable boat*, be my guest." He looked at her and saw that she did not, in fact, want to do this. "We're here to kill Gigadon. Anybody else wants to screw around with sharks or get themselves killed some other way, that's not our concern."

"Aye, sir." She hesitated, and it was as if Sean could read her mind.

"Yes, you should absolutely check with your captain. Whatever seafaring orders he gives, you should carry those out to the letter. But I bet he'll say the same thing I'm saying."

"Aye—"

"You're a good person. Hang on to that. The sea needs more sailors like you."

She bobbed her head, possibly blushing a bit, and retreated to the bridge, maybe to ask the captain about rescuing any shark hunters, maybe not. Sean didn't care one way or the other; it wouldn't be any of his mission's crew going out there, that was for damned sure.

There was chatter all down the rail, whispering in some cases, just plain talking in others, and a few were loudly jeering the shark baiters. He gazed at them for a few minutes, amused. Those weren't his people, so Cap could control them if he wanted. But why interfere with morale? It would be quashed soon enough when the sharks started arriving, which had to be at any moment now.

Quashed when they saw ships sustain irrevocable damage from frenzied great whites, people getting dumped into the chum-nasty water, people getting really and truly killed right in front of them and no way to do a goddamn thing about it. What, were they going to swim out and rescue the assholes? No, they were not. But they wouldn't pull away, either, when the screaming and the dying started at last.

Dying. It was going to be hard to look away, or would be if he didn't already know he'd watch until the end, see what any of his fellow professional and academic contestants did about it. If the other missions lost people, so much the better for the Bentneus expedition.

The thought of bloody death right before his eyes made him think of what he had told Mickey the night before. Why, he wondered, would he tell his mission chief such a thing? Did he think it would make Mickey more loyal or something? It was much more likely to create a distance between them, a confessing murderer and a good man who probably got into academic boat management from commercial fishing because he didn't even like to kill those nets full of fish.

Maybe he was testing that loyalty. Did Mickey know what Slipjack had in store for Sean when the winch chief sabotaged the cable? Did he know the cable was damaged in the first place? And if he did, why didn't he stop everything before Sean or Kat got killed? He might have assured Slipjack of his silence in exchange for ... well, for *something. Let me kill Sean Muir, and I'll give you this* something. Sean couldn't imagine what such a thing would be. But it had convinced Mickey to conceal—

Whoa, hoss. Sean had to physically shake the thoughts out of his head. *You don't know that Mickey was involved in any way. You don't even know for sure if Slipjack sabotaged the cable; admit it.*

That's why you test loyalty.

That cleared the doubts out of his mind. He'd see how Mickey acted now in front of someone he thought was a straight-up murderer. Maybe when Mickey came out to see the show.

Then he'd do what needed to be done. If anything needed to be done. When Mickey showed his lack of loyalty, maybe he'd take a bad slip into the water, thrash about nice and violently for the sharks. Problem solved.

If Mickey showed disloyalty, he scolded himself. *If.*

"Goddamn," Sean said out loud. "I'm not a murderer. I'm a scientist."

Like you can't be both, his smug asshole brain spat at him. *Like you aren't both.*

***

The tip of the fin of the first shark to swim into the circle was spotted not two minutes after Sean's traitorous brain finally shut the hell up.

One fin. Then two. And more until it wasn't possible to count them anymore as they crisscrossed the circle, sometimes going outside the line of the boats but always returning immediately. Some snouts were visible now, the man-eaters getting excited at all the fish and the blood and the smell. There were at least a dozen within five minutes of the first fin's appearance.

The water had begun to churn. There were a lot more than a dozen sharks now, some of them—most of them?—moving with agitation below the sharks appearing on the surface.

"Now what?" Mickey said at his boss's side, startling Sean.

"Shit, pardner, you almost made me jump into the water," Sean said with a laugh. And it *was* a laugh, not some kind of evil cackle like he was crazy. "What do you mean, 'now what'? I highly doubt Gigadon is going to make an appearance at this chickenshit party."

Mickey laughed now, although concern sounded in his voice as he said, "Me, too. No, I mean, these guys have done what they know how to do, attract a whole bunch of sharks—big mothers, too. So what now?"

Sean shrugged, but he'd seen a few induced feeding frenzies from both research and commercial vessels. "Now they swing the side of beef out into the middle and the sharks get crazy going after it. You've seen that, I'm sure."

"Yeah, yeah, I have, boss. But these guys are trying to attract a dinosaur—God, how many barrels of chum did they pour in?"

"I lost count. I'm thinking as many as each of those boats could hold. A historic amount of bait for the biggest fish—well, not a *fish*, but—"

"I get ya. The bigger amount of bait in an area known to harbor their target, the bigger the catch and the greater the chance it'll show up. But … am I wrong, or do the dinosaurs at the bottom not give a crap about shark bait?"

"All signs point to *no*. But sharks sure as hell do, and there's a *lot* of bait in that circle."

Mickey nodded. There were also a lot of sharks, now swimming quickly and aggressively among the boats. The chum had attracted, what, a hundred of them? With more to come, probably? But once the animals were in feeding-frenzy mode, you had to get that meat out there pretty fast, or all that frenzied energy was going to be directed at the only solid-looking things that weren't sharks.

Without actual prey provided to them, they would try to eat the boats. They would ram them and bite out the loose boards of a boat's keel, chewing because that's what feeding frenzies were: chewing on anything they could, trying to kill whatever was there by slamming into it, then chewing and biting and chewing.

"Why won't they put out the hook with the meat?" Mickey said, now seeing that exactly what he had predicted was happening more and more. The sharks nudged the boats, whipped their razor-sharp tails against the hulls, pushed up against them from below. They wanted their prey. "This is literally suicidal, man! *Put the meat out already, for Chrissake!*"

If the fishermen could hear him, his words did nothing. The bastards must have been waiting for their Gigadon—how could such a giant beast refuse such a massive meal?

"What the hell are they doing, boss?"

"It just hit me." Sean shook his head ruefully. "These guys know how to hunt sharks. Obviously, they do. And yet, they're not putting the prize out there to make the sharks crowd against it where they could shoot the predators with guns and harpoons."

Mickey waited. "Yeah? *And?*"

"They're extrapolating their shark hunting into hunting for an even-larger predator. The *sharks* are the meat on the hook, Mick. We were thinking that they put out the bait to get Gigadon's attention, but really they were drawing out the sharks so that they can dangle for a *Gigadon* feeding frenzy."

"Holy crap," Mickey said.

"But blood ain't gonna bring Gigadon, not according to anything I've learned. That means the sharks are the ones looking for a meal now. Hundreds of them, frenzied out of their prehistoric minds. This was not well-planned on their part." He let out a breath, almost in a laugh. "I mean, that's the understatement of the year, but people have to *think*—they have to *plan*."

Sean Muir had come through again, a scientist through and through, logical and brilliant. Mickey had no idea why his old friend was messing with him, but he didn't murder anyone. He *couldn't* murder anyone. It made no sense. It wasn't logical from a scientist's standpoint. Murder would have no possible benefit for an innocent man behind bars.

"Well, time to die," Sean said, his eyes never moving from the increasingly agitated pool of sharks, the creatures now knocking into the small vessels with greater frequency and intensity. "Horrible. Beyond horrible. But maybe there's a silver lining: I see a paper in this, maybe even a cautionary chapter in my memoir."

A *paper?* Mickey thought. *Letting all these people die just so you can write a—*

A *paper.* Sean Muir was thinking of the paper he could write after watching all this death he would do nothing to allay. Just like, maybe, he had murdered a man just so he could continue his research without distraction.

No, he's not killing these idi—people. He's just keeping the people in his charge safe. It's not the same thing at all. He was messing with me. Now he's just messing with everybody. Sean always did have a scientist's weird sense of humor. Inappropriate, that's all.

A scream now, from *Sharkasm.* It was Orville "Popcorn" Blum, the computer specialist, and he shrieked like it was his own tubby flesh being bitten, not that of someone on the smallest fishing boat in the circle. The doomed man also screamed as he was set upon by several sharks at once and went under, spouting blood from his mouth, never to return.

"Doctor Muir!" Orville shouted to his boss on *Spit. "We have to* do *something!"*

"What do you suggest?" Sean shouted back, but too calmly. Or maybe not. It was hard for Popcorn to tell when he himself was so freaked out.

The scientist had no suggestions, nothing to offer. But the stricken look on his face—and now, Sean noticed, on the faces of every member of the crew at the rail of *Spit*—told him that it was going to be detrimental to morale if he didn't organize an attempt to do *something* to help.

Sean picked up the comm and switched the frequency to include everyone on all the Bentneus boats. "I'm not a fisherman, commercial or amateur. Does anyone on this mission know what to do in a shark feeding frenzy?"

Silence on the comm.

"Yeah. Don't even bother getting on the radio to tell us your ideas, if anyone comes up with any. Just go ahead and do it."

Sean took his thumb off the comm button and said to Mickey, who looked almost gray with shock and helplessness: "You're the sailor here—*is* there anything we can do?"

Thank God you asked that. Thank God in Heaven, Mickey thought, literally sighing with relief.

Sean smiled, looking abashed. He shrugged his shoulders and whispered, "At least they're thinning out the competition, right?"

Mickey had an entire ocean to do it in, but he could make it only to the sink before vomiting. He ran the water and wiped off and rinsed out his mouth. *I quit. I have to quit. My friend has lost his freaking mind.*

"You'd think someone with your experience wouldn't get seasick anymore," Sean said with a laugh. "No, but seriously, what do you think? We have an armored hull. The sharks shouldn't be able to get through that, right? So, maybe we could … I don't know, use the winch to pick them off their boats, one by one?"

A loud creak sounded over the water, a bending stretched from inaudibility to ear-splitting, was followed by a hard *crack*, and a great white shark at least thirty-five feet long burst through the bottom of one of the wooden-hulled boats with a gigantic plank of painted wood between its teeth. The shark crunched the board and kept munching until it was splintered beyond recognition. It definitely looked like it was celebrating.

As might it should. Apparently, the section of hull that the great white had broken through and then broken off was an important piece indeed, as the fishing boat immediately listed to port and started sinking so fast that just a few of the shouting men onboard were able to jump from the boat before it vanished below the waves. The tiger sharks, great whites, blacktips, all of them converged on the fresh meat and dragged it under so fast it was hard to tell the churning of the prey being devoured from the churning of the water created by the sinking boat.

Bits of the boat floated to the surface, broken planks and bits of metal and plastic. And a shredded pair of trousers. And a head, although another shark came along and swallowed it almost before the dozens of horrified onlookers from the Bentneus expedition could even identify what it was.

And if the men and women safely ensconced on the large research vessels outside the circle of the fatally shortsighted fishermen were horrified, the yacht captains and commercial fishing boat crews and small craft mariners without exception were panicked into complete paralysis.

One boat—not wooden, this one made of some kind of metal-plastic alloy—was knocked sideways and stayed there. Its crew could do nothing while shark after shark hurled itself at them, dragging them out into the water like dogs with new chew toys. Some men and women remained inside the vessel as it finished capsizing, hidden in the recesses and cabins where the sharks wouldn't be able to reach them. These lucky sailors would die a lonely and horrible death as the oxygen ran out in their air bubbles inside the ship, but they were betting that death by shark would be even worse.

They were probably right.

It was impossible to keep track of which boat was nearest its doom as the sharks ripped right through them, knocked them over, even bit off the propelling screws, which killed them in the process ... but by then, the damage had been done and the boat was dead in the water. It would not escape.

In fact, it struck Sean as strange how few of the boats actually tried to get the hell out of there, how few tried to get away from the roiling blood sea they had helped create and which now was getting bloodier by the second. He saw opportunity after opportunity for a craft to get its motor running and speed away from the circle of death, but terror had seized the crews almost to a man, and Sean could see that they were mesmerized by the horrors around them. *They were supposed to be millionaires! They knew shark hunting like no one else!*

Amid the shouting and wailing on *Spit*, Sean yelled loudly to the rapidly dwindling number of living people on still-seaworthy boats, "Gigadon is not a giant shark, my friends! *Get the hell out of here and save your asses!*"

There were two boats—bigger commercial vessels with reinforced fiberglass hulls—which were being battered right and left, swaying in the water like they were docked in the middle of a hurricane. The special hulls wouldn't be able to stand much more direct pummeling from the dozens of sharks still unsated in the midst of their feeding frenzy—soon they would crack, and that crack would travel up and down the entire keel in seconds. The ships would then open like an egg and sink like a stone.

Sean was surprised that tears were coursing down his face. He wiped his cheeks and stared at the wetness on the back of his hand. So he wasn't a monster, happy to see the competition get taken out of the picture by way of death. He could even feel himself wishing there was something he could have done, any of them could have done, with their millions of dollars of equip—

Or *could* do. They had *everything* on this ship.

"*Mickey!*" Sean yelled, almost screaming. He whipped around to see where his mission chief was—*shit!*—which was standing right next to him, not having moved this whole time.

Despite himself, Mickey let out a startled laugh. "Right here, boss."

"Who's in charge of the big gun up there?" Sean said quickly, pointing toward the War-Mart machine gun atop the highest place on *Spit*. "Get them shooting! We haven't lost everyone yet! There are still boats floating! *We can save the dumb sons of bitches!*"

"It's Crockett, but I don't know if he's even awake—"

"*Move!*" Sean shouted, and ran all the way to the ladder, then scaled the height to the machine gun, which hadn't been loaded or primed. It could be done in thirty seconds ... by someone who knew how to operate a goddamn machine gun. "*Jesus Christ, what do I do here?*"

"I'm getting Crockett!" Mickey yelled and ran out of sight, toward the crew quarters. It was hard to believe anyone could sleep amidst all the screaming and shouting and dying, but sailors knew how to get to sleep and stay there until it was exactly time to get up, no matter what was going on around them. They responded to whistles and bells to get them out of bed unexpectedly, and screams weren't whistles or bells.

Watching the sharks roiling in the water, trying to swim over one another to get at the "prey"—the two luxury fishing vessels, the only boats still afloat from the circle—and they were rocking the two boats hard—Sean felt his stomach sink. Everyone thought he was a killer— he'd "confessed" things to his best friend and right-hand man to make him believe he was a killer. But he *wasn't*, not in his heart. And this was his chance to *save* people—idiots, yes, but still people doing the best they knew how to land what they saw as the most monumental shark in the world. He maybe could have saved them and many more if he had remembered that the Bentneus vessels were each armed to the teeth. But Crockett would never get up there in time, those yachts had to be close to going under—

"Get ready to start shootin'," a voice spoke right next to him, making him jerk out of his thoughts.

The voice belonged to Slipjack McCracken. Sean couldn't have been more surprised if Gigadon had been standing there. "Slipjack, Crockett is—"

"Don't talk to me," Slipjack said. "We can't wait for Crockett—he's probably on the shitter. I know this gun from the Navy." He pushed and pulled a series of levers, then loaded the massive belt of ammunition into the machine gun, and hit one final switch. "*Go!*"

Sean looked from Slipjack to the yachts under assault a hundred yards in front of them. "Thank you, Sl—"

He was alone again. Only now he could reduce the attacking sharks to a fresh batch of chum. He stepped on a pedal and brought the gun to bear—he remembered that much, at least, about how the machine gun worked—aimed, and pulled the trigger tight against the guard.

POWPOWPOWPOWPOWPOWPOW

The firing was so loud that the entire crew assembled at the rail fell to their feet, covering their ears. Sean thought both his eardrums would burst, but he didn't have time to worry about this, because after the first couple of *POW*s, the big gun took on a life of its own—its barrel swung wide, and when Sean tried to correct it, he swung too hard the other way. The deafening discharge of ammo never stopped, because Sean had the trigger mashed against the metal of its guard and couldn't think to let go as he swung around with the out-of-control machine gun.

The first casualties he noticed were the two yachts under direct attack from the sharks. Sean didn't see that he had hit any of the predators, but he did see that he and his out-of-control machine gun had blasted a seam open in the side of one yacht and completely wiped out everything and everyone on the other boat, which now sunk like it had been pulled under by the Kraken.

The crew of the still-floating yacht shouted and waved, screaming for Sean to stop shooting.

But he couldn't. He was too busy just trying to control the machine gun, feeling like he was riding a bucking bronco at the rodeo. The gun swung too far in one direction, and then, when Sean tried to correct, it again swung in the opposite direction, burning metal cutting everything down that was unfortunate enough to fall into the gun's line of fire. Both yachts, of course, but so much more.

That included *Sea Legs* to port. It just exploded, a fiery blossom shooting pieces of ship, communications equipment, and crew members.

It also included the UC San Diego ships a quarter of a mile away. Still unable to control the gun, Sean sent rounds through the crew cabin of their main ship, struck one of their support ships below the waterline, its crew jumping into the water before the whole thing could sink and take them down with it. The other support ship immediately set off its alarms and dropped lines and divers to recover their sister ship's crew before the sharks came over their way.

That done, the two surviving UCSD ships hit the throttle and were gone, out of sight and chugging back toward Guam in a matter of two minutes. *That crazy bastard Sean Muir is killing everyone he can!* they were thinking, Sean could feel it. *How could they let that murderer get hold of a machine gun!?*

Finally, mercifully, the ammunition ran out and only empty clicks sounded from where the booming of firing rounds was assaulting everyone's senses just a moment before. At this, Sean released the trigger, and the gun abruptly stopped swinging.

Crockett, the ordnance man, reached the top of the ladder with a face drained of all color. Behind him was Mickey, not looking that much better.

"I—I had to get shooting—had to get the sharks from killing everyone—I didn't know—Slipjack—"

"Boss, don't bring him into this."

"No, he loaded the gun; he set the switches and levers! He—"

"Doctor Muir," Crockett said, examining the position of certain of those switches and levers, "the feedback control is disabled."

"I don't even know what that is," Sean said, disoriented as he watched black smoke fill the sky from the destroyed vessels that had not yet surrendered and gone under. "It got away from me. I couldn't control it. Slipjack."

"Slipjack *what*, Sean?" Mickey snapped.

"Slipjack didn't tell me how to control it."

Crockett shook his head as he examined another switch. "I'll bet the gun 'got away from you.' Without feedback control, you can't hit what you're aiming at because every shot knocks the gun one way or the other, and when the gunner tries to correct for that, it swings the other way, and so on and so on. The feedback control keeps this from happening."

"But it was off? Disabled?"

"Doctor Muir, it is *never* disabled—unless someone deliberately switches it off. That would mean lifting the metal hood, thumbing the switch, and replacing the hood as it is now."

"Maybe I hit it with my foot while I was fighting it for control?"

Crockett shook his head. "Not unless your feet have opposable thumbs."

"Then what? How could it have gotten flipped? Unless Slipjack—"

"*Jesus Christ, Sean!*"

"—disabled it when he was up here loading the gun," Sean finished, undeterred.

"Did anyone see him up here with you?" Mickey asked, a bit remotely, keeping his distance after the revelation of murder made the night before, and now more than half of the competition for the Bentneus Prize just being blown to bits by the very same man. A man who was in prison for killing his wife.

"I—I don't know. They were all watching the sharks trying to sink the yachts, looking out to sea rather than up here. The gun was the only thing I could think of to save the yachts—I only wish I had thought of it sooner."

"Yeah, I bet," Crockett said.

"What the hell does that mean?"

Crockett shrugged. "That switch doesn't just flip off without someone intentionally doing it. Your foot wouldn't even reach it, Doctor Muir. *You* had to switch it off. Why, I don't know, but I bet a lot of the crew and the law are gonna see lots of motive in you 'accidentally' killing fifty people or so. People who were your competitors—and are now, way conveniently, eliminated."

"No! Slipjack must have done it when he was showing me how to use the gun! It's *Slipjack* who just killed all these people!"

Crockett looked at Sean with the most violent disgust Muir had ever seen. "I'll go ask the crew—and Slipjack—whether anybody was with you up here. Who knows? Maybe this was a plan all along."

"None of those fishermen were a serious threat to our success—"

"And yet, they're dead. At your hand. Them and the other crew most likely to bag the Gigadon, the one from UC San Diego. You want that billion dollars."

Mickey exchanged a meaningful look with Sean. Mickey knew what Sean wanted was *freedom*; the money would just be a nice cherry on top. But he remained quiet. He *did* still have loyalty to his friend.

Crockett made for the ladder, fire in his belly. "You can forget about that prize money, Doc. Bentneus will call off this contest as soon as word of entrants' deaths reach him." He continued down the ladder and out of sight.

"Well, ain't this a fine mess."

"Mick, you got to believe me—this was a total accident!"

"I don't know what to believe anymore, man. We all want to win, but you just committed a one-man My Lai out there. You killed, God, fifty at the *least*."

"It wasn't my fault. It was an *accident*. If Crockett had been up here, he could've saved people. But he couldn't get his bearded ass out of his bunk in time. That gave Slipjack a new chance to betray me—"

Sean saw Mickey's fist fly from out of nowhere right at his jaw; the whole world went white for a second, a horrendous *bonk!* filling his skull. Suddenly woozy, he hit the deck—the roof of the bridge—falling with his whole body.

"Don't say that name to me again, goddamnit. *Not* one *more time*. Not until we have this shit cleared up."

From the deck, his lip cracked and his jaw bruised, Sean nodded.

"And you know what else, Sean? I'm starting to wonder for the first time if you aren't *really* the one who killed Kat. I'll work with you for this mission, but after that I'm done with you. One way or the other, you're a *murderer*. A sociopath, too. No wonder Kat wanted to leave you." With that, Mickey visibly restrained himself from strangling his mission director right there and then and stomped off to the ladder. Sean lay there, feeling broken into pieces by Mick's punch and the fall, but for all that pain, his mind raced, thinking how he could keep Bentneus—and the American authorities in charge of this part of the ocean—from calling off the mission.

***

Messaging Jake Bentneus was the surest way of contacting him and getting a reply. His voice, such as it was, was reedy and very difficult to understand in person, let alone on the telephone. He could use his special eye-movement-based typing apparatus to operate and instruct a Web-connected computer in a fashion similar to texting on a cell phone, but his pride kept him from using it much.

In the time since the Bentneus Prize competition had begun, the man himself didn't have a whole lot to do, not much to "talk" about anyway other than his rapidly failing corporeal being. Most of the time he was awake, he watched cable news and discussed with his staff or the occasional celebrity visitor what was going on in the race to kill Gigadon; the 24-hour news networks had ramped up the profile of the story, putting it at the top and bottom of the hour and showing footage taken from the boats themselves as well as the occasional helicopter popping over. (They were not encouraged to stay after they had gotten their footage, the sailors thinking it would scare off the dinosaur.)

The actual competition followed dwindling discussion and news about Bentneus's speech, the billion-dollar prize, and whether anyone could actually catch or kill a "Gigadon"—or if such a creature even existed. That morning-show speculation had put Bentneus in a bad, bad mood.

No, Gigadon doesn't exist, Bentneus thought. *I attacked my own submersible with myself inside. The giant head and jaw of the dinosaur were CGI effects—or maybe even practical effects, since almost everyone on each of the ships saw what happened. NO WAY could Gigadon exist.*

Jackasses.

This morning, though, there was fresh action and, thus, fresh coverage. An aide who had authorization to enter the room as needed woke Bentneus up—he slept and woke at practically random times, his body having the same demands at all hours of the day and night, since the only change he experienced was new pieces of him failing to operate. The aide alerted him that he had an urgent message from Mickey Luch, who was stationed on *I Spit on Your Grave*:

MUIR JUST KILLED 50 PEOPLE WHEN SHOOTING AT SHARKS.

WHAT SHOULD WE DO? CANCEL THE MISSION?

"Tuhhhrn on the newssss ..." He was barely understandable, his artificial lungs having to work harder and harder to keep a steady pressure of air traveling over his larynx. The wheezing speech lent him an ever-more-pervasive appearance of decay and approaching death.

His aide swept up the remote control and pressed the button for CNN.

Oh, boy, Bentneus thought, impressed: this was definitely the story of the day. The news anchors must have been sitting in pools of their own sexual arousal, so hyped up were they that this *billion-dollar* competition to *hunt and kill a dinosaur* was exploding right in front of the entire world. It was manna to the 24-hour news channels ... which was all of them these days.

Here's what the newsholes were saying: In pursuing the Bentneus Prize, entrants' efforts had gone haywire in several different ways. Most all of the smaller fishing-boat contestants had joined together in an effort to use sheer numbers to catch Gigadon. They hunted it using techniques as they would have if it were just an enormous shark—chum and stirring up the water and all that. The only difference was scale—*huge* amounts were poured into the sea, the better to catch a *huge* predator with. But what they got was every goddamn regular-sized shark (some of which were giant themselves) in that teeming-with-sharks section of ocean.

Almost thirty boats were lost, since they were small and susceptible to capsizing when hit with the force of, say, a shark in the midst of a feeding frenzy. And the sharks were primed for feeding, so no survivors were found by Sea & Air Rescue helicopters that rushed to the area from their base in Guam. The whole fiasco was an idiotic act performed by people who maybe were very competent in their area, fishing—even to enter the competition, they must have made big money from commercial angling—but were total nitwits who had no idea what to do when faced with what they were actually supposed to be hunting. *They wouldn't know a Gigadon from a goddamn Eustreptospondylus*, thought an annoyed Bentneus.

But they didn't deserve to die. Nobody deserved to die. *He* sure as hell didn't deserve to die, but there he was.

Gigadon was a different story, of course. Bentneus's facial servos weren't powered up right then, but if they had been, they would have pulled his face into a big smile as he thought about how that big bastard *did* deserve to die, and very soon.

Essentially, many of the smaller competitors had ganged up to get the monster and split the booty, but instead called over every shark around, and those sharks then frenzied, destroyed the boats, and ate the people.

Terrible, but not spectacular enough to keep the interest of the ADD newsrooms.

Topping the "scores eaten by sharks" story was the piece on the actions of Bentneus's supposed ace in the hole, convicted murderer Sean Muir, and his shooting of more than forty-five people. The "victims" (that seemed a premature label, Bentneus thought) onboard the two largest ships in that grouping were both sunk by the machine gun's heavy artillery. The talking heads had all the gruesome details a cud-chewing public could want. Muir had reportedly opened up on the sharks—*or was it on the boats?* (their question)—with a Mark II forward .50 caliber M2 machine gun, *allegedly* (their word) in an attempt to kill the sharks surrounding those vessels. No matter what his motive (their word, again), Muir had single-handedly killed almost four dozen competitors for the Bentneus Prize.

Much of this information came from captured radio transmissions between Muir's communications crew onboard *Sea Legs* and Sea & Air Rescue command, and CNN reported that it relied on "citizen journalists" aboard some of the few ships remaining in the hunt. The sources claimed to be frightened that Sean Muir would turn the heavily armed *I Spit on Your Grave* upon *them* next.

Those same "journalists" (in addition to ones from every alphabet-soup news network ever to appear by satellite receiver) had been calling for hours, apparently, while Bentneus slept his shallow sleep. His representatives, to a person, told the media that Mister Bentneus was in conference with his top advisors to fashion the best response to this horrible tragedy, etc. and so on, and that he would issue a statement later in the day, once more facts were known. (The usual bullshit that he paid them to spew, in other words. They were getting a bonus for this hazardous duty, Bentneus decided, *if* everyone got through it with more than the shirts on their backs. Or, in his case, the pressure suit that kept his artificial organs from falling out. *Ha. Ha.*)

"Nancy Grace is calling for Muir to be extraordinarily renditioned from his ship and brought to Guantanamo for some 'enhanced interrogation,'" the aide said, not without a touch of snark.

Bentneus liked that. "Whhhat do the lawyersss sssay?"

"Actually, sir, I have your lead attorney waiting just outside the room. I'll bring him in?"

"Yehhhhsss ..."

The Bentneus Prize organization retained its own top-shelf legal counsel, and Lance Boyle was the best—and most expensive, not that the expense mattered to the immobilized billionaire. Boyle followed the aide to Jake Bentneus's bedside. In ten seconds or so, the immaculately coiffured and bespoke-suited Boyle nodded hello to each man and got right to work. "It is my understanding that no one knows for sure if Doctor Muir was trying to kill the sharks and save those two boats and their crews, or if he was trying to eliminate them, is that correct?

"Yehhhhhhhsss …"

"Excellent. We are relying on all the sources CNN has—more, actually—and they say it looked like Muir had completely lost control of the machine gun, and it was shooting wildly all over the place. *The machine gun* sank not only those two boats, but a couple of support boats from other expeditions, including the main vessel from the Cousteau Society's team.

"But with him being a convicted killer and all, others say they're sure that he was out to kill and thin out the competition, wanting to get the Gigadon before anyone else with any chance could even launch their submersibles."

"Whyyyyyyy … yyyyyy … "

"Mister Bentneus? Sir, are you all right?" Bentneus's aide gave his employer a look of concern.

"Tekkkkksssssst …"

The aide paused for a moment, not understanding the word, then said, "Oh, *text!* Of course, sir—it must be much more manageable for you to use your eye scanner."

Bentneus's gaze had to linger on a character on the virtual keyboard below the monitor for one half-second for it to register and allow him to move to the next letter, so any interlocutor would have to be patient while communicating with the filmmaker.

"Sorry, Mister Boyle, it takes a little while."

"No problem. I've had several conversations like this remotely, on my cell phone, with Mister Bentneus during his, em, *decline*. Also, don't forget that I am remunerated by the hour." The lawyer's smile made the aide's skin crawl. This made him confident that Boyle was a *very* good lawyer, indeed.

Eventually, Bentneus's message appeared on the larger green-text-on-black-background monitor facing them on the other side of his communication setup:

WHY WOULD MUIR SINK THE TWO COMMERCIAL SHIPS? THEY HAD NO CHANCE OF BEATING HIM.

"I can't think of a reason," Boyle said, "but, then, I also don't know why he would be firing a big gun that he plainly didn't know how to control.

"As bad as this sounds, blasting those two irrelevant boats out of the water could show that he did not do any of this with intent to weed out the competition."

A moment passed. Then, on the monitor:

CRIMINAL CHARGES AHEAD?

"Because the whole incident took place in American-controlled waters surrounding both Guam and the Marianas area, the United States is the only country that can arrest Doctor Muir for the deaths and destruction of property. There might be, however, public pressure to indict him and let a jury decide if the incident was murder, manslaughter, or just a horrible accident. Also, the nations where the sunken boats were registered, not to mention the nations from which the victims hailed, could very well call for his extradition to their countries for trial."

WELL SHIT

Boyle smiled again. "Don't lose faith in the United States just yet, Mister Bentneus. The U.S. has the authority not only to ignore domestic public pressure, of course, but also the special pleading of any other country. This is because, unlike almost every other seafaring nation in the world, the United States never actually *signed on* to the UN Convention of the Law of the Sea. That document is the go-to legal reference on alleged crimes at sea, especially in international waters. Because our country never became an official signee, and because the incident occurred in American waters, the U.S. is under no obligation to arrest Doctor Muir for prosecution anywhere in the world. We usually *do* cooperate with those other nations, but it's not automatic by any means. And this competition is of worldwide importance, its aim being to rid the oceans of"—Boyle motioned to Bentneus's elaborate life-support system—"what has proven to be a threat to human life and liberty on the seas."

GOD BLESS THE USA
WE NEED HIM TO FINISH THE MISSION

"Indeed, and I believe the monetary interests of every nation's participants would hold up any indictment until after the Bentneus Prize is won. The fact that he was just released from prison for causing a death, if not outright murdering his wife, is immaterial because he's not on parole or probation. He is as free as you or I ... he cannot be sent back to prison without an indictment and trial for committing some new crime."

LIKE MURDERING 50 PEOPLE?

"We don't know how many, if any, people were killed directly by the ordnance being shot by Doctor Muir. We don't know how many, if any, people died as a result of the boats sinking, such as by drowning or electrocution. And although the people who ended up in the water *were* eaten by sharks because of the failure of their vessels, I believe it could be successfully argued that the victims themselves created the conditions that ended in their deaths. In any case, the *sharks* killed them, not Sean Muir."

GOOD WORK THANK YOU

"It is my pleasure, Mister Bentneus," Boyle said. "Even in a worst-case scenario, Doctor Muir would not be arrested or indicted before the mission has concluded, whether in success or failure."

FAILURE IM NOT CONCERNED ABOUT
HE GOES BACK TO PRISON FOR LIFE THEN FOR YOU KNOW WHAT

Boyle's eyes grew wide for a moment, then he dropped his gaze to his briefcase, which suddenly needed fiddling with. "I certainly do *not* know what, Mister Bentneus. But, taking your lack of concern about legal ramifications following a possible failure of the mission into consideration, I will direct my team to focus on keeping him free and unencumbered by legal issues until the mission is concluded, and then afterwards if he is successful."

YES THAT IS ALL I MEANT OF COURSE
THANK YOU LANCE

Still visibly shaken, Boyle nodded to Bentneus and the aide and made for the door before anything else incriminating could be suggested.

The aide laughed. "Yes, sir, this is the morning. Muir is headed down to kill your Gigadon and bring his bloody head back home."

THEN I CAN DIE HAPPY

"Oh, sir, no, don't talk like that ..."

ARE YOU KIDDING? I AM COUNTING THE SECONDS

***

Two hundred miles from Bentneus's hospital room, Mickey Luch and his team were filling the bathysphere of *Ocean Vengeance* with the perfluorochemical liquid. Holly and Orville from the science ship were there on *Spit* to supervise.

Holly spoke through the opening at the top of the iron sphere, since Sean would still be able to hear her, and she wanted him to actually hear a human's words before this alien dive into alien waters: "When the level reaches your helmet, just count the seconds, then take a deep breath of the water. It'll be a shock at first, but don't resist it—get it into your lungs as quickly as humanly possible."

"Otherwise an instant pulmonary embolism will kill you," Orville added, but fortunately he wasn't near enough to the opening for Sean to hear him. Holly could hear, however, and gave Popcorn a damned sharp *swat*.

"All you need to do is breathe—if Gigadon or any of the rest of them come after your heat signature a little too quickly, we can pull you up faster without giving you the bends or turning you inside out."

"That is a good thing," Sean said, his nervousness and excitement betraying his attempt at a calm demeanor. "I've never actually seen any of my dinosaurs in the flesh. I've known for a long time that they were there, had to be there, but ..." His throat was closing up with emotion.

"You'll see them, boss. Now get ready to breathe like a fish. See you topside."

The not-exactly-water level inside the bathysphere was to Sean's chin now. Then over his chin, then his mouth—*should I start trying to breathe the water yet?* He decided to wait until the liquid rose over his nostrils and he would had no choice.

The liquid rose over his nostrils and, going against hundreds of millions of years of evolution, he took a deep breath.

Gah! Baccch! Shit! The oxygen-saturated chemical brew was *cold*—it was cold while it had been filling up the bathysphere, but his well-insulated diving suit spared him from the temperature—and at once his system tried to reject the entire attempt. But he held any bile down, feeling right on the edge of panic, and let out that first lungful of liquid breath.

Then he took another breath. In and out.

Then another.

Then he was just breathing. His body warmth compensated for the cold very quickly, and he knew the fluids surrounding him would warm up as the constant temperature maintained in the bathysphere rose back to stasis levels.

"Mickey here. This is it, Sean," came through his earpiece. "Do you read me?"

Sean raised a thumb. It felt weird to be underwater—the bathysphere was just about topped off, and they would be closing the hatch to keep the pressure at the right level—but now he was also full of water. He was now *Homo piscis*.

"Roger that. Now say something back to us so we know we can read you."

Sean remembered that any speech he tried to use would be completely incoherent because air would no longer be flowing over his larynx, as his whole respiratory system was now filled with liquid. That's why they had their robust communications computers. Sean typed:

I ROGER YOUR ROGERING. ROGER THAT. LOL.

He could hear the smile in Mickey's voice when the mission chief said, "Excellent. We read up here that all weapons are armed and all cameras and microphones are functional. It's a beautiful, perfectly calm day, as you can see through your little porthole, and so we're a *go* for submersion."

Again, Sean gave them a thumbs-up.

"Winch is raising you in three, two, one, *go*."

Ocean Vengeance shook a little as its greater weight challenged the winch slightly—but only slightly. But the stab of icy panic in his chest wasn't because of the shaking.

WHO IS OPERATING THE WINCH?

Mickey said in a flat tone, "Jesus, Sean, who do you think? *Slipjack* is. He's doing his job—y'know, *operating the winch*."

IS HE BEING MONITORED?

"*Sea Legs* has a dedicated camera on the winch and a dedicated crew member watching the monitor. Now pay attention, or I'll cut the goddamn cable myself."

SORRY, MICK.

Mickey took a deep, cleansing breath and let his frustration leave his body along with the carbon dioxide. "All good, Sean. Now why don't we act like you're *Doctor Muir*, the scientist, not the psychopath, okay? How are the instruments reading?"

ALL ARE GO.
THE LIFT FEELS EVEN.
GO FOR IMMERSION?

"Go for immersion," Mickey said, and relayed the command over the shared comm to the winch crew, *Sea Legs*, and *Sharkasm*. He put his hand over the microphone and said to Holly and Popcorn, "Thanks for coming over here. I need you to monitor his vitals—and the submersible's, too."

The geeks smiled. Holly said, "We could've done that from *Sharkasm*, Chief."

Mickey had shared their smile, but now it quivered and disappeared. "This whole mission is cursed. I know you science types don't go for sailors' superstitions, but I want you near me, here in the command center. I don't want to lose contact with you on the science boat."

"Chief Luch," Popcorn said, as usual unable to address him casually, "if you think you're going to lose *Sharkasm*, don't you have an obligation to bring the entire crew onto *Sea Legs* and this ship?"

"I don't *think* anything, Orville. I *feel*."

"I see. And, by definition, *feeling* is subjective experience lacking specific quantitative content."

"Sure." Mickey tapped into the camera feed on Slipjack and the winch. Nothing looked particularly sinister—but then, everything had gone smoothly with Kat's final dive until the damaged part of the cable came about. But there was nothing to be gained by thinking about that now. "Just tell me what you see, dinosaur-wise, and if something's going haywire with Sean or the submersible, okay?"

"Roger that," Popcorn said, sounding as much like a seafaring cove as he would a superstar rapper.

I hate everybody, Mickey said, and took another deep breath. How cleansing it was, he couldn't say, but at least he could concentrate again without dorks tempting him to throw himself overboard.

***

The world outside *Ocean Vengeance* darkened quickly. The extra weight allowed *Spit* to descend much more quickly than had the other submersibles trying to pull off this trick of reaching the bottom of Challenger Deep.

Unlike those missions, however, Sean Muir didn't give a rat's ass about historic dives—he was going down to keep Kat's death from being in vain, to confirm his theories with his own eyes, and to kill whatever he needed to kill to stay out of a prison where he never should have been in the first place.

Kat's death had not been his fault. Slipjack must have introduced some flaw into the cable sometime during the manufacturing process, a flaw which became apparent only once it was unspooled. *How* the little freak did it, Sean couldn't begin to guess; he knew only that he, Sean, had had nothing to do with it. They had tested the cable in every environment under the sea—freshwater, saltwater, laboratory conditions mimicking the PSI it would encounter at the bottom. No matter what the water conditions, the cable had remained coherent. It spooled back wet but completely operational.

There was no explanation except that Slipjack, wanting to get Sean out of the way to fulfill his pathetic dream of romancing Kat, had induced some split in the cable, every inch of which had been run through the harshest conditions before going on the giant spool. They *did* test the whole thing—there was nothing wrong with it at all. *How* Slipjack did what he did remained a mystery.

He put the whole thing out of his mind for now. He had descended amazingly quickly to the dysphotic zone, which monsters passed through on their way to kill near the surface. He typed:

WE'RE MAKING REALLY GOOD TIME.

Mickey responded, "We sure are. I don't know how fast we'll be able to haul you up with the liquid inside the sphere, but it'll be a hell of a lot faster than we could do without it." *Because it would kill you in the most painful way possible.*

Almost involuntarily, Mickey's eyes flitted to the winch monitor: nothing untoward there, Slipjack and his team watching the cable carefully—*very* carefully—as it unspooled, in position to stop the winch before any flaw got to the point where the cable couldn't be respooled and *Ocean Vengeance* brought back up.

That could be a ruse, though. Just *looking* like he was taking care.

Oh, for God's sake, man—you sound just like Sean now. Cut it out.

He nodded at his own thoughts and said to Holly, "How we doing? Anything out of the ordinary?"

"All systems seem to be working fine. The temperature is at the low point one would expect below the euphotic zone, but the submersible hasn't picked up the heat signature of the hydrothermal vents yet. It's not close enough."

"All right, good."

"You know, it's funny," Popcorn said, making Mickey and Holly turn their heads. "The Bentneus expedition, the Muir expedition— neither one ever made it all the way to the bottom. The 1960 *Trieste* dive as part of Project Nekton is still the only vessel to touch the very deepest part of Marianas Trench, the others ending in failure and tragedy."

"Yeah, hilarious," Mickey said. "That really helps alleviate my sense of doom. Thanks."

"I offer that merely as an obser—"

"We get you, Popcorn," Holly interrupted. "Maybe just work on your social interaction skills after we get done with this mission, 'kay?"

"I roger you," he said, and returned to observing the logical computer readouts and the submersible's thermosensitive-camera monitors, things that made sense.

Holly didn't have a whole lot to do at this point, Popcorn being in charge of science-related computer operations and there being nothing unknown yet to identify via her database uplink.

Nothing to do but wait.

Her blood ran icily through her system. She dared not speak it out loud—and was surprised a veteran mariner like Mickey had done exactly that—but her thoughts were clouded, too, by a pervasive dread of what would happen before they got back to shore.

She had watched the shark feeding frenzy along with everyone else, so she amended her thought:

If they got back to shore at all.

***

At the winch, Slipjack McCracken watched every inch of the cable unspool. It was moving faster than he would have liked, what with *Ocean Vengeance* descending full of that heavy-as-water breathing fluid.

But he could still keep up. He called Vanessa over to watch while he splashed in eyedrops every ten minutes or so. The salty air felt like it was burning right through his eyes. It was counterintuitive (actually, Slipjack's thought was "didn't make a thimbleful of piss's sense"), but salt-rich air could sometimes actually be more damaging than salt water, because of the constant wind adding to the salt's corrosive effect.

Slipjack paused, the Visine bottle still poised over his left eye. Something was floating inside his brain. There was something with the air, the salt air ...

"Chief, come in. Mickey, come in."

"Copy, Slipjack. What do you want?"

"Do any of the geeks have a magnifying glass?"

"A *what?*"

"A magnifying glass. You know, like Sherlock Holmes."

Popcorn said, "In the Conan Doyle stories, Sherlock didn't actually use—"

Holly cut him off and said to Mickey, "I'm sure we have one, but it's on *Sharkasm.*"

Slipjack heard her. "I think I know what caused the cable to come apart during Kat's dive! I need a magnifying glass, like, *right now.*"

"We're in the middle of a goddamn dive, Slipjack," Mickey said, his black mood not getting any lighter with the winch chief's going over ancient history.

"Exactly! Sean—Doctor Muir—whatever—could be in danger. *Serious* danger."

"Oh, and that would leave you heartbroken."

"Chief, I think I've realized what happened to Kat—"

"*You and Sean* happened to Kat."

"*Goddamnit! Shut your face* and get me a magnifying glass unless you want another disaster on your hands, you goddamn mook!"

He's serious, or he's a really good actor, Mickey thought, and covered the mic again to say to Holly, "We can't exactly send a jolly boat over to *Sharkasm* in the middle of a dangerous dive. Can you guys check all the drawers? Somebody's *got* to use a magnifying glass for maps and charts and shit."

Holly, Popcorn, and every crew member within hearing started pulling open drawers and rifling through cabinets. It took about twenty seconds to find a huge glass, five inches across at least. "Got it!" Popcorn shouted.

Mickey called to Holly, "I'll take it to Slipjack—you mind the comm."

"Roger that."

Mickey grabbed the magnifying glass from Popcorn and double-timed it to the aft of the ship, where the winch was letting out cable at a rapid pace. He put it in Slipjack's hand, and the winch chief immediately put it above the unspooling cable with his eye right up to the glass.

"Before I get pissed—even *more* pissed—tell me what's going on, Slipjack."

"I ain't a scientist, but I just had a You Ricky moment."

Eureka, *you dummy*, Mickey thought but just said, "Is that right? Is it something like, 'Hey, I just found evidence that Sean Muir murdered his wife after all'? 'Cause if it is, I *do not* want to hear another word. I'm about to stick the two of you in a lifeboat and let you fight it out to the death. Then *I'm* gonna kill whoever wins."

"Naw, man, there's a hairline crack in the cable. I can see it go by as the cable advances. We got to stop the whole thing."

"Why would there be a crack in the cable ... unless you put it there."

"*What?* Why would I do that?"

"Revenge, because you think Sean killed Kat."

"Would everybody *please* stop saying that? It's the stupidest thing I ever heard. Yeah, I hate that son of a bitch because Kat and me was in love. But I'm not gonna throw my life away on a skirt! I'm not a murderer—hell, this shows *nobody* murdered *nobody!* Look for yourself!"

Mickey took the magnifying glass from Slipjack's reddened hands while not taking his eyes off the winch chief's. Slowly he bent and looked through the cable passing through his field of vision.

"I don't see anything, Slipjack."

"You don't know the cable good enough," Slipjack said. "Look right in the middle, where the seam is? Then look just below it. There's a narrow crack right below it—it ain't quite even, see?"

Mickey did see. "All right, what does it mean? And if you say one goddamn word about Sean Muir doing this, I'll call Sea & Air Rescue to come and pick up a certain crew member who somehow got his jaw broken."

"It means that nobody did a thing to this cable. It's a flaw in the cable's own self—the whole damn thing has a crack running through it, start to finish, I bet."

Mickey stood again and handed the glass back to Slipjack. Then he said, "That cable was inspected, all 40,000 feet of it, before we left port. There was *nothing* wrong with it. It went through the saltwater test with every science and engineering team member watching it. That took *hours*, and they had magnification equipment like nothing you've seen. They pronounced it to be completely without any flaw, and they sure as hell would've noticed a hairline crack running through the whole damned thing. Care to explain that, Mister Winch Chief, the only person to have continuous access to this cable since it left the shop?"

"Toro and Vanessa had access to it, too. But they didn't do nothing to it, neither."

"I'm getting short of time *and* patience, McCracken."

"The iron armor did fine in the saltwater tests, and it was spooled when it was still wet, right?"

Mickey just waited, not saying a word.

"*Right* is the answer to that. But when it gets exposed to the sea air, the salty-ass sea air, it's still a little wet and the strong wind out here blows just enough corrosive crap to make the iron oxidate—"

"*Oxidize.*"

"You lost your *mind*, man? Who gives a shit! What I'm saying is the combo of moist iron combined with salty wind starts a crack as the cable unwinds into that wind. Enough crack, enough strain, and it'll open like a zipper."

"But just on our expeditions."

"What?"

"This shit didn't happen to Bentneus when he went all the way to the bottom. No problem with the cable whatsoever." He shook his head and turned to go back to the bridge and the mission.

But Slipjack got ahold of his shoulder and spun him back around. Before Mickey could even clench a fist, Slipjack shouted in his face, "*Sean and Kat developed this cable! It's patented! It ain't the same as what Bentneus used, man!*"

Mickey's anger and desire to engage in imminent violence slid away like raindrops on a window. In their stead was fear and dread. It wasn't Slipjack who damaged the cable when Kat got killed. It wasn't Sean, either, despite his trying to get Mickey to believe he was a murderer or just a garden-variety psychopath.

The whole goddamn thing was an accident.

"Slipjack, I …"

"Yeah, whatever—I'm stopping the winch—you get in there and call this shit off!"

"You know you're giving up millions of dollars with this. We both are."

"I ain't givin' up *nothing!* There's no way he's gonna be able to lure the dinosaur to the surface if the cable splits! We got to cut our losses, Chief!"

Mickey hesitated a moment—Sean "cutting his losses" meant the rest of his life would be spent in prison—but had to agree with Slipjack that they needed to stop immediately. Life was better than death, no matter where you spent it, wasn't it?

***

Breathing the perfluorocarbon liquid, heavier than air but suffused with oxygen, gave Sean Muir a pleasant feeling, like the relaxation of being high on pot mixed with the absolute clarity of perfect wakefulness. It was still dark outside the bathysphere, but the illuminated snow of detritus made him feel like he was inside a Currier & Ives Christmas card. However, he still remembered to check all his instruments and knew the exact sequence in which he was to execute the (he hoped) Gigadon-attracting measures. All was well—

He felt very heavy for a moment, then returned to normal. The snow outside seemed to be falling more quickly than before. He checked his depth. The number remained unchanged at 27,455 feet.

Ocean Vengeance had stopped descending. It was dangling, completely still, more than five miles below the surface, yet almost two miles above where he needed to be. "*Spit.* Come in, *I Spit on Your Grave.* This is Muir." The whole thing was kind of redundant for him to say, since his comm line was dedicated to communicating only with Mickey, who was of course on *Spit.*

"Copy, Sean. Let me—"

"Why am I stopped? Are you aware that the submersible has stopped? I'm too far up to shoot the missiles or even give Gigadon a whiff of heat."

"I'm the one that stopped you, boss."

"What? Well, get me going again!"

"There's a problem with the cable, Sean. It's developed a hairline crack, and Slipjack thinks it might cause the cable to lose integrity and snap, just like … um, just like *before.*"

"*Slipjack* said this."

"Roger."

"Restart the descent, Mick. Slipjack is trying to keep me from my goal."

"I saw the crack with my own eyes. It's too dangerous. We're gonna have to pull you back up."

"Jesus, Mick, *you know what that means.*"

"I do, boss, but you could very likely die if that cable splits."

"I'll take that chance. Restart the goddamn descent."

"I can't, Sean. It would be, at best, negligent homicide. That's twenty years in prison—"

"That's where you're sending me, you son of a bitch! Forever!"

"I'm sorry, boss, I really am ..." This was followed by the click of *Spit*'s comm mic being turned off.

That heaviness hit Sean again as *Ocean Vengeance* was tugged back up toward the surface. *No, no, NO! NO! NO!*

He was in full panic mode, now, with no idea what to do. He couldn't go back without Gigadon, without that big monster's head on a pike. *He couldn't go back to prison.* That would truly be worse than death.

His pleasant high now thoroughly extinguished, he scanned the instrument panels, the various locks and switches and circular levers, looking for anything that could help him. Finally, his eyes caught sight of a code-locked glass door, striped yellow and black to indicate *danger*:

CABLE RELEASE

Death would be better than going back to prison.

If they brought him back up now without Gigadon, he would go back to prison and likely never leave, since "chomos" didn't exactly receive the best treatment from their fellow prisoners.

Or maybe he would go to Death Row for killing forty-five fishermen, which definitely *felt* like an accident to Sean. Maybe it wasn't an accident. He couldn't tell anymore and it made no difference right then. Death Row *might* happen even if he *did* manage to bag the dinosaur. But prison was *certain* if he didn't.

He *would* descend to Gigadon. He would tempt him, somehow, to follow him.

He punched in the code—his four-digit birthday (security on that switch not a high priority during a dive)—opened the glass door, and yanked down on the lever inside.

Suddenly he felt *lighter* ... and the snow of a million dead sea creatures slowed down, then actually seemed to rise in relation to *Ocean Vengeance*.

He was descending again. Free-falling, really, although the density of the water kept his acceleration nominal. He would drift to the bottom, the liquid filling the bathysphere acting as extra ballast to cast him down, down, to the lair of Nothosaurus, of Megalodon ... of *Gigadon*.

He would figure out what to do once he got there.

***

Vanessa almost got her face whipped off by the suddenly loosened cable, the winch whirring at high speed now that its cargo had been cut loose. She fell backward as Toro ran forward, the two of them slamming together and knocking the wind out of both of them.

"Jesus God, what the hell did you do?" Slipjack shouted at them, running from the bridge, where he had listened to Mickey break the bad news to Muir. Of *course* Muir didn't believe anything Slipjack had to say, but *Mickey?* The boss thought *Mickey Luch* was against him? And what was with that whole going back to prison 'forever' shit? Slipjack had no idea what was happening, and seeing the winch go crazy just made it worse.

He knew Vanessa and Toro hadn't done anything—the cable must have snapped when they followed Mickey's order to stop the descent *immediately*. Toro had been at the controls and Vanessa had been doing the observation of the cable and winch to make sure it was actually stopping the submersible's downward progress. When the cable became separated, the winch was still pulling, and with nothing to provide an opposite force, the whole thing went into the serious recoil that almost removed Vanessa's face.

Mickey's face went slack, his mouth actually hanging open for a moment.

"What happened? What just happened?" Holly said as she rushed up to confirm what the instruments all told her—that they had lost *Ocean Vengeance*. The instruments had told her by all going out at once; the cable carried all data and communications, so now they had no contact and no way of knowing if Sean Muir was alive or dead.

"How will we know when the Gigadon is coming?" Holly asked Mickey and Popcorn and anyone else who might know anything at all. "We have to light up the maser, right, Mick? We have to get the cannon loaded with the Honeycomb, don't we? *It could be here any minute!*"

Mickey grabbed the panicking scientist by the shoulders and held her still. "Let's do all that, okay? I'll get Crockett on it right now, all right? But that's just to make us all feel better, Hol. I really don't think Gigadon is coming. Sean won't be able to leave a heat trail now for it to follow. Unless one of the other competitors is baiting ... it ..." He looked out through the window at the empty sea around them, not another vessel in sight, no fishing boats, no well-equipped academic teams, no (other) rich asshole's fleet of expensive ships ... nothing. "Except there are no other competitors."

They were alone. They were the only ones left, and they weren't going to win the Bentneus Prize, not with Sean Muir joining his wife at the bottom of the ocean, trapped in a bathysphere that would, like Kat's, serve as his coffin.

"Still, let's get Crockett to arm everything we've got. Why not?" He made the calls on the comm to get the ordnance teams ready; it wasn't like it was going to hurt anything ... so long as Crockett remembered to keep that anti-feedback switch turned on. "It's too late to save Sean and the rest, but ..."

Tears streamed down Holly's face as she silently wept. "Every time ... *every* time ... I can't do this ever again, Mickey. They just *keep dying.*"

Mickey put an arm around her. "This is dangerous, experimental work. These things happen. We ... we ..." he said, trying hard to keep talking, to comfort Holly, but he broke down and sobbed with her, leaning on her as she leaned on him.

With no information coming from the submersible, the bridge was as quiet as the deep.

"This mission *is* cursed," Popcorn said in a low voice, the first nonmaterialist opinion he had ever expressed.

* * *

Freedom.

Sean Muir didn't know how drifting to the bottom of the ocean was freedom, but it felt that way nonetheless. The liquid he was breathing inside the bathysphere would stay oxygenated for several more hours, at least, before he used it all up. So he could watch the sinking biomass pass by in the aphotic darkness, lit only by the lamps of *Ocean Vengeance.*

Because of Jake Bentneus's brilliant vertical design of *Ocean Victory*—on which Sean's own submersible's was of course directly based—the submersible stayed almost true as it fell and fell. Sean saw on the monitors from the cameras on the bottom of the vessel that it was still pitch-black below him, but soon enough he would see the pale yellow of the hydrothermals that were home to his dinosaurs.

His dinosaurs. Not Jake Bentneus's, not Kat's, not Mickey's. He knew they were there long before anyone else. He *knew.*

He would join them soon. If only for a few minutes before the vents boiled him or he settled down on the bottom and ran out of oxygen, he would join his discoveries, extinct and yet still alive. Then he would die, join Kat in death, and the creatures would continue their impossible existence, the best-funded expedition ever attempted unable to reduce their number by even one.

It was a shame he never got to use any of the toys built into *Ocean Vengeance*. He had lasers, concussion-grenade mini-torpedoes, even missiles pointed in the eight cardinal directions, at the top of the submersible, and even a couple on the bottom.

Smiling a dreamy smile, Sean broke the darkness of the deep for a few seconds by shooting the laser in a random direction. The true extent of the drifting organic matter was revealed by its reflecting the laser's path all the way to the vanishing point. He knew the laser wasn't powerful enough to kill, although it could burn the flesh of anything coming too near, make the curious or hungry creature back off and give him up as a bad job.

He shot it a few more times, aiming it here and there in the darkness. It was entertaining ... but there were other ways to pass the time until he joined his friends at the bottom. He armed and sent off a concussion torpedo. Unlike the laser, it was invisible after it shot out of *Ocean Vengeance*'s sphere of light. He knew it went off only when he saw the slightest flash of light—

—and seconds later his hands flew up to his ears as the concussed wave slammed into the submersible, the loudest thing Sean had ever heard. His hands flying to his ears actually flew to the sides of his helmet, but thank God he had that on—it absorbed enough of the vibration to spare his eardrums from bursting and leaving him in agony for the last hours of his life.

"Note to self: Concussion torpedo *bad*," Sean gurgled through the water, making him laugh at the sound of his own garbled voice.

His course to the bottom had probably seriously deviated from true, but it didn't really matter; he'd get there eventually. However, he was always a scientist first and foremost—hell, wasn't that why he had taken the fall for the exercise-yard stabbing in the first place, to get his own little research office?—and so he checked the instrumentation to see what the craft's attitude was, its temperature, its distance from the bottom.

It seemed that the concussion had in fact put *Ocean Vengeance* at a 25-degree angle from the vertical, but even as he watched, the attitude monitor showed that he was drifting back toward the true. That was interesting—he must've been falling faster than he realized, which meant the depth meter was malfunctioning and he was closing the distance between himself and the hydrothermal vents.

To test this hypothesis, maybe the last of his life, he shut off all the lights inside and outside the submersible.

And there it was, something he had never seen with his own eyes: the sickly yellow glow was just visible at the bottom of his porthole. The bottomside camera confirmed it, giving a view of that beautiful tear in the fabric of mundane reality.

But why wasn't he burning up? Now that he knew the heat vents were not far below him, he did notice that he was slightly warm, but the interior temperature gauges showed a level just one degree Celsius above the norm. However, the external thermometers showed 27 degrees Celsius (80°F) and visibly climbing, just as in the Bentneus dive.

Then it occurred to him that while water (or any similar liquid) was an excellent conductor of heat, it also warmed very slowly. He thought of the frogs in the pot, who stayed quite comfortable during the gradual increase in temperature—until they boiled to death. However, in this particular pot, the temperature had risen very little because the entire bathysphere—and his lungs—were filled with the liquid perfluorocarbon.

If he kept dropping pretty much straight onto the 700-degree vent, the temperature would probably go up a tiny bit higher. Like hundreds of degrees in less than a minute. It wouldn't be a pleasant way to go, but it would be unique, that was for sure.

A shadow blocked the brightening yellow light for a few seconds. Sean's eyes turned immediately to the monitor of the camera at the bottom, and that was definitely a large shape passing below *Ocean Vengeance*. It wasn't a tube worm or the other chemosynthetic life that fed the marine lizards; this *was* a marine lizard. This *was* a dinosaur.

But which?

He flipped on all the exterior lights and scanned each of the monitors. He had never seen one of "his" creatures with his own eyes and hoped one would swim past his porthole. If he could just see one, no matter which, he could die happy as a poached human.

And there it was. *There it goddamn was!*

Megalodon.

He watched it glide by the porthole, its near-albino stripes beautiful in the yellow light from below and the white light from the sub. Sean felt tears welling in his eyes, but he didn't know if they came out in the liquid environment. But no matter—he cried at the beauty of what he had always hoped to see. He was freer in the six-foot ball of iron than he ever was in his 9' x 11' solitary cell, or at the university, or when he was a child with the whole world in front of him.

He was with his friends. He was *free*.

Then a massive concussion struck *Ocean Vengeance*, much louder than the little torpedo grenade he had set off earlier. The sub was forced hard sideways, and Sean could hear the strain on the structure. His death might be more imminent than he had even expected. The Megalodon was gone. His ears were in agony.

A quick look at the external thermometer showed a temperature spike far above what should have been the 32 degrees Celsius (90°F) of his current location several hundred feet above the vents; the temperature was remaining in the 50s Celsius and not cooling down, being more than 120 degrees Fahrenheit.

What in the holy hell was that *shit?*

***

"What in the holy hell is *that* shit?" Mickey shouted from the bridge of *I Spit on Your Grave*. Water swelled not 300 feet from the ship—and right beneath *Sea Legs*, which rose fifty feet at the crest of the sudden prominence. The shock wave of the swell rocked S*harkasm* and *Spit* almost onto their sides but passed, and they righted themselves.

When the ships regained their upright positions, those topside could see the swell deflate like a popping air pocket on a baking pie, and *Sea Legs* essentially dropped straight down, unsupported by any water, from fifty feet in the air.

Popcorn watched with horror, calculating in an instant that (not taking any wind resistance into account) *Sea Legs* would hit the water at almost forty miles per hour.

He couldn't even form a first word to tell the others before the fleet's communications ship smashed into the water, immediately broke into shards, and exploded into a mushrooming fireball. This told Popcorn that the fuel tank had been breached and blown up and had almost immediately ignited the many onboard oxygen tanks, which also erupted. That created the yellow ball of flame. The heat generated from such a blast, not to mention the outward force of the hot gases, followed quickly by the collapse of the vacuum formed when …

It was not always easy being Orville Blum.

"*Mother of God!*" Mickey screamed, instinctively throwing a forearm in front of his face. The heat from the explosion—*Sea Legs* had been just a football field's length away—singed the hair on his arm. Veteran seaman that he was, he immediately scooped up the general comm and shouted for the watch chief to radio Sea & Air Rescue *now!*

Holly, intelligent woman that she was, hit the deck immediately. She didn't need to watch *Sea Legs* hit the surface to know that it would explode and that all of the friends she had made on that boat were now dead.

Popcorn's glasses steamed, and his face heated unpleasantly as if he were staring at the sun, but the glass installed to protect the computer setup from the corrosive salt air also shielded the scientist from the worst of the blast ... at least physically. His mind was abuzz with grisly details about explosions and bodies, and those bodies were of people he knew.

In seconds, however, Mickey's question came back around: *What in the holy hell was that?*

"Chief Luch," Popcorn said, "can you feel that? The heat isn't abating. The surface thermography readout indicates this heat source— not the one from the explosion, right?—is coming from below. Something is causing a widespread temperature spike that ... *sweet flying spaghetti monster, WHAT THE FRAK IS THAT!?*"

Even in the shocked and emotional state Holly Patterson found herself in, she very nearly laughed at Popcorn's words, which were possibly the nerdiest thing she had ever heard—and her world *was* nerds. But her slight amusement gave way to jaw-dropping awe as she looked out at the water. *What in the hell ...?*

"Hol, you know what that is?" Mickey said.

Astounded, Holly shook her head, her gaze never leaving the sight in front of them.

"It's the North Koreans."

The submarine must have been rising at a steep angle, because its nose burst out of the water first, followed by the rest of the gray cigar shape as it evened out, making a grand splash. When it had settled, a head popped out of the top hatch, and the sailor raised two small flags.

"You have got to be kidding me," Mickey said, and found a pair of binoculars. He put them to his eyes. "Goddamn if they aren't using semaphore." He had used semaphore many times on fishing vessels and during replenishment operations on larger ships, but what was this, 1950?

"What are they saying?" Holly felt like her mind had been stretched like a rubber band and had now snapped back. Two minutes earlier, she had watched two dozen friends die; now she was looking at a Communist country's Soviet-surplus submarine that apparently wanted to chat with them.

"He's repeating an 'X'—that means 'Stop carrying out your intentions and watch for my signals,'" Mickey said, remembering the old codes like you remembered how to ride a bike, the International Signal Code flag positions, which didn't rely on a common language.

"'Stop carrying out your intentions'? That seems a bit ... presumptuous," Popcorn said with an offended air.

The sailor now signaled a 'U.' Mickey had to think for a moment, then he remembered: "They say 'You are running into danger.' I think we done run into it there, son."

"Wait a minute," Holly said. "They're competitors for the prize! Are they trying to scare us off?"

Mickey kept the binoculars pressed to his eyes and waved for quiet. He mouthed words with a lack of comprehension. "Okay, they're making no sense now. 'L' means 'You should stop immediately.' But 'E' means they're turning to starboard. 'A'? They have a diver down? From a sub?"

"Oh, no," Holly moaned into the hand covering her mouth. She saw where this was going.

"What the f—'V'? Now they say they require assistance. It's all contradicting itself, it's gibberish. And another 'E'—they didn't even make the first turn to starboard!"

"Mickey," Holly said.

"Now he's gone back to telling us to stop immediately. *We're not moving, you stupid asshats!*"

"Mick."

"What is with the starboard shit? Are they cra—?"

"*Mickey!*"

That snapped him out of his loop, and he pulled the binoculars from his eyes. "What, for Chrissakes?"

"They're telling us to leave. L-E-A-V-E, get it? *Leave.*"

"Wh—*ohh*, I see." He smiled, then realized what she was saying. "They're *telling* us to leave? Do we have any semaphore flags? I'm gonna tell them to shove it up their ass!"

"Um, Chief? Hold on a moment, please. I don't think that would be the wisest course of action," Popcorn said, motioning for them to come look at his bank of monitors.

"I was just kidding," Mickey said.

"I see," Popcorn said. (He did not "see," but that was not a pressing matter.) "Look here on the thermography—there is that heat rising from below, as I said. That is a mystery for the moment, yes?"

"Yes," Mickey and Holly said as one.

"No, it is *not!*" Popcorn corrected. "Correlate the ocean swell that took out our frien … um …" He cleared his throat and finished, "… our communications vessel."

Holly smiled a little. Orville really was very sweet.

"Correlate that swell with the sudden rise in heat coming from below the surface and now the appearance of our North Korean Gigadon-hunt competitors, who are telling us the area is dangerous and commanding us to leave immediately."

"I'm correlating ... I think. I got nothing. Holly?"

Their chief scientist looked like she had seen a ghost.

"Jesus, Holly, what is it?"

"The North Koreans have a fission bomb," she said.

"Exactly right!" Popcorn said with enthusiasm. "It's pretty weak. It's not even as strong as the bombs that destroyed Hiroshima and Nagasaki. Judging from the displacement of the water and the fact that the submarine that exploded it is still in one piece although almost directly above the heat source, I would estimate the explosive power at about ten kilotons. Not very powerful compared to fusion weapons or even modern fission devices, it's true, but it gives off a lot of heat."

"A lot of heat," Mickey repeated.

"Yes," Popcorn said. "There is only one conclusion I can make from this evidence—"

"The North Koreans are calling Gigadon," Holly said.

***

Seven miles below the standoff, Sean Muir was almost becoming used to being buffeted around. The concussion grenade, the giant whatever-the-hell-that-was explosion that damn near shook *Ocean Vengeance* apart, and now ... now his submersible was being spun around by the very close passing of something beyond huge, something he couldn't really take in through his porthole or the camera array.

It swept within ten feet of him and then rose sharply, actually dragging the submersible upward a bit in its wake.

"Gigadon," he gargled to himself.

Could he shoot it with the laser? No, that wouldn't do enough damage, and besides, the leviathan was too far away already.

Maybe a grenade? Or one of the eight missiles mounted on his underwater coffin? No, there was no way a missile would go fast and true enough to even catch up with the damned dinosaur, no matter how much thrust it had ...

Thrust. Newton's Third Law. Every action produces an equal and opposite reaction. That's how missiles—rockets, essentially—worked in the first place: Fuel was consumed and created a force out one side of the missile, and so it moved in the opposite direction with equal force.

This thing had *eight* missiles on it—missiles powerful enough to move through the densest water on Earth.

But what missiles *were* was *independent rockets*. But it wasn't like *Ocean Vengeance* was like a space shuttle, with booster rockets attached to it. The missiles would detach from the submersible and then take off. Unless …

Damnit, where's Crockett and Mickey when I need them? Oh, right, they're connected to that ship I uncoupled from. Brilliant.

He had worked very closely on the design of his own expedition's sub, and of course he had been heavily involved in the outfitting of *Ocean Vengeance*, but the training he received on the sub's weaponry was pretty perfunctory, since nothing he had on the vessel would really hurt an attacking ginormous dinosaur. But he had paid attention, he had listened … hadn't he listened?

Apparently not, because he had absolutely nothing.

However, what he *did* have was the waterproofed—like everything inside the purposely flooded bathysphere, of course—checklist for each of the weapons systems. The whole sub had been floating upward in the wake of the Gigadon, but now he was inching back down again toward the hydrothermal vents and his doom. Noticing this, he hurriedly pulled from a pouch on the bulkhead a set of ring-bound, protected sheets—

Wait, hold the phone, Sean's mind said with disdain. *What happened to 'I want to die on the ocean floor, just like my beloved dinosaurs'?*

Sounding like a drain backing up, he said out loud, "I meant I was *prepared* to die. I didn't *want* to die."

But that wasn't entirely true, was it? When he was drifting downward to his death, he felt a sense of *completion*. A feeling that if he had to die—and everyone has to die, of course—this would be the perfect moment, at the apotheosis of his career, at the height of his vindication. No—his *redemption!* He would *not* be going back to prison …

…not for the accident with Kat, anyway.

But no loyal crew membered would be able to shield him from the fact that the world *watched* him shoot up and sink two fishing boats. Jake Bentneus may have been able to hold off arrest and prosecution until Gigadon was caught, but even a billionaire couldn't protect someone from the entire world's cries for "justice" for long.

But now, seeing the Creature to his Frankenstein—and Sean *did* create him while in his solitary cell as sure as the good Doctor brought that corpse to life, he *did*—pass so closely, Sean Muir *got it*. He could beat this thing. He could *win*.

Forget the billion dollars. He could *win* and be hailed for not only his scientific brilliance, but also his courage to hunt and destroy his own malignant maleficence.

He flipped through the stiff pages until he came to the checklist for firing the missiles. He skimmed the part that he knew, aiming and priming them, arming the weapon, firing them, but there was something he was looking for, something that literally was his only chance *not* to die down here with these goddamned abominations, a chance to return to the surface and get Bentneus his Gigadon's head on a platter. Maybe slaying the monster would calm the TV-watching lynch mob slavering to throw him back into solitary confinement.

Finally, he found it:

PROTOCOL OVERRIDE FOR EMERGENCY MISSILE LAUNCH

He remembered now that this protocol, barely touched on in his training but for some reason remembered in the depths of his mind, was to dissuade or even kill a dinosaur that was right up on your sub. It was dangerous, but not as dangerous as being crunched and spit out like Jake Bentneus.

Would this work? *This could work!*

First, he aimed each missile upward, locking in a straight vertical trajectory. Then he purposely skipped the step of setting the missiles to uncouple from *Ocean Vengeance* when they fired. This could melt his bathysphere, he supposed, but that was a chance he'd have to take. Again, he was relying on the liquid inside his iron ball to keep him from experiencing too rapid, too *fatal*, a rise in temperature.

Then he armed every explosive payload. Maybe it wouldn't work— maybe there was some kind of failsafe to prevent them from exploding so close to the submersible—but maybe it would work, maybe it *would*.

Finally, and this took some near-panicked fiddling to figure out, the ticking clock being the increasing yellow light filling the porthole as he fell toward the hellfire, he coordinated each set of missiles, one of each on opposite sides to keep him going vertically, to fire just as the previous pair ran out of juice.

The two at the bottom would fire last, boosting him—he hoped— hard and fast enough to get him all the way to the surface. But seven miles of dense water … hell, maybe it wouldn't work. *But maybe it WILL, you overgrown bucket of bait.*

"Ready, Teddy," he burbled, and lit the candle.

###

"Where's the Navy? Where's the battleships? Those sumbitches are in *American* waters and just set off a nuclear weapon!"

"Actually, chief, is was just a low-yield *atomic* weapon," Popcorn said.

"Whatever it was, man! We got goddamn *Communists* 200 miles from an American territory!"

"They were allowed to register, Mick," Holly said. "Brought the whole sub with them, remember? Maybe Jake Bentneus promised the rest of his fortune to powerful people who could have the U.S. make a deal with the North Koreans that they could hunt Gigadon however they wanted, but if their submarine was used to try to launch some kind of attack, we would erase their entire country from the map."

The semaphore flags went up again, and Mickey picked up the binoculars. "Now what ... he's using letters again. 'F,' okay, now an 'I'—write these down, would you, Holly?"

"Oh, I must be a secretary, 'cause I'm the girl."

"No, 'cause you got a pen in your hand." Mickey kept reading. "Now 'V,' uh-huh, 'E' ..."

Holly wrote down the sequence, stopping when it repeated:

F-I-V-E-M-I-N-U-T-E-S

"Five minutes?" Mickey read with confusion. "Five minutes until what?"

"I don't think I want to know," Holly said. "And yes, Popcorn, I know you would *love* to know."

Popcorn sniffed, but not without irony. "I would love to know all I can."

Mickey smiled ruefully and said, "I guess we'll know in five minutes."

"We can make an educated guess," Popcorn said. "It stands to reason, based on their earlier belligerent and threatening communications, that they will attack our two remaining ships if we do not show signs of vacating the Marianas area within the next five minutes."

"Oh, hell," Mickey said, a hand to his forehead. "I bet you're right."

"For once, I'd rather not be."

"I'm calling the captain over on *Sharkasm*."

"Wait," Holly said, "where's our captain? Where's Looper?"

Mickey raised the comm. "Captain Looper, come in, this is Luch up on the bridge." Silence. "Captain?"

One of the maritime crewman said, "I'll get him. He might be in the head." He went up the spiral steps to the Captain's quarters.

Mickey changed the frequency and said into the receiver, "Calling Captain Brady on *Sharkasm*. Captain Brady, this is Mickey on *Spit*."

"Copy."

"I'm gonna assume you saw the messages from the submarine?"

Brady sighed and said, "Never a dull moment around here."

"True. Sir, what did you take that message to mean? 'Five minutes'?"

"They obviously want us to think they're going to shoot at us or sink us or something horrible like that. When I was in the service, these brown-water Navy assholes were always threatening everybody, just like Kim Jung Whatever does every frickin' week. They just want us to leave in case their bomb—you guys realize that, right, they set off some kind of atomic device to generate heat?—actually does bring up the Gigadon. We aren't going anywhere, Mick. If the monster makes an appearance, our boats will bag it and bring it to shore. Subs don't have a lot of maneuverability up top like the three of us do." He paused. "Where's Looper?"

"We were just—"

"Chief! Chief Luch, *quick!*" the crewman shouted from the Captain's quarters at the top of the steps.

Mickey handed the comm to Holly and double-timed it up the stairs. The door to the captain's cabin was wide open, and Looper was splayed out on the floor, definitely dead. But that does tend to be the effect on a person when a massive explosion just 300 feet away shatters an unprotected window and a huge shard of glass buries itself in your brain.

"God," Mickey said, to the crewman but also, even primarily, to himself. "I think we should listen to the nice Communists and get the hell out of here before every single one of us is dead."

Mickey instructed the crewman to get a few men together to properly situate the late captain's body until (what he really thought was *if*) they got back to shore, notify the maritime authorities in Guam, and any other duties needed in a situation like this. Then he came down the steps and delivered the news. There was no response but covers being removed, heads bowed for a moment, and a respectful silence.

In that silence, the *chop-chop-chop* of the Sea & Air Rescue helicopter from the mainland finally could be heard. Maybe their video cameras, always on and recording when the 'copter was on a rescue call, could capture the insanity of what was happening and maybe at least get the government to dissuade the North Koreans from blowing up the remaining boats.

Popcorn broke the silence. "Please excuse me, everyone, but four minutes and forty-five seconds have passed, at my mark … *now*."

Holly rolled her eyes.

Mickey barely heard a word his computer supervisor said. In his mind, he could see Sean Muir dead at the bottom of the ocean. He saw Captain Looper, admittedly a bit of an alcoholic content to stay in his quarters and let Mickey do the driving, with his head shot through. He saw every one of his good friends on *Sea Legs* die violently and horribly.

And who was responsible? Not Sean or Kat Muir, not Slipjack, not even the North Koreans with their idiot bomb, not really.

The great and terrible *Gigadon* was responsible. It was unnatural, it was unholy, and Mickey could hear the words of the Bible as he contemplated the agent of their doom:

> *"Come see," he said, and I saw: behold,*
> *an ashen beast; and he had upon him the*
> *name Death; and Hell followed with him.*

No sooner had the words resounded in his head did he hear all around him his shipmates screaming as the North Korean submarine launched a torpedo that, in less than ten seconds, reached *Sharkasm* and blasted it to splinters.

Chaos ensued on *Spit*—some sailors tried to commandeer the ship to get it the hell out of there, others blocked them and insulted their manhood or, in one case, her womanhood. The two scientists stared, shocked into silence, on the floating debris, all that was left of *Sharkasm*. The vessel had sunk so quickly that its fuel and oxygen tanks never got the chance to explode. It was just … *gone*.

Holly sank to the deck, mumbling and chewing on the ends of her fingers.

The SAR helicopter was there, hovering several hundred feet up, and Mickey couldn't even imagine what they were thinking. Except they were definitely thinking of not getting any closer—he could hear that the *chop-chop-chop* wasn't getting louder anymore. Maybe *they* were calling in the Navy, or asking for airstrikes, or whatever the hell was supposed to happen when this kind of shit hit the fan.

Popcorn did the only thing he could think to do amid the horror and the bedlam: he slowly stepped to the computer monitors and observed what data he could.

"Chief Luch," he said, his voice seeming just to float out of him. "Look at this … if you want."

Mickey's feet felt like they were made of iron and the deck was a powerful magnet. Still, he made his way over to Popcorn and looked at the sonar image the scientist indicated: a huge, *huge* mass was hurling toward the surface.

"That's got to be the Gigadon—we can still kill it! We can have our vengeance—*Chief Luch, give us our vengeance!*"

"Have you lost your mind, Orville?" Mickey said, understanding only gradually the words his friend was saying.

"Yes, I think so!" He seemed downright thrilled by it. "Mister Crockett is at the big gun, right?! And Holly can fire the Honeycomb!"

"The what?"

"*The Honeycomb!* That foam-filled cannonball that expands exponentially when it hits salt water—*you're* the one who told me about that thing! *Thing! Ha ha,* I can't believe the imprecision of my speech right now! Holly knows the cannon! Let's do it! Let's *kill* that ...that ... that *very bad animal!*"

"We have twenty-two professional sailors to keep this ship afloat. They can keep everything running," a woman's voice said from behind them. It was Holly, and even as she wiped the tears from her face, she finished: "while we send that pile of shit back to the goddamn *Pliocene!*"

Popcorn patted Holly on the back very gently, keeping any further words to himself but quite chuffed that she had correctly referenced the era during which their enemy had most likely evolved into its present form.

"The only question now is—"

POWPOWPOWPOWPOWPOWPOWPOWPOWPOWPOW

Every person on board *I Spit on Your Grave* ducked by pure reflex as the Mark II forward .50 caliber M2 machine gun on the roof—the massive weapon that Sean Muir used to kill two boats full of merchant fishermen—made the entire vessel rattle like it would come apart. And it was *deafening,* maybe sounding extra-loud without the noisy chaos of a shark feeding frenzy.

POWPOWPOWPOWPOWPOWPWOPWOPOWPOWPOWPOWPO WPOW

"That's Mister Crockett!" Popcorn shouted.

They all stood again and looked out to see what their weapons man could have been shooting at.

"He's blasting them!" Holly said with joy. Mickey's brain insisted on amusing itself with the almost feral behavior of the scientists.

Splashes near the North Korean sub were followed by the *tink! tink! tink!* of large-caliber ammunitions striking the thick steel of the outdated vessel, the sound reaching them a second after each visible spark of a hit.

It didn't seem to be doing the Koreans any damage, but Mickey bet it sounded like Armageddon inside that tin can.

"Is the maser charged? Did anyone prime it?" he called out to the crew, some of whom had been trained on the different anti-dinosaur weaponry.

"No, but I can do it now," one voice responded.

It was Slipjack. Innocent of murder, but still an asshole most of the time. Fortunately, this was not one of those times.

"Thank you, Mister McCracken," Mickey said with a smile. "You may very well save our asses today."

Without response, Slipjack made his way to the stern of *Spit*, where the maser cannon was still in its protective nylon-steel case to keep it from damage by the salty air. It would take a minute to take the case apart and then another minute or two for the gas to be primed, but then they would have something that could cut the submarine in two.

For that, however, they would have to get closer. *Much* closer. And Mickey didn't know if it was worth the risk to get within 200 feet of the submarine, where a torpedo could strike them before Slipjack was able to even aim his weapon.

"Popcorn," Mickey said tightly, "science me. What are we looking at?"

"The mass I've tentatively identified as Gigadon is very near the surface now. Well, in the euphotic zone, which makes up a small fraction—"

"*Stop*. Holly, what do we do when that thing gets here?"

Die? she thought, but said only, "Shoot it with everything? Hope it's as hollow as Jeffrey Plaid's video made it look and hope we can puncture it or something?"

"*Gigadon is almost here!*" Popcorn shouted, even though he was just ten feet from Mickey and Holly. "What do we do?"

Die? Holly squeezed her eyes shut and pushed that out of her mind. Its likely accuracy was irrelevant at that moment.

Over the comm came Crockett's voice: "They're firing again! *Incoming torpedo!*"

Popcorn cried, "Gigadon is about to break the surface!"

The torpedo splashed as it was ejected from the submarine and now zoomed in a straight line right at *I Spit on Your Grave*. They had maybe ten seconds until it hit.

Mickey: "*Oh, shiiiiiiiiiiiiiit!*"

Popcorn: "*Gigadahhhhhhhhhhhhn!*"

Then, very near the North Korean sub, a massive gray *presence* under the water grew impossibly large, impossibly quickly, and

Gigadon's familiar crocodile snout and jaw, as tall as a four-story building, breached the surface, and its enormous body broke the water line …

… right behind the zooming torpedo, which shot forward unimpeded in its deadly trajectory.

Some on the exposed deck of *Spit* thought of diving off the boat; some inside the boat considered ducking down and covering; and some on the bridge made the decision to start running, wildly, in any direction; but every one of them stayed frozen in place, their couple of seconds of remaining life seeming like an hour.

"Yeeeeeeeeeeeeeee-ahhhhhhhh!" a voice from the stern shouted like a banshee, and the torpedo magically split right down the middle, each side angling sharply and in different directions underwater, the explosive warhead going off deep and still distant enough to rock *I Spit on Your Grave* while not causing a scratch.

"Yeah, baby! That is what I'm talkin' a-*bout!"* Slipjack screamed with triumph, his hot maser spent and smoking from having let loose the intense, radiation-boosted, amplified-microwave beam of destruction. *"Slipjack saves the day, bitches!"*

The winch chief was loud, but the cheers and hollers from everyone else onboard drowned him out. He strode on the deck with both arms raised and a cigarette hanging from his mouth.

But the cheers were instantly replaced by shouts of shock and awe, eyes widening and hands covering mouths as they looked back to the submarine and the surfacing Gigadon. It breached almost half its body— its tremendous, aircraft-hangar–size body making the submarine look like a toy floating in a bathtub.

The gigantic dinosaur turned as it breached—maybe turning to expose more of itself to the hot sun—and fell mightily back toward the water, its untold tons of flesh crashing down directly on top of the North Korean submarine.

"It was too much heat—Gigadon went into a frenzy! The fission heat and the lingering radiation rising just under their sub—they made themselves Gigadon bait!" Popcorn yelled as he simultaneously *whooped* and checked his computer readouts.

"Will the submarine just come back up and shoot at us again? Or maybe it'll just get the Gigadon now?" Holly said to Mickey, her eyes not leaving the spot where the DPRK submarine had been just a moment ago.

"No, no, no," Mickey said, a big and possibly inappropriate smile on his face. "That sub is squashed flatter than a cardboard box with an elephant standing on it. Not one commie survived that, I guarantee you."

"What is with that 'Commie,' Mick? You running for Congress in 1954 or what?"

He laughed. "Actually, it's a funny story with me and the Commu—"

"Chief Luch," Popcorn said as calmly but firmly as he could manage, "it's turning around."

Mickey squinted out at the 10-foot "ripples" radiating from where the dinosaur had come down. "What? There's no way the sub could have survived—"

"Not the submarine, Chief—*Gigadon*. It's coming our way."

Into the comm, Mickey shouted, "Crocket! Get shooting, man!"

POWPOWPOWPOWPOWPOWPOWPOWPOWPOW

Then, to Holly, he said, "Can we stop it before it rams us and eats us?"

Holly shook her head. "Not according to Newton's First Law of Motion: *A body in motion will tend to stay in motion.* Gigadon has seen us, yes he has, but he's a big son of a sea cow. It takes him time to build up momentum. But yeah, Mick, without a countervailing force, he'll bust us up in 60 seconds or so."

POWPOWPOWPOWPOWPOWPOWPOWPOWPOW

It was like they didn't even hear it anymore; the machine-gun fire certainly wasn't doing anything to discourage the floating island from moving toward them.

Popcorn said, "You're kind of conflating the First Law with the Second Law there, Holly."

Both Holly and Mickey looked at Popcorn in unmistakable expressions of threatening serious violence upon his person.

"Um … but Newton's laws really *are* intertwined, you know, so, no problem. What we need is a force traveling at a velocity opposite that of Gigadon's vector, but it might be enough if we could introduce even a perpendicular force to arrest its vector progress toward us. Its, um, linearly *increasing* vector progress toward us. T-minus 30 seconds, I'd say."

The comm still in his hand, Mickey flipped a switch and called with a smooth and calming voice to everyone aboard, "May God and the Spirit of the Sea bless every one of you. It has been an honor—"

"Chief Luch," Popcorn said from his place at the sonar monitor, "we got something shooting up toward us."

He took his thumb off the mic button. "*Something?* Shooting *up?* What are you talking about?"

"I don't know," Popcorn said. "It just *is.*"

"A missile or torpedo from another sub down there?"

"No, nothing like a submarine is appearing on the sonar. Just the bullet."

Mickey turned away to watch the beast closing in. "It doesn't matter. We'll be dead before whatever the hell 'it just *is*' gets here. Goodbye, guys."

Holly was too choked up to respond, and Popcorn didn't even hear the farewell, so engrossed was he in his final seconds on Earth trying to figure out what that weird bullet was that was currently rocketing in a straight line toward *I Spit on Your Grave*.

The last two rockets, the ones at the bottom of *Ocean Vengeance*—which Sean had now renamed *Ocean Vindication* in his mind—ignited right after the third set of two spent their fuel. He was just entering the euphotic zone, and Sean didn't know if he had ever seen such beautiful light. The pressure was far less now than it was from the hadal depths, and the two last missiles were accelerating him to the surface so quickly he was actually pulling an extra G or two inside the submersible.

The light was enchanting, the sun making the small choppy waves above into a sparkling promise. As he got closer to the surface, however, two objects above blocked some of that sweet light.

One was Gigadon, its size and shape like nothing else in the sea.

The other was a boat. It was the only boat he could see anywhere in the area above.

Gigadon was moving toward the boat, picking up speed as it swept the water with its forked tail. This decided it.

He would die a hero. For science, but also for the two things he was about to do, now just 50 feet from the surface and the shapes upon it.

The first thing he did was hit the release switch for the portside bottom missile, uncoupling it from the sub. It zoomed off into a random direction away from the monster and ship above, harmless since its explosive payload was not armed.

I can spare that one. There's a lot *of BOOM left for you, big boy.*

This made the submersible move at a sharper angle to starboard, aiming the tip of *Ocean Vindication*—which was as sharp as an arrow—right at the middle of the continent that was the dinosaur's body.

The second thing he did was arm every one of the seven remaining missiles. As soon as they struck anything solid, it would be "Smile, you son of a bitch" time for Gigadon.

He hoped. The thing was essentially hollow, so it wouldn't suffer the destruction that ensues when solid muscle (or fat, for that matter) got hit by a bullet, sending out liquefying shock waves to all organs in the area.

But it was hollow: a sharp violation of the monster's bodily envelope (as Popcorn would say—in other words, *stabbing that mother*) would shoot the explosives right up into that envelope, and he was hauling ass toward it.

Five seconds to impact, Sean thought with excitement and pride. *Five seconds to freedom.*

By the time he finished his thought, the final missile rocket pushing *Ocean Vindication* shoved the sub's sharp tip right into the center of Gigadon's massive body, violating the hell out of its bodily envelope, and all the missile payloads exploded as one inside the beast, lighting up the cavernous darkness with an intensity the formerly smiling but now vaporized Sean Muir would have very much appreciated.

With no time to save or rescue anyone, the SAR helicopter crew still hovered in the same spot all through the unfolding events. They were tuned into *Spit*'s radio frequency and heard what was being said and how people were screaming, but they couldn't make heads nor tails of it.

They did see the Gigadon hurl itself halfway out of the ocean, breaching right onto the North Korean sub and creating a noise of such volume that it made the helicopter wobble in the air. And then they saw Gigadon itself—the largest thing short of a battleship either had ever seen in the water—come about and target the remaining boat in Jake Bentneus's fleet. There was nothing the crew could do that wouldn't kill themselves and destroy the 'copter, and that wouldn't rescue a soul.

So they did the only thing they could: they watched in horror, and captured the whole thing on video.

From the bridge of *I Spit on Your Grave*, Mickey Luch listened to Orville Blum narrate the impending T-bone collision of the rapidly rising mystery object and the leviathan rushing toward them. "The bullet"—he called it that because damn if it didn't look like a bullet shooting up from the deep—"is five seconds, four, three—"

"Holy shit!" Holly cried as she got a look at the sonar monitor, "That 'bullet'—*it's Sean Muir! That's* Ocean Vengeance*!*"

They all could recognize it now, their leader somehow not only alive but *rocketing*—

"—zero."

A muffled but still massively loud explosion swelled the central body of the Gigadon even larger. This explosive expansion tore its flesh, and the body collapsed in on itself. This forced tons upon tons of foul water and air out of the dinosaur's mouth, creating a loud lowing from the beast. It was an otherworldly sound, haunting, fit for this nightmare from another world.

Gigadon was dead.

Cheers erupted on *Spit*, and Sean's name was shouted from high and low as if this were a wake in his honor already.

Acrid black smoke poured from the dead dinosaur's mouth and from where its eyes had been before they were blown out of its head. The stench of burning chemosynthetic biomass was unreal—

Popcorn said in a low voice, "It's still coming at us."

—but worse was that the entire momentum of the dead Gigadon still kept it moving swiftly at them, like the world's largest barge about to break *Spit* into very small pieces. Its speed had been only partly arrested by the arrow shot into it from below and the pressure of the explosions.

"Oh, goddamn, man!" Mickey groaned at the giant carcass. "Give us a break already! Holly, we—"

But the scientist was gone, only her sneakers squeaking on the steps to the weapons area indicating what direction she was headed.

On the comm, Mickey said firmly, "Prepare for impact! All hands, brace yourselves!"

The fast-drifting carcass was only 20 feet away now, and even though it wasn't moving at terrific speed, its tons upon tons would broadside *Spit* like it was a locomotive striking a '78 Pinto stuck on the tracks.

Kerploop! A round turd from the sky splashed into the narrowing gap between the drifting carcass and *I Spit on Your Grave*.

"What the hell was—*ohhh!*" Mickey said, his brain shutting off his mouth as he watched the Honeycomb cannonball bob on the water for a moment.

"She tossed it—she didn't even need the cannon!" Popcorn shouted in a bit of hysterical glee. *"Brilliant!"*

Almost instantly, its coat eaten by the salt, the sphere ripped open and honeycombing nanofoam expended and multiplied to fill the gap, pushing the boat sideways to starboard gently as the honeycombs surrounded it and held it fast.

On the other side, the foam pushed against the Gigadon, first bringing it to a halt relative to *Spit*, the whole mass of carcass-foam-boat now drifting to starboard as one unit. Then, having expanded as deep into the water and under the floating objects as its nanofoam could reach, the Honeycomb had created a de facto "underground sail" that dragged in the water and brought everything, finally, to a stop.

Completely spent, Mickey dropped into his seat. Popcorn rested his hot forehead against the cooler metal computer rack. Holly came shakily down the spiral steps. The crew was cheering and letting out its pent-up energy. So much—so *many*—had been lost … but the battle had finally been won.

The radio crackled and the pilot of the Sea & Air Rescue helicopter called, "*I Spit on Your Grave*, come in, please."

Mickey switched his comm channel to the right frequency and said, "We read you, Sea & Air. We're all alive down here. Well, except the Gigadon." (And Captain Looper, and Sean Muir, and the crews of *Sea Legs* and *Sharkasm*, and and and …) "Over."

"Do you require assistance? Over."

Mickey thought for a moment as he took it in the extent of the buoyant Honeycomb surrounding them and actually lifting their boat a few feet out of the water. "We could use a tug," he said. "Our whole little island group here, just to the beach, where the boss can see what we caught for him. Over."

The pilot laughed and said, "Roger that, but I don't think there's a tug powerful enough to drag that whole monstrosity anywhere. We can send a boat out to pick up you and the other survivors. Over."

"No, thanks—just send the best tug you've got. We'll think of a solution. Out."

"A solution?" Holly said, sitting down now herself, her leftover adrenaline keeping her shaky.

Mickey smiled and switched the comm back. "Slipjack, read me?"

"That's an affirmative, Ghost Rider."

"You got the maser primed again yet?"

"Naw," Slipjack said with lightness, "I was too busy trying to apologize for every bad thing I've done in this life before I died. I don't think I made much of a dent in the list."

Anyone within earshot of the comm speaker laughed at that, some because it was exactly what they were doing in the face of imminent death, others because they bet Slipjack had a list of sins he couldn't finish in a day, forget about 30 seconds.

"I can prime it now, though. Take five or ten minutes. What do you need the maser for? It's dead, ain't it? We're gettin' our billion dollars, right?"

"Yeah, we are—if you don't mind doing some wet work. The whole carcass, which we are connected to by that foam what won't let go, is gonna start sinking very soon, and it'll pull us down with it—unless you can use the maser to slash our trophy's head off its body ."

"*Haw!* Consider it done, Chief." There was a moment of silence from the comm, and Mickey was about to put it down when Slipjack added, "Um, everybody, I'm sorry about Doctor Muir. I thought he killed his wife on account of me. He thought I was trying to kill *him* on account of my being in love with her. But neither one was true, you guys, okay? We know that now. It was an accident.

"It was an accident and I'm sorry," he finished with a tremulous voice, then said, "Sean Muir is a hero." Another pause. "Anyway ... maser time." He clicked off.

"Tug'll be here in a few hours, *I Spit on Your Grave*," the pilot called on the overworked comm. "They'll get you to shore. Over."

"Roger that, and thank you, Sea & Air. Over."

"We might go sell our footage to FoxNews or CNN or somewhere—let's make that our 'cut' of your prize money, yeah? And you guys are all going to be famous."

"And rich," the copilot said. "Over."

"Yeah, right now we're still appreciating being *alive*. Thanks for everything. *Spit* out."

Popcorn giggled. "*Spit out!* An infelicitous double entendre there."

The high-pitched *whirr* of the maser started up, and within two minutes, Slipjack had sliced through the tough but empty hide of the Gigadon, the dinosaur's head floating atop where the Honeycomb had expanded underwater. The body was not thus supported and so was already drifting away and slowly sinking.

"All we have to do now is wait," Mickey said, letting out a huge breath he hadn't realized he was holding. Then he reached into a drawer under the command station and pulled out a sealed bottle of Kraken Dark Rum. "And we're not driving, so ..."

Everyone on the bridge got a cup and they all drank to their colleagues' safe passage into the next world. All onboard who were with the expedition crew thought of their lost friends on the other boats, and then of Sean Muir, who had single-handedly saved their lives and won them the Bentneus Prize.

Even Slipjack McCracken, still out on the deck in the front of *Spit*, raised his trusty flask of whiskey to the man he had wrongly hated for so long.

"I hate to be mercenary," Popcorn said to Mickey and Holly, who believed him without hesitation, "but do you have any plans for your ... em ... well, Doctor Muir has passed, and we have 23 people left onboard, so ... what are you going to do with your roughly $45 million cut?"

Mickey smiled at this. It was always the conversation after a commercial (or perhaps mercenary) job had been done, although this was a historic amount, to say the least. He thought and said, "I'll have freedom to do whatever I want, right? So I'm gonna start my own charter boat service. That takes tourists to an island I'm gonna buy. That would be a *different* island from the one I buy to live on, of course."

"Of course," Popcorn said. "I've been thinking about it, too, and my plan is to take some time off from computer work."

"*What?*" Mickey and Holly said in unison.

"It's hard to believe, I know, but I'm leaving computer work behind me. I need to be free of the grind of sitting at a screen all day. No, ahead of me is building my own hyper-parallel quantum-based neural-net computer system."

Holly was stunned ... but she also wasn't. "So, you are leaving computer work to do different computer work."

"I know, it sounds crazy, right? But now I will have the money!"

Mickey said, "Well, at least you'll be able to spend less hours at it than you work now."

Popcorn laughed, but then saw that Mickey was serious. "Fewer hours? No, this is my chance to spend *more* hours at it, no interruptions except for meals with Mother and the Sunday RPG. It's going to be more fun than one man should have!"

His compatriots blinked a few times, then smiled and raised a cup to him.

"How about you, Holly?"

"I am going to create, endow, and then chair a new Department of Oceanography at whatever college is nearest Rugby, North Dakota. *Total* academic freedom."

This made Popcorn almost laughed grog through his nose, just managing to get out, "That says a *lot!*" Holly joined him in laughing.

"What ... what am I missing?" Mickey asked, completely confused. "*North Dakota?* That's about the farthest away from the ocean as you can get!"

"Actually, it *literally* is, Chief," Popcorn said after collecting himself a bit. "The town of Rugby is famously the exact geographical center of North America."

"That's a tough place to study the ocean," Mickey said, still not getting it.

"That's why whoever invented books—"

Popcorn interrupted without having to think, "That would be King Neferirkare Kakai, of the Fifth Dynasty in Egypt."

"—invented books," Holly finished with faux annoyance at her colleague. "I'm going to endow, with my own fortune, a two-year program, one where students can learn everything they need to know about the ocean before going on to a big oceanography institute somewhere on one of the coasts."

"I love ya, Holly, but that is frickin' *bizarre*."

"Not really," she said. "Not if you *never* want to see the ocean again. *Ever*."

###

It was approaching dusk on the last day of Jake Bentneus's life. The technology that kept him alive was working exactly as designed, not a glitch in the whole system.

No, it was what was left of his body that couldn't do it anymore. It had gone downhill *fast* after his broadcast, maybe sensing that calling the world to kill the monster was the last, best thing he would ever do.

His ability to speak was gone, less and less sustenance was being absorbed by his body, and his sight, although still acceptable with the corrective lenses they had put on him, was fading fast as well.

But it would last long enough to see what the news video told him was coming.

In fact, although he couldn't turn his head, he was able to shift his gaze to the window as he heard the news choppers and heard the long hoot of the tugboat pulling the head of his Gigadon.

He watched for it, waited for it. He just needed to hold on, to will the machines to keep his blood circulating for just a few minutes more the way he once could will his crews to make the biggest movies of all time. If he had still possessed a heart, he would have felt it beating harder and faster.

The tug appeared first, followed by *I Spit on Your Grave* on its pillow of Honeycomb … and then …

Pulled slowly into his view was the face that had haunted his nightmares: that awful snout packed with rows of teeth, the eyes missing now but the dark holes still seeming to glare at him, that head as big as a drive-in theater screen. Then, into his field of vision came the end of that head, cut off raggedly, maybe even savagely.

Gigadon was dead. Bentneus had achieved Victory over the ocean, Vengeance against the eternally black water ... they belonged to him now and forever.

If his eyes could have produced tears, his face would have been wet with them. But as it was, he cried with joy deep inside his conscious mind, the only thing he had left except for his victory and his vengeance.

Not much later, this last of him faded away, and Jake Bentneus slipped forever into the darkling deep.

The End

CHECK OUT OTHER GREAT
DEEP SEA THRILLERS

MEGA
by Jake Bible

There is something in the deep. Something large. Some-thing hungry. Something prehistoric.
And Team Grendel must find it, fight it, and kill it.
Kinsey Thorne, the first female US Navy SEAL candidate has hit rock bottom. Having washed out of the Navy, she turned to every drink and drug she could get her hands on. Until her father and cousins, all ex-Navy SEALS themselves, offer her a way back into the life: as part of a private, elite combat Team being put together to find and hunt down an impossible monster in the Indian Ocean. Kinsey has a second chance, but can she live through it?

THE BLACK
by Paul E Cooley

Under 30,000 feet of water, the exploration rig Leaguer has discovered an oil field larger than Saudi Arabia, with oil so sweet and pure, nations would go to war for the rights to it. But as the team starts drilling exploration well after exploration well in their race to claim the sweet crude, a deep rumbling beneath the ocean floor shakes them all to their core. Something has been living in the oil and it's about to give birth to the greatest threat humanity has ever seen.

"The Black" is a techno/horror-thriller that puts the horror and action of movies such as Leviathan and The Thing right into readers' hands. Ocean exploration will never be the same."

CHECK OUT OTHER GREAT DEEP SEA THRILLERS

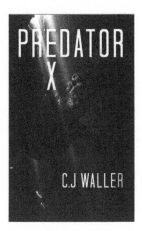

PREDATOR X
by C.J Waller

When deep level oil fracking uncovers a vast subterranean sea, a crack team of cavers and scientists are sent down to investigate. Upon their arrival, they disappear without a trace. A second team, including sedimentologist Dr Megan Stoker, are ordered to seek out Alpha Team and report back their findings. But Alpha team are nowhere to be found – instead, they are faced with something unexpected in the depths. Something ancient. Something huge. Something dangerous. Predator X

DEAD BAIT
by Tim Curran

A husband hell-bent on revenge hunts a Wereshark...A Russian mail order bride with a fishy secret...Crabs with a collective consciousness...A vampire who transforms into a Candiru...Zombie piranha...Bait that will have you crawling out of your skin and more. Drawing on horror, humor with a helping of dark fantasy and a touch of deviance, these 19 contemporary stories pay homage to the monsters that lurk in the murky waters of our imaginations. If you thought it was safe to go back in the water...Think Again!

CHECK OUT OTHER GREAT DEEP SEA THRILLERS

MEGATOOTH
by Viktor Zarkov

When the death rate of sperm whales rises dramatically, a well-respected environmental activist puts together a ragtag team to hit the high seas to investigate the matter. They suspect that the deaths are due to poachers and they are all driven by a need for justice.

Elsewhere, an experimental government vessel is enhancing deep sea mining equipment. They see one of these dead whales up close and personal...and are fairly certain that it wasn't poachers that killed it.

Both of these teams are about to discover that poachers are the least of their worries. There is something hunting the whales...

Something big
Something prehistoric.
Something terrifying.
MEGATOOTH!

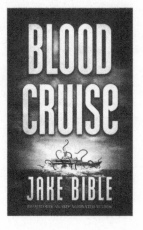

BLOOD CRUISE
by Jake Bible

Ben Clow's plans are set. Drop off kids, pick up girlfriend, head to the marina, and hop on best friend's cruiser for a weekend of fun at sea. But Ben's happy plans are about to be changed by a tentacled horror that lurks beneath the waves.

International crime lords! Deep cover black ops agents! A ravenous, bloodsucking monster! A storm of evil and danger conspire to turn Ben Clow's vacation from a fun ocean getaway into a nightmare of a Blood Cruise!

CHECK OUT OTHER GREAT
DEEP SEA THRILLERS

SEA RAPTOR
by John J. Rust

From terrorist hunter to monster hunter! Jack Rastun was a decorated U.S. Army Ranger, until an unfortunate incident forced him out of the service. He is soon hired by the Foundation for Undocumented Biological Investigation and given a new mission, to search for cryptids, creatures whose existence has not been proven by mainstream science. Teaming up with the daring and beautiful wildlife photographer Karen Thatcher, they must stop a sea monster's deadly rampage along the Jersey Shore. But that's not the only danger Rastun faces. A group of murderous animal smugglers also want the creature. Rastun must utilize every skill learned from years of fighting, otherwise, his first mission for the FUBI might very well be his last.

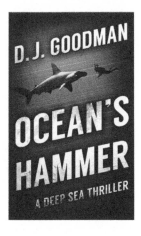

OCEAN'S HAMMER
by D.J. Goodman

Something strange is happening in the Sea of Cortez. Whales are beaching for no apparent reason and the local hammerhead shark population, previously believed to be fished to extinction, has suddenly reappeared. Marine biologists Maria Quintero and Kevin Hoyt have come to investigate with a television producer in tow, hoping to get footage that will land them a reality TV show. The plan is to have a stand-off against a notorious illegal shark-fishing captain and then go home.

Things are not going according to plan.

There is something new in the waters of the Sea of Cortez. Something smart. Something huge. Something that has its own plans for Quintero and Hoyt.

Made in the USA
Coppell, TX
19 October 2020